Little Ro<

Book Ten
The Elizabeth of England Chronicles

By G. Lawrence

Copyright © Gemma Lawrence 2021
All Rights Reserved.
No part of this manuscript may be reproduced without
Gemma Lawrence's express consent

"All my life I have spent in little rooms."
Queen Elizabeth I

"Have mercy upon me, oh God,
According to thy loving kindness:
According unto the multitude of thy tender mercies,
blot out my transgressions.
Wash me thoroughly from mine iniquity,
and cleanse me from my sin
For I acknowledge my transgressions:
and my sin is ever before me.
Against thee, thee only have I sinned,
and done this evil in thy sight:
That thou mightest be justified when thou speakest,
and be clear when thou judgest.
Behold, I was shapen in iniquity;
and in sin did my mother conceive me.
Behold, thou desirest truth in the inward parts;
and in the hidden part thou shall make me to know wisdom.

Purge me with hyssop, and I shall be clean:
wash me and I shall be whiter than snow.
Make me to hear joy and gladness;
That the bones which thou hast broken may rejoice.
Hide thy face from my sins,
and block out all mine iniquities.
Create in me a clean heart, oh God;
And renew a right spirit within me.
Cast me not away from thy presence;
and take not thy Holy Spirit from me.
Restore unto me the joy of thy salvation;
and uphold me with thy free spirit.
Then I will teach transgressions thy ways;
And sinners shall be converted unto thee.

Deliver me from blood guiltiness, oh God.
Thou God of my salvation;
and my tongue shall sing aloud of thy righteousness.
Oh Lord, open thou my lips;

and my mouth shall shew forth thy praise.
For thou desirest not sacrifice;
else I would give it:
thou delight is not in burnt offering.

The sacrifices of God are a broken spirit:
a broken and a contrite heart, oh God,
thou wilt not despise.
Do good in thy good pleasure unto Zion:
Build thou the walls of Jerusalem.
Then shalt thou be pleased with the sacrifices of righteousness:
with burnt offering and whole burnt offering
then shall they offer bullocks upon thine altar."
Psalm 51, as spoken by the Earl of Essex before his death.

"These wall stones are wondrous, calamities crumpled them,
these city sites crashed, the work of giants corrupted.
The roofs have rushed to earth, towers in ruins.
Ice at the joints has unroofed the barred gates, sheared the scarred storm walls have disappeared.
The years have gnawed them from beneath.
A grave-grip holds the master crafters, decrepit and departed,
in the ground's harsh grasp, until one hundred generations of human nations have trod past.
Therefore this wall, lichen-grey and rust stained, often experiencing one kingdom after another, standing still under storms, high and wide, it failed…

The wine halls moulder still, hewn as if by weapons penetrated…
The strong-purposed mind was urged to a keen-minded desire in concentric circles; the stout-hearted bound wall roots wondrously together with wire.
The halls of the city once were bright: there were many bath houses,

a lofty treasure of peaked roofs, many troop roads, many
mead halls filled with human joys until that terrible chance
changed all.

Days of misfortune arrived, blows fell broadly, death seized all
those sword-stout men, their idol-fanes were laid waste, the
city steads perished.
Their maintaining multitudes fell to the earth.
For that the houses of red vaulting have drearied and shed
their tiles,
these routes of ringed wood.
This place has sunk into ruin, being broken into heaps.

There once many men, glad minded and gold-bright,
adorned in gleaming, proud and wine-flushed, shone in war
tackle;
There one could look upon treasure, upon silver, upon ornate
jewellery, upon prosperity, upon possession, upon precious
stones,
upon the illustrious city of the broad realm.

Stone houses standing here, where a hot stream was cast in a
wide welling;
a wall enfolding everything in its bright bosom,
where there were baths, heated at its heart.
There was convenient… when they let pour forth…
Over the hoary stones countless heated streams…
until the ringed pool hot…
where there were baths.
Then is…
that is a kingly thing..
a house, a city."

The Ruin, (incomplete, poem partially lost)
Author unknown, Anglo Saxon.

"For God's sake, let us sit upon the ground,
And tell sad stories of the deaths of Kings;
How some have been deposed, some slain in war,
Some haunted by the ghosts they have deposed;

Some poison'd by their wives; some sleeping kill'd;
All murder'd; for within the hollow crown
That rounds the mortal temples of a king
Keeps Death his Court…"
William Shakespeare, Richard II

"My crown I am; but still my griefs are mine;
You may my glories and my state depose
But not my griefs, still am I king of those."
William Shakespeare, Richard II

This book is dedicated to the protagonist of this series,
Queen Elizabeth I
One of the most remarkable women of history
A true survivor, pragmatist, trickster and political creature
Master of ambiguity
Who survived death many times, but not the last.
A fascinating and flawed woman, whom I admire.

After writing about Elizabeth for many years, in this book I must say goodbye to her,
A hard task, to bid farewell to a heroine

Prologue

Richmond Palace
February 1603

"The end," I say to Death and all ghosts watching, waiting for me. "Every story has an end, a close, yet we see it not often. When do we know the end has come? Sometimes signs are there for certain, grey hair and memory slipping, the sound of an assassin coming by darkness, slinking up the stairs. We know for we are held in prisons, little rooms where we feel the world, once large, closing in, becoming small until the only escape is death. Sometimes we know not the end is nigh until it is upon us. It was that way for Robin, for my mother. My sister, my father, they knew the end had come, they had time to prepare. I too have had time."

I look to the window, a finger tracing a line along my sore gums. My teeth, these implements supposed to aid in eating, have turned on me, so no more can I bite down. Life now will bite me with death, I can bite back no more. Once we warred, equal foes were life and me, and now I am without weapons. Surrender is close, yet still I do not surrender. There is fight left in me, and to fight is to live. There are words left in me and those I will speak, until I become silent in death, as death.

For Death does not speak, not to me or any He takes. At times people call Death cruel, but truly He is not. His voice would scare more than silence, so silent He remains.

I take my finger from my mouth, as though I have become a child again who no more wishes to suck fingers pretending they are the breasts of my mother, the mother who died before she could know me, and before she died was not allowed to feed me from her own breast. I remember the stories, how she tried and how my father stopped her, saying she was no commoner who fed children herself. Sometimes it seems to me that whilst their lives are harsher, common people have more freedom than those of us born to gold and glitter may boast. We are kept prisoner without knowing it, bound to ritual and convention for no real reason but that it sets us apart from others. Such a simple, natural act, to feed one's own child, but my mother was not allowed to be simple or natural. All that she did and all I was born to was unnatural. We never were allowed to be but ourselves. That was not enough for the Crown.

"The end," I say again. "Many people through history, and I ever was a student of history, watched the worlds they knew, all that was familiar, crumble into nothing. Invasion, sickness, famine, the changing, whirling weather of their times, things they could not control and their gods could not appease spreading through lives, houses, the very worlds they had built until there was nothing, until they either died with those places or fled and tried to make a new world. We look at the stone of our houses, my palaces, our roads and streets and we think this life we have built, these mighty kingdoms and all the little rooms they contain, are permanent. Yet all permanence is illusion. A few days, an army, a sickness that spreads too fast, and all is gone. Empires, once mighty and great, invincible so men claimed, tumble to dust, are forgotten. People who did great things, and awful things, are lost from memory. Civilisations which knew more than we do now are gone, their wisdom lost, drifting in scraps and fragments amongst dust and wind. So many have watched their empires fall, but we all witness our worlds as they crumble. That is what happens as we die. The world we knew, that we loved, that held us safe turns on us; friend becomes foe. The end may come gentle or brutal, but life turns on us in the end because it must, because death is the way all stories end. Because we all must watch our cities burn, our kingdoms fall, our thoughts decline. Cities of mind or reality they may be, but all comes to an end, in the end."

I look around with hollow eyes, my throat and mouth paining me. "The kingdom of our minds is vast. All these little rooms inside our hearts, our heads, rooms where we store memories and parts of ourselves, rooms meaningless to any but us, precious only to us, eventually all those rooms waste and fall, dust upon the floor."

I turn to those who watch, all these eyes on me. "Sometimes I know not which is worse, having time to prepare for the end or not. Is it better to know, lay plans for the time when you are not here, to put into place things and missions, to feel you still have a hand upon the world you are about to leave? Or is it best to slip away? Fall asleep one day in a chair before it even feels as though your time has come, and die and never wake, never knowing a moment of fear that you are to leave life, all you have known, behind and enter the vast and unknown darkness that comes when we close our eyes and enter the void of death?"

I sigh. "Yet even for those upon whom the end fell sudden, this peaceful end of no fear was often not the way their deaths came. My mother knew fear; I was told that by plenty who witnessed the last weeks of her life as she became a caged falcon in the Tower. Robin…" I look at him. "…You were one of the fortunate who died swift, perhaps knowing little of what was coming for you. Yet the truly fortunate are so rare. Most of us know what is coming, even if we know it only for a day. Sometimes a day of fear is enough, is it not?"

"I have known for years." I turn to Death. "I knew you were coming, footsteps getting closer every day. You were too curious, old friend, too eager. I felt you many times near me when I was a girl, when I was Queen, but the last three years I knew. I always said I would not live long enough that I outlasted my usefulness to my country and my people, yet I felt I did. I became a memory, a pale shadow of an age long passed, young eyes of a new generation watching me as though I was some ghost from a tale of romance or a page come loose from a tome of history, fluttering in the wind. A relic of the past I became, wandering amongst them, a fragment of something lost, that none remember but in myth and fairy-tale."

I smile. "Perhaps I did well enough in these last years to say that I was not useless, but I felt like a guest who has tarried longer than three days at a house and now the chamber he is in and the place at the table he takes is no more welcome to him, but is resented. People want the rising sun, not the falling star, and that was what I had become." I laugh. "They will flock to my godson when he comes, tell him how glad they are to have him, to have youth and masculine energy upon the throne once more, yet in time his perfections of sex and age will wear thin and they will remember me, and they will miss me. In death I will become perfect and since he lives they will note all his flaws. What changeable, fragile creatures we are to forget those once we loved with such ease, and to remember them with the same ease and regrets, only when they are gone.

"Fickle we are, more often than faithful," I say and many ghosts agree, nodding. Some do not. They frown at me.

"Scold me not, Kat, Robin, Cecil," I say to those ghosts who frown. "Take your example from Blanche who does not seek to censure me for the things I think, but accepts them." I nod to the ghost of my very oldest friend who smiles. "She knows I speak not of all of *you*, but of my experience of people in general. You are too quick to take offence at something not directed at you, old friends. I was fortunate to know many who were faithful, and when I speak of fickle friends I speak not of you." I smile wider. "Although the ease with which you take offence makes me think that you feared this of your own selves, and this is why you do not like me to mention it."

I think this is the way, often what we are offended by, assuming that someone speaks of us when they talk of people who have done something wrong, is what we fear about ourselves. If we did not think ourselves at least a touch guilty of the sin or crime spoken of, why would we be offended by the mere mention of it? Offence speaks plain of guilt. In showing offence we demonstrate clearly that we are, or hold ourselves, guilty of something, yet at the same time do not want to admit it even to ourselves. Indeed, admitting it to ourselves can be the hardest part of any road to acceptance; it is after all the first step, and always the most difficult since we have small momentum behind us. We should mark what we are offended by, for uncomfortable though it might be our indignation points to truths unspoken and unexamined inside us, faults that require eyes, honest and open, upon them. How else are we to learn, unless we learn to see what is good and bad within us? What we are most offended by is what we fear lies inside ourselves. Our own flaws and crimes are the ones we are most afraid of, afraid others will see. And yet there is one who sees all, one we cannot hide from.

"Wisdom to see and accept our flaws and crimes comes at the end, if we are fortunate," I say to my ghosts, this legion of loved ones I have in life found, and lost. "And if we are not. If fortunate, before we die we understand what we have done wrong, go to the Almighty prepared to answer for our crimes, our sins, for all we did wrong. Perhaps we may formulate excuses, or reasons, or know enough to simply come before the one who made us and say we know we did wrong and will stand to accept our punishment. So perhaps those who know the fear of death coming for them are more fortunate in the long run than those who drop sudden from life without fear or warning. Perhaps having a time to think of all we have done is good, to prepare."

I look to them. "For we all must answer for all we have done, for the good and the bad and mediocre. We all must stand before one who knows what was in our hearts when we did what we did, one to whom there is no point in lying, in trying to make ourselves sound or feel better. There are no lies told to God that He will not see through. He knows our most secret hearts, every impulse that drove us, every emotion that bound us. We all come to answer for all we have done, and for those who ruled, who chose what countries and armies did, who lived and who died and who was pardoned a crime and who was not, there is more to answer for."

I look to Death. "I have much to answer for," I say.

He stares at me a while, and then He nods His head.

"The end comes of our little worlds lived in little rooms," I say. "All must watch their cities burn, their crops wither and their kingdoms fall. The worlds we know, our empires, become lost to time and memory. Inside us all the kingdoms of self and spirit fall to our enemies and even to our friends. Inside us all there comes to be but one thing left, where we are called to a place we all dread, that we might answer for all we have done."

Chapter One

Greenwich Palace
Autumn 1598

Leaves whispered, gold and red above me, a little, light breeze floating through them, ruffling what life there was left on the tree to speak words barely heard. I swallowed tears, only too ready to come that autumn. In all that I experienced every day, in each moment I experienced loss. Grief had opened holes in me, wounds that would never heal. My father had rent his leg once, and that wound festered for the rest of his life, giving him no peace from pain. No wound showed on my body, yet I carried the same festering pain inside me. People had torn holes in my soul as they were torn from life, and those wounds gaped in me, baggy, bloody mouths speaking of agony that could barely be expressed. There were no words for what I felt. People say grief should be shared to be dealt with, yet I had no words to share what I felt. I stood alone, a ragged person ripped too many times and ways. I stood alone, missing too many people.

So many friends I once had, so blessed I had been and barely known it. One by one they were falling. I was become a tree of autumn, leaves drifting to the ground in washes of glorious colour as she stands on, alone, no one paying attention to her barren, skeletal fingers, her plain colours of bark and branch not as wondrous as the fallen leaves upon the ground. So often what is left living in autumn is not as noted as what dies. All that dies blazes in colour, metal shining, glorious hues burning, and all that remains alive is like the pale, plain peahen to her cock; dull and unremarked. I knew why the trees did not change colour as they lost their leaves. They were in mourning, and mourning is a place for plain, simple colours so we may hide and Death will not note us as He wanders past. We hide in grief, hoping to live. Sometimes I wondered why. I was thinking that day I would rather join the ones I had lost than carry on as I was.

I put a hand to the tree, as though she and I could feel each other's hearts and draw strength from one another. I was lonely. My Spirit gone, some days I felt like a hollow husk, a stalk from which grain has gone, tumbling into the wind, leaving just the grey-brown stalk to stand in storms of autumn, waiting for winter when it will fall to the earth, become trodden underfoot.

I looked up at the tree. Cecil had always loved that noise, the noise of leaves in the wind. He said it was like the sea, and was it not strange that the sound of waves hissing on the shore should be so akin to the noise of wind in the trees? Was it not a sign, he said, of God's touch upon the world, that that self-same noise was in wood and water, that that noise was perhaps the sound of God's fingertips softly stroking the world? Cecil had smiled when he said that, and he had said it almost every autumn, more frequently as he got older. I think sometimes he forgot he had already said this to me, imparted this wisdom, but I did not tell him he had repeated himself. He liked to be a teacher still, even though I had long outgrown his schoolroom.

Do the dead love, even though they are not alive anymore to feel the strains upon the heart which love offers? Was Cecil here, a part of all he had loved in life, and now by death was set free of mortal bonds holding spirit inside flesh and bone, to live as one with all he had loved? If I wanted to believe anything, that I wanted to believe; that by death the living are set free to become part of all they held dear in life. It was a nicer thing to believe than to think that he was simply gone, part of this world no more.

The leaves rustled anew and I thought again of the affection in his voice as he spoke of his love for that noise, strange perhaps since it also sounded like gossips spreading rumour, something Cecil always had hated. The lives of many of us would be easier if others remained silent, did not suppose, judge, slander or ridicule, making small events into something other than they were through exaggeration and fantasy. People are often so bored with their lives they must make those of others miserable too, creating stories about them so the ones spreading rumour feel better or more worthy by comparison, or so they may sleep at night thinking at least such and such did not happen to them. Some lives have even been ended by gossip. It only takes a slanderous tongue to be believed to wreck lives, shed blood, begin wars; take a mother from her child upon the blade of a sword.

Gossip is so very pointless; a moment of excitement, then the feeling of being soul-dirty, talking of others when we should be leading our own lives. So much of life that we think urgent and important we find is, in the end, not. We create grand stories about small events, and in doing so miss what actually is important. Significant moments and times we miss, passing them off as everyday, commonplace. We spend time looking ahead, failing to regard what is in front of us. We think about new friends to be made, or those we have lost, and we forget the friends standing with us, never shifting from our side. We miss much of present life by gazing back or looking ahead. There is in truth naught but the moment we have, for we never know if it will be the last we ever have. Cecil, my dear Cecil, had had his last. There was no more future for him, only a past, only memory.

I sighed in sorrow, looking away from the tree Cecil had ordered to be planted in my garden so many years ago, a tree that even now he was gone was providing shade for me. The present is important, but glancing ahead and back can be beneficial if we do not stare too long into those places. My good friend had thought so far ahead that his careful plans cared for me still. "Thank you, for thinking I would need shade, or a place to lean my hand, old friend," I said to his ghost.

I could not bear to hear people speak of Cecil; everyone at court had been urged not to say his name aloud in order to save my sanity, yet here to my gardens I came each day and not just to walk. Cecil's hand and his heart, his sensitive touch was in my gardens. Plants he had raised at his house he had brought to court for my men to plant. When I stood amongst plants Cecil had raised, trees thoughtfully planted, I did not feel as though I had lost him, but more as if he was simply elsewhere, at his London house or in the country perhaps. Mayhap he was inside the palace, his poor aching back hunched over a stack of papers as normal, whilst I walked outside. I was not alone. He had not gone. A fiction it was, but sometimes it helped for a while. Sometimes just a moment of not being wrapped in grief is enough for those who grieve. We all need respite, we all need rest. Even though emerging from fantasy was painful, for I entered the world again and found my friend not here, it was a break from sorrow. Sorrow is so weighty. Relief is required or the back breaks.

Of all the people I had lost, and there had been so many, Cecil was the hardest to understand. It is the odd thing about death; we know an end has come but our minds cannot grasp it. Often we forget a person has gone, for me it came most often when I woke, and when we remember we feel the first surge of grief all over again, a cruel torment. One day we have a friend and the next we do not. They are gone, walking far ahead on a path we, as yet, cannot find. It is a hard thing for the mind to comprehend, and my mind, strong and deep though it was, was no different in this regard. I could not understand death, or my loss. Sometimes I was not sure I understood life anymore, either. Without the people I had loved, I was not sure I knew what the value of my life was. The best things of this world are often people, just as the worst are. Even the beauties of the world are enhanced by sharing them with someone.

I looked up at the palace, at all its little rooms, little rooms that made up one huge palace. The palace was as my mind. We all must make compartments of our lives. Prison cells, chambers, palace rooms or kitchens, waiting rooms, places we store treasure and rooms where we rid ourselves of waste.

This is how we cope with life, with ourselves; a different self for each room. A thousand spirits stored away. In rooms we store moments of happiness in golden memory of joys past, and in such rooms we keep our sorrows locked away as prisoners, so they cannot destroy us.

Little rooms. All my life I had lived in little rooms. Spirit was stored in one, as Robin was, as Kat was, as Walsingham, as Blanche, as Parry, Hatton, Drake, Catherine and Henry my cousins, and as was my mother, my father, my sister, my brother. I had to store them away, my many dead. If I did not I would be too surrounded by ghosts. The rooms of my mind had grown into a palace bigger than any I possessed in life, winding corridors of memory linking each one, servants to serve all the dead I had loved bustling around this palace of my mind. In each little room inside my soul I could keep a person safe, a person I had failed to keep safe in life. In each room inside myself I could keep a piece of my heart, a piece of my heart that might have been lost to death with them, had I not snatched it back from Death's hands. This was how I held on to all of them and did not go mad. I could visit and I could tuck them away again, carrying on. I retained people, love, and kept hold of myself too, the parts of me that had tried to fly away to death with them I had locked in my little rooms.

But Cecil had been harder. With the death of my Spirit, I had lost part of my soul, a large part. So gaping was the hole in me I was not sure what was left that was solid.

Spirit had been so much a part of my day, of myself, that I kept forgetting he was not with me anymore. Even Robin I had spent more time away from. I had more experience of being without Robin from times when he was banished, when he was at war. Cecil was different. Since I was a girl, before I took the throne Cecil had been there, always, just the distance of an arm away from me or so it felt. More father to me had he been than my own, his mind so often thinking the same thoughts as mine that I rarely had to explain myself. If you do not understand how rare that is, think of every time you have fought with someone you loved, and every time you found the argument, truly, was about you failing to understand what they said, or them misunderstanding you. Then consider a friend known so well that never do you have to explain yourself, and then think of losing that friend. Enhance that feeling with all the power of the sun and stars, all terrors of the endless night and wishes of the heart most lonely, and you might draw close to how I felt without Cecil.

Spirit was gone, and with him part of my soul had gone to its rest too. Yet nothing in me was at peace.

And here I was, continuing on. At times I wondered why and what or whom for. I could tell you of my country, my role as Queen, that I had to guide the foolish young, or misguided old, for neither wits nor years aid men in finding the right path. I could tell you I was a symbol and I was alive and therefore I would live, but oftentimes of late I had tarried with the thought that death was not something to fear. At a certain stage, it was but another part of the tale to look forward to. Plenty of times over the past months of the end of that year I had come to think that a long rest might be not only well deserved, but overdue.

I had worked hard all my life, and been fortunate enough to play too, taken amusement where I could. I had been proud of the work I had done, yet I wondered sometimes at the pride we take in work and the shame in leisure. Why did I take more pride in a bill or law and less in the time I had spent laughing with a friend? Was it that the former might benefit many, the latter only two? I could not tell you that I thought I should have more pride in laughter than law, but perhaps it should be that they were equal. That any good we bring to the world whether for one or one hundred people is equally important. That at the end of my life I was thinking I might be more content had I laughed more with friends, worked just a little less.

Hindsight is never a friend. Inevitably it means we are looking back and regretting, otherwise the ability to gaze into the past is simply called memory. Hindsight is an ugly word, implying we got something wrong. Of course we did. Perfection is not a human trait and the world would be a grandly boring place to live if we were perfect. We live, we make mistakes, if we are wise we try to learn from them, and then we die. This is life, or so I was thinking that day under Cecil's tree.

I stared up at the tree feeling tired, something not unusual for me. I had always been a light and troubled sleeper, too many horrors in my childhood and youth had trained me to be suspicious of closing my eyes, becoming entirely vulnerable for hours upon hours each night, but since Cecil had died I had felt my lack of slumber more. I had wrested to fill the long hours of night. I used to get up and work if I could not sleep, used to sit at my desk or read at the fire, but since Cecil had died I had not wanted to, and often now spent hours each night staring into darkness, not asleep and not awake, thinking of the past. When I rose, I did so tired. When I worked I no more felt the invigoration of excitement in my plans. Death had made me weary of life, and losing my partner in so many projects had made me lose enjoyment of so much more. I had no one, not even Cecil's son, Robert, to share that with now. Robert was a good man, a steady, hard worker, but he was no William Cecil. I would not share a jest with him about this plan or that as I had with his father. My Spirit would have understood me in a moment, but his son would need jests explaining to him.

It is what no one ever says about death, that when you lose someone close to you, you also lose all merriment once between you two alone. All your private jokes and japes are gone, and there is no one else to whom you might say just a word or phrase to, which to you and the dead one recalled a time or place of amusement, but to anyone else is meaningless. With every loss of a loved one, other connections too are gone. So much between people is private, and once they are gone those moments of private joy are too. It is a hard thing, to lose a person, and to lose all the joy you two shared. So much becomes buried when we place people into the earth.

What I had been left with did not seem to recompense for all I had lost. Increasingly I seemed to be the only adult left in England, a mother who never had wanted children presiding over a court of infants.

My women were not far away. They at least were adults. Anne Dudley, Katherine Hastings, Katherine Howard and Helena Snakenborg, who I should get used to calling by her married name of Gorges, but somehow never could. She suited the serpent-like name of her foreign family. Snakes may have a bad reputation in the Bible at times, but they are creatures of wisdom, symbols of healing. Women too have a bad name in the Bible, that does not mean we should hold them all to be beings of sin.

Helena had come to England as a lass of sixteen in the train of Princess Cecilia, whose brother the King of Sweden had been trying to woo me. I acquired no husband through this round of negotiations, but I gained a friend and that made me far happier. Romance is a brief-fluttering wing, but friendship is a bird entire, made for long journeys to distant lands and back again. Although Helena had grown out of the habit of aping me in all things, her signature was not exactly like mine anymore, she still wore clothes in the same styles as I wore, but in black and white as I asked all my ladies to. With pale skin and red hair, dressed in gowns that looked like mine, she seemed a younger version of myself wandering court. A long time she had admired me and I her, and although we had fallen out occasionally over the years, about her choice of husband mainly, we had managed to mend and make do, and I thought had become stronger for all the ways we were now sewn together. Sometimes a patch may come to be stronger than the original garment.

Anne Dudley was Countess of Warwick, and possibly, especially since Blanche had passed from life, the most powerful woman of court under me. Wife of Ambrose Dudley she had been, and in some ways I thought that made us sisters-in-law, for if I had ever married anyone it would have been Robin, Ambrose's brother. When he was alive her husband had often complained that I paid no wages to Anne, but she had other ways to feather her nest. She had always been important, but since Blanche had died Anne had become the one within my chambers who took petitions from without. She filtered the requests made of me, and brought to me ones I was likely to support. She knew her job and although people thought it unofficial, I had in fact asked her to do this service for me. It was better people thought she was simply able to ask much of me, being so much in my love, than the truth; that I had asked her to be my sieve for petitions, as Blanche had been. I had not the time nor inclination to spend all my time on such things.

Anne also had a fine network of spies in England and about the world. Her connections with merchants, due to her title, brought much of this about, and Ambrose had been a soldier and a commander, so she had men loyal to him in her little web too. She was clever at making friends with ambassadors, who ever were slippery folk, and many of them were pleased to send information to her in return for the most minor of information on me, and she only shared that which was not important. With these two talents, Anne had become both a link to the world for me and a way of shutting much of it out. Through her I could hear people but did not have to listen to them in person. Since by that time I was finding many people were more tedious than could be borne by my ever-slender temper, Anne was invaluable to me.

The two Katherines, one Hastings and one Howard, were the other two of my closest women. Katherine Hastings was Robin's youngest sister, and the wife of Lord Huntingdon, and although I had long been fond of her she had not had a place at court in a permanent way until after Robin died. It was her choice more than mine, for she had enjoyed quiet in the country more than the clatter of court, but as Robin had gone to the grave I had called for her more and more until she decided she might as well reside at court, for as soon as she left I was bound to call on her again. She was dignified and polite in company, but she did not yearn for others as many of us do; happier she was with her own self, something I often wondered at and was jealous of, for she seemed to have made a close friend of herself many years ago, and therefore was always in company with a friend, a person she liked, even when alone. With Katherine Hastings I could remember times no one else could, for we had known each other since the start of my reign. We both had lost people precious to us. That, in truth, was one of the aspects of friendship that bonded me to all these women; they all understood sorrow, as I did, and they all carried it each day, as did I. We all knew the weight of grief.

Katherine Hastings, indeed, had been so lost to grief when her husband died I had thought it might steal her senses. I had delayed in telling her he was gone until I could do it in person, and she, left without a husband and having no children, had felt most alone. We were usually with one another at least once a day, talking of the past. Katherine, like all those I liked the most, never abused the power she had or our friendship. She stayed at court out of love for me, and I was grateful for it.

Katherine Howard, *nee* Carey, was Countess of Nottingham, my first lady of the bedchamber and eldest daughter of Baron Hunsdon, Henry Carey who was now dead. In life he had either been my cousin or my half-brother. In whichever way we were related, Katherine looked so like me that I had sometimes asked her to don my gowns and pose for portraits that my men insisted I have done for the people of England to see. Being younger than me she made an excellent model who brought the illusion of youth I so needed to maintain to pictures of "me". This would have been enough for me to love her, but there was more. We shared people we had loved, but we also shared a love of people who others would not class people. Oftentimes I found solace with creatures who had fewer words than me and decidedly more hair, and Katherine loved them too. She was in charge of my wardrobe, my jewels, but also my animals, and there were many who spent time in my rooms with me and my ladies, and many of them had better manners than the young gallants of court. There were many horses I would have preferred to spend an afternoon with than with wooing princes flourishing poor poetry, and some apes I had known were demonstrably more intelligent and courteous than lords of this realm. Only one who has no interest in happiness ignores the creatures who share this world with us. They may seem simple in their emotions, yet if they had chosen to be so I believed it was so they might understand few emotions well, better than we with our churning minds and souls ever will.

I nodded to my ladies, who were starting to hover close to me, like bees to a cup of sugared ale they came. A little space they offered me when they knew I wanted it, but too much and they would come after me. I would never become lost when they were with me. I had lost many friends, but those I had left were what kept me from losing myself.

They were with me often, all the time in private and standing as my personal guard in public. More use to me they were in truth than Raleigh's guards, the Gentlemen Pensioners, for my women protected me in ways men could not. They guarded my emotions and protected my fragilities. Since Cecil died they had rallied more than ever, gathering about me as though they were become feathers on a hen's wings and I was a last, lost chick they had to protect. They were ever with me by night and day, making sure I was not reminded of Cecil in public for such would make me break down and they knew I did not welcome the shame of that. Women are so often expected to be creatures of emotion, yet always are looked down on for expressing emotion; a strange paradox.

My women clustered about me when they could see I was sad, so others would not see. They encrusted my face with thick cosmetics to hide the years, made only more obvious by grief and weariness upon my face, and hid the grey skin, made grey by the very cosmetics meant to conceal defects. The ritual of putting on my mask of paint and my gowns in the morning was as though I was being prepared for battle by them each day. They were my Spartan warriors, fiercest fighters of the ancient world, who loved the fellows they marched into battle with and fought only harder to protect them because they did love them. That was what my women did, what they were. Their care and ministrations protected me from a world which would look on an old woman and see nothing *but* an old woman. Youth was lost to me, what beauty I had possessed being eaten by time and by the cosmetics meant to preserve my looks. My figure was still that of a young lass in her prime, and my mind was sharp as an arrow, but eyes saw my skin and hair and they saw my age, and age is not respected upon women as it sometimes is in men. Even then it is rare. Too often the young are so busy feeling sorry for the aged that they hear not a word the aged ones say, heed nothing they do. So many times a woman is ignored through life because of her sex, and now I could add age to the reasons people would try to pass me over too. I was fortunate, glad to have friends who respected me still, listened to me and would do all they could to maintain an appearance of more youth than I possessed, just so my people would continue to hear me.

Yes, my women were my soldiers, for in life we fight many kinds of war and the majority of our conflicts are not ones of blood and broken bone, but little battles fought each day against those who would judge us, against prejudice and foolish beliefs, against the trials of grief and weight of sorrow, against those who would misunderstand us and not take the time to understand. We all need soldiers, guards who stand with us in loyalty and life. I had mine and I thanked God for sending them to me.

There was a ritual now that began each day, a ritual that prepared me to face a world I was growing tired of and people I had small interest in spending any of the precious time I had with. People often say the old become intolerant, and it can be true. Those of us with any sense know that we have little time left, and spending any of that time with fools is hardly a good use. The young can afford to be more magnanimous. They think they have much time to waste, so they do, just as they waste their bodies with wine and food, and their hearts by loving those who deserve not their love. Time I had was not wasted, for I spent much of it with women I loved. In part our morning and evening rituals of dressing me for court, and undressing me, took so long because I needed more adornments those days to dazzle my people, and in part they were longer because I wanted to spend my time with my women, with my friends, rather than in my Presence Chamber, fools and imbecilic infants dancing about me, trying to gain favour.

Each morning my women dressed me in more lavish and more garishly coloured gowns. My ladies were to wear only black and white, so they became to me as the wood surrounding a portrait, plain colours making mine only more brilliant. This also meant people noted them less, and so my ladies could discover information without being seen to be doing so; perfect spies in plain sight. People always supposed I did most things I did out of vanity, and it was as well they supposed so, and so wrongly. The supposition that I was a vain creature, who did everything out of a desire to appear beautiful, covered up a great deal I was doing behind the backs of such judgemental eyes. The plain colours of my ladies made them uniform, so people did not note immediately when one of my closest companions was near, listening to what was said, and it made them fade behind me into one, which also gave them the ability to hear and see much others missed. I had an army of spies and they stood right in front of all eyes at court. Fools could think what they wished. When I adorned myself it was not for vanity, but survival. People had to think me always full of health, or they would start imagining my death.

My head now entirely bare of hair, I wore wigs. Once I had worn those that matched my own colouring, reds, and they concealed a head of thinning grey hair, but of recent times I had started to wear wigs in colours that did not exist in nature, for if one must be bald, one might as well have fun with it.

Each morning thick layers of cosmetics were applied to my face. I looked younger than I truly was because of this makeup, and it was also the fashion, as Italians, always the leader of what is sophisticated, were wearing their makeup thick. Early in my reign I would have flinched from so much cosmetic on my face, but now it was needed. Paint and powder I had worn over the years had discoloured my own face; my skin was slightly grey, yellow under my eyes. This, along with discoloured teeth from my love of sweet treats, gave me an aged appearance, one I could not have. If I looked old, my people would look at me and see death, they would see an end, and in doing so they would commit treason for it is treason for a people to imagine the death of their king. It was also dangerous for me because the moment people start imagining that you are dead, they can see a world without you, the moment people start imagining you are not there they think of who they will put in your place. I had enough enemies. I did not need to make my own people my enemies by allowing them to imagine a world in which I was no more needed. This is why I had to preserve the illusion of youth. If I was young then I would not die, this is one of the foolish lies we tell to one another. People forget that many aged carry on living long past the time anyone thinks they will, as they forget that youth is no shield against death. Plenty who are young die young. But these are the illusions we believe, the lies we tell to make life acceptable.

Once I had been washed, perfumed, cosmetics caked upon my skin and salves upon my lips, ointments on my face to make my skin shine, once I had been cleansed, treated, my entire face, neck and hands painted with ceruse, my lips and cheeks washed with a red paste of beeswax, cochineal and plant dye, my eyes lined with kohl, once my body was enclosed in silk and velvet and jewels so numerous that I shone like the night sky had been hung on every available piece of my body, once I had good gloves in hand in winter and a shawl in summer, when a wig so tall and thick it towered over my head and wobbled in the breeze was upon my bald head and a wash of white had been applied to my yellow and blackened teeth, then I could face court, then I could appear before my people dressed in my own armour, bearing my own weapons.

In such armour and with such weapons, people might still believe I was young, or at least not soon to die. For one thing the effort all this took and the time should show I was hale enough, for it was a trial of endurance merely to be dressed each day.

And in such armour and with such weapons people might still deign to hear me, not ignore me as so many people ignore the old, *because* they are old, and the young *must* know more than the old. Another fantasy made of lies.

In truth, age must speak loud not because their own ears are faulty, but because the ears of all younger than them cease to hear them. The more wrinkles one has, the fewer ears and minds open to listen to you; the more grey hairs, the less important your thoughts become. The young declare they listen to wisdom passed on but in truth they are so busy shouting such things that they hear nothing at all. And if their ears hear you not, eyes drift past you too, as though you have in age become a creature of transparent skin and no substance. People start to see you as a memory, begin to pass you by as though you are a ghost wandering through your own life, at the end of your own story.

The reason they do not want to see or hear you is because you remind them of their own end. You stand, a ruined monument to an age lost, but people do not want to wander about your ruins, for you are too close to them, their own empire and their own world. Too close is not comfortable. To look upon you is to look upon their own end, the end of the world, their lives, and the crumbling of their kingdom. You are a reminder of death they do not want, even though in truth you may be further from the hand of Death than they, these foolish, bold youths are. They dance with death all the time, taking hands with Him to go to war, or to bear children. Those who reach a great age do so because they are either cautious or lucky. The young could learn much from the old, but they never do. So few people learn anything. All people should be students all their lives, for then they would learn a fraction of the knowledge the world contains, but so many do not learn a thing. A life is wasted that is not spent, at least in part, lost in the sin of curiosity and the virtue of knowledge. This was in my mind in particular that day, for I was thinking of a man who learnt nothing no matter how many lessons he was sent by God and me. I was thinking of Essex.

It was November. I had just ordered Southampton, fellow Earl and friend of Essex, home from the Continent after learning his mistress Elizabeth Vernon had given birth to his bastard daughter in the countryside. "At least she went into hiding," I had muttered when I heard the news. One maid of apparently most dubious honour had given birth to a bastard child in the Maidens' Chamber some few years ago. Could no one keep control over themselves anymore? It seemed all my maids had forgot their honour, tossing away virtue on the hollow promises of men who simply wanted to use them to scratch an itch of desire, and all my men had surrendered the notion of honourable behaviour and were instead impregnating women of court then scampering off to other lands, presumably to do the same there to other women. Essex had come to plead for his friend, even though I thought he had plenty else he should be thinking of.

"Should you not be more occupied with thoughts of war, not of love or in this case *lust*, my lord Earl?" I asked, deeply annoyed, when Essex came armed with one of his flowery, familiar speeches to defend his friend. The mention of his title, which I only used with my men when I was in anger with them as mothers and fathers may shout names entire of offending children at them when they are in a rage, should have warned him, but Essex never could take a warning, or wisdom, from others. He knew everything, you see?

"Majesty, most gracious lady, pearl of this world and guardian of all graces, Southampton is not at fault in this matter," Essex declared as I winced at the false flattery that slipped so easily from his pretty lips. "The woman, Mistress Vernon, was so lost in love for him that she would not let the matter rest until he had concluded her desire with his."

I arched an eyebrow. "What, the strength of England's men is lost, is it, my lord Earl? Are men like Southampton so fragile that a woman may overcome them? Southampton is at the very least three times the size of Mistress Vernon. Is his strength so feeble that he could not hold her away, or are his legs faulty, my lord, that he was not able to run from her or even walk? I think if Southampton had wanted to resist, and barring the notion that Mistress Vernon drugged him, he could have fended her off," I said, my tone so dry it could have outmatched the deserts for lack of moisture.

Essex barely heard me. He had become accustomed to talking and being heard, but seldom offered such indulgence to others. As he launched into a list of Southampton's virtues, and declared that he wanted him for the coming campaign in Ireland so I could not *possibly* throw the man into jail for deflowering and dishonouring one of my ladies, as if a military need outweighed any crimes Southampton had committed, I held up my hand.

"Cease," I said, closing my eyes to pull the strength that darkness held into my soul. "Go, prepare for the command you begged for, my lord Earl and desist from throwing yourself into business that concerns you not. Into your hands I am setting the greatest force I or any of my ancestors ever sent to Ireland in order that you might quell the foul rebellion there led by Tyrone, and therefore into you I am setting more trust than with any man, yet you are here, pleading for one man who cannot manage to keep his breeches buttoned when around a pretty woman? For Southampton you are expending energy when I, your sovereign and master, have entrusted you with more power than any other Lord Marshal ever was given?" I arched my other eyebrow. "You make me regret my choice of commander, my lord Earl, and you are not even in command yet."

With that, he was gone. He could not risk the notion I might decide to take his commission away. That would strike too deep at his pride, and pride was what ran in his veins rather than blood.

"For the day at least," I said to Anne Dudley when she told me the Earl had departed my outer rooms. "He will be back tomorrow when the idea he can persuade me by shouting at me comes to him again. When the itch to dominate me rises, he must scratch it."

She smiled a little, sad smile for she knew what I said pained me. I never had welcomed those who, dog-like, try to dominate by barking, and Essex made me sadder and sadder each time he tried, for it not only showed a lack of imagination and intelligence, and I was sure he possessed both, but a growing desire to overthrow me, in will if not in reality. "You could still appoint another commander, Majesty," she had said. "If you are unsure about Essex for Ireland, you could send someone else."

I almost laughed. "No one else wanted the position, Anne, and all found excuses not to put themselves forth," I said. "In truth, there was no one in title or blood or experience better suited than Essex to this role, and that is why he has it." I looked at her. "I place him in this position not because I trust him more than others," I said. "I place him because I have no one else, and he knows that, as does everyone else in this country."

I had looked to the window. The country had lost a father with Cecil, gained nothing but an unruly child with Essex. Sometimes I wondered why God was testing me so much, when I had little strength or will left. "You should have tested me when I was young," I said to my Lord in Heaven. "Then I would have had more time to prove myself, Father."

I sighed, under my tree. Thinking of these troubled matters did little good. The present had to unfold to future, and we would see what Essex could do when to Ireland he went. Pulling my shoulders back, I walked away from the tree Cecil had planted. I looked back as I came to the palace gate, the steps leading to the Privy Chamber. The leaves were still dancing in the breeze but I could no more hear the sound of their whispers. Yet still the shade he had wanted to create for me was there, a dark shadow on a knoll of soft grass and chamomile. Seeing my face fall, Anne and Helena appeared beside me, their hands there to guide me up the slippery stone steps, through the walkway that smelt of cold, damp stone, just as their hearts were there to stand beside my own, valiant hearts of stoic strength there to bolster my courage.

Little food and rest did I take in those days, but I had another source of sustenance. My ladies fed me courage and compassion, and I ate gratefully from their hands.

Chapter Two

Greenwich Palace
Winter 1598

"All men become experts the moment something of moment occurs," I muttered, hearing two young gallants of court discuss tactics Essex *surely* would use in Ireland against Tyrone and his rebel lords. Only a fool, said they, would ignore the fact that the Irish used the terrain so well, knew it so intimately, therefore my lord of Essex, not being a fool, would need native guides to show him where and when he would be attacked.

Right they might be, but fools they remained. It is so much easier to give advice than it is to take or act upon it, much easier to be on the outside looking in than to be the one who must decide which path to take. Men like these two gabbling in the hallway of my palace were suddenly everywhere, all talking of Ireland, of Essex, of what would happen. On the basis of nothing but the arrogance of certainty in their own minds, many had become experts in the art of war.

The truth was Ireland was trouble, especially for one who did not weigh up all that might or could happen. It was true the enemy knew their territory, were experts in it, and managed to sustain themselves on very little food. Although I would have called this necessity, the apparent supernatural powers of the Irish led some of my soldiers to name them *ghosts*. Yet we had enough problems in this realm of existence before worrying about another. Communications in Ireland as well as supplies were taxing as often the roads were impassable to wheeled carts, and rain fell with unnerving persistence. Corruption was a demon which haunted our troops in Ireland. When pay, always in arrears, was short, soldiers often sold arms and even clothes to Irishmen who then sold them on to rebels and made profit. This meant we English were, inadvertently, arming and clothing the rebels we fought. Some Irish who joined the English army changed sides whenever they wished. Englishmen found this shocking, but I did not. What cause had the Irish to be loyal to England? My own family had treated their country badly enough, and we were just the latest in a long line who had viewed Ireland as some provincial backwater full of savages. I was sending an army to Ireland now not because I was affronted that rebels had risen, but because it was too dangerous to England to allow them to do so. Allow Ireland to fall to enemies and England, which had to be my first priority, and sadly often rulers must pick such a thing, would fall too. Gaining the loyalty of the Irish was not something that would in my reign happen. That was a task future kings would have to undertake. What I required was obedience, but I was under no illusions that the Irish would obey me willingly.

The truth was Ireland was the back gate to England, and our enemies such as Spain and Rome wanted to sneak in through this unsteady entrance. The gate had to be closed and locked, secured, and that was what I was sending Essex to do. His armies would subdue the rebel leader Hugh O'Neil, *the* O'Neil as he was called, Earl of Tyrone, and a military presence would prevent Ireland from rising up again. I did not believe this would win England friends in Ireland, especially from the common people. It was an ugly task, and a hard one, but for the sake of my kingdom entire it had to be done.

I walked to my window and stared out. Snow had fallen the previous night, and now covered everything. Dusk was falling again and more snow had come to join the army of winter spread across my lands. The vast whiteness of the snow, flakes that sparkled as stars before my eyes as they fell from light to darkness and then to light again, and the darkness beyond their light, filled my eyes. What was beyond that darkness? In waking days I would tell you there were fields and houses, the river and her boatmen, there were shops where food could be bought or the bridge where people would wander, but in that strange half light and darkness there could have been anything beyond. I stared onto a border between our world and the world where dreams are born. In these late days of my life I always seemed to be seeing borders, boundaries, places where realms of old and new met, and I found myself wondering what lay beyond that I could not see? Part of me itched to slip on boots and race away into the gardens, then beyond, never to be found again. What a jest that would be, that one day the aged Queen had just kicked off her fine court slippers and run off, and to where no man knew but there were tales she had been seen in britches and a wig, running off to join the pirates plundering the New World. "A pirate Queen, Rob," I whispered.

I chuckled a little, thinking that destiny my friend had once promised me when we were children would be fine and sweet, easier than all I had to do in this life I had been handed to exist in. "If only I could transgress those borders as I so wish I could," I whispered to the ghostly reflection of myself. "I would have adventures such as you would not dream."

She looked wry, the woman in the window. Her eyes were lecturing, telling me I had already lived adventures such as many would love to boast of, and had survived them to tell the tale, a feat even more impressive. *Be satisfied with all you have done, Elizabeth of England,* she scolded. *Many have lived lives much smaller than yours, and been less honoured than you, you ingrate!*

Of course she had a point, but there are times all of us, even old women whom many would look upon and think the fire had gone out in their bellies, dream of a new and different life, a life of adventure and freedom.

I breathed in, deep and long, turning my thoughts back to business, where they should be. Tyrone was one of the most successful of Irish rebel leaders, who had been able to unite his forces and arm them with pikes and other weapons most modern. We English should have been superior in organisation and technique, but fighting in Ireland was very different to fighting on the Continent, and few people had developed the specialist talents and skills which were required to put the Irish down. Essex had belief in his own abilities, and he was one of my more seasoned generals, but he was no expert in the kind of fighting that would be required in Ireland. It had been agreed that his most important operation was to lead his army into Tyrone's power base of Ulster, make a garrison there, and then seek to pull this troublesome rebel plant out by the root. Essex swore he would do this, as he swore he would personally kill Tyrone. There were already too many boasts for me to rest easy.

"My lord of Essex will, of course, need much horse for the campaign too..." a voice from the hallway echoed as another set of fools talking war wandered past. "The best would be the ponies the Irish themselves use. My lord Robert of Leicester always said they were the best horseflesh in the world."

"The Arab horses are faster," said another.

I shook my head. "Go tell those men if they cannot keep their voices down when they wander outside the Queen's chamber then I shall be pleased to take their tongues and make a gift of them to their wives," I said to Paul, one of my pages. "I am sure the possession of such waggling, annoying things would bring great peace to their poor wives."

He grinned, relishing the task, and ran off to relay my message.

They were not alone, these fools of Englishmen talking of war and getting involved in much they should have stayed out of. There had been some of Spain too, interfering where they should not. On his deathbed Phillip of Spain, my enemy, once brother-in-law and even betrothed, albeit something promised in a secret agreement I never had intended to keep, had written to Tyrone and encouraged his rebellion. "How sweet that his last thought was in truth of me, albeit of my destruction," I had said when I heard of a letter Phillip sent to

Tyrone, mayhap written in the death-throes of Phillip's life. "Phillip never could stop thinking of me, even when married to my sister."

My ladies and gentlemen had laughed, but there was a truth to what I said. Phillip had been obsessed with me for much of our adult lives, and if he could not possess me in marriage, subdue me in that way, he would destroy me. He never succeeded.

Many had said his successor, another Phillip and his only living son, would be mild compared to his father, but it was not so. Robert Cecil's spies, already a good network the young man had built along with others inherited from his father, had been busy. The new King of Spain intended to continue his father's mission, or fixation, to invade England. No matter that they had sent almost more Armadas over the past years than anyone could count and each one had either been seen off by our navy, or more often by the weather, the Spanish kept on trying. They altered their plans but a little, always seemed to be setting out into our seas at the wrong time of year, and their ships fell to waves, to water and to wind before ever having a chance to challenge us for England. One might think they would learn, but Phillip never had, and his successor looked set to follow the same path. How many of us make mistakes in our own life by seeking to fulfil the wishes of our parents?

"His son might have a different notion, however, Majesty," Robert Cecil told me.

"How so?"

"Using Ireland as a way into England."

"That is not new, Phillip his father did it before."

"I know, Majesty, but it would seem, from all I have heard, this is where the new King will concentrate his efforts rather than aiming for the mainland at all."

"And with Ireland in revolt, it is not a poor plan," I said. "Get reinforcements to Tyrone, and he and Phillip of Spain combined could be dangerous."

Which was why the choice of commander sent to go against Tyrone was becoming increasingly important as time went on, and why I was worrying that Essex was not the right man. But what was also true was no one else wanted the commission or had volunteered for it, that Essex had the right as Earl Marshal to command my forces, and that he was the only one with blood high enough to be commander. I had to admit there were times I chose men solely for their titles and families; it was, after all, the way it had been for hundreds if not thousands of years, for if I was chosen by God to rule then men had to be chosen by God to be noble. Yet many times I wondered. My father had rewarded and promoted men of use as well as title, and I had done the same where I could. Commander of my armies was not a post I could hand to just anyone, but there were times I wondered if God was jesting with me when He offered only Essex as commander. Mayhap it was a test, and I was supposed to pick otherwise, break old rules of blood and title in combat. Or perhaps the Almighty had a plan for Essex that would, in the end, have him confronting the ghost of his father's failures in Ireland, a phantom which long had haunted him, and see him rising to glory. Who knew? I was as endlessly baffled by the mind of the Almighty as I was awed by His creations.

I felt often I was being tested more in these late days of my life than I had when I was young, and all I could bring to bear upon such challenges was the patience and perseverance I had learnt. The trouble was that I had supposed that through hard work and diligence in His cause, which to me was to bring peace upon a world much troubled by war, I might be rewarded, yet all I seemed to encounter were more challenges, and any period of peace was short. I also seemed to have lost more people than many others, and I wondered why. I had tried many times to avoid war where possible, and there never had been the kinds of persecutions in England over faith that there had been in other lands. I had dealt with traitors where I had to, but especially compared to my contemporaries and forebears had taken few lives. I had shown mercy sometimes to my detriment. Mentioning this once to Cecil before he died, he had smiled. "God sends work to those He knows will complete it, Majesty," he had said. "And God's work is never done. The Almighty created the world in seven days, but He has been tinkering with it ever since."

Perhaps my old friend had had a point, and God sought out those already busy to hand more tasks to, knowing that if you want something done you should always ask a busy person to help you. Those who remain un-busy remain so for they do no work. But even so, even if continued challenges were a compliment sent by God, honouring my abilities, there still seemed to be a level of unfairness I struggled with. I began to think I would like to be tested less, and sometimes have a clap on the back when I did well, rather than be handed another office to perform, or another trial to endure.

Another concern came with another King. James of Scotland, my godson and the man most favoured to succeed to the throne after me, which many gazing upon my old bones murmured would not be long now, seemed to have been making friends I would rather he did not. Since I was his godmother and his mother was dead, albeit at my hands, I thought I had some right to say who I thought my godson should play with, and the people he was apparently communicating with in Ireland did not please me. One was rumoured to be Tyrone himself.

"My godson began the year by insulting me before his Parliament," I grumbled to Robert Cecil. "Then, when I complained about this James demonstrated a coward soul by sending a letter to say he would not engage in the *sport* ladies excelled at; *insults*, thereby insulting me once again in a craven and covert manner. And now, this!"

We had no direct proof James was in communication with Tyrone, and certainly none of a conspiracy, but there were other things going on which led me to trust him less. The fact that James's wife, Anne of Denmark, appeared to have decidedly Catholic leanings of sympathy was one thing, but James seemed to be using his wife's religious sympathies to foster hope amongst Catholic nations and leaders, the Pope most of all, that if he succeeded me he would convert his own religion, and England would be no more a free Protestant state, but under the purple boot of Rome again. I doubted he would actually go through with it. I thought all of this mere posturing to secure more support, but it was not pleasing to me. I had worked hard to throw off the yoke of Rome's power, set about England's neck once more by my sister after being cast off by my father, and I had no intention of allowing any successor of mine to bow to the Bishop of Rome again. England was and would remain free and independent. Let other countries genuflect before a man of gold like the Pope, and let England be ruled by the monarch sent by God to lead its people.

But James liked the support, of course, and was building links with Spain, another thing I did not like. The new King of Spain was sending an ambassador to Scotland. Word was they were to talk of how Spain would support Scotland in claiming the throne. What I wondered was if they were talking of after my natural death, or if they would create a death unnatural for me, to speed succession along.

"We intercepted letters that may be from James, sent to Tyrone," Robert Cecil told me later that night, coming to share time with me at my fire as his father had.

"*May* be?"

"The seal is imperfect and signatures suspect," he said, one finger rubbing his temple. "And yet, James may have done that himself in case these letters got into English hands."

"Ormond tells me Tyrone would work with James," I said, speaking of Tyrone's former tutor who had offered much information on Tyrone to Robert. Since the rebel Tyrone had been educated at the English court, he knew much of our ways of warfare and tactics. To my mind it was only fair we should have the same on him, so I had enlisted all who had spent time with him when he was in England as a lad, to tell tales to my men that we might learn about him. Anne Dudley had been taking care of this for me. "*Would* James work with the O'Neil rebel?" I asked. "Is he so impatient for the throne he cannot wait for my natural death?"

"Your Majesty is in the best of health, perhaps James does not want to wait," said Cecil, looking up from his papers, a pile in his lap.

"Do you think I should feign illness to make my godson more loyal to me?" I asked, and laughed. But soon I stopped. "Would he join with my enemies, Robert? Make me abdicate, as men did to his mother? It would be a perfect revenge for me taking her head, would it not? He could turn Mary's fate upon me, make me feel the pain and humiliation she endured."

"There is always the danger of impatience, Majesty, especially in young princes who see a great destiny just out of reach, and you do not name him your successor, so he may fear you will name another."

"Like whom?" I snorted. "Arbella Stuart, or the Infanta Isabella? Much as I would relish another woman on the throne, neither of them are suited to this position, and men of England want a king after me. Two reigns of women have been enough for them. I think sometimes they care not really who the one to follow me will be, as long as he possesses a shaft. People tire of the same dish, and I have been served to my people every day for forty years now. They seek a different flavour. James must know he is the favoured candidate, the one many of my people hunger for."

"There are few who support the Infanta, since she is of Spain," Robert agreed. "But there are some who would favour Arbella, spoilt and sullen a woman though she is, for she was born in England."

"Many people were born in England, Pygmy, that does not mean they all should sit upon this throne. It would collapse under the weight."

Robert laughed, but I shook my head. "Arbella was born noble, not royal," I said. "And she would be awful for the kingdom, you and I and any person of sense knows that. Arbella Stuart would treat England as a plaything, as something to further stoke the flames of vanity and arrogance within her. She would drape England about her shoulders like a fine fur, leave the people to starve as long as she had gold rings and fine boots enough. England to her is not a calling or a duty, it is a toy, and when she is done playing with it, it would lie broken upon the ground."

I shook my head. "James is who I would pick, though I will never say so before another or Parliament. Imperfect though he is, he was born to be a King and understands the sacred duty the crown bestows. James is aware of the griefs and losses that come with a throne, and therefore he would never treat it lightly. But he must wait for the power he covets, for it is mine at the moment. I have no intention of being forced from my throne at this stage of my life. My enemies would deny an old woman her chair? Such rudeness is not to be borne."

"I believe, Majesty, if James is in communication with Tyrone it is so he might gain information on what is going on in Ireland, and what may happen in England. It is the same as his use of his Queen's religious sympathies for Catholics, if they are in fact true at all and not a feint. James uses Anne to reach men who would not otherwise talk to him, since he is a heretic like all of us, and through pretending to be or become something, he gains information." Cecil was looking at me oddly.

"What do you want to say that you fear to?" I asked.

"I was going to say, Majesty, you yourself would like as not do many of the things James is doing if you were in his position."

"That he is as capable of deceit and tricks as I am, is not something I welcome," I said and rubbed my own temple. The games went on, sometimes I thought them endless. "Make James aware that I have heard of these rumours, and tell his ambassadors I have been shouting about them. Say that I am in great anger, that everyone at court flees from me, and that I have shouted I lust to create a law to exclude the sons of Scotland, or her daughters, from the English throne because of continued treachery against their own blood. That should scare James enough to make him back away from any plans forming between him and Spain, or Ireland."

"It could push him further towards them," Cecil warned.

"Then, much as I will regret much of what will occur, we need to ensure Ireland is crushed, and cannot be a go-between between Spain and Scotland," I said. "That means Essex must succeed, and if he does not he will answer for it."

As Cecil left I shook my head. Once I had felt surrounded by allies, if not friends, but now as true souls died I seemed only to have enemies; wolves at my door, crying out for my blood in the darkness of the long winter night.

Chapter Three

Richmond Palace
Winter 1599- Spring 1599

I looked up from pages of paper and scribbled notes; a veritable sea of thoughts, many half-formed and few fully realised, were spread out in enjoyable chaos before me. Lost in my task I had been content, until life interfered. I scowled at the one who had interrupted me. A messenger, sent by Essex with yet another message of thanks for my granting him his position as Lord Lieutenant of Ireland. "Thank you," I muttered, taking the note and handing it straight to Anne Dudley without reading it. She would have it in the fire soon, the best place for platitudes.

I pressed inky fingers to the brow of my nose, pinched, and closed my eyes. "Tell my lord Earl that he would do better with his time to plan out his ideas for Ireland than to send endless notes thanking me for his commission," I said to the messenger. "He has the position, so there is no need to keep fawning for it. Let it be clear that if he fails I will not be pleased. This position he may not thank me for so much when he begins the work it entails."

The messenger clearly did not want to give such a message to his master, but I waved him away, understanding a watered-down version of my words would be in the ears of Essex soon enough. No doubt the messenger would say I had *praised* Essex, *simpered* over his letter of poetic thanks. No doubt, for the characters of young men are fragile and need much pampering. Like spoilt hounds they pester for treats, and those treats make them fat and useless. I had had enough of pandering to them. Let Essex understand he had what he had asked for, and let him begin to work for the glory he desired to come of it. I had worked all my life to take and to hold the position I had been granted by blood. The younger generation needed to learn the same was true for them.

I exhaled long and deep, wishing that day was one of the ones I rode on, but it was not. I was sixty-five years of age, and rode out to hunt every other day. This was a goal, indeed a pleasure I had set for myself and it was keeping me in good health. But if I did not rest for a day between rides, I felt it keenly. Virgil was my companion on rest days, and normally I was happy with him, but young men such as Essex were always intruding on my times of peace and pleasing occupation.

In truth it was not just annoyance at Essex that was making my temper frayed. As I aged, I was finding it harder to control unruly young men of court. Once I had delighted in them, finding their spirited manners and boldness enticing, enlivening to my blood which then was young and bold as theirs was, but now I found them tiring more than anything, ridiculous occasionally, and every now and then, dangerous. Essex was too popular. The people, looking upon his handsome face, his fine figure, and feeling his charming ways warming their souls, wanted to believe in him. What they saw in Essex was an image of a past that in truth had never truly existed, which granted them hope for a future that never would be. They saw chivalry in him, because of the idealistic way he spoke and the foolish way he boasted, and chivalry was an ideal of a past when knights protected maidens, commoners, and the rights of all free men. Yet this past had never been. It had been made up by men like my father who had wanted to believe in times of romance. It did not take much effort for you to turn a few pages of history and find within them that knights had never been these men of honour as they are so lauded in annals of myth. Codes of chivalry were agreements between knights, there to protect the rights of noble men, men with coin to buy swords, and no one else. Most knights had cared not a ha'penny for the rights of others, certainly not for those of men or women, common or not, who they exploited more often than protected. Yet people want to believe. They want to believe in a world of myth and fairy-tale where good prevails, where the evil are easy to recognise; where noble men are honourable men, simply because they are noble. My people wanted to believe in Essex, because they wanted a future full of romance and he was a romantic figure. The trouble was, he was never going to give them what they wanted, for all he embodied was fiction. Fiction rarely comes true. Reality has a habit of getting in the way.

In truth, the reason they wanted to believe in him was darker even than that which I have just explained. People want to believe that their rulers are good, as they wish to believe that their fathers, their husbands or any who have ultimate control over their lives are good. If such people are *not* good that means that those under them, wives, servants, those bound to lords and subjects of the Crown are in grave danger. This is why those who are abused by others spend their time blaming themselves for their abuse. Wives who were beaten by husbands say that they *must* have done something to deserve it. Children beaten by their parents blame themselves. Servants of the Crown blame the advisors of the king, not the king himself for all wrong that is done in his reign. If the one in ultimate control of us is wicked or evil or foolish, there is no hope for us in the future. We may as well be doomed.

The fact that the people wanted to believe in *Essex*, and were blaming me for his failures rather than blaming him, did not bode well. It might mean that the loyalty that so long had been mine was mine no more. More people worship a rising sun than a falling star, and, despite the layers of paint upon my face, despite the glorious gowns I wore, the thinness of my waist, the hale and hearty strength with which I could leap in the dance, it was not hard to see that my part now was the setting sun. Upon my reign dusk was falling. Yet a man like Essex was still young enough to carry on past my reign, all things being well, and he would live into the reign of the one who followed me.

And that was dangerous. As I was aware of this, as I suspected he was, then it meant he was already envisioning my death, was already thinking of what he would do when I was no more. When people start to imagine your death, one day imagine a world without you, they start to think of you as disposable. They start to think it would be better to be without you now, not just in the future.

I turned back to my pages, translations of Virgil, a man I should never grow tired of reading as I was tired of reading the letters of Essex and he had not left England yet.

"Some say this will be Essex's ruin, madam, and that is why his foes are so eager he should be sent." Anne Dudley was near me, setting the paper into the fire without me asking her to. She knew me well.

"His friends declare it will be his making, and that is why he asked to be sent." Helena was there to offer the other side of the argument.

Half of my heart which still thought of Essex as my son, kin of my heart as well as blood, sighed with sorrow over the first argument. The part of my heart which knew him for an enemy arched an eyebrow at the second. That was the trouble with Essex. He enraged me and I knew he had scant respect for me anymore, but still hope, that enemy of reason, lingered. Still affection, that fool who keeps on falling for lies, wanted to believe in him. I needed him to succeed, England did, so wishing he might turn out to be the hero many thought he could be was not entirely foolish. The trouble was, he had had many a chance to be a man, let alone a hero, and chose to remain a boy. I had a sinking feeling of defeat already, and he had not left England's shores yet.

"The Earl *asked* to be sent," I said, scribbling a note against a word that might be translated two ways, with very different meanings, on a side bar of my work. I felt as though I had explained Essex's commission a thousand times now, and was getting weary of repeating myself. "He pleaded for the command time and time again. I am not so light and foolish that I can afford to throw away good order in one part of my kingdom in order to merely teach a rash young man a lesson, and my Councillors, whether they support Essex or not, know Ireland is a perilous place to fall into disorder. It would be a simpleton who would want the Earl sent to Ireland *knowing* he would fail, and I do not surround myself with fools. Life is too short to waste on the opinion of braying monkeys who use only half the wits God granted them and spend the rest of their time gossiping and whining about those who achieve more than them."

I looked up at them and tapped my fingers on the table. "Essex *asked* for this command. He will do well, do badly or do something no man will think to mention again, it being so dull a tale. This command is *his* and he is responsible for its success or failure. No other but he. It is about time the pup learned to be a wolf, about time the boy learned to become a man and accept responsibility. Not until we are ready to own our actions, mistakes and flaws can we claim our successes and virtues, and not until then are we grown. Not many achieve it, which is why there are so many children wandering this world thinking they are adults when they are not." I frowned. "And children can be dangerous when they do not grow up."

My women knew what I was talking about. That February a work had come out on the life and reign of King Henry IV, with the book dedicated to Essex. Already people had drawn parallels between Essex and Bolingbroke, the man's name before he made himself Henry IV by usurping the throne from his cousin, Richard II. The fact that I had been compared to Richard in the past, and Essex was now being compared to the man who overthrew Richard, was hardly welcome. This dedication seemed like a warning shot, as though enemies who might see me off the throne and another upon it were signalling their intentions. Essex, fool though he was in many ways, had been worried by this dedication, but I think he had also been pleased. He was the darling of the people, far more popular than I was at that time. Youth and beauty carry much currency with popular imagination. He might not be considering usurping my throne, but becoming the power behind my throne or that of my successor was not something Essex would dismiss. In some ways he saw himself as my successor, the one who would lead England when I was gone, even if it was from behind the robes of another king. And he wanted to rule now, when I was still alive. Essex believed he had power over me, because he believed I loved him still.

He was much mistaken.

The author of this work, called *The First Part of the Life and Reign of King Henry IV*, was Dr John Hayward, and I am not sure he was or had intended to become one of my enemies. He might have had a simple interest in history, but intended or not, his work aroused dangerous thoughts in people. I had been furious to see the book published, even though aside from the dedication there was little in it drawing parallels between me and Richard, or Essex and Bolingbroke. The author had been made aware of my intense displeasure, and the book was not circulating openly at court, although I had no doubt that, like all books banned or looked on with displeasure by the ruling power, it circulated well enough underground.

"Cannot this John Hayward be prosecuted for treason?" I had asked Francis Bacon who had training in the law, and came more often to advise me in those days than he had his former master Essex.

"Not, I think, for treason, madam, but for felony," he replied, a tiny smile inching up the corner of his mouth.

"How so?"

"Why, he has stolen so many pages from Tacitus!" Bacon laughed a little.

I had suggested to Bacon that Hayward be arrested and that he be shown the rack to make him talk, to see if men bent on causing trouble and working treason had put him up to writing this work. Bacon dissuaded me from the rack, but Hayward was arrested and condemned in the Star Chamber for having dared to write of the fall of a sovereign at the hands of a subject. He was imprisoned in the Fleet for the rest of my reign, and I hoped there he would learn not to write any more books.

I turned back to my own books, and tried to regain the comfort I had felt, yet itching thoughts came like errant, gnawing fish nibbling the toes of dead, drowned men. If Essex was Bolingbroke, why was I handing him an army?

*

On the 12th of March, I signed Essex's commission. He had leave to return from Ireland when he thought fit. He had powers unprecedented in other ways too; in one clause I had authorised him to prosecute or conclude the war at his discretion, even to come to terms with Tyrone if nothing else could be done. Essex himself had convinced me that this expedition alone could save Ireland for good, and he needed more power than any other Lord Lieutenant had ever been offered before.

And I had given it to him. Essex himself declared it the best warrant that any man had, and indeed he had the best army. He was almost ready to leave.

Some said I feared Essex greatly, and was therefore sending him to Ireland in the hope he would die. Why I would need to do such I had no idea. Did people think me such a coward? Essex had given me reason enough to arrest him in the past and I had shown mercy. Perhaps gossipmongers thought I would not dare now, since Essex was so beloved by my own people. They might have had a point, but I would not grant someone such a large army and such an important commission as controlling Ireland on a whim, hoping they would be murdered in a bog somewhere, lost to all time in a miasma of peat. People said if it was not me behind this, it was Robert Cecil, for he hated Essex greatly, the Earl being far more handsome and charismatic than the dull hunchbacked younger son of William Cecil. I had no doubt Robert did dislike Essex, they had long been rivals, but he too was not dullard enough to want to send a man off on such an important mission simply so he would fail. If Essex failed, we lost control of Ireland. Spain or perhaps the Scots would seize that control, and England would be undone.

The fact so many people thought Essex was being set up to fail, and he had not even begun his mission yet, also boded not well. If even his supporters had this little faith in him then I had perhaps chosen entirely wrong. Yet he was so popular with his own men, with the vast army I had put together for him, so I thought there was some hope. If men believe in the men they serve they will fight for them, and may well die.

Essex seemed enthused about his mission, which gave me a little more hope too. In truth I had handed him more power than any other commander I had sent to any place in the world, so he had little cause to be miserable. His forces were the greatest ever sent to Ireland. If he succeeded or if he failed it was on his head. He had no excuses that his men were not enough, not experienced enough, that he had not enough support, so if he succeeded then the victory was his, and if he failed it was his responsibility entire. I wanted him to succeed, and had given him all I could to ensure that outcome. My doubts of faith were also true enough, but I was giving him one last chance to prove himself.

And I had no one else.

I suppose it was a test, of kinds. But it was more than that. I was tired of hearing, when Essex failed, of how it was the fault of *everyone* but him. I was sending him to Ireland with all he could ever possibly need to succeed, and if he won I would allow him to claim all glory of his mission. But if he failed this time there would be nowhere to hide, and all my people would see that, as would I, as would my enemies, as would all who supported Essex. A test perhaps, indeed, but it was not unfair.

I had set him up to win, and if he did not that was on his head, or possibly neck might be a better word.

Many, naturally, did not believe the Earl was being given all he could be. Some already were making excuses in case he failed.

"People say I am setting the Earl up for failure, madam," said Robert Cecil. He looked weary of the accusations being whispered about court. I understood how he felt.

"Odd is it not that so many already suppose he will not succeed that they seek someone to blame in his place?" I asked. "Is it a sign of how much they love Essex, or how little they believe in him?" I smoothed my skirts and pulled on my sleeves, using them to cover and warm my hands. "The Earl was the choice we made, due to blood and title for Ireland, and for all the anger between you two, all the boyish resentment and then adult arguments, I know you would not waste men and money to destroy a man. People think when a person is high they will play games with anything, at any cost, but the truth is that the wiser of us know the stakes only too well."

"If Ireland fell to Spain or Rome, so England would follow."

"My worries are as strong as yours, for if he fails then we will be in danger great, and in a way if he succeeds I may be in worse. They call him Bolingbroke. Should I wait for a dark knife at my back, or the day I will be stolen away from my own palace and thrown in a cell, to wait for death?"

I walked to the window and stared out. Sometimes I felt as though I was being watched, and not just by all the eyes of court, that winter. Richard II was young when he died, but I had lived long, through many dangers. I had felt Death close to me many times, sometimes a hand almost touching my shoulder. That was not how I felt then, not immediate danger. I felt more that He was waiting for me, as often He had done, yet this time Death knew the end was not so very far away.

"Not far away," I whispered, "but not yet here, either." I shook my head at the mist creeping over the park.

"Get you gone," I said to Death. "I am not ready to take your hand."

Chapter Four

Richmond Palace
Late Winter 1599

In the weeks before he was to depart England, Essex became as two men, one a boaster and one a cringer; one suffused with unbounded confidence in himself and all he would accomplish, and another who believed with the same amount of confidence that he would fail, that all relying on him would see him for the fraud he was, and then that the skies would tumble, the seas boil and the world would end, because of him.

It was frankly exhausting and not a little unnerving to talk to him, therefore I began to avoid him. When I heard he wanted to see me I slipped like a forbidden lover in the night from my chambers and marched into my gardens. When I heard his braying voice in the corridor I turned about, went the other way. It would not do to meet him and betray the annoyance I was feeling to all my subjects; I hardly wanted Tyrone to hear we English were divided before Queen and Commander had even parted ways, but I could bear little of Essex at that time. He was making me nervous, weary and worried, for backing out and naming another commander, one I would likely have to force into Ireland, would look feeble, yet I might be sending a weak man to do a hard task. The mere thought of him made me want to close my eyes and sleep for a thousand years, like some princess in a fairy-tale. *Perhaps what never was said in those tales,* I thought, *was that the princesses who slept eons away did so to avoid conversations with men both dull and irritating.*

Every day there was a crisis, mostly of his confidence. I found myself wishing he would leave for Ireland simply so I did not have to see him or hear his bleating, mewing voice again, or at least not for a while.

Neither the man of confidence nor man who cringed was helpful to my new commander, *the Hope of England* as people called him. The one was too far one way and the other too far the opposite, and Essex was left in the middle, hopeless, helpless, staring at one demon and then the other, knowing both whilst trying to help were just as likely to destroy him. Perilous though hubris can be, more often, as with most of us, he took the hand of the low spirit, and it did him as great a disservice as overwhelming pride would have.

Such is the way of depression and worries, one ill spirit takes our hand and leads us down twisted and darkened paths where all that we imagine could ever go wrong will indeed go wrong, and there we meet more ill spirits and worry only more, winding our way down spiralled paths in the forest, never finding the way out of the woods. Fears breeds its own kind in the darkest places our hearts imagine, and more often than not we can make those fears real by obeying what our imagination tells us is inevitable.

Of course, the worst is *not* inevitable. If it were, you would not be reading these words or I speaking them. The worst would have happened to us long ago, the first time we ever thought of our own deaths, and we would be dead. The dead sadly read little. What more often happens is not the very worst that could occur, or even the worst after that. Most events turn out fair and fine, perhaps not the best that might be, but not the worst. The truth is that the reason we imagine the worst almost every time we set out to do something is because our minds want to preserve us. They cannot exist without us, after all, so they make us plan for the worst outcomes our fearful minds can conjure so we might survive them. But just because we can imagine something does not mean it will come true. The trouble is, by concentrating on the worst fears we have, sometimes we *make* them come true because we refuse to imagine there can be another possibility. This is why those who think always in terms negative believe themselves to be realists; they *make* the worst into reality by refusing to countenance another possibility.

It is wise to think of what ill things might happen, but just as wise to consider the best and the middling sorts of possibilities. We should be aiming for the better outcomes, not making the worst into certainties by feeding them with our belief. Gods and heroes, heroines too, fall or succeed because of the belief people have in them. It is a power we never should underestimate, or misuse.

But if the worst truly happened the majority of the time, most people of this earth would be dead or at least dismembered, all countries would have fallen to enemies or demons, and all that we shiver to think dwells in the dark would have overrun daylight, bringing chaos to the world.

Yet it could not be denied that Essex had good reason to fear what he was about to set out to do. If he failed he had nowhere to hide this time. Perhaps his mind was wise to prepare him for the worst, but the mind of Essex had ever been an odd country, a strange kingdom where skies shifted between high confidence and hysterical joy, then lowness would fall as mist upon him sometimes for weeks, where he was rendered so low as to be able to sink into death without any sickness dragging him there. Few were the times my lord of Essex was temperate and had settled somewhere in the middle of the two moods, as most of us most often do. More often he was high or low, joyous and bouncing from the walls or low and slinking along the ground like some kind of crippled eel seeking the safety of a pond. He had not the ability to hold himself between the two states, and I knew it was not a choice for although his periods of highness could be said to be most productive and helpful, the much longer periods of darkness where he had no energy sapped him, made him think all was hopeless. I doubted anyone would choose to live in such a way, even considering the benefits of the high times.

When low times struck Essex he became convinced that whilst he was in Ireland his enemies would poison my mind against him. He began to say that even if he won the war success would only lead to other men suspecting and envying him, therefore working for his destruction. He seemed to think that men would steal his mistresses, even his wife, and I never saw a woman more devoted to a man, sadly, than Frances, Countess of Essex was to her Earl. Also sadly, other men encouraged these paranoid beliefs, and for no other reason I could see than trying to ingratiate themselves further with the Earl, to win his love by sharing his fears.

Soon Essex was saying he wanted to make the Earl of Southampton General of the Horse, and his stepfather Sir Christopher Blount a member of the Council of Ireland. I told him neither appointment was acceptable, as Blount was unqualified and Southampton was still in disgrace for impregnating one of my ladies, and his gloom deepened. Essex began to blame me for the failure of a mission he had not yet begun.

He complained to anyone who would listen of my lack of support for him and my failure of understanding, and began to whinge and whine to everyone at court that he was being sent out to perform a most difficult task, a feat beyond the reach of most men, without any kind of comfort or demonstration of my favour. Essex in truth was so busy tumbling into a miasma of self-pity, convinced that even if he succeeded he would fail, that his eye was not on the task in hand. I told him many times what he should be concentrating on, but the wild visions his brain vomited out obscured his ability to reason on what he should be doing and separate it from what he feared would happen. By the time he was ready to take up his duties in Ireland at the end of March, he was in a mood most despondent.

"He has no stability in his mind," I said one day when Essex had left after another round of moaning to me that I was not supporting him enough. I had gritted my teeth for a while, then exploded. I believe the entire court heard me shouting at him that I had given him more men and more trust than I had any other soul and if that were not proof enough of support I knew not what was. "Were he a peasant, people would call him mad and make his family lock him away, but for being born a lord and sometimes seeming a useful man, he wanders my court."

"Not for long, Majesty," said Helena, pulling a thread of gold through her embroidery.

Not for long was true. He left for Ireland not long after. On the 27th of March Essex, dressed somewhat plainly for him, rode out of London at the head of his enormous army, cheered by watching crowds of English men and women who cried out, "God bless your lordship!" Some of them wept, called him a hero. Some named him a god.

"Why do they love him so?" I asked Anne Dudley as we stood watching the line of men march out of the city. "What has he ever done for them?"

"Perhaps it is as much about what he has not done, yet they hope he will do, which they love, Majesty," she said, smiling sadly as she put a hand on my crimson sleeve. "People want to dream, they want to hope. Sometimes all it takes is a talented teller of tales spinning yarns they want to hear to make people fall in love. You yourself have believed in him, hoped he would do much for himself and for England."

"Love makes fools of many of us," I said.

The sun was shining as Essex and his men rode out, yet just beyond Islington a thunderstorm broke over their heads, which many held as an ominous portent. With Essex rode Southampton, who I was unhappy to send to Ireland since he was still in disgrace, and there was also Lord Mountjoy, and John Harrington, my godson, both useful men. We soon had word that their crossing to Ireland had been made difficult by storms upon the sea, and on the 15th of April my new commander arrived at Dublin complaining of pains in his joints and swelling in his fingers.

"I am sure Tyrone is shitting his fine rebel breeches," I muttered angrily upon reading the report. "Could Essex not have arrived and sent out reports he was hale, even if he was unwell? Must he appear weak from the outset?"

He sets up excuses from the moment he is at his post, said my mind.

He was supposed to make straight for Tyrone and engage the rebel leader, but as soon as Essex was in Ireland my commands drifted away on the breeze which flowed over the sea.

"The Irish leaders have convinced him to wait until a favourable time, and capture other places before heading for Tyrone," Robert told me.

It was May when Robert said that. Without informing me, Essex had decided to listen to men rather than his master, and march his army into Leinster and then through to Munster to subdue rebels in those provinces before he went for Tyrone. The plan had changed the moment he got to Ireland, and it did not please me. He had forgotten immediately that he was supposed to be communicating effectively with me, his master and ruler. Essex, convinced that everyone in England was making war against him whilst he was absent, was failing to make war in Ireland as I had told him to, to bring about success. Tyrone's Ulster base of power was the most important target that my arrow of Essex was supposed to aim for. But the Council of Ireland persuaded him to postpone the march until later in the season and first deal with troubles in other provinces where rebels had been reinforced by Tyrone. They might have thought this the best plan and perhaps it was for their people, but it was not the best plan for England. We needed Tyrone rooted out, other rebels could wait. But Essex, perhaps suffering lack of confidence, listened to other men and went after lesser targets.

I pursed my lips. "I knew this would happen," I said. "And I take no pleasure in being right."

*

There was even less to please me as April came rushing in. We heard that against my express orders, Essex had been creating knights. He had also elevated Southampton by giving him the position of General of the Horse, which I had also told him not to do.

I did not want Essex making knights. He had done it before when in command of an army and I had not liked it then. He had been warned and threatened because of it, and informed it was not his right to do so. The trouble was, Essex was holding to an old ideal of his power, and men in the same position had created knights before. I did not like men making knights. I myself only did so when men had proved themselves through long and careful service, when I was certain of their loyalty. Essex made men knights before they had done anything of use, hoping to bind them to him in loyalty, and there was the problem. He was binding them to *him*, not to me. Those knights would follow him because their reputations and titles were bonded to him. I wanted men loyal to me, not to Essex. I had ever thought his habit of disregarding me in this matter boded not well, and now that men were calling him Bolingbroke it was even more sinister. Was he making men of nobility and war so they would support him? He could of course be seeking simply to bind his army together, but I had forbidden what he had done. If he could disobey me in this, what else was he happy to rebel against?

"I am Richard II," I muttered to myself when I heard. I had often said this, for there were similarities. We both were the last of our houses, both known to be intelligent and well-read, inclined not so much to war as peace. Richard had held Lollard sympathies, and I was Protestant, and both believed in the translation of the Bible. He had been a radical thinker for his age, as some had called me, my moderate stance, radical too. He had loved and been betrayed, as I often had.

"But I, unlike Richard, have an example of what happens to a king who fails before me to learn from."

I turned to Cecil. "My lord the Earl Marshal *will* revoke all new knighthoods handed out to his men upon my order and he *will* demote the Earl of Southampton since I expressly told him I would not suffer that lecher to take a command position in my army. If he cannot be trusted to keep his seed inside himself and not in my ladies, then he cannot be trusted to command my men."

Essex refused to revoke the knighthoods, and would not take away the position of Southampton either. I could threaten and bluster all I wanted, but he was far from me and if he defied me and people heard, I would lose power in their eyes. Essex refused to revoke their positions on the grounds that it would encourage Tyrone and his rebels to see that the English were not united, and that I had no trust in my commander. But this was a poor excuse.

My own personal Bolingbroke thought himself far from my arm, and outside my power. My own personal rebel, was rebelling. My most personal danger was drawing close.

Chapter Five

Whitehall Palace
Spring- Summer 1599

"My lord of Essex should be bought a compass," I declared, "for our enemies are north yet he marches south. Does he think to confuse them by playing the fool? Or does he think to play me for a fool?"

It was May and I had no doubt Tyrone was laughing all the way from the north of Ireland, hearing of Essex scampering along the south. I also had no doubt that all enemies of England were looking on the actions of Essex and declaring all men of England were indeed cowards, as they had always thought they were. Essex had set off on a circular tour of the south of Ireland, some said he meant to go as far as Limerick. It was as though my lord of Essex thought he was on progress and was a king, rather than a commander in charge of my army sent to bring down a dangerous rebel leader. I had heard that in various towns he had been welcomed by the townsfolk as though he was a hero of old, with men making grand speeches and rushes and flowers thrown at his feet in the streets. No doubt this pleased the vanity of the Earl, but it did not please me.

He was supposed to be setting up a permanent garrison in the north of Ireland. The position we had chosen for the northern garrison could be accessed by sea, and, modelled on the notions of Cadiz, would have given England a permanent foothold in the north of Ireland, allowing us to march about Tyrone and come at him from two places at once.

Yet Essex spent that spring marching south.

There was no reason, as far as I could see that the one plan excluded the other. Why could he not establish the northern garrison as well as send men south? One of his commanders could have marched out to take on the lesser rebels, as Essex went north to challenge Tyrone. But Essex seemed to think that he needed to be with all his men all the time. He had 20,000 men, and not all of them had gone south with him. Why have men sitting idle?

The truth was Essex was ill-prepared and ill-motivated for the command he had begged so hard to have. The Irish fought as do all others when in their homeland, using the terrain to their advantage because they knew it so well. Communications were, as ever, taxing, and the troops he had taken did not want to be there. Swiftly we had reports that our men were despondent, and had been selling their arms and clothes to the Irish, who were in turn selling them to the rebels. Irish men who joined our army deserted and changed sides as they wished, and their commander was apparently unable to keep control of them.

"Essex complains he cannot establish the northern garrison because we have sent the supplies for his men south," Robert Cecil informed me. "Yet he announced he was to march south, so that was where supplies were sent. We dispatched the allies and the reinforcements he asked for further south for the defence of Dublin.

"He says he needs more horses and at the same time declares they are useless in the bogs and marshes the rebels use to fight in. He says he cannot use his best men for he does not want to risk them, and the poorer kind of men he has are deserting. He accuses some of us, me most of all, of sabotage, but I swear to you, madam, we were responding to the information he himself sent."

I touched my lips and raised an eyebrow at Robert. He spread his hands before me and shook his head. He knew what I was asking and he had answered it. I was asking if he had hampered Essex on purpose, and he was telling me he had not. It was not beyond the realms of possibility that Robert might have decided to scupper Essex by sending the supplies to Dublin rather than to the north. It would, however, have been an exceedingly large risk to take, especially with rumours of a Spanish fleet on its way to join Tyrone. Ambitious Robert Cecil was, certainly capable of being ruthless, but gamble his country and her freedom for a chance to undo Essex? There was small affection and much annoyance between the two of them, but all the same Robert was unlikely to lay his country down as a wager on a bet that Essex would fail. It was nonsensical.

"I actually diverted the supplies to aid the Earl," he went on. "My informant, Sir Geoffrey Fenton, told me to do otherwise, and concentrate on the north, sending them to Lough Foyle so we could take Ulster, but I obeyed the instructions of the Earl of Essex, and now I find I am blamed for doing so."

"Wallow not in self-pity, Pygmy," I said, clicking my tongue at him. "It does not suit you. In truth self-pity suits no one for it is an ugly cloak. I am well aware of what the Earl will do to avoid blame, and to shift it to others. It will not work this time."

The best months for any campaign were late spring and early summer, but Essex wasted those gadding about in the south of Ireland. Though Leinster to Waterford he went, and then to Munster where he took one castle. Munster was valuable as it was said that was where the rumoured Spanish fleet had thought to land, but the seizure of one area was not enough.

Soon he was complaining about horses again. Carriage horses were supposed to be being sent, he whined, annoying me. "I said we would consider further expense when there was evidence of success," I snapped when Cecil told me of this latest complaint. "There *are* horses in Ireland, are there not? He has twenty thousand men to go find them. I believe my lord could, with the money he has and the resources he owns, send men or go himself to find pack ponies able to drag his wagons, or carry his soldiers. Let him do that, show some initiative, rather than mew and beg and moan about me not spending even more money on him."

As Cecil left I paced to the window, then back, then back again. "Excuse, excuse, excuse," I said as my boots tapped on the ground. "That is all there is with you, boy."

One of the greatest paths to evil and to repeating evil in our lives, comes when we do not accept our flaws but instead blame everyone else for our failures. And Essex could not fail, there were too many dangers. "He needs to set himself and his concerns aside and do his task," I muttered to myself.

Rumours were growing of another Spanish Armada set to sail and this one was to head for Ireland, and if this one should reach that land whilst it was in the grip of Tyrone, and certainly not within the power of Essex and our men, there was a true and great danger to the people in Ireland and on the English mainland. I sat down and wrote to Essex, trying to impress some sense upon him of the responsibility he had and the power I had given him.

"If you compare the time that is run on," I wrote to Essex, *"and the excessive charge that is spent, with the effects of anything wrought by this voyage, ... you needs must think that we, that have the eyes of foreign Princes upon our actions, and have the hearts of people to comfort and cherish, who groan under the burden of continual levies and impositions, which are occasioned by these late actions, can little please ourselves hitherto with anything that hath been affected... Whereunto we will add this one thing, that doth more displease us than any charge or expense that happens, which is, that I must be the Queen of England's fortune, who hath held down the greatest enemy she had, to make a base bush kern to be accounted so famous a rebel, as to be a person against whom so many thousands of foot and horse, besides the force of all the nobility of that kingdom must be thought too little to be employed."*

Yet even as I wrote these words, a most unpleasant thought came to me. Essex was leaving Tyrone alone. Either Essex was incapable and afraid of the rebel leader, which would only make Tyrone bolder, or my commander was deliberately leaving the rebel at large, which pointed to darker and more sinister aspirations.

What if Essex had decided to follow me no more, but sought another master or sought to make himself his only master? Was he Bolingbroke in truth? What if all of this bumbling was not bumbling at all, but in truth had purpose and that purpose was to knock me from my throne?

And if it was treason, what was I to do about it? He was far from my reach, and I myself had given him an army. If I fell and men told this tale after my death they would name me a fool, for I had handed Essex the means with which to depose me. "Perhaps some might be kind, say I was betrayed by one I trusted," I murmured, yet I knew even if some were kind most would look on me with harsh eyes, glittering with all the knowledge of their present existence, and judge me harsh for this. It is the way of people. They always think they could have done better than you, of course they do, for those in the present are armed with knowledge of the past, when to you all this is future. When you know what will unfold, it is easy to be clever. Not so is it in the moment. People forget this, for people are fools.

I had small option but to continue to hope Essex was my loyal man still. Recall him and much hope for settling Ireland would be spent, and if he was a traitor he would be alerted to my distrust, making him more careful and less easy to catch.

I told Essex he must put the axe to the root of the tree, meaning he was to make good all he had promised and go for Tyrone, for with the end of Tyrone, a charismatic and clever leader, other resistance would fall and Spain would have no ally. I told Essex he had assured me that he alone could prevail in Ireland, and now that he was there he was retreating from that boast, which made him and England appear craven.

I knew he would not like that, and I hoped that calling him a coward would, as it does with most boys, spur him on to prove otherwise. Yet it seemed to have little effect other than angering him and pushing him deeper into self-pity, and I wondered if this emotion he showed was true, or if it was another tactic to delay until Spain got there. What if he had made friends and terms with Tyrone, terms with Spain? Had Essex offered himself to Philip of Spain as a puppet King of England? Was I about to become Richard II in truth? Or was he true of heart, simply ineffectual in practice?

But the more he dithered the more troubles came, and soon we heard that sickness was spreading through our English camps. The longer he delayed the sicker his army, at that moment all but useless anyway, would become, and then no attempt could be made on Tyrone that would not end in defeat. I had sent him with well men, hale men, but sickness always spreads in armies, and commanders must use their men before they get ill. It was said by some that on the way to Agincourt the Welsh bowmen had worn no breeches, for they all were suffering so from the flux that there was small point; better to shit down one's legs, have the rain wash it away, than to mess breeches that would require washing. And yet those men had marched on, bottoms bared naked and sick to the wind and rain, and had aided their King to win that fateful battle. Some men, it seemed, could inspire sick men to fight and fight well, but not Essex. He could not even inspire the best of his men to fight. They all seemed to have persuaded him that they should not be used in small encounters, and no large ones were being risked. The best of his troops he was not using and the rest were growing sicker by the day.

I sent word for him to stop wasting time. He was to take on the root and not the branches, cease wasting time on lesser rebels. To make my point I added something at the end of my letter. I revoked his licence to return to England.

Essex was not to come home until he had done what he had promised to do, or die in the undertaking. And he was not to come home until I could trust that when he came he would come as a loyal Englishman, not as a traitor and puppet of Spain.

Chapter Six

Greenwich Palace
Summer 1599

"Spain at our back gate and the man sent to keep the door closed spends his time bleating excuses at me through the wooden panels!" I shouted. Trembling hands of anger quivered at my wig, for all I wanted was to rend my hair, but wigs are not made for expressions of rampant fury. Through sheer force of will I brought my hands down to my sides, bunched in fists. Then I slammed them into the table in my room, making my ladies and Council members jump in fear.

The fourth *Gran Armada* to be sent by Spain, demonstrating not only that people know not when to stop doing foolish things, but also that fools like Phillip breed sons who are fools too, was rumoured to be setting out for Ireland.

Cecil's sources, Anne Dudley's too, many eyes watching over many clifftops and hills, peeking from ports and in markets, said sixty great warships accompanied by 120 more small ships, and 3,000 soldiers were ready at Coruña. Our forces in Ireland should have been more than a match, but combined with Tyrone's, and if the Spanish came from the south and he from the north, our enemies would be too many. My men would be outnumbered, outgunned and surrounded. Once our forces in Ireland were crushed, and the island was in the hands of Spain, Spanish and Irish forces combined would sail for England. I had sent the bulk of our army to Ireland. We would have little left to defend ourselves with.

And Essex was doing little but to sit at his desk penning increasingly frenetic, agitated letters all about how none of this was his fault. Other men had let him down, his soldiers were sick, supplies and horses had not arrived, Cecil was out to scupper his boat. The list went on, and I was tired of listening to him moan.

I was also afraid, for the more Essex dithered the more I came to suspect it was on purpose and he was working with my enemies.

"Nottingham!" I screamed, beside myself with fury. "Bring me Nottingham!"

I sent word to an actual adult I knew I could trust. The Earl of Nottingham, at that time Lord Admiral, was sent instructions to rally his men. He was made Lieutenant General of the Kingdom, holding supreme command on land and at sea. "At least I know I can trust your husband," I said to Katherine Howard, when I had calmed down.

"Of course, Majesty," she said, her voice calm yet her eyes wary. "My Lord husband would serve out of loyalty if he was not moved, as ever, by love."

Nottingham and Cecil worked together well and in no time a fleet of navy ships was patrolling the Channel and all ways into Ireland, and another forty ships, mainly armed merchants' vessels, had been brought in to act as supply and support ships. Across the Thames a barrage was built by scuttling eighty or so small ships and boats, and all ports and beaches from Cornwall to Norfolk were on high alert.

"And our field army?" I asked some days later, nervously playing with my sleeves. We were stronger at sea than on land, I knew, but we needed a plan in case the Armada landed.

"We have estimated we may muster twenty-five thousand men, and since this was done before, when the first Armada came, we are better prepared for the logistics now, Majesty," Cecil told me.

"Are our enemies headed for England or Ireland?" I asked. Reports had been confused.

"We remain unsure, Majesty."

As were others. That August there was almost a riot in the streets when a false report that the Armada had landed at Southampton reached London. People panicked, and merchants shut up their shops. Many fled, thinking the Spanish were on our doorstep. But it was a false report. Lookouts on the Isle of Wight had spotted ships in the night sailing eastwards towards the Channel, and fired their beacons. Not knowing this report was false, and thinking indeed we were about to face invasion, I found myself bundled into a carriage at dusk and driven at a ridiculous speed through London, bound for St James's Palace, where I had taken refuge before. "Surround Her Majesty," cried Raleigh as we entered, his hand on his sword and a swagger of importance in his hips. "No one comes into these chambers!"

"Aside from my women," I sternly told my Captain of the Guard, as I walked to the window. Stars were starting to shine in the gloaming, fires in houses not far away were glowing red, casting light into the cobalt blue skies. "None of them are agents of Spain or Ireland. If you are to keep me prisoner in a little room, Raleigh, my women must be allowed in and out."

It was agreed, and I spent a fractious few days recalling how I had been kept prisoner at Woodstock, under the command of my sister. "Little rooms," I said. "We think they keep us safe."

"You are safer in here, Majesty," said Helena.

"Some rooms we think are safe," I said. "Yet my mother was kept in little rooms before she died, Helena, the self-same ones that she had waited in before she was crowned. They should have been safe for her and yet were not, at the end. Richard II was kept in a little room and starved to death."

"But Your Majesty is now surrounded by friends who will keep you safe, not by enemies who plot your downfall," she protested.

Perhaps she was right, but I knew much of little rooms. Some little rooms keep us safe indeed, and some become traps. We build castles of our souls, hide parts of our fragile hearts, memories, people, in each little room. We keep ourselves safe within cold walls of damp stone. We build castles to protect us from the end, the crumbling dust of destruction we all know is coming, as we will find ourselves hiding in little rooms from the end, from sickness, war, famine, hoping that last room will protect us, and yet that last room is where Death is waiting, for that room was built for Him.

We try to hide Him away, not realising that by doing so we make a trap in our labyrinth of protection for ourselves. We try to keep ourselves safe, but we keep Death safe, give Him a place to wait for us in comfort, in patience. And when we enter that room, the castle falls. One day people will wander past, stare at the ruins left behind, half-fallen towers and windows bare of glass or cloth that stare out as hollow eyes upon a world so changed we would not know it. Youths and maidens will walk amongst the fallen stone, the briar and bracken creeping through tumbling masonry, and they might think to ask who we were and what we did, or they may be consumed with the lights and loves of their own lives, and ask nothing of us. Our little rooms, shattered and broken, remain as our castles, wrecked and fallen, stand but only as husks, as ash, as memory, the rest of us is gone.

One day if we are fortunate, people will see the ruins of our lives and they will ask who we were, and if we are not lucky they will simply walk past, and only crows nesting in the broken windows will keep our lonely ghosts company through all the eons of time.

Little rooms, some keep us safe, some are prisons holding us until the end.

*

Three days later we found the ships were merchants, simply going about their business.

"I think we should point out to any vessels we can reach that England is on alert," I said waspishly to Cecil. "Otherwise we might find that honest merchants whose ships and trade we need will find themselves attacked and sunk to the bottom of the sea." I massaged my aching brow, "and send word again to our friend Sultan Mehmed of Turkey," I said. "I want to try again to persuade him to enter the war and fight Spain with us. Walsingham always thought it a good idea."

The previous Sultan, Murad, had always told us that he had larger problems than Spain to deal with. He was often busy with rebellion about the Danube in Moldova, or Hungary where the Ottomans had resumed their war against the Habsburg rulers. A few years ago however, Sultan Murad's son and heir by the Sultana Safiya rose to claim the throne. His mother was named Valide Sultan, the most important and powerful position after that of Sultan itself, and Safiya wielded immense influence. When I offered amity, a swift reply came from the Grand Vizier, but he wanted me to send him troops and money first before he would reciprocate. My ambassador in Istanbul, Edward Barton, had sent a translation of this document, but he left out the last passage demanding troops and money, thinking it would anger me. I had heard of these terms through subtle spies of Anne Dudley rather than through my own ambassador. Sultan Murad had however, when Philip II's second *Gran Armada* had sailed, said that he would not want my war effort to be compromised by a Spanish attack on Marseille and if the town fell he would send a fleet to restore it to France. This was self-interest, as Marseille was one of the chief hubs for imports of Ottoman goods into Western Europe. Since that time, diplomacy with the Ottoman Empire had slumbered, and we had restricted ourselves to friendly letters reporting victories, trade alliances and other minor matters. But now rulers had changed, and things might be different.

I decided at that time to write to a woman rather than a man. The Valide Sultan Safiya wielded great power. Attempting to use the Sultan's mother as an intermediary, I tried to persuade her and her son to make war on Spain. I sent gifts; one was a jewel of my own picture, a miniature set with rubies and diamonds, along with three great gilt plates, and garments of cloth of gold, as well as a case of fine glass bottles decorated with silver and gilt. In time, Safiya replied. *"Let there be a salutation so gracious,"* she declared, *"that all the rose garden's roses are just one petal from it and a speech so sincere that the whole repertoire of a garden's nightingales is but one stanza of it"*. Safiya sent me a gown of cloth of gold and a kirtle of cloth of silver along with a girdle of work made in the Turkish style, rich and sweet.

I wrote again sending more gifts. One was a richly upholstered coach for the Valide Sultan and a mechanical organ for her son. These were paid for by the Levant company. I tried to avoid spending my own money as far as possible. Safiya responded by telling me that she would intervene on my behalf with her son, for the benefit of mutual trade, and she thanked me for the coach. I was told she rode out often in it, with her son. Although none of this was a sure promise of help, it gave me hope for the future. If the Ottoman Empire would join with us, we could stand against the might of Spain. And with their armies willing to fight, I could risk fewer sons of England, I could sacrifice fewer of my children.

Yet at that time the aid became not so needed. The Spanish fleet went elsewhere in the end, and headed for the Azores. Our allies the Dutch were, it was rumoured, waiting there for the Spanish New World treasure fleet and if the new King of Spain did nothing about the Dutch he would lose a great deal of revenue.

"People always asked me where the benefit was in aiding the Dutch," I said to Anne Dudley when this occurred. "They must be short-sighted, more so than me with my poor eyes, for in this time of our need our allies divert the Spanish from coming for us, just as they aided us the last time."

I shook my head. "People think being selfish and self-contained aids a country, but it does not," I went on. "The friends we make, the ones who will and do come to our aid, they are the benefit of the risks we take for them. No doubt the aid of the Dutch will be forgot by many, but I shall not, just as I know they were not forgetting all the times we sent money and men and aid to them when their need was dire. We are none of us so strong that we do not need help from time to time, and when you have aided others, they are happier to help you."

With a view to making more friends, and since they were in a weaker position now than before, Robert Cecil opened negotiations with Spain for peace. Phillip's ambassador arrived on the 20th of August, but the main demands of Spain were in truth means but to weaken the Low Countries. They would offer no religious toleration either, so negotiations broke down fast. Spain's ambassador left with our countries no more friends than they had been before he arrived.

"Sometimes people do not understand," I said. "But when people make friends, they must each give as they each receive. Only in this manner of sharing can people truly be said to be friends, and countries are the same. Spain has become too used to ruling as master of the world, the kings too accustomed to tyranny."

"They set out long ago, madam, to conquer the known world," said Helena. "They know no other way but this, their way and no one else's."

"The world is not enough," I said, twisting a gold ring, once a present from Robin, on my finger, "that was Phillip's motto, such an ungrateful one which dishonours God and all He gave us, and Phillip's son will keep to it too, trying to make the ghost of his father proud." I cast my eyes heavenward, looking at the gilded ceiling. My father had ordered those decorations painted, little stars and suns made of gold and silver which still cast light upon me. "How many mistakes in life do we all make, trying to appease phantoms of the past?"

But if nothing else, opening negotiations with Spain had distracted them from making war upon England through Ireland. Men of the Low Countries, our allies because I had sent men to aid them in the past, were now taking on the ongoing role of distraction.

I had once more aided Essex. He now had only the Irish to deal with.

*

"I am paying the man so he might strut about the countryside like a cock!" I shouted.

Essex, again. He still had not gone north to face Tyrone despite the fact I had ordered him to. I had ordered him to Ulster and all he had done was take one small castle, not in Ulster. I was not satisfied with his manner of proceeding and I did not like anything he had done, little that he *had* done. To Cecil I said I was allowing him 1,000 pounds a day for going on progress. He had returned from southern Ireland with nothing to show for it, and he disobeyed my orders so thoroughly I began to wonder if some mischievous fairy or sprite had intercepted every single one of my letters and changed their meaning, for in truth it seemed as though whatever I said Essex would do the opposite.

All I heard from Essex in place of victory, or of obeying my commands, was increasingly hysterical letters in which he blamed others for his own mistakes.

He spent all his time writing to me telling me the failures of the campaign were not his fault, yet he was failing, himself, me, Ireland and England, just as his father had before him. The most ridiculous thing I heard was when, rather than march out his men, Essex sent a challenge to Tyrone, single combat. It was a way to end this in one go, I supposed, but why Tyrone would accept such a risk when he was clearly on the winning side I knew not.

"The Earl declares he will denounce Tyrone as a coward," said Cecil. Aware of how annoyed I was, he was trying not to laugh about the ludicrous challenge.

"He may do what he likes, but the fact is it is those who win who write what history remembers," I spat bitterly. "So Tyrone will soon be able to render any page that mentions this ridiculous duel blank, and Essex will be capable of doing nothing about it."

Feeling increasingly irritated with young men who knew not what they were about, I snapped at Lord Hunsdon that summer when he asked if it was wise for one of my years to ride horseback all the way from Hampton Court to Nonsuch on progress. "My *years*!" I roared into his face causing him to step backwards sharply. "Maids! To horses quickly!" I shouted, striding away from the lord, who for some days said he believed he would be sent to the Fleet at any moment.

I refused to speak to Lord Hunsdon, my cousin's son, for the next two days. Within those days it was said about court that *my* Majesty was in the best of health and had enjoyed *very* much the ride from Hampton Court to Nonsuch. People said, their voices scandalised, that many false rumours had been put about, about me, which troubled me, and yes, they all were *obviously* untrue since I was clearly in the best of health. I made it my business to ride as often as I could after that, just to show how well I was. Even on days where there was a roaming rumble in the skies of thunder coming I rode, even on days when warm air floated above cold, when heat closed in on us and I knew there would be a storm, I rode.

After I read an intercepted letter wherein it was said giving up long voyages was noted to be a sign of great age, I deliberately extended my progress. I was tired of men telling me how I ought to feel, and thinking they knew better than me.

But there was still no good news from Ireland. Essex was again found on another little progress of his own, off into Lannister this time to go against minor rebels of small importance. He was then obliged to return to Dublin when he suffered a defeat at the hands of the Irish rebels at Arklow. He sent his secretary Henry Cuffe to inform me that the Irish Council had advised him it was now too late in the year to push north against Tyrone. Cuffe stood before me and boldly informed me that the weather in Ireland was truly terrible and that out of Essex's 16,000 men only 4,000 were left. The rest had been slain in conflict, had deserted or were dead of disease.

I stared at Cuffe until the man managed to look ashamed. "Are you telling me twelve thousand men are dead that we sent to Ireland?" I asked.

"Some are deserted, or sick, Majesty."

For one of only a few times in my life, I was rendered without speech.

Horrified though I was to hear that Essex had only 4,000 of my children left under his command, I sent reinforcements. 2,000 men were sent in August and on the 10th I wrote to him telling him that I expected to hear in his next letter that he had gone against Tyrone and I would have no more excuses. I said he was not to leave Ireland until he had completed his mission and accomplished what he had been sent to do, and what he had boasted no other man could do but him. I said he must cease wasting his resources and my men on inferior rebels who were not going to win him the cause of Ireland. *"We require you to consider whether we have not great cause to think that your purpose is not to end the war,"* I wrote to him. I did hope it would make him think, although I was beginning to wonder if that was a feat beyond the abilities of my lord of Essex.

Essex, I had been told was ill, having problems with his kidneys and also with the flux. He was demoralised, men said, and hesitated now to face Tyrone knowing that he was weakened and that his men were too, and therefore he faced defeat. Yet I insisted that he do as he had promised, and added in my letter that *"no good success ever attended a man who refused to heed sound advice."* Up and down court people were now marvelling that Essex had done so little, and Francis Bacon himself, once a great friend of the Earl, warned me personally that leaving Essex in Ireland and leaving power and arms in his hands might be a kind of temptation to make him prove unruly. "I would urge you to recall Essex, Majesty," Bacon said to me.

"I begin to think, Bacon," I said, "that you are starting to be the voice of my own dark suspicions."

I was sent messages by friends of Essex, saying that the Earl was becoming obsessed by fears of what Cecil and his friends were doing in England to undermine the Earl's influence. I had appointed Lord Buckhurst as Lord Treasurer, taking the vacant post that my dear William Cecil had left. Essex had apparently taken this as a nefarious sign that Robert Cecil was about to overtake the Council, for Buckhurst was Robert Cecil's friend. *Everything* Essex took as a sign that someone was against him. He never seemed to think that some matters had nothing to do with him at all, and I might have simply chosen the man I thought best for the post. But this sort of thing would never occur to Essex, for in Essex's head Essex was the centre of the universe and the rest of us merely revolved around him.

I heard a rumour that Essex was considering coming back, as certain men on the Privy Council were against him, he claimed, and he had to get me to see this. Some said he meant to come to England with his army and force me to get rid of his enemies on the Council. I heard rumours that Essex was to take two or three thousand of his men and land in Wales, but whether this was so he could come to reason with me about his enemies on the Council, or whether in truth the Earl was planning actual invasion, I knew not.

Not knowing how much of this wild and foolish plan might be true, and knowing Essex much of it might be, I sent word. A command, or rather a repeat of one. He was not to abandon his post in Ireland until the north was safe and under our control. The previous allowance, that he could return to England when he wanted to consult with me, was formally revoked.

I did have some hope when I heard Essex had finally headed for Ulster and Tyrone, but what I heard later gave me no hope, no hope in the Earl or what he might do for England.

Chapter Seven

Nonsuch Palace
Summer's End 1599

"Come in, Cecil," I said to Robert. "Sit, take wine."

He did so, and watched me. I did not look well, I knew. Essex was tiring me, and Spain and her constant attacks were bearing upon me too. A great deal of my weariness I could hide under paint and powder. Some of my waning strength I could conceal by riding every day and dancing before people. But there were times, like that evening, when the truth of my age and the weight of my fears pressed upon me, and perhaps my suspicions of what Essex was doing or might be doing had led me to think more of when my end would come.

"I grow old, Robert," I said.

"Majesty, you are hale, beautiful and well!" he exclaimed and went to say more.

I held up a hand to ward off the inevitable compliments and denials of my years. "Stop," I said, staring into the fireplace where flowers and green branches sat in place of flames. "Whilst it pleases me when most men dance about like lunatic chickens to flatter me, it does not please me now. I am old, my time is become limited and that is a fact, and I have come to a conclusion."

I looked into his eyes, so like his father's. There were times I wondered if I trusted Robert Cecil so because sometimes, for brief moments when I looked into his eyes, it was as though I had not lost his father. Robert Cecil was not William Cecil. No one could compare to my dearest Spirit, yet at times I had reason to wonder if the spirit of William Cecil had lingered in his son, an imperfect ghost but still a fragment of the greatest jewel I ever had possessed. I do not think that even I, who never had been one to waste people or time with them, had appreciated how much I had leaned on Cecil for counsel, friendship, for companionship. A great deal of solace in life had passed when he had.

"Your father, my beloved friend, put me on this throne," I said. "It was mine, but right of blood and name and title does not make a claim so. Your father and my good friend Thomas Parry, they were the ones to make it happen, and happen smooth. England was in good hands with them, without fear, and I would make it so when I leave this life. I would have you support my chosen successor, ensure that they come to my throne in peace, as I did. This is for the sake of England.

"I cannot name a successor, it would be too dangerous for me and it would be an act that would fill the time I have left with worry, uncertainty and danger, for sometimes men want what promise the future holds to be delivered to their present, without waiting, but I want you to ensure the man I choose gets to this throne unhindered, and I want you to make sure that before I die that same man behaves himself, keeping me and England safe."

"You mean James of Scotland, Majesty?"

I nodded. "I do. He is royal and of my blood, my godson and the only successor I would choose. But I cannot name him for it would hasten my death, if not at his hands then those of his supporters, and I feel I have use yet for England. So I want you to perform this task in secret. If ever you ask me about this conversation before others, I will declare it never happened and I will threaten you with gaol. But know that you have my trust to complete this most important mission which, if all goes well, may well be the last mission I ever give to any of my men, for I will not see the end of it, so I will hope and pray for its success."

"What would you have me do, Majesty?" His face betrayed excitement, though he tried to hide it. I was not surprised, it was an exciting mission to be handed. To become the man who would ensure the throne for the next monarch? A position of power indeed, and he was being given licence to do so *by* me, not something I would trust just anyone with. Even his father had not had this power.

And why hand him such a power now, even a secret power? Necessity. I would have trusted William Cecil with the task, of course, but now he was gone his son was the true heir to his position, and it felt right in another way, as though the duties of one generation were being handed to the next. As his father had ensured my succession was smooth as silk, he would do the same for James.

Robert, Essex and James were in truth my sons in many ways, each taking on a part of soul and heart I would have wished my own son, should I have had any inclination to have one, would have possessed. James was wily and canny, Tudor in bone if Scottish and French by blood. Robert Cecil was clever, shrewd and careful, the best mind out of them all. Essex had all the flamboyance a king required to impress his people. He had the dreams and the romance that would inspire people to fall in love with him, just as they had with my father who had possessed attributes akin to those of Essex when he was a young man, and even as an older one. Had all these traits been placed in one man, no one would have been able to resist him, but shared between all these men there was potential for the future. Perhaps the times when all these traits existed in but one man were gone, and perhaps the world would be better for it.

"I would have you communicate as if in secret from me and *actually* in secret from other lords, except those you trust, to bring this about. James is my choice for the throne after me, but he cannot know I have chosen him for it would make him feel too secure, and therefore England would not benefit from what Scotland might offer now, during my reign. James must be hopeful, but not too secure, hungry for the throne and offered titbits from you to keep his beak sharp and appetite keen. I want him to support me through to the end of my reign, and you to bring him to the throne after."

"Majesty, Essex is in communication with James," said Cecil. There was a question in his voice, and I knew what he was asking. Many of us had known for years that Essex had started communicating with Scotland in an effort to make friends with its King, so he would start the race for favour ahead of all others once I was gone. Cecil was thinking that a man as charismatic, as charming as Essex, would impress James more than a man like he himself could. Cecil was thinking Essex was already too far ahead in this race, and he could not win.

I inclined my head. "I know," I said. "But James is clever, often more so than he seems when he stands before others. He is one who hides his intelligence, for such a tactic has kept him safe. He will come to realise that Essex is too volatile, and you, dear Pygmy, are not. As your father guided me to my throne, you will guide my godson, and whilst you will know power you will be content to wield it in the shadows behind the throne. Essex is not the man for that, he would claim power and fame himself and this does not aid a king. He is not the advisor I would offer James when he comes to rule England. Essex will not counsel James on what is best for England, but what is best for Essex. You have the humility of soul to know when to act for your country, and not solely for your own best interests."

I smiled and set my hand on his. "A Cecil must stand at the side of the throne," I said. "The blood of the Cecils must stand behind the blood of the Tudors. It is the only way for England to be safe."

"Whilst I am honoured by your words, I think James would not welcome me, Majesty, as an advisor or friend," said Robert, his brow furrowing. "My father was instrumental in the death of his mother, and from what I know of James he is flamboyant, a royal in the old sense of the word. Whilst you, taking after your father, know the worth of men who hail from common blood, Majesty, James seems to prefer the old ways, the promotion of nobility. I think he will follow Essex sooner than me."

I shook my head. "James is a wily fox, holding true to my blood in that way," I said. "The death of his mother he *must* lament in public, or he will appear unnatural and a king cannot afford that, but in truth I think he welcomed her end more than he mourned her death. She was deposed and he became King, and he never knew her as a child. He was raised to be King and she threatened his claim with the possibility of her return, which is why he never truly fought for her release. Had she ever returned he might have had to share his throne, which no king wants. As a prisoner she was an embarrassment, and her reputation before her death was not one he welcomed, even though what men said of her was false. Now, Mary is talked of as though she is a saint, but before she died men called her whore and changeling often enough. In death she has been made into a different story, but in life she was defamed before she was deposed. All that was shameful to him, to his reputation as King, for men will look at a parent and suppose their children are like them. I do not think he mourned her end as some say he does, I think he saw the necessity of it, and if he would blame anyone he would blame me, for he knows I would have been the one to give the order. He knows it was a lie my men acted without me."

I walked to the window, looking out on the countryside, onto a grey-blue river under the rolling skies. "And James may hold true to old ways, but ways of old change, as all does. He will see that no matter the worth in the blood of Essex, there is more in the mind of Cecil to aid him. He will see this, just as I did, if he is wise."

"And if he is not?"

I turned to Cecil. "Then you, for the sake of England, must make him wise," I said.

Chapter Eight

**Nonsuch Palace
Autumn 1599**

"Do you know the year of history where there were five emperors of Rome?" I asked Cecil.

He started as I turned from the window. I had been staring upon colours gay, brought into being by the talented brush of autumn, greatest artist of all seasons of the year. Red and yellow, brown and ochre glowed the world, a thousand shades of gold and green adding to silver, copper and iron, as though the world became a battlefield of old, where swords and pikes lay upon the floor, their hues blending back into those of the world. The world in autumn becomes as a death of metals, a glorious rusting of the skies and trees, the earth under our feet, as from summer's life we fall towards winter's death. Autumn is a warning of horrors and trials to come, but such a beautiful warning, as though in dying the world has one last chance to throw on her best gown and dance through chilly mornings and frosty nights, beautiful and fragile, garbed in her colours of death approaching. Autumn is the last hurrah of life.

That morning I had been walking the paths of Nonsuch, the early morning oddly warm, almost like summer and on those gritty paths, dusty and white, I had encountered butterflies, golden and red, sunning themselves. They rested, wings spread, upon the white dust, allowing the sun to seep into them. As I walked to them they flew into the air, and one came close to my face. A breath of butterfly wing brushed past my cheek, the tiniest of winds, and before an errant hand could rise, thinking to bat it away, it was gone. I felt kissed by some spirit of the sun and autumn, and for a moment had forgotten all that I was or was doing, and simply felt blessed by the world, by God, content in my heart.

For a moment, until I returned to the palace to talk to Cecil about Ireland.

Robert Cecil looked at me, surprised by my mention of ancient history, and no wonder. We had been talking of more recent, most important events. An edge of light, a suspicious illuminance, came into his eyes, something I often caught a glimpse of nowadays. There was a thought in his brain that my mind was slipping into dotage. *The old baggage has forgotten what I said already*, he was thinking, I could almost see it.

Yet this baggage of old bones had not forgotten. Recent events reminded me of ones long since passed. Little man does is original. Become a student of history if you wish to see a catalogue of mistakes man has made time and time again, punctuated here and there by moments of brilliance and success which refresh the soul and make us forget all we did wrong. So many things we think done for the first time, here and now, were done first hundreds if not thousands of years ago, and often better, bigger, and more astounding than what we manage to accomplish, for good and for ill. Become a student of history, everyone should. Eventually then, one of us will do what few others have, and manage to learn from the past. If enough of us attempt the same feat then mayhap in time mankind will actually learn from our collected mistakes. What a world we could make then!

"Do you know of Albinus, the general and commander of Britain who decided he would be Emperor of Rome?" I asked. Still looking from the window I saw birds, their undersides turning against grey clouds, white and silver and black flashing above me.

"Madam, we were talking of *Essex*, meeting secretly and in private with Tyrone in Ireland," Cecil said, that edge of condescension in his voice again.

"I am well aware of what we were speaking, insolent pup," I snapped. "Now answer me. Do you remember your ancient history?"

"I recall the name, although admittedly, Majesty, the fall of Rome was never my favourite part of its history."

I laughed, a scoff slapping the end of my chuckle. "Of course you, being young, would glory in the days of the might and power of Rome," I said. "But if you are wise, Pygmy, or want to become so, you need to go back to the end. Study the fall of kings if you want to see kings of your land succeed. See the dangers that came that people then did not see."

I played with a pearl in my ear, a gift from France to my father in times long past. The pearls in my ears had once hung on necklaces he had worn, then given to his wives, tokens of affection bestowed in the fleeting days of his love. These ones once had been Katherine's, his first wife, so they must once have hung on my mother's body too, and every wife who followed her. When I walked they rattled against my starched ruff, a little reminder of the fragile nature of love, and of man. Jewels live longer than any of us do. I wonder how many hands they remember touching them, how many bodies they have felt the warmth of? Since the first day a hand found them nestled in the dark earth or plucked them from the rolling seas, how many lives have each of them touched?

"Albinus was a general, given command of Britain," I said, leaving the window and beauty behind as I went to stand near my advisor. "In the year of the five emperors, as men rose and fell so fast, he allied himself to one, Septimus Severus, who handed him much of the Empire to rule. Later, Albinus came to think that he had what it took to be sole Emperor, and declared himself so. His men, believing in him, declared him Emperor too. The actual Emperor, Severus, was not happy about this, for he knew Albinus was a danger." I stared into the serious eyes of my companion. "He knew that any force of men large enough to control and subdue the British Isles was also large enough for something else."

"What, Majesty?"

"To capture Rome," I said.

Cecil stared at me a moment, finally understanding my meaning. Essex had gone to meet Tyrone against my express orders, and what was worse was that the two commanders had met first in private. None of my other commanders, the spies Robert had in Essex's army most of all, knew what had been said or agreed between them.

At a second meeting, held this time before others, they agreed a six-month truce, which was also not what I had commanded and was against all his present instructions for Ireland, let alone his many grand boasts. I had told him to come to terms with Tyrone *only* if the rebel could not be subdued and Essex had not even made one attempt to do so. He had gone out to conquer, but he was the one running to our enemy with his tail between his legs, fawning for scraps. And much as the Roman general who had decided to make himself an emperor, Essex commanded a vast army, one large enough to take Ireland, but if he decided to turn traitor, large enough to turn on England, on me.

"What happened to Albinus?" Cecil asked.

"He waged war against his Emperor, and he lost," I said. "Albinus fell on his own sword, tried to make his end his own, but he failed in that too."

"How so, Majesty?"

"Emperor Severus cut the head from his corpse," I said. "And executed his family."

"So the Emperor won."

"Indeed, yet easily could have lost, for he raised one up who would turn on him, gave him men who would follow him." I looked over at the window again. "And I have done the same, with Essex."

We were at Nonsuch still, and news had come from Ireland. When Essex had marched north to Ulster I had thought he was on his way to make war on Tyrone, yet that was not what had occurred. Essex had told everyone he alone could deal with Tyrone, but I had not realised in what *manner* he intended to deal with him. Dealing with him meant, apparently, making a deal.

It seemed the Earl had been in secret contact with Tyrone, and had exchanged messages via an intermediary with the rebel O'Neil, and Tyrone had been making promises that if my deputy would follow his lead then Tyrone would make Essex the greatest man that ever was in England. This would have been enough treason on its own, yet there was more. Essex marched his army north to Louth, a town between Ardee and Dundalk. Tyrone was just out of range, apparently, displaying the strength of his forces.

It was said that Tyrone had offered his submission, and suggested the two commanders parlay, so Essex met Tyrone at the Ford of Ballaclinch. Essex led his horse to the edge of the river, and Tyrone was on the other side. Tyrone brought his horse into the water until it stood chest-deep, and the two men had talked for half an hour in private with no other ears upon them. Apparently the rushing of the water had hidden all that passed between them.

That no one knew of what they spoke unnerved me, and the fact that Essex had said nothing of arranging to meet with Tyrone worried me still further. At the least Tyrone would have demanded freedom from English domination, something I could not deliver.

"We know not that he made any underhand deal with Tyrone, Majesty," said Cecil.

"His failure to retake Ireland is enough, even if there is no deal. I like not that I have heard of James communicating with Tyrone by letter, and now Essex is too, and we know Essex talks to James. An unholy trinity is forming just beyond the borders of our England, and men line up to combine strengths, and I wonder if they will use that strength against me."

There was silence for a moment, as no doubt the same thoughts of treachery had been within the mind of Robert Cecil. Essex had sent no word about this meeting but at a second meeting held on the following day other men had been present, and we had been sent word of what had been agreed. A truce lasting six weeks had been promised, which was renewable for periods of six weeks, lasting until May 1600. That meant that we could end up in limbo in Ireland for years. I was told Tyrone had indeed demanded freedom from England, and it had been denied, and had also demanded liberty of conscience and religion, which had also been denied. But the rebel had squeezed much out of my feckless commander.

What had been agreed was that at present the rebels would remain in possession of all territory they had seized up until the date of this agreement, and that we English would create no more garrisons or forts in Ireland. I heard also that Essex had spent time spilling his heart out to Tyrone, telling the O'Neil how little he, Essex, was appreciated by his own Queen. I had no doubt the clever rebel leader would have leapt upon this opportunity, using Essex's dissatisfaction and self-pity against me and England to his advantage. What had been promised between them? No one knew what had been said in private. What I was in ignorance of scared me more, perhaps, than what I knew.

I shook my head. "What was agreed was bad enough. The rebels will remain in possession of all territory they have stolen, and we will establish no more forts or garrisons? This is madness for an English commander to agree! Why supplicate ourselves before a rebel when we have an army sent to squash him? I hear Tyrone is heading into the midst of his territory and I have no doubt he will laugh all the way, for he knows he has made us look ineffectual and foolish, even if Essex has not grasped that yet."

I feared this unholy trinity. I knew Essex was writing to James, that he had been for some time, that he had offered himself to James as the King of Scots' true knight. William Cecil had warned me of this on his deathbed, and he never was one to be overly dramatic. I could not help but wonder if all these mistakes in Ireland were not mistakes at all, but were deliberate. I had to wonder if Essex, impatient for power just as James was, was not seeking to subvert the power of my throne by destabilising Ireland. If peace was made between Ireland and Scotland, and England were disabled by the actions of Essex, then England might become weak enough for James, Essex and Tyrone to shake. In that shaking, would I fall from my throne?

My brow furrowed deeper. "And if my worst fears are not mere fantasy dreamed up by my mind, which always must think the worst for that skill has kept me alive more often than any other talent I have, and if these fears are real then James of Scotland and Tyrone of Ireland and Essex of England are as one, working together. Perhaps Spain is with them too. Tired of a woman on this throne they would have a man. Tired of waiting, my godson will depose me and steal my throne, and Essex would help him, that is, if the Earl is not intending to place himself, as Bolingbroke, upon my throne."

"The message Essex has sent makes it appear he thinks he has done good work in your cause," said Robert.

"But is that Essex's fantasy, his fool's thought that he has actually achieved something for me and for England, or is it a mask put on to conceal darker designs?" I asked. "If he truly is unaware of the bitter shame he has cast upon England through this retreat and surrender to an enemy, an enemy he has not made a whit of an effort to best before rolling over and showing his belly, then I pity him. If he is working for others than me, for James or himself, then I fear him." I ran my anxious fingers down my gown, gold shimmering under my wrinkled hands. "Send word to all your men in Ireland," I said. "Try to find out what was said between Essex and Tyrone in private, and get more information from Scotland. I need to know, Robert, to know if the general I sent to subdue Ireland is about to come back and challenge me for my throne, or if he is merely weak and ineffectual. Either way it is not good, but one situation sees me in immediate peril."

"Majesty," he said, bowing as he went to leave.

As Cecil left I was deep in thought. For a while I was barely even angry, a morose temper falling upon me, bringing thoughts of old and new dangers. But as I thought of Essex and all he had done I grew fractious with wrath, and took up a pen to write to him.

"We that trust you with a kingdom are far from mistrusting you with a traitor, yet both for comeliness, example and your own discharge we marvel you would carry it no better."

I said the only way I was to know what had passed between the two men was by "*divination*" since Essex had not thought to furnish me with any details, and if he thought he could trust Tyrone then he was much mistaken. *"… we shall doubt you do but piece up a hollow peace, and so the end prove worse than the beginning."*

Essex never got my letter, for he was not where I sent it. My lord of Essex disobeyed yet another command that autumn. He left his post, and came home to England. The first I knew of it was when a man burst into my chamber one morning as I was dressing.

Chapter Nine

Nonsuch Palace
Michaelmas Eve
Autumn 1599

It was early, and I never was one for mornings. Sometimes, when I had not slept I would be up in the hours before dawn or just after, already dressed from the night before and walking in my garden, after having worked all night.

As I walked in a fresh morning wind, mist rising slowly on the horizon or about my feet, the breeze would awaken my mind, fuzzy and hazy with sleep or lack of it. As I walked I would watch the trees in my park, flowers along the borders, and I would know peace for a while. I always felt more peaceful outside with space and air about me. I did not like the inside where it was stuffy and warm and where people closed windows for fear of spirits of sickness that might come and make me ill. The place I felt freest, as I suspect many of us do, was amongst the wind and wild of the world, and even though the wild within my own pretty gardens was tamed and subdued, there was still a small echo of its fierce howl on the wind. There was enough for me to feel free, at least for a while, until my mind was awake enough to deal with the world and all its troublesome, noisy people. After a night of work, I did so need solitary time to feel fresh of soul again. When one is ever and always in the gaze of the public, time alone is necessary to renew spirit and courage.

Some would praise such industry that was mine, say my ethics of working long hours, frequently into the night were fine and true, markers of a soul of diligence and morality, but I never worked all night because of ethics. It was for my sanity. My childhood and youth had passed in danger and I never had slept well since first I had brushed close to Death and saw the shape of His shadow cast upon my bedroom wall. Horrors came in my dreams; people I had loved and lost, people I had sent to death, people I had failed, and that list of people, like the players in all of the London playhouses, only grew as time went on. I could bring to bear my good acts upon memories that haunted me, all those I had helped, saved, looked after, but the hours of night are long for those who cannot sleep and they are not filled with friends. The night is when our mistakes come to haunt us, keep us awake, when people we let down stalk our dreams, trooping in noisome and rowdy to jeer and taunt us. I had helped many, and many I had failed. Against every good act I had done, my mind could march in a million mistakes. People had died, if not at my hands then because of my orders. For every friendly ghost there was an army of men sent to die in other lands who could come to haunt me. For every anonymous person one of my laws had helped there was a member of my own blood and kin wailing to me, screaming for me to help them.

Night was not an easy time for me.

Dreams were where I saw my mother, her elegant hands reaching out to me as I stood in the window my father had at Greenwich, staring upon her, scowling on the day before she was arrested. Dreams were where I saw my cousin, Mary of Scots, walking to her death, where I found myself holding the axe that had beheaded her. Sometimes I was the terrified dog who had hidden under her skirts. Sometimes I was Mary herself, and she was the one waiting to cleave my head.

Dreams were where I found Robin asking me why I had told God I would sacrifice anything to save England when the Armada came, leading God to take Robin in payment for victory. I saw Blanche sick in bed, Kat beside her, and I would run about with useless potions, spilling them on the floor and watching, helpless as skeletons tore my oldest friends apart. Walsingham would shake his head at me buried in a mountain of papers, Cecil would gasp for my aid as the earth of England herself suffocated him, and Lopez, my poor innocent physician, would scream as his insides were ripped out, over and over again.

Those who sleep in perfect peace must have blameless lives, or meek consciences. Only the very best of people and the very worst sleep peaceful, without mistakes of the past coming to haunt them.

Often therefore I stayed awake and worked, not because of some deep devotion to England, but because working for England through the night aided me. It was not me saving my kingdom that kept me at my desk, it was my country saving me.

That morning I had not been up all night working. It was one of the mornings after I had passed a night attempting some sleep, and had as usual failed. Three hours or so I believed I had taken in rest, and the remaining night was spent either dozing and starting from half-begun dreams of falling or phantoms screaming, or staring at the ceiling wondering how the women who slept in my bed and upon my floor slumbered with such ease. You will never know true jealousy until you know what it is not to sleep. Nothing so simple is ever coveted so greatly as when one who does not rest looks upon the peaceful face of an innocent in deep, untroubled slumber. Lack of sleep can make the best saint in heaven into a demon of hell. Some nights I would happily have committed murder upon women I loved, simply for envy that they slept so deep and peaceful.

When I had passed a night such as that, I needed my morning to hold me gently. Fragile and fractious, my mind wandering in mist and fog, belly troubled and eyes burning, I needed time to rise, my old bones creaking and popping, neck crunching, from bed to wash and eat a little, getting ready to present myself to court and country as the glorious creature of myth I was supposed to be. I needed peace, quiet, and gentle steps taken about me. It took time to find my wits, lost each troubled night somewhere under my bed, and time to sharpen them. Time to paint my face so I did not look as tired and aged as I felt. Time to sweeten the skin on my body so men could not smell sweat that had pearled upon my flesh as demons chased me in doomed dreams.

My women understood. It was their role to protect me, and mornings were when I felt the most vulnerable, unpainted, raw and naked before them. No man was allowed into my chambers at that time. Women alone had been entrusted with my body since I was a girl, and that was the way it would be.

But one man cared not, not for my privacy, my sanctuary, my sanity. And as Essex came bursting into my chamber that morning, I had to wonder if he cared for my life.

I was just sipping a little broth, talking quietly with my ladies, when the noise began. There was shouting outside. There was the sound of footsteps in the corridor, of men yelling, swords and daggers being drawn. My head darted up, for this is the sound of the death of kings.

The door flew open. Essex crashed into my bedchamber. From the look on his face, I wondered if he was there to kill me. Mud-splattered, wild of eyes and face, red of cheek, he looked like a feral creature.

I did not know it at the time but whilst he was in Ireland Essex had made a decision. He had decided his enemies were poisoning my mind against him, and he had to get me to see how impossible the task he had been given was, how rumour and gossip was ruining his name at home. He could not stay in Ireland another day. On the 24th of September he had handed his responsibilities to Archbishop Loftus and the Earl of Ormond, and with the Earl of Southampton in tow along with a small group of other knights had set off on a lunatic dash for home. They had reached England and ridden hard down through the Midlands, and by the early hours of the 28th of September they were in Westminster. Finding I was at Nonsuch, Essex had crossed the river by the Lambeth ferry and had ridden hard through the Surrey lanes through mud and rain and wet leaves, to reach me. He meant to take me by surprise, to get his story into my mind before anyone else could defame him, so that I would believe him. That Michaelmas Eve at ten o'clock of the morning, Essex arrived at the court gate, rushed up to the Presence Chamber then into the Privy Chamber. He burst into my private bedroom where he found me only just risen, and in a state of undress.

My women were only just about their work, preparing my cosmetics and my jewels, and cloths for washing. Ladies were brushing down my fine clothes and some polishing jewels so that I could face the world in my armour and with my weapons. No man was allowed in my bedroom, it had always been that way for queens, and especially so for me. Once when I was young a man had invaded my bedchamber and had sought to take much from me. I had sworn ever since that time with Thomas Seymour, a wolf in a man's clothing, that I would allow no man, unless he was a physician, within the confines of my personal bedroom. Until that moment that promise had been kept, and my walls had kept me safe. But no more. My little room, my sanctuary, was violated.

"Majesty," Essex cried as my guards tried and failed to hold him back. "God save you!" He fell to his knees at my feet.

"Essex?" I said, half rising in fear and wonder. I wondered for a fleeting moment if I had slept indeed, and this was the start of a nightmare. Essex would fall at my feet and as the Duke of Buckingham had once meant to before my father, would draw a dagger from his sleeve and stab me through the heart. "What do you do here?"

I wrapped my nightgown around my frail body, suddenly fearful, and shamed. Unclothed I was not, I had a nightgown and cap on, a robe too, but I might as well have been naked. This was the least clothing any man had ever seen me in since I was a baby. I felt vulnerable, embarrassed, and fearful. Naked I was not, yet I felt so. The shame of weakness pressed on me, the terror of my vulnerability choked my throat. Flashes of troubles past flew into my mind. I was in the

Tower again, waiting for death in the same small rooms in which my mother had waited for hers. I was standing beside Edward, my brother, being told our father was dead and there was no one left to protect us anymore.

Then came a memory stronger than all others. Thomas Seymour. Once more the predator of my youth was before me. He was in the eyes of Essex, his scent, a musk of exhilaration and excitement, was upon the skin of my once-favourite. For a brief moment I was not the Queen of England, I was a child again, standing alone and helpless, no guards, no sword, no parents, no means to defend myself against a man bent on taking much from me, a man determined that his desire was more important than my wishes or rights. That was how I felt as Essex stood there, panting, staring at me, his eyes wild and fixed. I felt I was about to be raped, and if not raped then murdered. I was not sure in that moment which was worse, for both held that I was important no more, that I was a person no more but some tool for his will to exert itself over the world. Essex looked on me as Seymour had that day I thought he would rape me against a wall in his own house, the house of my stepmother. Essex and Seymour, two souls become as one in that moment as Essex stared at me. If ever you saw a cat, pupils wide and black as night, watch a mouse, you know how he was looking at me. Any move I made he would see. If I tried to run, he would pounce.

One might say that the position of a queen means that she exerts her will over her people, and to an extent this is true, but I had never tried to drive windows into people's souls, and when I had kept order by force it was so the kingdom might be in order, not arbitrarily to exert my will upon my people as an expression of my personal power. The way Essex was staring at me that day, having violated my most personal space in this world, having come to stare at me, see parts of me that I alone should have the right to choose who saw, I knew that the man standing before me had no respect for me. He did not care for my rights, my wishes, my will over my own life or body, and if he could violate all these things most sacred to a person, he would not hesitate to violate other things, such as my life.

He is here to kill me, I thought. *And if not now, in this moment, then to take me prisoner, so I may die quietly in some little room where no one will ever find my blood, my bones. They will find but my hollow eyes staring up, asking God how it came to this.*

Finally the wild cat staring at me moved, as I almost flinched backwards. "I had to return, Majesty," he cried. "There is a plot against your life, against this very Kingdom of England and I feared I alone could save you. They would tear us apart, Majesty, make it seem I do not love you and do not work for you, make it seem I fail when I succeed. They would undo me in your eyes and then when you are stolen from me they will sell England to Spain! Enemies are all about you!"

"My lord," I said carefully. "You speak wild, and without cause."

I looked about, cautiously. A cold feeling was upon me. Many times in the past kings had been taken captive by those who came to them suddenly, speaking of perils only they could save them from. Thomas Seymour had tried to do this to my brother, entering his rooms late at night, telling my brother he was in danger and only his dear uncle could rescue him. A lie it had been, and Edward had been fortunate, but I knew not that I would be. Others had not.

Into hands of men who claimed they were friends kings and princes aplenty had gone, some unaware of the danger they were in as they wandered blindly, innocent as lambs into the hands of enemies and then Death, and some aware, and worse, unable to do anything. And if Essex had me captive, he could kill me or he could do more. He could rape me. You might say I was past the time a man would desire me, but rape is about power, not desire, and he wanted my power. There was another reason beyond my subjection and humiliation that he might do this. Through rape he could force marriage on me, for some still held the only way for a woman to escape the shame of rape was to marry her violator. In this late stage of my life he could make himself King, then have the chance to be named King, or Lord Protector after my death. A man had dared to do this to my cousin of Scots, so why not to me?

I tried to inch to one side, look from the window, to see if there was a force of men about Nonsuch. I could see little. Early mists of autumn surrounded the palace. Was there an army outside waiting to take possession of me? Would I be marched out under the lie that I was being saved from evil men, and taken to an evil fate? Would my ladies be brought with me? Marched as prisoners too from this place? I knew not, but somehow I had to find out. I had to find out if the man truly was here because he thought I was in danger, or if he was here because finally he had decided to join with Tyrone and Spain, or possibly James of Scotland, possibly all of them, and turn on me, take me prisoner, and kill me. It would be said my imprisonment was for my own protection, and then I would be taken to castle after castle, further and further away, to a great chamber first and then little rooms, smaller and smaller, until I would one day simply vanish as Richard II did, and Essex would tell the world I had named him King. One day my bones would be found stuffed into a chest for arrows, like that which held my mother, and people would see I had a knife in my back, and on its hilt would be the sigel of Essex.

And I could not let him know what I suspected. If he was here to take me prisoner I had to play along, find a way to escape. If he knew I suspected him, I might have less time or opportunity to discover what this was all about, less time to save myself.

"Wine, for my lord of Essex," I called gaily to Katherine Hastings, who had frozen in shock. "Katherine," I said, "come close." As she leant forward I spoke loud of some herbs and spices to be added to the wine, but under my breath I quickly whispered. "Find out if Essex is alone, or if his men are upon us."

I did not know whether the entire army that I had roused and sent to Ireland was with him. When Bolingbroke rebelled against Richard II, the people had risen with him. When Albinus declared himself Emperor of Rome his soldiers had declared him Emperor and sailed for home, for the heart of their own country, to place their choice of master upon the throne. I needed to know if I was dealing with one possible traitor or an entire army of them. I was vulnerable and Essex, who knew so much of the palace and of progress, knew that too.

Progress had been a space and time many of my enemies had considered and thought it offered opportunity. I was at a small palace, away from populated areas, and only a handful of guards did I have. Loyal men they were, trained well by Raleigh, but they were no match for an army, as I was no match for the Earl of Essex. I could not call on my guards or my people to come to my aid. My ladies would be small help in a physical fight, and I could hardly wrestle Essex to the ground. Flight was a possibility, but only if I could get away from Essex for a while. As it was, if I was surrounded I was in a place and position most vulnerable, and was likely to be captured.

I could not allow him to know how afraid I was, could not allow him to know that I had seen his treachery, if treachery it was. If he was here to capture or kill me I had to play along, to placate him, for playing the trusting fool was the only way I might lull him into thinking I was indeed a fool, giving me opportunity in the future to escape.

I had played the fool many times in my life, for often pretending to be foolish may save a person where being wise will not. I played it when I was a child pretending I did not understand accusations of lewdness levelled against me when Seymour tried to ruin my name as he had tried to ruin my body. I played the fool when my sister accused me of treason. I played the fool many times when men proposed marriage, so they would cease pressing for my hand and yet never cease to hope for it. I played the fool when my cousin of Scots went to her death, for I could not be seen to be guilty of regicide. And now I would play the fool again, and for the same reason; to survive.

In this dusk of my life, I had to resurrect games of youth.

I turned back to Essex and smiled, allowing it to reach my eyes. Robin would have known it was a false smile, but Essex did not. He did not know me as well as Rob had. "My lord, come to the fire and talk to me." I sighed as though suddenly content. "I missed your face, Essex," I said. "My heart is made glad to behold you again."

He smiled in a boyish fashion, and looked relieved. Taking his hand, I led him to sit at the fireside.

I was kind and friendly, which astonished my women, but they understood in time. I did not know if he was alone, did not know if this talk of treason, of Cecil selling England to Spain, was real, in Essex's mind, or if it was a lie told so he might take possession of me. I had to placate him, woo him, soften him. And I did, hating myself every moment and for every kind, sweet word I spoke. Had I been strong in body or in guards I could have hauled him away, stabbed him through the eye with his own dagger, and yet I could not. I was weak, I was vulnerable and I was in danger, how immediate I did not know.

The dragon who had entered my chamber had to be lulled back to sleep, so the princess of this tale had to sing to it, soothe it into slumber so she could escape.

"Bring my wig," I said to my women. I wanted something on me. I felt exposed with just the cap on my head. I was not even wearing my cosmetics, and no one for twenty years or so had seen me without them. Had he come across me in the wilderness and stripped me of my clothes I could not have felt more exposed.

"You need no adornments to be beautiful in my eyes, Majesty," he said.

His old charm was there and I smiled, but its appearance just exaggerated something I knew already. I did not care what *he* thought of how I looked. It was what *I* thought that mattered. He was here, a soldier ready to fight, but I had not my armour or sword.

He told me that Cecil and others were out to ruin the country and him, and he had come back to ensure this did not happen. They had ruined his chances of success in Ireland, he said, saying nothing of his woeful mismanagement.

"But why are you here, when I asked you to stay, beloved?" I asked, my tone appeasing, pacifying. Until I knew what the situation truly was, I could not risk angering him.

"My men said coming back to you was madness and if I landed with my men it might lead to civil war, but you must be aware of what these men are up to Majesty, and must be protected!"

He reached out to grasp my hand. I almost flinched. It took all the power of will I had not to, and to allow him to kiss my hand. The touch of his fevered lips upon my skin made my flesh crawl. I wanted to pull my hand away from this false gesture of love, of loyalty. He thought I would see it as proof that he still adored me as he had so often claimed, yet many a traitor has pressed their lips to the hand of the one they intend to kill. Many a sweet kiss has come before bloody murder. Many a false friend has claimed to love their friend more than any other is capable of, and but a moment later stabbed them in the back.

I found myself looking at his dagger, for he had rushed into my chamber still armed. For any other man this would have meant death, but my guards had not had time to take it from him. I had to wonder if this was how I would find death. Upon a blade my mother met her end. I wondered if fate and time would repeat themselves and steal me from life too upon the edge of a blade of metal. Perhaps to die upon the sword was a fitting end for a king, princes many have died in battle. Perhaps it was also fitting that I should die in my chamber, my death combining two ends for princes, the first to die in battle as all heroes of old did, and the other to die in their beds, as sensible people might wish.

I stared at the dagger upon his hip. Was this where my life would end?

How fragile a thing is the body, and mine was aged. Even as a young girl with fire and youth on my side I would have had trouble with a man like Essex, but at my great age I knew there was no chance. If he tried to overpower me I would be overpowered. I could command all I wanted, but if it came to a trial of strength I had not enough. I had many times in my life felt vulnerable, but never more so than in that moment. I knew my own weakness and his strength and it scared me.

And in that moment and after it I hated Essex for it. I hated him for the humiliation of it, for the truth of my weakness laid bare before me, the truth of my age, my years and my fragility. I hated the truth that I could and would die, and that I could be overcome, that when it came down to it my power meant nothing if men decided it did not.

I hated him for revealing the illusion of power. My power only existed when men lauded it. When they honoured it and me no more, I had nothing. It was not as though I never had known this, I was no fool prince who understands not the fragility of the crown, but never had my power been presented to me as more of a farce than in that moment. He was showing me he could take everything from me, he was demonstrating that he could undo me, and I knew part of that display that morning was purposeful. He had come not only to reason with me, as he claimed, but to force me. He was showing me his power over me, and it was a spiteful, bitter display I saw that morning.

All that morning I sat there, listening to him, hearing whispers from my ladies when they could, reporting that no one had been seen marching upon the palace. All that morning I pretended I heard him and was his friend, but I heard nothing and I was not his friend. In all my dangerous life no one scared me as he did, for at all other times I faced the possibility of death so close I was young, I had strength on my side. At all other times I had had the chance to flee on young, swift legs and even when I had not that I had my wits to save me. I knew if he decided to take me then and there I would have nothing to save me. My women and guards could not, I had not the strength, and no wits of the world would help me to escape a man who meant to take me prisoner.

I knew I would not stand more than one blow from this man. I feared him, and I hated him for it. Never was I called on more to pretend, to play false, than on that day.

And I swore, as he left with my sweet, false promises in his ears, I swore I would make Essex pay for what he had done.

Chapter Ten

Nonsuch Palace
Autumn 1599

"His soldiers and most of his men appear to still be in Ireland, Majesty," Cecil told me when he and the few others of my Council who were at Nonsuch had been gathered to me, in secret, later that afternoon. Voices hushed and faces pale and worried, we talked. Locked away in one of my smaller chambers, it was as though we were the conspirators, rather than Essex. It was not only me who suspected Essex, thought we might be on the verge of a *coup* such as my reign had not seen before. "It would appear the Earl has told the truth and came back with but a small body of men to convince you to set me and others aside and retain only him."

"I am not sure if I fear more the paranoia of the Earl or his politics," I said. My voice was firm but my heart was still shaking, with both anger and fear. Every drop of my blood was howling for revenge. It was hard to contain myself.

"Truly, Madam, both are dangerous and have led to Ireland now being abandoned by the man sent to tame her, but at least it would seem you are not in immediate danger."

I was not so sure of that.

Cecil was whispering, even though Essex was far away, sent to other chambers for I had told him he should cleanse himself and eat, drink ale to steady his nerves, and I would hear all his arguments for the preservation of my life when he had rested and was able to fully explain himself. I do not flatter myself when I say that I had put on the pageant of a lifetime in telling Essex he needed to take some time to gather himself. I had, in the past, many times thought that if I had not a queen become I might well have cropped my hair, bound my breasts and donned the costume of a young lad, that I might have taken to the stage and become a player. I think during that time with Essex that morning, as I sat contemplating my own death whilst pretending to be great friends with the man I feared would take life from me, I proved my worth as a player. Master Shakespeare would surely have risked the displeasure of the law to have me perform his plays.

"You are sure Essex is alone?" I asked. "You are certain that my army is still in Ireland, not in hiding somewhere about this very palace? You are sure that they are not near my London, that they are not seeking to claim England in the name of Essex?"

"We have men riding through the countryside this very moment, Majesty," Cecil replied. "For the moment I cannot be sure of England, but I can assure you there is no one here at Nonsuch but Essex and a few of his men."

So he had not come to depose, murder or kidnap me but had, like a great child, run home to tell tales of other boys before they could tell tales of him. Why had I, with no wish to breed, been granted so many children to raise? I felt, although I could prove nothing, that he had come to impress his power on and over me. I felt as though I had been pissed on, a patch of land a hound decides is his, so marks it with his scent. Anger, that great friend and fellow of fear, rose in me as a wave. Swiftly I was become the ocean, and in my depths Essex would drown.

For ten years I had waited for boy to become man, for ten years I had saved him when his successes were few and failures many. But no more. A morning of fear, of thinking he was on the verge of kidnapping or killing me, had shaken me to the core. My old friend survival had kicked off her house slippers and set on good boots, ready for a campaign. Long she had slumbered inside me, relying on others like Raleigh, like my guards and my people to ensure I was safe. But that morning I had seen I was not. It took but one man who could gain entrance to my person and I was undone. It took but a moment, and what life I had left would be no more.

Sometimes life sends us warnings, and if we are wise we heed them. I had been warned about Essex, and would pay attention.

There is a moment in a relationship soured where it seems as though the skies open and dawn has come. In any relationship it is hard for one to truly know the feelings of the other, and this was so for me with many people, and especially so with Essex. With Robin I had known a part of him, a large part, loved me true for the woman I was without my crown. With other favourites, like Hatton and Raleigh, I had known that a part of them held honest admiration for me. This was not so with Essex. I had always wondered, had hoped that part of him did feel for me, that a part of his soul had linked to mine, but now I thought not so. He had seen me as a step, a convenience, and had used my hope in him, as a favourite, as a surrogate son perhaps, then as a replacement for Robin when my love died, and he had used that weakness against me. The skies opened on the day he crashed into my chamber unannounced. He had not thought of me for a moment, though he protested he did. He did not love me, for he would not have shamed me, infiltrating my most private space at my rawest and most honest time of day, would not have scared me, even to protect me as he claimed.

A man who loved me would not have made such a display, showing me how powerless I could become if he decided to make me so. Love does not seek to reduce the one it adores, but upholds and honours them. There was nothing honourable in what Essex had done to me. In all ways but the last he had violated me.

I saw all he had done for a lie, and wondered bitterly and fleetingly why he had put so much effort into it. Robert Cecil saw me for a tool too, although I did believe he was coming to have some grudging respect for me, the old baggage, but Robert never plied me with words of charm or sweet moments of endearment. Perhaps it was that Essex wanted to believe he loved me, and I him. Essex had thought I would fall in love with him as so many did, and for a while I had been blinded by his charm, but this moment changed all. He had not come to depose and kill me, capture me or carry me away, but the fact was that had been my first thought when he entered my rooms, mud-stained and wild of eye. And if that was my first thought, then that was what my mind and heart suspected he was capable of.

My father had sent many a man he suspected to the block. Women too. I doubt he often had full proof, but simply listened to the horrors of his mind. They told him what to do. My mind was telling me to arrest Essex, but I never was as spontaneously thoughtless as my father or forebears.

"I want him to justify himself to you, my Council," I said. "I do not want to be the one to question him, for he will use me against myself, and some fool's hope in me might seek to quash my fears by believing him, and might forgive." I looked at Cecil. "I need you and the others to do it," I said.

"Will we arrest him?"

"I believe that should depend on what he says, and you believe," I said. "I do not want to see him. You will ascertain his guilt."

"Or innocence, Majesty?"

I stared at Cecil. In my eyes I was sure he could see I thought there was no innocence in Essex. He had come here to subdue my will, and if he had not come with an army that did not mean this was not his purpose. He had come here to lessen me. Crashing into my bedchamber was, I believed, purposeful. He had *wanted* me vulnerable, had wanted me exposed, raw, naked, he had wanted to exert his power over me. He wanted me low so he could rise high, I was now no more than a stepping stone to my Lord Essex. He wanted me to be afraid of him so I would do as he wished. I knew that, as did he. But he would not get his wish. That nasty, low and bitter moment of total vulnerability he would pay for, and I would not work his will out of fear, by God I would not!

"Majesty," said Cecil, "I would advise that you do see him one more time. Have him to dine with you, that he might be lulled into thinking you believe him entirely."

"To give you time to scout the countryside further?" I asked.

Cecil nodded. "Very well," I said. "The Earl shall dine with me and I shall play friends once more, but no more than that."

I had got rid of the Earl within an hour of him bursting into my chamber, and then within the next hour he was back and remained with me until dinnertime. Despite the advice of Cecil I could not stand the idea of eating with a man I suspected, so Essex was sent in state down to dinner in the Great Hall. I persuaded him it would be better for the court to see him, to know he was in my love. His great friends the Earls of Worcester and Rutland, Lords Mountjoy and Rich marched with him, and once he was in the hall ladies and gentlemen of court gathered around him, asking to hear tales of Ireland. Also at dinner were Cecil, Raleigh, the Lords Grey and Cobham, the Earl of Shrewsbury, the Lord Admiral and Lord Thomas Howard. Although others clustered about Essex wanting to hear tales of bravery and chivalry, these men stood a little apart, for they knew he had acted in such a way as to scare his Queen, and to rouse the suspicions of all honest Englishmen.

That afternoon Essex returned to me, but he found a more honest creature waiting than the one he had met that morning. He seemed surprised by my change of attitude, my coldness which radiated from me as it does from a sheet of ice, not understanding, apparently, why such a change had occurred.

He did not understand I now knew his army was not about my palace, that I had more men than he did, and in the knowledge of my present safety I was prepared to bare my teeth. Fully dressed, a wig on my head and jewels on my body, my ladies at my side and all the Gentlemen Pensioners Raleigh could find at the door, I faced him.

"I want to know why you have returned," I said. "Why you have abandoned your post, duty and my men."

"Your Majesty knows why I have returned," said Essex, his face betraying shock. Obviously I had acted better than even I had thought.

"I do not know," I said, "or I would not have asked. I am not satisfied by the manner of your coming away, leaving all things in so great hazard in Ireland. It would seem to me and to many other lords, my lord, that you have run home to *mother*, apparently relying on my previous affection for you to save you from your own mistakes."

He flinched at that. No man likes being called a child, after all. I walked to my window, still talking, so he had no opportunity to interrupt. "For ten years, my lord, I have put up with your infantile tantrums and poor manners, your arrogance and broken promises. I have put up with these ill things because I had a natural affection for you, but you let me down, Essex, time and time again you fail me, you fail England and you fail yourself.

"You begged for this command, my lord, begged to be put in charge of my army. You told me that you alone could subdue Tyrone, could win Ireland back for England, and could save England from Spain and from her landing on our shores, yet the moment you were in Ireland you forgot all commands I gave you, as you forgot all loyalty to me. You created knights when I told you to make none, made Southampton a commander in your army and General of your horse when I forbade both. You did not go to meet Tyrone in battle when I commanded you to, but marched fruitlessly and fecklessly into the south of Ireland where no man who was your commander and your master told you to venture. You came home when I told you to stay at your post, abandoned your men when I commanded you to remain with them. In every way in this campaign you have failed me as you have failed your own expectations of yourself."

I turned back to him, my face as cold as winter's end. "Even your father never disappointed me as you have done, and he disappointed me enough."

"Majesty…" Essex stuttered, "but, you said this morning you understood what I had said. I had to come back for I am in great danger and so are you."

"You seem to have confused yourself with me, Essex," I said calmly. "Do you think we are one and the same? Do you think yourself king, Essex? In imagining my death so many times in your own head have you come to believe that I am already dead, that you as Bolingbroke have usurped my throne?"

He stared at me as though I were a stranger. "You will leave now," I said. "I must consult with my Council, for in truth I need minds other than my own, for if my mind had its way you, my lord, would be already in the Tower."

Essex tried to plead with me and I would not hear him, I was tired of hearing him. There comes a time when words are not enough, when we know all that comes from a mouth is false and therefore there is no point in listening. I knew this man not, that was now plain to me. I wondered if I had ever known him. I wondered if anything I saw in Essex had been anything more than a dream I had dreamed of hope; a vision of something old and good in England that before that time had only existed in myth. He stumbled to the door, for once the pride that ever had held him upright failing him.

It was the last time I saw him. It was not intended nor did I plan it, but that was how the dice fell in our game. Sometimes we see the end coming, sometimes it sneaks up on us, an unwelcome surprise hiding around the corner. Sometimes we see the axe, sometimes we may escape. I did not know that was the last time I would see him, but I did know it was the last time I wanted to set eyes on him. There are people who cause trouble, noise, distraction, yet are worth keeping in our lives. More numerous are those not worth the effort. More numerous are those who should be left behind. We can only carry so much, and only some of the hearts we meet in life are worth the pain for our backs to bear.

As he reached the door he turned. "I know not what it is you accuse me of, Majesty," he said, his temper rising. "I demand to explain myself to the Council."

"Since that was what I was going to order in any case, my lord, your request is approved."

He was made to stand bareheaded before the Council table and my men. Cecil outright accused him of disobeying my will, of deserting his men and his command in Ireland, of acting against direct orders, of making "idle knights" and intruding in a way most bold and unwelcome into his Queen's chamber. For five gruelling hours Essex stood before those men, none of whom had any friendship left for him anymore, and he sought to justify himself. He was then informed he was being dismissed so that my Council could adjourn to discuss his crimes. They debated the matter for only fifteen minutes, then they came to me with one recommendation; that Essex be arrested.

That night at eleven o'clock I sent a command to my lord of Essex saying that he should keep to his chamber. He was under house arrest until his conduct had been investigated fully by my Council. The next morning when the full Council, summoned from London and from their country estates, had assembled at Nonsuch, Essex was brought before them again. The clerks were sent out this time and the doors closed. For three hours they questioned him and afterwards I was told he had conducted himself with seriousness and discretion, which showed that perhaps he understood the gravity of his position. When Cecil came to inform me of Essex's answers to the charges set against him I said nothing. The Council members finished speaking too, and stood around me, looking at each other, wondering when I would speak. I simply said I would think on the matter.

By that time court was on fire with rumour, and many people were still expecting that Essex's army might arrive and still attempt a *coup*. By the morning of the 1st of October it became clear that the army was definitely in Ireland and our fears were hollow. I gave orders for Essex to be handed over to the custody of his friend Lord Keeper Egerton, and the Earl would remain under house arrest at my pleasure at Egerton's official residence of York House on the Strand. Essex was permitted two servants and no visitors, not even his wife, who was pleading with me to see her husband. I wanted no one with him who might take messages from the Earl to any of his supporters.

The only person I did allow Essex to see was Francis Bacon, for I thought if anyone could get the truth from him it was Bacon. Francis consoled the Earl, saying that he thought his present trouble was a mist that soon would clear away. Bacon went on to encourage Essex not to try to pretend that the truce with Tyrone was anything but inglorious in an effort to make me think that I should send him back to Ireland. Bacon also told him to continue to seek access to me. Even Bacon, who was no fool, did not grasp how much I *never* wanted to see the Earl again, not only because of his behaviour within my bedchamber, not only because of his failure over the Irish campaign, not only because of his failure in general, his ill manners and his arrogance, or because I had grown tired of setting eyes on someone so ungrateful, but because I had grown weary of loving someone who did not love me back.

Or perhaps Bacon did see this and that was why he said all this; because he knew the danger the Earl was in.

There is only so much the heart can endure before it turns, and rarely does it turn back to face in the original direction. This is what those who abuse the love of others do not understand, that one day there will be nothing left to abuse, and if the one abused can manage it they will walk away, they will leave the bully, and therefore the bully will become nothing for what is a bully with no one to pick on?

That Monday morning I sent word that Essex was to be formally placed into the keeping of the Lord Keeper at York House and there he would remain until I had decided what I would do with him. That in itself made my displeasure manifest and all people could see it, and at the same time I needed to extract the flames from this fire. Essex's enemies were ready to take his head, and I was no less eager, but I wanted there to be a time of peace so I could think, so I could understand exactly what he had been up to in Ireland and what he had agreed with Tyrone. If he had decided to work with my enemies then to execute him immediately would not be in my best interests. A corpse cannot any secrets spill. If there was a plot about to unfold in which James of Scots or Philip of Spain was a part, then I wanted to know, wanted to know all, and Essex would be the weakest link.

My godson John Harrington, one of those who had followed Essex home and one who was in receipt of one of the forbidden Irish knighthoods, came to see me but found me not in a good mood. Normally when I saw Boy Jack I was merry, for he was one of my favourite godchildren, but not that time. "What?" I said, "did the fool bring you home too?" I snorted at my godson, "Go back to your business!"

As Harrington watched me I walked fast to and fro, scowling at him and when he came to kneel before me I caught his girdle, shook him and leaned into him to say, "By God's Son! I am no Queen; that *man* is above me. Who gave him command to come here so soon? I did send him on other business."

I insisted upon seeing the diary which my godson had been keeping during the Irish campaign. I wanted to know what Essex's men thought had happened there. "By God's Son," I said. "You and Essex and all others, Boy Jack, you are all idle knaves and Essex is worse for wasting our time and my commands in such ways."

"Majesty, there were particular difficulties and problems that we met with in Ireland…" Harrington tried to say but I almost exploded at him.

"Think you I know nothing, boy?" I shouted. "Think you that men like you know all because you can don armour and climb on a horse? Think you that Essex did well in this campaign of failure and humiliation? For if you do I shall say you are no godson of mine, for I do not play godmother to dolts spare of brain matter or courage!"

I drew in a shuddering breath, valiantly trying to control myself. "Get out of my sight, Boy Jack," I said, "for I still have some affection for you and I would not want it spent."

After five days I sent my godson a summons to come to Whitehall, and when he was there I asked him more about the Irish campaign. I had heard he had been one of those who had visited Tyrone after the truce had been agreed, and had been entertained to many dinners with the rebels. Boy Jack became nervous, noting that my anger still was there, albeit boiling under the surface rather than overflowing as before. I did not feel satisfied by his answers, and I was less satisfied still by the fact he defended Essex. I told him to go home and he did so swiftly, saying to one man before he left that if all the Irish rebels had been at his heels he could not have taken better speed for he now fled from one who he both loved and feared too. Sometime later my godson sent his wife to plead his case with me, instructing her to say, and to blackmail me, by saying that she kept her husband's love by showing her love for him. "Go to. Go to, mistress," I growled. "You were wisely bent, I find; after such sort do I keep the goodwill of all my husbands, my good people. For if they did not rest assured of some special love towards them, they would not readily yield me such good obedience."

I did agree that Harrington might return to court, but when he did so I still was angry at him. I teased him mercilessly before others, not in a sweet and pleasing way but in a form of malice. I threatened him frequently with the Fleet prison, although I did give him a gracious audience in the Withdrawing Chamber at Whitehall, where I acquitted him of blame in the Irish campaign. Boy Jack, well aware of the danger he had just been in, and also aware that my affection had saved him, was wise enough to thank me and keep his head low for the rest of that year.

But I had larger troubles to deal with.

Essex was sent into house arrest, and when he reached York House people of London were there to cheer him. No more my darling, he remained the darling of the people. I pitied them, for they like me had been charmed by his daring and his looks. They like me had been fooled.

Essex was like my father, who always had wanted to be the good knight, never seeing he was, in truth, the dragon.

*

"Of course he rearmed," I said. "I understand not why anyone at this table looks surprised."

Tyrone, of course, had rearmed and was ready again to seize Ireland from us. And we had fewer men there, for many had left Ireland when their commander had, and London was full of deserters. It was also full of supporters of Essex. The man himself, struck down with a flux, and some said with a *broken heart* for the way I had treated him, was at Egerton's house, ill. Messengers had come to tell me the Earl was close to death and wished to see me before he went to Heaven, but I would not go. If I saw him ill, or feigning illness, I might succumb to pity and forgive him. I could not forgive him. He was too dangerous to me, such had been proved now.

Sadly, whilst I had seen through the fantasy the Earl of Essex had managed to throw over himself, a cloak of shining illusion, the people of England had not. They still believed in Essex, still wanted him to be their hero, and it is hard when we have a hero to abandon them, even when we are presented with truths which prove them not hero but villain. All of London was talking about Essex, all of London it seemed was defending him. Every alehouse and inn rang with cheers for him, and all people spoke his name in the streets. Having once been one of them, one of the fools ready to believe in a man with charisma but no character, I could pity my people. But that belief in Essex was dangerous to me, perhaps even more so now that he was wounded. A creature who sees danger in their sights is more dangerous than one unaware of the existence of the end.

I retained a suspicion that Essex had been in contact with Tyrone before he even set out for Ireland, which although it could not be proved, was high in my mind. If this was true then his offences were even more serious than those he had been detained for, and if this was true he would certainly lose his head. I had not shared this suspicion with any of my men, for if I did they would demand Essex should be executed immediately, and if he was working with Philip or with James then I needed to know, and for that I needed Essex alive. It was also only a suspicion, not enough to secure a conviction on that basis. I remained unsure as to what I should do with Essex, for I could not merely keep him in prison, and to try him was likely to be dangerous. And yet the people needed to understand the seriousness of his crimes, as they needed to understand he was not this Golden Boy they thought he was.

At the Accession Day tilts on the 17th of November, I appeared before my people in glorious clothing, presiding over the jousts for hours. I did my best to make it appear that I did not care for Essex and did not care he was not there. A week later I sent word to Lord Mountjoy and my Council that Mountjoy was to replace Essex as Lord Deputy of Ireland, and he would go there as soon as was reasonably possible to see if he could do better than my lord Earl had done.

But even as crowds roared on my Accession Day out of love for me, there were many in the streets still talking in support of Essex. If I was to punish Essex or try him, do anything against him at all, I needed to make it plain to my people why I was doing so. Perhaps it should have been that as queen I had no cause to justify my actions to my people, yet I did, for if I simply went against Essex in this matter they would not understand. Blinded by love they would support him and not me.

I therefore wanted Essex to be tried in public. If my people were to be disabused of the notion of Essex's heroism they needed to understand his crimes against me and against them. They needed to understand Essex was not this man of action they thought he was; that he was in truth useless to them, to me and to England. They needed to understand that he was not acting for them, nor for the glory of England, but was acting solely for himself, and he always would, and a man so selfish could not be trusted with their faith, or trust. A man so centred on himself could not be called upon to be the hope of England. Essex was a false prophet. He had sold himself to England on the basis of tales and stories, on their hope that, like sleeping King Arthur and Merlin, days of lost magic that once were the everyday of England would return. There was no magic left. It was about time that my children of England grew up. It was about time they chose heroes who could be of use to them.

But when I spoke to my Council and to my men of my decision to try Essex in public, there were opponents.

"You should not try him in public, Majesty," Frances Bacon said to me. Bacon had for some time been Essex's greatest supporter, but no more. Bacon was no fool and he could see the wildness of Essex would not aid him in his career. He had tried for a long time to tame the Earl, but like me he had failed and like me he understood now the limitations of this lord.

I had not liked Bacon a great deal before this time, particularly when he was working for Essex. I had always thought he was out for himself, which had proved to be true, yet Bacon did seem to possess a genuine interest in aiding the people of England. When this was combined with his own ambition, he would work well for England. No man is perfect, and this one had a mind, a strong mind, useful to England and to me. He had become one of my advisors. I ever held that in life all people should remain students, that we should always be willing to learn. Oftentimes I had learned important lessons from men I did not like overmuch. I cannot tell you I had warmed to Bacon, but I had thawed a little.

"I should, for the people must come to understand," I said.

"The Earl speaks well, and with charm," he said, playing with his sleeve on which there hung a pretty pearl surrounded by gold. "Majesty, if you put him on trial I believe he will come out of it only more popular than he is now, no matter what evidence there is against him."

"Once you advocated for the Earl," I said. "You advised him. Yet now you abandon him."

"I do not mean to abandon the Earl, Majesty, but the man will listen to no one but his own mind and when that mind is high and seething he is wild and when it is low and angry he is dangerous. I have tried to be his advisor and I have tried to be his friend, and neither does he listen to. I firmly believe that if he could temper the wild spirits inside him he could be one of the most useful men of this realm, a true asset. But as he is he cannot be worked with, so I work for and with you, in the hope you can change him."

"No one and nothing changes because of the influence of another," I said. "Long ago I learnt this, and yet I have fallen for that honeyed trap many times, thinking that if I forgave enough, loved enough, gave enough chances, that one I wished would alter themselves would, but they do not, Bacon. Only inside influence can bear upon a soul to bring it to alteration. Only we can change ourselves. All else is fruitless work, sure to bring on one thing alone, disappointment."

Bacon nodded. He looked honesty sorrowed, and I did understand. There is nothing worse in this world than the squandering of potential, however great or small it may be. Essex who could have been so much, chose to be so little. I think now, looking back, there were too many expectations upon Essex. The people, many lords and nobles of my kingdom, they all thought he would save England, make her new and glorious. He never could achieve all people wanted of him. That meant he feared failure, and never could accept it. The expectations of others prevented him from becoming a better man, the man he should have been destined to become.

But we all have a hand in destiny. We are not mindless souls swept along by the waves of fate. We all can strike out hands and legs and swim in those seas. We all can change what is destined for us, and where we are headed. Essex never chose to swim. For those who will not swim, there is only one option left.

On the 29th of November, the Star Chamber assembled to try Essex.

Chapter Eleven

**Richmond Palace
Winter 1599**

Bacon thought I would lose in this trial, not by Essex proving himself innocent of failing me in Ireland, but that I would lose something more precious; the love of my people.

It was something I feared, and it was a fear that had been growing in me. When first I came to my throne I was young, pretty, and people knew I had wits. I was easy to believe in. They lined the streets when I rode past, cheering and crying, for they pitied me for the loss of my mother. Even those who had hated her knew anything she had done was not my fault, and they pitied me for the strangeness of my father's changeable love, the loss of my title as his legitimate daughter, for the hatred of my sister, and then perhaps for her love which at times seemed just as dangerous. They looked on me and saw youth and potential, and many had come to admire and love me for my actions of mercy, wisdom, or friendship. But that was then. Things had changed.

The people who were young or of middling age when I came to the throne were now old or dead, and those generations that had come after knew me too well and at the same time knew me not at all. Some of them had grown up in a time that rarely had known peace, for we had been at war a great deal over the past ten years. To some, I was a monster who would not allow them to keep their faith.

I was familiar and my people, especially of the young generations, knew and remembered my mistakes. For some of my victories and triumphs they had not even been alive, and to some tales of my bravery before I took the throne were just that, tales, and they wondered how true they were. They noted all I did wrong and forgot with ease the good I had done. It often is the way. When we live people catalogue our failures and only when we die do they think to list our successes. I was not dead, was hanging on as an old woman to the throne. Many were looking to the future, and I would not be long in their futures.

Essex was different.

He was young so appealed to the young, was handsome so appealed to eyes and to the wish we all carry that what is beautiful is also good. Essex was a man and a noble man so appealed to those of a conservative bent who wanted the ways of old to be restored, with men in charge, and he possessed a kind of idealism that few had and fewer still truly believed in. He was a dreamer, a romantic, and people admired him for it. They might not have wanted him as their leader or king, but they wanted him to be one of the men driving England's future, for Essex was one of those who can shout ideas out that others dream of, who could convince people he could bring England's dreams to reality. He never said *how* all this was to be done, just that it *could* be, and people like the notion there is an easy fix to all trials of life. We know in truth that nothing comes without work that is worthwhile, but we all want to believe this is not so, and one day all we need and want will be there, fairies placing it before us in the soft hours of the long night.

Essex was one who could make people believe in magic, for he had magic in him. I had seen now the sleight of hand that made up his tricks, the smoke and the mirrors, but the people had not. They were still staring where he told them to stare, as the trick was worked behind their backs.

So Bacon was right to fear I might lose this contest. That Essex would, by now being the underdog, be loved only more and more than me, by England's people. But I had taken off my blindfold to see Essex clearly, and the people needed to too. It might not happen right away, but in time, mayhap even when I was no more, perhaps people would see through this fantasy he exuded. He had done wrong, failed me and his country and not for the first time, and he needed to learn that failures such as his must be answered for.

The boy needed to grow up, become a man, and the only way we do such things is to learn to be accountable for what we have, and have not, done. We must learn to open our hearts and be honest, not pretending to be something we are not, or to love where we do not. In some ways his deception about Ireland, how he passed all his failings off as those of others, was like the deception of his love for me. I would simply have preferred him to turn about, tell me he never did love me either as woman or Queen or surrogate mother, or friend, admit that he had used me, taken advantage of my hope in him, of my need for him when Robin died, as a means to achieve his own ends.

Foolish though it would have been for him to admit such, I would have preferred honesty, a sign that he could grow, but as the Star Chamber examined Essex all he offered was blame for other men. Not for Essex, never for Essex. He could not face his flaws, could not accept the worst parts of himself. He was a man always to be lost in an illusion of how the world should be, because he was lost in a fantasy of himself. There was little reality to Essex. He was a dreamer, lost in dreams.

Hard though it is for any of us to face the worst aspects of ourselves it is, in the end, the best way to better ourselves. When we can look our demons in the eye and recognise them is the first moment we can start to struggle against them. It is a war which never ends. Sometimes the demons win a battle and sometimes we do, but the important thing is not to ignore the dark impulses inside us, to strive to see them and rise higher than them, to try every day to be the best of ourselves we can manage. Yes, a lifelong struggle, but the one we were put on earth and into this life to undertake. This is our quest, and it is an honourable one. The trouble with Essex was that he was too afraid to look inside himself, recognise his failings and seek to redeem them. And by running from his demons, he made them only stronger, enlivened by the chase.

When the Star Chamber came to try him, to give an explanation to England as to why its most beloved and popular Earl had been imprisoned, they were ready. We needed to be prepared since the people of England were starting out firmly on the side of Essex. There was no question in many minds that he was innocent, and boring, dull and ugly men like Robert Cecil were simply so infused with jealousy for England's darling that they were seeking to undo Essex. People had been calling for his release and reinstatement, without punishment. It would have been the easier path, certainly better for my popularity to do so, but I could not. This was the moment of the dog fight where we stood panting in exhaustion, both bloodied, staring at each other. If I backed down now I would have been subdued, my power lost to Essex. He would always win in the future, knowing my weakness. The people had to see his crimes, had to understand this trial was not the work of jealousy, had to understand that Essex posed an actual danger to me, and to them.

Lord Keeper Egerton began by saying that many had brought forth false rumour about Ireland, and were seeking to slander me by declaring I had neglected the needs of the Earl, perhaps on purpose, to bring him down because I feared his popularity. These people were traitors, Egerton said. All justices of the peace and judges were charged to make effort deep to bring any who spoke against the Crown, and Queen, to answer for such crimes.

Egerton declared I, as a wise prince, had sent my most famed commander against the Irish, an appointment Essex had pleaded for himself, and one that had been a great honour for me to bestow. Egerton then explained that Essex had gone against my commands time and time again, had "frivolously spent" my money, lost much of his army, and then came the most serious charge; Essex had met in secret with our enemy,

Tyrone, offered peace that was detrimental to England as well as to future peace in Ireland, and had deserted his post against my express order, and returned to England, encouraging other men to do likewise. The cost of the Earl's campaign was 300,000 pounds, all spent between April and September, and England had not a thing to show for this money. The Lord Admiral chimed in at this point, saying with such an army Essex could have marched through Spain.

Cecil spoke, gave a long speech which few actually heard as he mumbled and stumbled his way through it. I know not if it was nerves, for Robert did better in the company of few people rather than many, or if the thought of what this might do to his old rival and adopted brother, a man his own father had once loved, made his courage stumble. Robert Cecil had the ruthlessness his father had possessed, I could see it in him, but it had not yet been fully tested. He too might have worried about the love of the people for Essex. Cecil was not popular, was dour rather than dashing and careful rather than charismatic. He never would inspire men's hearts or win great love. Respect he would win, in time, but not love. People thought he envied Essex, coveted all he had, and therefore they thought Cecil had made all this up, or made it sound worse than it was, to destroy a man he envied. Cecil might well have feared what the people would do to him if they believed he was acting against Essex with spite. People in love can do terrible things.

Fortunately, at that time their love was not wild enough to do much, but they did a little to hurt Cecil. People who loved Essex scribbled insults on walls about Cecil on the night of the day he spoke in the Chamber, all over London, and even on my palace walls. I told him to read what was written, and to understand it was not about him. "But if you can face the worst said about you, and carry on, believing in what goodness there is inside you, you learn a great deal, Robert," I said. "I have heard and seen much written about me, and all of it stung whether true or not, but facing it allowed me to know I cannot please all people at all times, that I have enemies, and that the things they think about me are not made into truth just because *they* believe them."

There were seven charges read against Essex in total, and for most men in the days of my father, just one would have been enough to lose them at least their position. Essex answered well to most of the charges, but his discussion with Tyrone was deemed serious enough that further investigation was required, and whilst this went on he would remain in custody, under house arrest.

Perhaps showing how desperate he was, Edward Reynolds, Essex's secretary, instructed the man named Cuffe, who had come to tell me how many men Essex had lost in Ireland and since then had become famed for inflating the Earl's good deeds and minimizing his bad, to search through Essex's private papers and look for anything that might clear his conduct in Ireland.

"The trouble is, Majesty," Bacon said to me as we walked the long gallery one wet afternoon, "if Essex wants an end to his troubles then he ought to show humble respect to Your Majesty, but he will not. He continues to contest all evidence brought against him, to act in arrogance, to speak with high praise of himself and not accept any responsibility for all he has done."

"Indeed, Bacon," I said, pausing to look from a diamond-paned window where rain ran like tears down the glass. "Essex once asked whether princes might err, but forgets that mortal man may as well."

But whether Essex was indeed as confident as he appeared when facing my men was something else to be seen. As I have said before he was always a creature of high and low spirits, one taking control and then the other. During the trial Essex became ill again. A flux which had dogged him in Ireland had followed him as a faithful hound home.

"Although at times it would seem," I said to Bacon, "that the health of my lord Earl is much responsive to my temper. When I am happy he is well, when I am vexed at him he wanes as the moon, as pale in face as his sister in the skies."

"Your Majesty's favour and love are like the sun," said Bacon. "When the cold night comes men become wistful thinking of the gentle warmth of day."

"You should set that clever pen to poetry someday," I said.

By the first week of December Essex was very ill. He was too weak to get out of bed, his doctor said, his legs had swollen and his strength had fled him. Essex's sympathisers said that he was truly seriously ill, made sicker still because of my hard treatment and lack of compassion for the trials he had faced. They said it was my lack of gratitude which had rendered the Earl so ill that now he might die, for what man wants to do all he can and is capable of, only to be told it is not enough? Men shouted for the Earl, said he truly was at death's door, but I knew not what to believe.

Robin had often enough used illness as a way to reach me through paths forged by sympathy and pity. Essex, as Robin's surrogate son and perhaps mine, knew the tricks of his father well enough, and knew my foibles well too. It was possible his illness was honest, war and campaign are dirty places, full of dirty acts and dirty times. What was just as likely was that it was a feint dreamed up to inspire my pity and to rouse that of the people of England too. They loved Essex, and now he would create fear that they would lose him and that would make them love him more. It is said often we know not what we have until we have it no more. Essex, like all those who would abuse emotion in order to gain what they want from others, was more than happy enough to play the fears of the people like a lute. I wondered whether his wife knew if his illness was true or not, for Frances, poor child, loved him true. Many other men could not boast such a thing as a woman who loved them for who they were no matter what they did, yet Essex could. But because he had her love he cared nothing for it, and it was not worthwhile for it was already his. At that time I was accused often of taking Essex for granted, but he committed that crime truly, and not only against me. Essex never understood the treasure he already possessed. The love of Frances Walsingham was worth more than all the gold he ever could seize from enemies of England. She begged to see her husband, even though she knew he had never been faithful and she, carrying his children and only having just given birth to another, was always a faithful heart.

"I want to know he is truly sick before I send Frances in to see him," I said. "And when I do allow her in, for contrary to what some say I do own a heart, she will be let into his house under cover of night. I will not have any mercy I show to Essex, or indeed his wife, to be taken as a sign that I will forgive him and all he has done." I rapped my fingertips briskly upon the table and looked at Cecil. "And when she does see him," I continued, "they will be listened to, so I will know all of his designs if he attempts to use his wife, who after all was the daughter of a spymaster, as a tool for his ambitions."

Word Frances had visited him still managed to leak out, and it was said it was a sign I would pardon Essex.

Not everyone believed I would show mercy. Some said I would still cart the poor man to the Tower, would have men pick up his sodden and stinking sickbed and drag it through the streets to the place my mother and so many others had died. But I was not about to do that. Although some of England had been convinced he had acted poorly now, the sight of a sick man, and Essex would no doubt go out of his way to make himself look sicker, being carted off to the Tower would end any love the people had for me.

Chapter Twelve

Richmond Palace
Winter 1599

I did not go to see Essex. He sent letters dictated by others, apparently, because he was too sick to talk most days, but I could hear his voice in those letters, and I knew he had recited them to clerks. All those letters asked that I see him, so he could explain himself in person for we were being kept apart because of wicked men and their wicked designs on my kingdom. Essex thought if he could get to me in person he could control me. Although it had worked for him in the past, the last time he had tried that trick it had not worked well for him, but Essex was not one to learn from past mistakes.

And I was well aware of the trick of making yourself appear sicker than you are in order to avoid punishment. In my youth I had been a master of it. Many of us pretend to be things we are not in order to get what we want, or fit in. I had done it, so I could always see when others were attempting the same trick.

Once when I was young and my sister held me as a prisoner, carting me to London to answer charges of treason, I pretended sickness so I could delay the journey there, giving me more time to think so I could prepare to face my enemies. So I knew, I knew what Essex would try to do. When we are in danger and our enemies are closing in we must use all weapons and tricks we have.

I did understand there could be another twist in this tale. When I employed the trick of pretending illness, the stresses and strains of my capture and imprisonment by my sister led me to *actually* become ill. Sometimes what the mind envisages, the body accepts as truth. Indeed when men are low in spirits their bodies sometimes can become sicker than their minds, leading them on darker, deeper paths into woods of illusion and reality combined from which they may never return. We can sometimes, out of our own fantasy, forge traps for our minds, prisons for our bodies and in them we throw ourselves; we can become our own jails and the bars about our own cages, can become the very keys that can set us free or keep us captive inside prisons of flesh and bone.

So whilst I remained suspicious of Essex's illness, wondering whether it was genuine or whether it was a genuinely good *act*, for he would have made a worthy player himself, I could not know for certain whether he was truly sick, whether he was faking, or whether he had been faking but had made himself actually ill through faking illness. And such was his popularity, I could not afford to have the people see me as cruel and him as the victim of my cruelty.

"I wish I could know whether it was the truth or not," I said to Helena.

"Call his doctors to you, Majesty," she said.

"Those in the pay of the Earl will say what he wants them to say," I said.

"Then send your own doctors, Majesty," said Helena. "And make them aware that you suspect the illness of the Earl is not genuine. Loyal to you and your coin, they will find the truth."

"Wise snake," I said.

"Be as wise as serpents, as gentle as doves," Helena said with a smile. I noted a new wrinkle about her mouth, and immediately loved it greatly, for it was caused, clearly, by smiling. Not as old as me, for few were, Helena was advancing in years and growing each day more beautiful in age. I had thought her captivating when she was young, but now she was an older woman I knew not how anyone failed to fall in deep and devoted love for her. "Your Majesty taught us that lesson as well as any priest. It was ever a law of your life, and as Your Majesty knows I delight in copying you in all things. This is a worthy thing to ape."

"Worthy indeed," I said with a laugh. When first she had come to England, Helena had aped all I did, my clothes, mannerisms, even my signature. She had calmed a little in this, but not entirely. Some women I would have thought envious to copy me so, but never her. It was, in all ways it was done, the most sincere flattery; emulation free of envy.

I ordered eight physicians, leaders of their art, to attend to Essex. My doctors went out and came back. What they had to tell me when they returned I did not know whether to find pleasing or not. It seemed Essex was not lying, that he was truly sick. Whether he had been made sick by pretending sickness the doctors could not tell me, there being still much mystery in medicine, but they thought nothing was faked now. So he was not lying, which was good, but actually was sick, which was not. Since he was ill, pity would be felt even more for him by the people, cries for him to be pardoned without paying for his crimes would increase, and worse, should he get sicker or die, the people might turn on me. Besides, no matter how angry I was with a man, I had never liked to see things suffer, and never had enjoyed as some do watching something suffer at my hands even if it deserved it.

Sometimes when I was out on a hunt my ladies stood amazed watching me as I took a knife to dispatch an animal in pain, bleeding on the ground. Some of my ambassadors also thought it remarkable that a woman should have such bloodlust in her. Yet it was not lust that drove me to take life when an animal was suffering, dying before me. It was mercy.

People think of death as being the worst end anything can come to, but it is not so, the worst ending is one that is long, lingering and full of suffering and pain. When I dispatched animals who I had had a hand in wounding, it was for mercy's sake, not for the sake of relishing the sight of blood or the feel of its sticky liquid upon my hands. And it was the same way with anyone I ever had to execute. I always tried to mitigate the fear, pain and suffering of executions and never took delight, as my sister did with her fervent faith burning her and any near her, in killing people for their faith or as my father did, punishing traitors for having worked treason against him. Death was enough punishment. To lose this world, this life, every morning and every dusk, every rain and sun? To lose the sight of the shine on a horse's neck, the soft patter of a moth's wings beating against a window, to lose the first breath of summer, fresh and sweet infused with all flowers blooming on the morning before a hot day? To lose the castles of night that clouds make in the skies when the moon reigns, or the crisp frost first fallen of autumn? To lose evenings laughing with friends and the feel of an arm slipped into your own, inspiring the warmth of friendship in your heart?

To lose all that is glorious about life... was this not punishment enough? Many will tell you that life *is* suffering, that it is endless pain punctuated by moments, sheer brief moments of joy, and therefore we should look to have happiness only at the end of life when we are in Heaven. But I think if this was true then God would have taken us to Heaven immediately, not left us here a while simply to suffer. How cruel a parent do people think their God is? I do not believe, as some do, that this world is but a test to see whether we are worthy to go into the next life. I believed this life was a gift, given by God, and one we should relish. Therefore the taking of life, even the wickedest or laziest, from it should be an act of moment, nothing hastily done. And therefore when something is suffering and dying, when it is losing the world and all that is left of the world for this creature is pain, turn the dagger swift. Send that soul to God, and to the Lady of Light who serves at his side.

It was not therefore to my satisfaction to find that Essex truly was unwell. I did not like to see any creature suffer, even one like him who had deserved it.

"His liver is all but perished, Majesty," reported one of my doctors. "His guts are exulcerated and we can take only the most gentle measures with him, for so much is wasted in his body."

I sent soup I drank often when I was ill, my own recipe of chicory, leek, caraway, parsley and cider vinegar. It was a recipe I would not share with just anyone for it was a restorative I took many times, and many times I believed had saved my health, but I would not go to Essex. "Tell him if one day I might, with honour go to see him, I will," I said. I meant when he apologised.

People said I would forgive him, others cried out he would be dead soon. He had to be lifted upon sheets out of bed, for he could not stand, and his bed was full of blackened, foul-smelling waste which spewed from his bowels. I had him moved to the Lord Keeper's room, and allowed his wife to see him. Poor Frances. It is the fate of many a capable, intelligent woman to fall for a hapless, charming man, and it never does one of those women a shred of good. They could be so much, and settle for so little, hoping that the man they see in the boy before them will come to be. It always ends in disappointment.

I think at times this happens because those women do not believe in their own selves, and think these charming men possess all these women would need were they to drive forth their own ambition. The confidence they see in men, that privilege of knowing the world was for *them* created, is what draws useful women to hapless, charming men. If only women were permitted by law and freedom to have the choices men have in life! If that happened I am sure that these women would fall no more for the charms of hollow men who possess little but self-confidence, for those women would know they could order and control their own lives.

Yet you are one with freedom and power, said my mind, *and you have fallen for fools often enough, too.*

At least I never bound myself to them in marriage, I retorted. *I kept my freedom. I knew how rare and precious it was.*

Frances had only just given birth, yet rose to the challenge of caring for another child, her husband. I permitted her to go by night so that she could see him, but Cecil and his spies listened to all that was said between the couple. I did not think I needed to worry about Frances, like her father before her she was loyal to me and to England. The only time truly she had disobeyed me was by marrying Essex, and although her blood was no match for his, my main concern about their marriage had been to spare her the pain of marrying a faithless man. Essex would never know how fortunate he was to have a wife like her, so he was constantly unfaithful, hurtful and careless with her love. She never returned the favour in kind, never took revenge; Frances just gave more love. Sadly, although such people as Frances make the world a better place, they rarely make their lives easy. They give and give, and because they do, others take their generosity for granted. Often people like Frances start out full of love, and end up filled with bitter hate, for having the gift of their love disregarded.

Essex never did see how many people loved him more than he deserved. If you want to know who loves you honestly, find the person who comes to your bed when it is full of your own foul waste, the person who seeks to cheer you in your darkest moments. Look for the person who is there when no one else is. I had no doubt that the moment he was well he would be back spending time with his mistresses, and yet not a one of them came begging to care for him or pleading for his release. Frances was the one who did that, and she would be unrewarded, as usual, by the man she wasted her love on. Perhaps I should have not allowed her to see him, I banned others, like his sister Lady Rich and his mother, the odious Lettice. Perhaps I should have saved Frances from herself, but it does no good, people have to make their own mistakes and she had married him, so in sickness and health she was bound by promises made to God to care for him.

It might be that her quiet ministrations and talk of encouragement was what saved him in truth, rather than just her care for his body, for I thought this illness, although perhaps real, was in truth a projection of the swamp of his mind. Always he suffered low and high times, and this failure brought on one of his worst, and the sicker that Essex appeared to be the more the pity of the people rose for him, a storm wave breaking over glistening rock, a wind curling in the skies, sending errant clouds to tumble as performers at court before a feast. He knew that the men of the Star Chamber and of my Council were still gathering information on him, trying to find out what he had said alone to Tyrone. I have no doubt he feared what they might find.

At Christmas I had to send word to churches to cease performing public prayers for Essex. It was hardly fitting since he was under investigation for betraying me and England. Rumours grew that he was dead, but he was actually getting better. Soon I heard he was up, eating broth in his bed. Was it broth of chicory? I knew not, but whatever pottage his doctors had brewed it did Essex good. Soon people were saying he was on the mend, would mend his reputation and his relationship with me, and then would go on to mend England. "Suddenly my lord of Essex is become a tailor," I said dryly, "they think he has but to thread his needle and any cloth he will mend."

But it takes time to learn to mend things, and it also takes care; not a thing all are capable of. Any fool may stitch together pieces of cloth, but only a true tailor or seamstress may patch two opposing cloths and make them look as one. If one is not careful, the tear always shows. Cloth is much like skin in that way, scars show on the surface, yes, after wounds have healed. Some scars never fade.

Chapter Thirteen

Richmond Palace
Winter 1599

We moved to Richmond for Christmas, and I passed the season in an outwardly merry mood. I danced with men of court, and all people present feasted. Often I was found playing cards with Cecil or my other Councillors, or watching my ladies perform country dances. I offered no sign I missed Essex and neither did anyone else. I wanted him to know, as he recovered, that life was going on without him, that I did not need him. It was the truth, and truth was a thing he needed to start to see.

On the 19th of December it was rumoured that Essex had died, *again*, and church bells across London began tolling for a dead man not dead. People began talking in the streets, wailing that the son and hope of England was dead. I told my chaplains to desist from praying for the Earl, for I had heard he was certainly not dead and definitely on the mend. But on that same day someone wrote on the door of Cecil's house *Here lies the toad*, showing that many found him to be culpable for the crimes, and illness, of Essex.

We continued with the Christmas season as always we had in the past. On the Eve servants trooped into palace gardens and brought back bundles of evergreens, holly, mistletoe, and ivy, which they wound in garlands up the bannisters of the palace, and around the stairs, the walkways, making inside the palace become as green as the wood outside. The smell was glorious. There is nothing quite like fresh-cropped green leaves and twigs to make something smell new, full of promise. Hope seemed to spring from the scent of greenery in the palace at Christmas, the hope we all have, that somehow the turning of a year will make all things possible, so we may start again, might right mistakes of the past, might finally get life on its correct path so we can be happy. It is strange in many ways, for the turn of the year is just the turn of another night and day, yet we fill it with meaning. In truth it was just another day, and the scent of the greenery just another smell, although to me the scent was enough to be grateful for.

Oftentimes in my palaces, beneath the scent of perfume, fresh rushes, herbs in those rushes, and the wafting scent of pomanders knocking against the legs of ladies as they walked, beneath those smells sometimes could lurk ones not so sweet. The scent of bodies, of sweat old and rank, the smell of cheap perfume, reeks of food and wine and soured wine and food, the stench which rose from the palace jakes, the scent of the river, particularly in summer, all these things could linger beneath sweeter smells, reminding one and one's nose of the rougher things of life. Yet when Christmas came, and my halls were filled with all the glory of the woods, there was no smell in the palaces but that of the fresh forest.

All through Christmas I appeared in good spirits before my people. There were plays and Christmas pies to digest. Pembroke's heir, a young man called William Herbert, was often with me and there was talk that he would become my new favourite, because he was sweet and kept to the old traditions of courting his mistress. Yet although I simpered before him and flirted I found him dull, in truth. He was one of those who preferred reading to dancing, and whilst I had always loved to read and loved my books, that did not mean I ignored the diversion of the dance when it came, when I had opportunity to enjoy myself. All things are to their seasons suited, and there is a time for reading as there is a time for dancing. No one wishes to do one thing all the time, we are creatures who desire diversity. I flattered him to make people understand Essex was gone, but had small interest in truth in taking another favourite. That position had, in all honesty, died years ago, gone to the grave with Robin, the only man who had loved me true.

As the Christmas season drew to an end, and Essex's illness appeared too on the wane, those men who stood against the

Earl on the Privy Council had continued to collect evidence against him. They came to me. "And you have found nothing?" I asked.

Cecil looked uncomfortable. "It is not that we have found nothing, Madam," he said, "but we have found not one thing damning enough on its own to justify a treason trial. Our investigations are inconclusive."

"And what of this portrait that Essex had made?" I asked. "It would seem he would set himself up to rival us in fame and power."

The portrait of which I spoke had been a commission from Essex himself to Thomas Cockson, one of the finest art engravers in London. It was a portrait of Essex in armour and on a horse, modelled on an image of Robin which had included an inscription below his image, and behind him scenes of the defeated Armada and the Battle of Zutphen, Robin's great triumphs.

Essex had had himself set against a similar background using his "triumphs", if one could call them such, in Cadiz and the Azores, and Rouen and Ireland. Below Robin's portrait there had been a list of his titles and honours. Below that of Essex there was something else. His inscription called him, *"Virtue's honour, Wisdom's nature, Grace's servant, Mercy's love,"* and worst of all, *"God's elected".* If using the term *God's elected* which was only used for princes was not enough, the Earl had also recently chosen to circulate amongst his friends handwritten copies of his letters exchanged with Lord Keeper Egerton written in the year before. In that letter Essex had asked *"Cannot princes err? Cannot subjects receive wrong? Is an earthly power or authority infinite?"*

"Is this not enough to charge him with treason?" I asked Cecil. "He calls himself *God's elected*, asks whether I can err, he asks whether he is wrong, and he questions my power, my authority."

"The evidence that we have collected against the Earl, to do with Ireland, is not enough to prove treason, Majesty," replied Cecil. "But I do believe we could bring to bear upon him the evidence of the portrait and the letters he has copied and handed out."

I walked to the window and looked out upon the world. It had snowed. The roads had been cleared by men with brooms, working hard so that my servants could get in and out of the palace, yet sometimes I wondered why, when we were safe inside and had no cause to go outside, as so many common people did. At such times when there is danger all about us, is it not more sensible to remain inside, where it is safe, and as many animals of the briar and bracken do, curl ourselves into little balls in little rooms that we may sleep through seasons of danger and emerge when there is food and warmth once again upon the world? Why put so much effort into making the world appear passable, as though nothing has changed? Why pretend dangerous times are not dangerous?

"Essex does not appear to understand how close he steps to the block," I said. "He does not see that by challenging me in such a way I will have to rise and he will have to fall."

"The Star Chamber will assemble to try him, Majesty," said Cecil.

I nodded. "Let it be so," I said. "Let him be tried."

When Cecil had left me I sent word to Bacon. I told him that for the sake of the love that had once been between Essex and me, and that had been between Bacon and Essex, that he should warn the Earl. "*He does not appear to understand the gravity of the situation into which he has placed himself,*" I wrote to Bacon. "*I would like you to make him aware. The Star Chamber cannot inflict the death penalty but it can impose unlimited fines and life imprisonment upon the Earl. I understand how this would wound Essex, and whilst I have little true affection left for him, I made a promise to his stepfather that I would protect him, for Essex was Robin's son as he was the son of his own father. For William Cecil, Baron Burghley, too I would protect the boy, if he would protect himself."*

When I had sent the missive to Bacon I went again to my window to look at the snow. Flakes were falling again, little darts of light dancing against the darkness of the night. It was as though the stars had come to dance around the palace, surrounding my castle and me and everyone else inside with a miasma of light and darkness, shadow and spirits. There was nothing there to offer me an answer to my riddle, and you might well ask why once again I chose to try to save a man who would not save himself. In truth it was as I had said, and if I loved Essex no more, indeed feared him more than ever I had loved him, I had made a last promise to Robin, to try to protect the boy and to honour him.

The boy we had raised together, this boy in truth who had for years been a man. He had never outgrown infancy, and whilst it is a sad truth it remains the truth, that in this dangerous world not all children live through the years of their infancy and survive to see the other side.

"Some children die without ever having become adults," I whispered to the whiteness of the world.

Chapter Fourteen

Richmond Palace
New Year 1600

If I gave no sign I thought of Essex that winter, he sent plenty to me, or perhaps in truth to the people of England, of which I was one. Often an easy thing to forget, that the queen is also one of her own people. All people of England were my subjects, yet I too was subject to the Crown.

Essex was sending many a clear message to all people of England that year; the message was he was being neglected, and I was being cruel. He sent gifts at New Year, letters aplenty besides. He convinced men to speak for him, women too. In exile from court, he used his charm to continue to have a presence in England. The worst of it was, Essex was convincing many.

If I ignored my favourite, but he was sending gifts and letters and love to me, then *I* was the poor-tempered beast in this pageant Essex was trying to play to my people. *I* was the one who would not forgive, who was at fault, who ignored coldly all effort on his part to make amends. Of course, he could have admitted culpability for Ireland, admitted he was wrong in the way he had behaved towards me but that firstly was not the point, and second was a step too far. Any real effort was too much effort for Essex. He was not seeking my good opinion in truth, but that of the people. An appeal made of popularity and forged in false display of devotion this was, and it was all to make him more beloved by my people; just another exterior show with nothing solid underneath. If he could rouse their pity and make me the monster, he would win, for I would have to take him back and I would have to apologise. I could see this feeble plotting in every letter he wrote and every gift that arrived in my unwilling hands. I wanted nothing he sent, for none of it was for me, not really, but I was polite, courteous, yet remained cold.

He sent presents to me for New Year, and I received them, thanking his messenger as I would any sent by a lord offering tributes to his Queen. I did not send gifts to Essex. I knew what he was trying to do and all I could do was maintain my stance. He was trying to make me look unnatural, both as a monarch and as a woman. The fact is people expect men to act in one way and women in another. As a woman, even if I was a queen and ruler of England, I was supposed to be warm of heart, clement, forgiving, sweet and mild. Such nonsense. If men are permitted a range of emotion, women should be too.

As a monarch, and especially had I been a man, I was allowed regal coldness towards those who thwarted me, but as a woman no such grace was mine and when a woman wears a crown she is always woman first, not monarch. Of course fools who wanted me to behave as they thought women should would have been the same people who would have been horrified had their sovereign lord behaved like a woman, showing womanly weakness. We cannot please all the people of the world, it is a task impossible. If we are sensible we will seek to please ourselves, for on this lonely journey through life we are our only companions. And to my mind, so-called womanly virtues such as compassion, and kindness, mercy most of all, were not indicative of weakness, but of strength. It is far harder to show mercy than it is to take revenge. That is why our Lord offered the other cheek, knowing that act was beyond the abilities of most of his people, therefore something worth attempting.

But mercy has its limits, like anything. Show mercy to Essex before he had learned a single lesson, and I would regret it. The only way I would accept him back at court would be if he changed his character, accepting culpability and responsibility for all he had done and failed to do. I had small faith now that this miracle would ever occur, and if Essex did not change, he remained a great and growing danger towards me.

On Twelfth Night I held a feast in honour of a newly arrived Spanish ambassador who seemed to find the whole evening quite amusing, reporting gleefully that the Head of the Church of England and Ireland had been seen in her grey hairs and a garish gown dancing like a young lass. "Can servants of God not rejoice in the world He made?" I asked, and that man and his limited opinion was not the only irritant that season.

"Lady Rich, desist," I snapped one day, exhaling sharp and long as I struggled to control my temper. "Your incessant pleas on your brother's behalf are driving me to distraction. I have half a mind to banish you both, simply for being annoying."

"Your Majesty," she said, wringing her pretty hands earnestly. "A year ago, on this very night, you danced with my brother before all your people and declared you had no greater friend. What has changed?"

"Much," I said. "You would do better to support your lover, Lord Mountjoy, who is to leave soon for Ireland, rather than your brother. Mountjoy at least has a chance to succeed, to put right all that your brother failed in."

Lady Rich was driving me quite wild. She would not desist from speaking for her brother, and was apparently in great fear for her lover. And I knew well there was a secret plot afoot in which she was playing a part, which hardly endeared me to her. Southampton and Essex's other friend Sir Charles Danvers had decided the best way to help Essex was to recruit the support of James of Scots, by informing my royal godson that Robert Cecil and his allies were working to prevent his succession. "They tell James that his only hope of wearing the crown goes hand in hand with the restoration of Essex to power. And they want my godson to put forth an army into England to bring this about?" I asked Cecil.

"Indeed, my lady," he said. "They sent a message saying if James would put together a show of armed strength to bring about the restoration of Essex, then Lord Mountjoy would bring from Ireland an army of around five thousand men, and you would be forced to agree to their demands."

"And one of those demands will be the restoration of Essex and the naming of James as my legal successor to the throne?"

"Indeed, my lady," he said. "That is precisely what their terms are. The King of Scots, however, does not share their enthusiasm about the plan. He has shown little interest in the proposal, and my spies tell me he has not answered any of the letters they have sent."

"When one cannot rely on Englishmen," I said, "but yet we can rely on the loyalty of Scots, I wonder what my country has come to."

"Do you wish to not send Mountjoy to Ireland?" asked Cecil.

"No," I said, "send him. He is the most likely candidate who can do any good in that country, and the campaign, if he is planning to betray me, will be punishment enough for his disloyalty."

"Mountjoy himself does not seem overly enthused either about the plan, Majesty. The ease with which my spies found out this information suggests to me that Mountjoy himself intended them to know of it, and he is therefore playing both sides, allowing Essex to think he is his friend, but also allowing me to have this information that I might bring it to you. I think his loyalty therefore is true."

"True it will be to whoever he thinks will win," I said. "I know his sort. Although they have many times changed the course of history for better or for worse, I like not those who sit on the fence and dangle a foot on each side."

Mountjoy was not alone. Essex's mother was up to something too, sending me presents and trying to see me. I did wonder if Lettice had been sent by Essex to distract me, for he knew I loathed her. Perhaps he was hoping that my intolerance of her would lead to mercy for him, if I came perhaps to think of him as the lesser evil, but all her attempts did was annoy me. Anything that came from that obnoxious woman was poison to me. I gave her gifts away to maids in my chambers, and made it known that I had. I wanted nothing from Lettice. Anything she had touched seemed to burn me with hatred.

But if Essex was here in England, the mess he had left remained in Ireland. "Mountjoy will have the post," I announced to my Council. "He is most suited in blood, and he has a sharp mind, which may be a match for wily Tyrone."

They all looked at me with troubled brows, and I knew why. Mountjoy did not want the post, no man of sense would. The only one who volunteered had been Essex and he was the only one fool enough to believe he could do something in Ireland. Most other men had no hope.

The other reason, as some were aware, was the secret talks going on between Mountjoy, Essex and James, although James was still ignoring my former favourite as well as the man I was about to appoint to go to Ireland. Men on my Council, like Robert, thought it a mistake to send Mountjoy if we knew not if his loyalty was true or not, but I believed that as long as I remained on the side with the power, Mountjoy would remain true. That is the thing about men who follow power rather than people; you can judge more easily which way they will bend when the winds change. Besides, Mountjoy was the man most likely to be capable of sorting out this mess Essex had made. It was worth the risk to gain his skill, and capture Tyrone, or crush his rebel armies.

"I must away to entertain the Archduke Albert of Austria's envoys," I said to my Council.

Archduke Albert of Austria had sent envoys to court in October of the year before. This was important, as Albert's wife was the Infanta Isabella, who many times had been named by my enemies as the woman who should be sitting on my throne rather than me. She was also the sister of Phillip of Spain. The Archduke and Isabella now ruled the Spanish Low Countries, and their envoy had come secretly to London and in the spring of that year representatives of both our side and theirs were to meet in Boulogne. I doubted the talks would go anywhere, for Isabella and her husband still had the same mentality as her father had; that the Low Countries, and the Dutch people were their villeins rather than their subjects, and deserved to be put down rather than held up.

Although a little unsure of their purpose, I wondered if it was a way for Spain to make friends with England after a decade of war. The envoys were apparently secret, but I wondered if Phillip had asked his sister to send them, a way of saving face if peace were to be made. We heard Spain's people were weary of war, the high taxes set upon them, and of course the danger to their outposts and ships. Isabella and her husband were now the Hapsburg choice for regents of the Low Counties, and I had therefore informed our allies the Dutch that they had sent men to my court, and informed them also that nothing that was detrimental to them or our friendship would be agreed.

I stood, brushed down my crimson and gold gown. "Send word to Mountjoy and talk him into it. Essex has failed in Ireland, but England must not." I left to sound out the ambassadors, discover their purpose.

They were unlikely to offer the trading concessions in the Spanish Americas I wanted, which was something I had demanded as vital to the talks. The fact remained however, that whilst I could keep Isabella and Albert talking, dangling concessions and promises before them, they were less likely to set into motion any plan to oust me, or cause trouble in England. I had many times in my long reign used tactics such as this. In truth sometimes *not* coming to a decision, eking out talks so they went on for years if not decades, keeping people dangling and agreements unagreed, could be more beneficial than all the treaties signed throughout all the eons of the world. As soon as a treaty is signed it can be broken. But the treaty *unsigned* holds all the potential and none of the peril, for those involved. Keep men talking, women too, and all that is possible remains possible. Sign promises to paper and parchment, agree clauses firm and with resolution, and soon they will become as dust in the wind, as ashes are the promises of man, for the hearts of men are as changeable as the skies that God placed to roam over us each day and every night.

Some said I maintained chaos by refusing often to agree on something, but in chaos there lies possibility. God used that chaos and possibility to craft a world, yet my intentions were humbler. I simply sought to keep peace in parts of God's glorious world, by maintaining possibility through procrastination.

Chapter Fifteen

Richmond Palace
Winter-Spring 1600

As winter creaked through the gateway of spring, Essex was allowed to leave house arrest under control of my men and return to Essex House, his London seat, but I would not have him there as once he had been. For years he and his sister had been setting themselves up in Robin's old house as heads of a court to rival my own. Both that time and my patience were spent. Essex would go home, and it would be the home of a lord of England. He was not a prince, and would not return to a palace. No court would he hold there. I would have no more suns in my sky. An old sun I might be but I alone would blaze and he would dwell in my shadow.

I sent orders. When he returned to Essex House he would find it stripped of signs of power. No petitioners would go to him there, and only family and those friends I allowed would visit. He would find himself lonely, and perhaps with time alone with his thoughts he might discover a scrap of wisdom, understand how his mighty power, this flame that ignited his ambition, could be extinguished by me, for if he was a flame I had the tinderbox in my keeping.

I still wanted a public trial, more public and more damning than his examination in the Star Chamber had been, but the fact was Bacon was right, and had been right before. Little had the Star Chamber's examination added to my cause, and Essex's illness during the trial and after had led even those who had started to believe in his guilt over the matter of Ireland to pity him so greatly that guilt no longer mattered. What mattered was the life of the darling boy of England was at stake. The Queen was simply being cruel, kicking a wounded pup when he was down. Essex had gone up in estimations, and I down. It was not only annoying, frustrating that I could not pull the blindfold from my people's eyes away as I had pulled away my own, but it was worrying. The rising tide of affection for Essex was making me wary, costing me more hours of sleep, a debt I could not afford. I had little time to repay it, after all.

My doctors said I needed rest, that I would grow ill, and they were right. Mouth ulcers plagued me that winter, and I had lost weight again when I had little to spare. Many creatures put on weight for winter, fat stored from pillaging crops and stores, but I never did prepare my body in such ways. The worry over Essex and strain of pretending all was well, the aching cold of the winter, took a toll. My mouth was sore and painful too because of my teeth, for I never would have teeth pulled until the last moment, so much did I loathe the experience itself and to have to look afterwards in a mirror, only to see an old hag, toothless and baggy-mouthed, staring back at me. My mouth sores made me not want to eat, and strains and worries added to my problems. Some people eat when they are sad and under strain, but I was one of the other kind. I sometimes wondered if my body wanted me always lean, lithe so I could flee if danger came. My body seemed to forget that most times that had happened I had been kept still, a prisoner in houses, in the Tower where my mother had seen her last days, at Woodstock when my sister tried to shut me away from the world. There was something of the hare about the way my form wanted to react to danger. One day, sniffing peril on the wind, I would turn into a hare, I thought, and away fly to a hilltop where I would simply vanish. Sometimes I thought that a fate that sounded better than anything I would face in truth.

Richmond helped me a little. It was a cosy palace, with smaller rooms and chambers, close walkways. It kept heat in, Richmond. It was where my grandfather had died, and where Kat, dearest Kat, had too. Perhaps it was the warmth or the dark chambers, the thought that it was the closest I would ever come to a return to the soft womb of the mother I had barely known which made me affectionate towards Richmond. Perhaps it was because it felt safe, that my grandsire chose it for his last days and that it had held Kat safe, too, as she died. If there were ghosts at Richmond, they were kind ones. I slept better at Richmond than any other palace, a good thing when winter came and the nights stretched longer. In my endless winter nights when I was awake, I was often thinking of Essex, and what I was to do with him.

If I wanted Essex to stand trial in public, I was not alone. Raleigh, my Captain of the Guards and Essex's old enemy, kept badgering me to follow my own instincts on this matter. Partly he was disturbed by Essex gaining entrance to Nonsuch, for which he had been soundly reprimanded since Essex had got past his guards, but I knew that in truth Raleigh was out only to further his own ends, for as Essex had fallen from my good graces it might have seemed that Raleigh had risen. I spent more time with my Captain of the Guards than almost any other man, but this was out of necessity, not desire. I did not feel safe, and the safest place was with Raleigh, even if he had failed once. With that failure, showing he was a man unlike Essex, he had learned, and security about me had increased. It did make me feel more secure, but it was also keeping me in more than out, and I had always felt freer in the outside world.

But I did not spend time with him for pleasure or friendship. His handsome face held few graces for me by that time. Raleigh had betrayed me by marrying in secret. His wife too had betrayed me. If I knew in my secret heart I could no more trust Essex, I also knew I could not trust Raleigh. There are only so many times you can set faith in a friend and have that faith let down. Few keep trying as a weight of evidence builds. Most surrender. There are, as false friends often forget, many other people in the world, and many of them are more worth the effort than false hearts who only wish to use others to gain their own wants.

But there are different kinds of trust. Trust Raleigh to always follow my orders, evidently I could not, but I knew I could trust him to protect my body. His career and life depended on it. As Captain of my Guards it would have been a dereliction of duty to allow me to fall to the knife of an assassin, or a soft pillow pushed over my face by night, and he had failed me once already, with Essex. He would defend me to the death, Raleigh, give his life for my own. In that mission I could trust him. Perhaps that was enough. I had others I could claim friendship with. Besides, pretending to be the best of friends with my bodyguard would only annoy Essex more, a thought I relished, for the two men loathed each other.

That March, as Essex returned to Essex House, I met again with the special envoy of the Archduke Albert at Richmond Palace. There had been polite dancing and feasting before, and now there would be talks. I had reassured the States General of the Low Countries that I would do nothing without agreement with them first. Whilst peace with the Archduke Albert and his wife Isabella might well be beneficial to England, men of the Low Countries had been our allies longer, and many times had come to our rescue when England needed a friend. The Dutch were friends worth keeping, whereas their Hapsburg masters were questionable at best. Their ambassador was equally questionable. I disliked him from the first, and my instincts were rarely mistaken.

The special envoy of the Archduke, Lodewijk Verreycken, might well have expected me to fall at his knees, take his feet and kiss them in exchange for a chance at peace with the woman my enemies wanted on my throne and her husband, but he would have an unpleasant surprise. The man irritated me from the outset, coming into my presence in an arrogant, overconfident manner. He had a lofty way about him, always commenting how *quaint* things at my court were, which was intended as a back-handed insult I did not miss. I had heard that rather than prepare for the interview between us he had been dining with my lords and nobles of court, and attending performances of Shakespeare's plays, the most notable being *Henry IV, Part 1*, a tale of Bolingbroke, not likely to please me.

"You talk so assuredly of peace between our countries, as though it were a sure thing, ambassador," I barked, interrupting him as he launched into a list of how valuable his master's friendship would be to England. He did not mention the worth it would have for Isabella, Albert or Spain. "Yet your letters of credence are signed only by Archduke Albert, not by Philip of Spain. I have a peaceful agreement with men in the Low Countries already, sir, but Spain is the enemy we have been at war with, who sends ships time and time again to be scattered on our shores by the holy breath of God."

"My lady, I was given to understand..." the ambassador began but I held up a hand.

"*Lady*, my Lord Ambassador, is the very least of my titles," I growled, my tone so tart it could have baked lemons and eggs and presented them at my table at court. "Here in England, although the fashion or I may indeed say, *manners*, may be different in other countries, all men do call me *Highness* or *Majesty*. I would suggest if you wish to be heard, my lord, you address a person by their right and noble titles. I would also suggest if you intend for me to remain here, receiving you as sovereign lord of this country, that you remember to address me correctly."

The ambassador rushed to call me *Majesty*, and I ignored him by moving on to talk about the weather currently present in Europe and asking how the Infanta Isabella was coping, for "in moving from Spain to freezing Brussels," I said, "she must be finding the weather taxing. I understand she is not of a hardy constitution." The ambassador was left unsure what to say, other than to agree with me.

After I had left Cecil, Nottingham, and Buckhurst took the ambassador aside and ripped his proposal of peace to shreds. The ambassador was demanding that my remaining auxiliary troops be withdrawn from the Low Countries, and all trade between England and the Dutch cease. My men greeted this proposal with a deafening silence. The man clearly had not been prepared properly. He had been sent on a mission as though we and the Dutch had surrendered.

My Councillors inquired as to whether Philip of Spain would allow English merchants free passage in the East Indies, and his ambassador refused. He then refused to promise that no Spanish forces would be sent to reinforce Tyrone's rebels in Ireland. The meeting ended there.

"Send the man back to Brussels," I said. "Send him with a letter that the Archduke needs to revise all his peace terms, and that he has a month to send a better answer to me than the one he sent with his ambassador."

"Will we still meet with his men at Boulogne in May, Majesty?" asked Cecil.

"If our allies the Dutch will meet with them, then we will. But I think these negotiations will go nowhere, Pygmy. Spain and the Hapsburgs of the Low Countries seem to be labouring under some misapprehension that we have lost the war. Send instructions to Sir Henry Neville, our new ambassador to France, to make it clear that there will be no removal of our troops from the Low Countries, and no agreement to any hostile move made against the States General of the Low Countries. Tell Neville also that free trade to the East Indies will be considered a test of the true friendship of Spain, and if this is not offered we will hold them false friends. I like war not, but I have no intention of making peace in ways detrimental to England or our allies."

Realising that his tactics of delaying me had failed, for I could see no other purpose in sending the odious ambassador to England other than to irritate me and waste my time, Philip of Spain was apparently soon making swift plans to invade Ireland, where Mountjoy, who had gone in February to meet Tyrone and to engage him as much as Essex had failed to, was actually doing very well. Lord Mountjoy was herding rebels into Ulster. Soon they would be surrounded.

"That is the way it should have been done," I said. "That is the way it could have been done by Essex, had he but concentrated on something other than his own pity, for his own self. Oftentimes, in truth, the best way we help ourselves is to look outside ourselves, help others, complete tasks that need doing. Essex could have reaped this glory, but instead wrecked it, and his name."

He was not the only one causing wrecks all over the world. As our delegates and those of Spain and the Low Countries headed to Boulogne, Tyrone cried out for Spanish aid. "And will Philip send men, ships?" I asked Cecil.

"We have heard, Majesty, that Phillip declared that to protect and help these Catholics of Ireland would be an act most worthy of his greatness. His men have told him that he will be able to copy what we English have done in Holland and Zealand, in other words he can support our enemies as we supported his, at very little cost," said Cecil. "However they do have a problem, Majesty; Spain barely has enough money to pay the Archduke Albert's troops in the Low Countries, and Phillip's men warned that if he sends but half troops to Ireland, they will regret it."

"We shall make him regret *any* action he takes against us, Pygmy," I said.

Yet soon enough, despite Phillip's poor purse, there were rumours of yet another Armada to be sent into English waters. Phillip wanted to cause trouble for me in Ireland, as, as he saw, I had for him in the Low Countries. He would take revenge on England and on me, using Tyrone.

Chapter Sixteen

Greenwich Palace and Whitehall Palace
Summer 1600

That summer Essex stood to answer for his crimes, not before a public tribunal but a special one. It was not a public trial, yet it was not exactly not. As close as I could come to compromise was it, and as close as I dared to step in disgracing him.

"If I could only make my people see him for the dangerous child he is," I muttered to my own reflection, a pale ghost of Elizabeth, hovering in the window. She looked on me with sad eyes, knowing the pain I had felt and still did feel, when it came to Essex.

It would be easy to think that I, being Queen, could put someone away, banish them or put them in gaol, and forget them. Yet not always is this true, even for Queens, even for the most powerful.

I had escaped him and I had not. The lies that I now saw plain were still wrapped about others, making them blind. It is so hard to make people see what you have, so hard to make them understand that a person might be not what they think they are. People are capable of putting on acts before others, revealing their true selves only rarely, and Essex, like many who fashioned power in his hands as clay, was talented at this. To one person he wore one mask and he had others to put on before other people. His mask had been stripped away for me, yet still he had power over me through my people and still a little through my pity. He had more power over my people, many lords and ladies of court, too. He still had good disguises to wear, and he used them.

He was setting me up to be the abuser in this pageant, deflecting all blame from his actions to rest upon me, and the trouble was, people believed him. I felt the same as when a woman cries out her husband has hit her more savagely than the law allows, and he pulls back his sleeve to show a bruise inflicted by his work, and claims she hit him first. Who is to say which one is telling the truth unless they were there, and saw it with their own eyes? Those who abuse are so talented at making people believe they are innocent and the *actual* innocent is guilty. They know how to isolate their victim, not only in reality but through making them appear to be something they are not, by making people doubt them. That was what Essex was doing to me.

The woman in the window could see what I could, and she would stand by me, but so many others would not. They saw me, the Queen, as the one with the power, therefore I must be the one to blame, yet I was not. In truth my only ally who knew what Essex was, was myself. All others, even those who did not support him, did not see him for what he was. Those who wanted him gone wanted such to further their own ambitions, and those who wanted him reinstated wanted it because they had fallen for the mask, the sweet honey he spoke coating his bitter lies.

When one has come out of a relationship that was poor and poisonous, it is so easy to see the traps one fell into. But the fact is until you can see such things you always are blind to them. Hope can be a good friend, and a dangerous enemy. When we have hope for the future, for ourselves, it can be healthy. When we hope someone will change, will treat us better when we know they have become accustomed to taking pleasure in our abuse, hope is a fool who takes our hands and leads us, often willingly, into chaos and danger. I was free of Essex's web now, but others were still in its strands and like struggling moths in the spider web they could not see how they were held, bound to him. He had power over them and they did not see it. They thought he loved them, would do well for them, but all good Essex would do for was Essex, and often he was not even capable of that.

"One day he will in his own web catch himself, hold himself," I said to Katherine Hastings. "One day he will stare, as Narcissus, into a pool and catch sight of himself, wasting away whilst watching this vision of perfection he so wishes to be."

"Yet you still sound sad, Majesty," she said, putting her soft hand, warm with compassion, on mine. "Often you say you have run out of patience and love for the Earl, yet some must remain for you to sorrow for him."

"I often think when I love I never cease to love, no matter what the person does or how little they deserve my affection," I said, one of my fingers curling up to stroke hers. How warm her hands were and how cold were mine! I felt the cold in those days; even when it was warm I felt I needed layers of fur. "I loved my father and still do, yet he cut off my mother's head and declared I was no legitimate daughter of his seed. I continued to love men who betrayed me time and time again. I have loved plotters and murderers, men who tolerate nothing but their own kind and their own people. I have loved women who stole from me, and I have loved my people, even when they turn their faces from me."

I looked at her. "A part of me will always love the Earl, for a part of my heart is a fool always wishing and hoping that the ones it loves will not let it down, if it gives and it gives and gives with honest affection it will be returned. I have known that part of me a long time, and I know how to silence its foolish prattle. But the part that sorrows now is not that part, it is another. It is the part of me, an old woman, who looks on all that youth squanders with so little thought and cringes from it. The part that knows where this is heading, and wishes it did not."

"What do you mean, Majesty?" she asked.

I shook my head, unwilling to answer. There is an old belief that sometimes to say things aloud makes them come true. If I could do anything to make the fears of my heart not come true, I would.

I was unwilling to explain myself for another reason. I was tired. Many times in my life I had felt weary for good reason, and there was good reason now; I had been tested, England had been too and we had risen time and time again to strike back against our enemies, and even those who had claimed they were our friends. But friends I had lost along the way, and the people who had replaced them could never be as close to me as the ones I had lost. I did not share the same amount of time with the replacements as I had with my beloved originals, and perhaps it was a prejudice within me, but I felt I had had the privilege to know some of the most remarkable people who ever walked upon this earth, people who were irreplaceable and not just to me. Essex, certainly, had been a poor replacement for Robin.

The last years had taken their toll, through death, through disappointment but because of another reason too. It is a thing important to treasure the present, and to be present in that time, for we know not what is coming or how much time we have left. But something which is also important, intrinsic to the strength and will of the human heart, is to know that we have things to look forward to, plans to make, people and places to see, new things to set our eyes on that we might be refreshed in our thoughts, that we might find new beauty in a world we so often take for granted. For the past few years, I had felt increasingly that I was running out of time, out of future, and that I would enjoy plans and trips less now because I had not the people I wanted to share this experience with anymore. Life can become most stagnant and ugly when we do not have things to look forward to. In some ways since I had lost Robin, since I had lost Walsingham and William Cecil, since I had lost Blanche, I had come to think I was running out of things to look forward to. I made plans, I went on progress, I set in motion things that would make

England great and help her and her allies, yet sometimes I felt hollow. A great deal of the excitement and exhilaration had gone out of these proceedings because I wanted to share them with the people I loved, and so many of the people I loved were gone.

I was also so very tired of feeling tired. I wanted to know joy in the enjoyment of looking forward and planning for something. I wanted to sense my heartbeat running a little faster at the thought I would go to a place I had never seen, and see it. I wanted to feel again that I could take the hand of a friend, walk along a path unknown and unknowable, not knowing what was at the end but simply walking the path so I could spend time with that friend. I wanted to look forward to things again, but something in me told me that time of my life might well be passing. I could continue to try, and I would. I would never do God a disservice by treating this beautiful world He made as commonplace and replaceable, but without sharing these experiences with those I loved I knew not if those experiences would bring me joy. I still had friends, but many who understood me and understood every part of me, were gone. Those friends I had now, though good and true at heart, had not shared my childhood of danger, had not been there in the Tower with me as Kat and Blanche had, had not supported me through all the perilous times of my sister and brother's reigns as Cecil had, nor stood beside me in times of peace and war as Robin had. I did not share with the friends I had now the longevity of life and existence that I had shared with the friends I had lost. And therefore I did not share as much closeness, as much understanding of soul, as I had with those who now lay in cold graves beneath the earth.

If anything could prove this to me, it was that I was about to put a former favourite on trial.

On the 5th of June 1600 Essex appeared before a special tribunal of my privy counsellors and judges at York House. Lord Keeper Egerton was the chairman and was to hear the charges against him. Essex was to give his answers and there would be judgement. There were to be no witnesses and no formal record. This was a concession to Essex, and there was another. I had allowed this trial to be held in a private place. That was my concession to Bacon and his warnings. However, since this was an exercise not only to bring judgement upon my lord of Essex but also to make the people of England aware of his crimes, an audience of 200 people who had been chosen for their influence within the community were invited. They were there to see justice done upon the man who had failed me.

Essex went to trial, and as he rode there the crowds screamed his name in adoration, and in love. Such fools we are when we love, and when we love the ideal of love in particular.

The case against Essex opened with a reminder of my generosity towards him. I had forgiven Essex time and time again for many things, let alone 10,000 pounds' worth of debts owed to me which I had waived before he left for Ireland. I had given him as much money again to purchase horses and to outfit himself for the campaign in Ireland, and even considering this I had not put him through an ordinary criminal trial. My generosity was such that I had allowed his failings to be held in judgement before an honourable and selected Council who would give a full hearing, and yet showing respect for the Earl, would also do this in private. "Generous, indeed," I muttered on the day the trial opened.

The Attorney General gave a list of complaints about the campaign in Ireland; this included his appointment of Southampton as General of the Horse, which was stated was in defiance of my express orders. They went through his failed journey into Leinster and Munster which had ruined success in Ulster. There was his creation of knights in disobedience of my direct orders again, and his dangerous conference with the rebel Tyrone. There was his abandonment of his post, against my express orders, yet again. It was said that before Essex went into Ireland he had boasted loud that none but he could deal with Ireland and Tyrone, but that when he arrived in

Ireland he ran away, did anything but fight with the rebel leader.

The Solicitor General chimed in with a lengthy document on the state of Ireland, the state in which Essex had left it. Tyrone had become more arrogant and confident than he had been before Essex came to Ireland, he had rearmed, and was now fighting Mountjoy, and so chaos continued to march across Ireland.

Bacon, now working for me as my learned counsel and not for the Earl, rose to speak and complete the case of my Government against the Earl. He expressed the hope that all lords there present would understand that any duty Bacon owed to the Earl had been laid aside, for Bacon now was working for the Crown, which was, he said, his first and true loyalty. He spoke of two other matters not brought up before; Essex's letter to Egerton at the time when I had boxed his ears in which he had said *"cannot princes err,"* and his patronage of Hayward's history of Henry IV, which had led many to suspect Essex saw himself as a second Bolingbroke, a usurper come for my throne.

Essex rose to speak. Not his words, but the manner in which he spoke surprised many. He demonstrated great humility, spoke with tears in his eyes of the huge sorrow that had fallen upon him, and of the horror of his inner remorse in failing his country and his Queen. He admitted I had been gracious to spare him the humiliation of a public trial, and declared he had resolved to surrender all thought of trying to justify his actions.

"Someone must have warned him," I said upon hearing this. "For this is not the Essex I know."

If only I could believe that this Essex was the true Essex, and the man before had been but a pale shadow of the man he might become. But I could not believe it. In a way I cursed myself for having sent warning of the danger he was in to Bacon. Bacon claimed he had said nothing to the Earl, hoping

Essex would reform by himself, but I wondered if this was true. Bacon had not wanted to stand and give evidence against his old master, and it was possible he had indeed warned him. Had I not sent that warning, I might have known whether this abrupt change in character was true or false. But now I did not know, and I suspected it was a show to save his life. Someone had finally managed to convince him that he was in danger of losing his head, not just his wealth and his name.

Essex, at first kneeling before his judges, and then, after Archbishop Whitgift showed mercy because of his late illness, leaning on a chair, declared he would freely acknowledge with grief and contrition his faults of either negligence or rashness, but he said he would freely acknowledge whatever faults *it pleased Her Majesty to impute to him*. So he would accept the crimes I attributed to him, but did that mean he actually thought those crimes were his, his fault, or was he just bowing his head to be scolded, and would under his breath mutter that I was mistaken?

That little declaration of his spoke to me, saying that once again Essex did not hold himself culpable for any crimes. He would simply accept the charges I laid against him, believing that *I* believed them, not that he did. This meant he had not changed. When someone offers an apology true, they acknowledge their part, their fault in the argument, in what was done. They say, "I am sorry for what *I* have done." But there is a canny slip that some choose to use, and often those who try to avoid blaming themselves use it. They say, "I am sorry *you* feel this way." That is simply a way of deflecting the blame once more upon the other party. They are not admitting fault, they are saying they are sorry that you feel the way you do, not that they did anything to bear upon that feeling.

Essex went on to say that his loyalty had been called into question and he wished to justify himself as an honest man, for if he did not he would be doing God and his conscience a great wrong. Essex spoke with passion, charm and sincerity, apparent sincerity, in any case. He cried out that he would tear the heart out of his breast with his own hands if ever a disloyal thought had entered his heart or his mind.

Sadly the charm of Essex was strong, and Egerton hurried on the proceedings for he was aware that Essex was winning people over. He pointed out that no one there had accused Essex of disloyalty, but that the Earl was charged with contempt and disobedience of orders. Therefore protestations of his loyalty and passion were completely irrelevant. Essex subsided like a pudding taken out of the oven too early. He began a pathetic plea asking that his former allies would make an honourable report of his disordered speeches that day, which were the best he could perform to them having both an *aching* head and *weakened* body. He was once more trying to make people feel sorry for him. Few amongst his accusers were deceived by this play on their emotions.

One by one each of the eighteen members of the tribunal gave their opinion of the case and all agreed that the Earl was guilty of dereliction of duty. It was said he would be suspended from his offices of court and campaign and would remain under house arrest until such a time as I was pleased to release him.

Many of the 200 people called to witness Essex's trial were weeping as the verdict was read. Many said it was the most pitiful and lamentable sight that they had seen for many a year, and yet this trial at York House had managed to show Essex to many as what he was, or at least to show to people that he was not as useful to me as he claimed, and therefore not useful to England. What aided me even more in this matter was news from Ireland where Lord Mountjoy, along with his commander Sir George Carey, was making good progress against the rebels, and proving that this was not an impossible task. They, with fewer resources than Essex had had, were doing better than he had. Mountjoy demonstrated patience, persistence, and determination. Essex had ridden in hoping for swift victory, for he lived not off meat but myth. Mountjoy's success proved another thing; if others could succeed where the Earl of Essex had failed, then he had not been set up to fail, but had managed that feat all on his own.

Essex was sent back to Essex House, and I was sent the verdict. I was to decide what would be done with him. I knew what I was to do with him but I would leave it for a while. People said that I had made my point and therefore I would forgive the Earl, for it was clear I could not do without him. But I had absolutely no intention of delivering my friendship, already too beaten and abused by this man, back into his hands again. He had had enough chances, had had enough of my love, my patience, enough of my friendship. He had taken every single one of those virtues for granted, and he had used my natural love and affection against me. I could not trust him, and if I could not trust him I did not want him at court, and without court the career of any man of noble blood was nothing.

Essex would never return to my side. I would not have him near me, I would not have him at my court. His days of power were done. I had shown mercy by not taking his life, but I would punish by stripping away all that he held dear in life.

"Light punishment, considering his crimes," said Cecil, as I told him what I had decided.

"Perhaps for some men. Not for the Earl," I said. "Loss of power and public eyes on him is worse than death. He knows not who he is unless he hears men crying out his name."

Robert laughed a little, but I was serious. This would wound Essex. I hoped it would, and would teach him a lesson. This was the last lesson I had to offer. I could not all his life be a tutor to him.

Essex lost his seat on the Privy Council, and was stripped bare of his titles of Earl Marshall and Master of the Ordinances. At court, about country, in war or times of peace he no longer had a role in England. People were already saying the country would fly apart but for him. I intended to show them this was not so.

It could have been worse. Had I put him through an ordinary trial, which I would have done but for fear of his popularity, he could have lost all his wealth, his freedom and most likely his life. As it was he kept his life, lost his titles, and was kept under house arrest at Essex House. I had considered freeing him, but many lords, mainly his enemies who no doubt feared what he might do with more freedom, persuaded me not to. Thinking that, in Essex's head, I was most likely now one of his enemies too, I agreed.

Although he could have lost more, what he endured was a grand humiliation, the worst I could contrive. His public career and power were gone, and all titles but those inherited from his family were too. He had no reason to be at court, no say in the future of England or its present. I had cut off his hands and his feet by taking his positions and one might say I had made him a eunuch by ripping out his power. He might have welcomed the actual loss of his head before this, for now he had to live knowing he was cast out of the bright halls of power, that he had a mouth but no one would hear aught he said. For a man as proud as he, this was the worst punishment. I had rendered him silent and ineffectual. I had made him impotent.

It was important he knew I cared not for his pain. I went about my normal routine. I danced and I laughed, entertained ambassadors and sang. I played the virginals for my ladies, rode and hunted each day. I pretended I cared nothing for the trial of Essex but it was not entirely so. I had won, of course I had, but that did not mean it had cost me nothing. I felt cynical and old many times when I was pretending to be caring for nothing. At times this leaked out of me, a seeping sap. Ten days after the trial I was at Blackfriars, it was the 15th of June and I was attending the wedding of Anne Russell, one of my favourite maids of honour, to Master William Herbert. There was a masque afterwards performed by eight ladies of the court dressed as characters of allegory. Such things were common entertainments. But somehow although I was at an occasion which should have occasioned joy, I could not feel it.

The ladies were dancing, dressed as characters meant to invoke love. Yet I, as I was supposedly watching them, was thinking of other matters. This occasion of love, this wedding was set at Blackfriars, the very place where my father had brought his first wife, a woman who he had claimed he loved for more than twenty years, and here in hallways once roamed only by monks my father had set out a case against Katherine of Aragon, saying that their marriage was cursed by God because she had been married to his brother before him. Everyone knew that was not the reason he wanted to set her aside and take another wife. He wanted my mother, Anne Boleyn, and no other than she would do. So Blackfriars then had been a place where love of twenty years, loyal and sweet, had been destroyed as my father sought to take a new love, one he believed truer than the first. Perhaps it had been, for who is to say what lies in the heart of another person? For seven long years he battled to have my mother, made himself Head of his own Church, freed England and did some things that were good, but in truth all of these things were done so that he could take the woman he loved, or declared he loved, into his bed, into his arms. Three years after he had that woman in his arms, he cleaved her head from her body, then he took another wife, and another, and another, and another, and might have considered another, had he gone through with arresting Katherine Parr. *So much for love*, I thought glumly. *So much for fidelity and loyalty.*

As I sat there thinking of these dark matters which brought about my birth, Mary Fitton, one of my younger maids, came up and asked me to dance. I gazed upon her costume. It was usual to have the name of the character each lady depicted sewn or embroidered upon a banner and wrapped about their body. Mary was not wearing one, so I asked what her costume represented.

"Affection," said Mary, beaming an innocent smile upon me.

"Affection!" I snorted. "Affection is false."

For a moment poor Mary merely stared at me. I knew she was thinking that I might well upset the joyous festivities of this wedding, which was something no young person, nor yet the happily married couple, would want. Mary Fitton, and so many others there, simply wanted to enjoy the happiness of the day, wanted to dance and lighten their hearts, forget all the troubles that had been and were coming for them. I felt heavy with my own troubles, and with visions of the past which came to me, but I took a deep breath in and I smiled. I stood, said nothing more that was cynical or detached. I took Mary's hand and I danced before my people.

Sometimes the best thing to do when one is sad is to dance. If one cannot feel light, one can have light heels and leap upon the earth, showing sorrow that it has not yet won, not every battle in which it is pitched against us.

Through the end of August and into September I was hunting every day and dancing every night. I was in good health, though perhaps cynicism kept me feeling as young as my daily rides did. I was to become sixty-seven years in that autumn, but I did not feel it. Keeping busy kept much of my mind together. I felt lonely, I will admit, a great deal of the time. I had my women, like Anne and Katherine, Helena too, but there were few who remembered the days of my youth, who remembered all I did. I yearned at times to speak to someone, recall those times even though many were fraught with pain and troubles. But in this late stage of my life I knew I could be alone and survive. I knew being alone would not kill me and could not hurt me, other than a pang to wish to talk. At times I shut myself away for days and saw only my women, made of my chambers a cocoon in which I could rest and transform. But even on those days when I was so lonely I wanted to be alone, I made sure I was seen, out riding, dancing in a gallery. I would not have Essex smirk, thinking I was sad because of him, and he was arrogant enough to assume that if I was sad at that time, he would be the cause. He never assumed that some of us had things other than him in our hearts and minds.

That July I had done something else to please my heart, and stripped away the knighthoods Essex created in Ireland. It was the correct thing to do, and it was a balm to my spirits. In some ways it felt as though I was erasing him from England by doing all I did. But he had his life and could do something with it. He could live a smaller life, perhaps a happier one, or work to grow great again in time. Many would have taken his head, but I did not. In part so I was not the one to destroy him, and in part because I knew there are worse things than death, and some people deserve them.

I had destroyed his kingdom, burned his palaces down. Essex had watched his world tumble to dust. There was his punishment, and it was deserved. What came next, what he made of this new start, was up to him.

*

"A fine day," I said as I came back to the palace, throwing my gloves, stained with blood, gaily to a maid. Her face blanched at the splattered blood and I laughed, feeling quite content.

I was hunting every day, and feeling hale for it. At the end of each day I would sit at my fire warming my aching muscles and creaking bones and I would feel tired for certain, but refreshed at the same time. Movement enlivens the senses and awakens the body's sense of joy. There is some sad irony in the fact that when we are low we wish nothing more than to curl up in a heap and move nowhere, yet to move would do us the most good. At times I watched my hounds at the fire, always those who performed best would be allowed to spend the night in my rooms in comfort. It horrified my women who liked not the smell, but I welcomed the dog as a teacher. Seeing hounds curled up at the hearth, wanting nothing but the fire in that moment or the woods in the daytime with their scent of game, I could learn much, I thought. The hound wants nothing more than the best the present offers, and this is why he is happy. So rarely do humans appreciate all we have, just in that moment, and so we remain discontented.

So much, too much of life is spent looking forwards. We will be happy *when* we do this, *go* there, *have* that, so we think. *When* we know this we will be content, *when* we have that person or do this thing to impress. We forget we can be happy by looking at what we have, what we are, all we have learnt already. When you know you have not so much time left, you end up forced to appreciate the present more because you have less future. And I tell you, it is a happier state though death might be closer. The moment a person might look around and say, "this is well, what I have here," is the happiest moment of life. Contentment is much underrated.

The unsatisfied never are happy, they always look for something more to fill a gap inside them, and they never will find it, for it should be filled with the present and the now, the all they have and the treasures already in their possession, but because they are too busy looking elsewhere, these precious things they never see. My father was one for this, always thinking what would make him happy was just about the corner, but when he turned he always found an empty space staring back at him. He tried to find happiness in his wives, his children, seeking always the perfect one. Even he knew Edward was not his perfect son, and never did he find a perfect woman for they do not exist. I think my mother came closest, for she was perfect for him, but he could not keep a woman who failed to give him a son, and could not bear a wife who dared to question him. He destroyed his own happiness, by always seeking a better happiness just out of reach. Such is the terrible power of illusion. Such is the danger of thinking happiness will come sometime *when*.

Death forces us to live in the present, and if we are wise we will come to understand we might die at any time, so we should all be doing this even now. Most would take this as an excuse to get drunk, stray from work or fidelity, but that is not what I mean. There are many ways to enjoy life, and becoming insensible with drink or fornicating with someone you care not a fig for are not pastimes I would choose, for there is more satisfaction in work and achievement than in a bottle, more happiness in a friendship that spans years and understanding, more peace in a love that holds respect than one that just harbours lust.

So I watched the happy, tired dogs at my fireside and I tried to learn the lesson their kind learnt eons ago, to be merry in the moment, content with all the blessings you have. Sometimes it worked for me. Nothing works all the time. Sometimes the darkness feels too long to see the end of, even though if we are sensible we know we will emerge eventually. Some days it was not enough, and for others it was. That, in itself, was something to be grateful for.

Yet it was not a good year for all, as for the seventh year in a row the harvest was set to be poor. Years of war had depleted the reserves of England, and I could not tax people more. More Crown property and my own jewels were sold off to make amends for my debts and for the needs of court. I could not take from my people when they had so little to give. When even my father's Great Seal was sold, and many courtiers were surviving on favours given to them, monopolies of trade on wines and other imports, I felt England was slipping into debts we never would repay. But there was little else I could do. Cut, cut, cut I had at court, so my courtiers paid for my court in the summer by hosting us on progress, and in winter the feasts and celebrations grew more and more spare. Parliament complained bitterly about the monopolies of certain courtiers, favours granted where they controlled imports of salt, sugar or wine, but with little of my own to offer them as rewards for loyalty I knew not what else to give.

On the 26th of August Essex was told he was free to wander where he wanted, as long as it was not to court. As much as I did not want him at court, many others, and Cecil most of all, did not want him there either. The reason being Essex was attempting, through his friends, to unseat Cecil from his posts near me, thinking Cecil was the reason he had power no more. It seemed I was not to blame anymore for all Essex had done wrong, yet he could not be, so someone else had to. Essex's designs to unseat Cecil were, however, fragmented at best. Most people were refusing to get involved with Essex's schemes anymore. Bacon had sent a letter to his former friend, apologising for his part in the trial, but few others would think to do the same. They had not the inclination, as most had run out of pity for the Earl as I had, and many were glad, thinking that Essex had, in truth, known too much power and his present position was just deserts for all he had done. But Essex had not surrendered. If me he could not reach, he would reach into the future, and approach my successor.

"He is still sending letters to James?" I asked.

"It would appear so, Majesty," said Robert Cecil. "The Earl is claiming that England is to be handed to Spain, and that I am working on this plan, and this is proved enough by our recent, secret talks with the Archduke Albert and Infanta Isabella. My men have intercepted letters to the King of Scots from Essex, which claim James of Scots needs to be aware that Essex is his only friend and supporter, his only hope of gaining the throne of England."

"Essex said he would to the country go, and live quietly," I said. "This sounds like an attempt to return to an unquiet life."

"Some men cannot live without noise," agreed Cecil. "Some of his friends, Blount his stepfather in particular, are trying to rehabilitate the Earl with men of court, although there are whispers of more direct action."

"It would be a shame if Blount got involved in this," I said. "And if he does it will no doubt be the fault of that harpy he married, Lettice. He has shown promise in Ireland. It would be a good thing for him to concentrate on his own career, rather than the lost and failed one of his stepson."

"Blount and others are saying that Jesuits are being treated with greater leniency by me and others, Majesty," he said. "And this shows that I and others mean to one day place Isabella, a Catholic, on the English throne."

"Clever, for that will scare James," I mused. "He has shown he is aware of the need for support from Catholic nations, by promoting his wife as a papist sympathiser, and he will be aware too that Catholic kingdoms would more readily support an actual, known Catholic than one apparently in hiding." I tapped my fingers, making an irregular beat upon the table. "Curse Essex!" I said. "He is undone yet still he would cause trouble for me! Perhaps I should have indeed locked him away or taken his head."

"Whatever he chooses to do is not your fault, Majesty," said Cecil. "We can only do what we think is right. If, with the liberty and generosity you have offered him, Essex chooses to act wrongly that is on his head and conscience, not yours. You acted with kindness when you had no cause to. That virtue and its reward is yours."

"Sometimes mercy and pity, even kindness, lead people to only do worse to us," I said.

"Which is why they are only more admirable when undertaken," said Cecil, offering me a small smile. "We could simply throw all who oppose us in gaol or take their heads, or we can strive, as you always have, Majesty, to act fairly, in accordance with the wishes of God and not with the strains of fear."

"You speak comfort, and I thank you for it," I said.

"I speak truth. My father often told me, especially when I was young, how he admired your generosity. He said you were different to many monarchs because of it, and although sometimes I may go against you on certain matters, Majesty, for the safety of England, I think the same as my father."

"You Cecils ever were a wise and cunning breed," I said. "Unlike my lord of Essex." I sighed. "What a fool is a fool who cannot stop doing foolish things," I said.

"Do you want us to lay charges of these crimes against the Earl, Majesty? Conspiracy?"

I shook my head. "I know Essex is false," I said. "But it will do no good to lock him away again. I want to know what James will say in reply to Essex. I want to know if all men are false, or if it is just the ones I place my trust in."

I looked up to see Robert looking somewhat hurt, an expression most unusual on his normally stoic face. "I do not mean you, Pygmy," I said.

"Thank you, Majesty," he said. But the expression of hurt remained in his eyes, and I knew why.

Robert Cecil was as far from a fool as it is possible for a man to be. He knew I did not hold him in the same affection as I had held his father for so many years. It was impossible for me to do so, for William Cecil had been as a father to me, as a friend, as a part of my own soul. The son was more than aware not only that I did not love him as I had his father, but that I also did not love him as I had loved Essex. Robert was a good man, a solid, clever, ruthless when it suited him, man. He was a skilled adviser, and I worked with him well, but it would have been taxing to call him a friend. He did not have the same respect for me as my men of old had, and I did not have the same affection for him. Work together well we could, but bonded to one another as I had been to men of the past and they had been to me, we never would be. He was more than aware of this. Sometimes I thought he was glad of it, having seen what devotion to me brought some men, and sometimes I think it pained him, seeing he was not, and never could be as great as his father had been in my eyes.

As autumn came people said I would forgive Essex and bring him back, but they did not know of his letters to Scotland, wooing my successor as though I were already in the grave. And what was more, Essex knew not I knew of his letters.

"Forgiveness may benefit me more than you," I said to him in the dark one night, "that is what they say. And yet I cannot be so foolish, for nothing in the pup has changed. When milk he cannot get from her, still he tries to bite his mother."

Chapter Seventeen

Whitehall Palace
Autumn 1600

It was Michaelmas, the anniversary of the day Essex burst into my room, and a decision needed to be made. There was a choice before me, to either maintain someone who had betrayed me, or not.

The revenue of sweet wines, a monopoly on trade that I had bestowed upon Essex to increase his income was due to be renewed. Once this had belonged to Robin, and although I cannot say he ever had a care with it, being like all men of my court more a spender than saver, I never thought Robin might use such funds against me. Essex was perilously in debt, somewhere around sixteen thousand he owed to creditors and that was not including all the money I had loaned him and he never had paid back. When he had been in a position of power his creditors had fawned, been prepared to wait, but now he had lost his places at court and in the army, as well as my love, they were growing agitated. If I did not renew his grant on monopolies of sweet wines, Essex would be in serious trouble, at last forced to confront the realities of life without my affection.

I hesitated a short while before making my decision, however, for I wondered if I was acting in spite. I had crippled the Earl already, had sent him to trial, which although not as public as it could have been was still a humiliation. I had stripped him of his titles. I had cast him from my court, so he was in exile from all that was most important to him; his positions, his power, his place in the world. All of that had I taken from him.

But I hesitated, wondering if I should take more. I wondered if I was in truth lost in revenge, whether I was seeking to hurt him as he had me. But in the end the decision came, and the decision was made in my interests. Guilt assailed me, but I spoke to the guilt within me, told it that it had no cause to be offended, for I had done everything I could for this young man. I told it to be silent rather than speak, for I had done the best I could for Essex, and no one can ask more than that. The best interests of Essex were no more my concern. I had taken more pains with his reputation, with his life, with his ambitions and with his sense of self and confidence than Essex ever had. I had done more for Essex than Essex. And I had been repaid badly.

"I cannot renew the revenue to Essex," I said to my Council. "Now, as he is stripped of power, he becomes perhaps more dangerous, and with money more so again. I am not sure it is deserved in any case. Such favours as revenues on goods and imports are given to men who work for England as a reward, and because he has lost his power he has done nothing for the country for a year."

Precious little he did for England before that time, said a voice in my head.

Some men about my Council table looked disturbed. They, like so many others, had believed that Essex would be back at my side within a month of his trial, and I would be once more simpering upon his youthful arm. Yet to find that he had been stripped of positions and power, his place at court and now his most lucrative source of income, worried them. It was not in truth concern for Essex that inspired brows to furrow, but concern for their own selves, their own power. When the example of one who has erred is before others, and when that one is punished, men become concerned the punishment of one might become the punishment of many if they do not live up to the potential of their own minds. They feared for their own authority as they watched the destruction of all that had made Essex powerful, for if one man so powerful can fall, then so can anyone. Essex had become a kind of fable told to men of influence, showing them what happened when that power was stripped away. It was not a fable any of them wanted to hear.

There was another reason I did not want to renew the monopoly. Essex had written many times at the end of that summer, telling me he loved me, adored me, missed me more than the sun misses the earth as night falls. So many missives had come recently, and I had been a little lost in his words… until I realised what he had, that the renewal of the sweet wines was approaching. "Oh, foolish boy," I said sadly, shaking my head at the letter. "You think you are so subtle, you think you can charm your way out of anything. You think I am so desperate to hear you love me that I will miss the canny timing of your letters of love." I crumpled the letter in my fist, threw it to the fire. "You almost had me tricked, Essex, almost but not quite."

It was all another lie, his gentle affection and passionate longing for me, and hardly a clever one. He sent sweet words to gain control of sweet wines and all the sweet money that came with them. His words and letters meant nothing, he was just trying to win my favour and his funds, that was all.

It was such a hollow feeling that came with that realisation, and I wish I could say it had come with surprise, but it had not. I had not understood at first, had thought he might have truly missed me, and then I had remembered the grant, and that he might lose it. At that moment I understood the fakery of his words and sentiments. I felt no excitement in the revealing of that knowledge. A hollow feeling indeed, just another disappointment to pile on top of all the others.

So I took back the revenues of the wines, kept them for the Crown since I was short on funds. I would not reward his lies and his falseness. An untrue heart was his, beating with the iron-ring of money and not with love.

When Essex heard, he was not happy and seemed genuinely surprised, as though he thought that grant would be his for life. It was not. Such grants were gift and favour of the Crown and it was up to me who was rewarded with them. My godson

John Harrington went to see Essex not long after the news was out, and said the man seemed honestly distraught that all his missives of love had been so ignored by me, and despite all his declarations of love I remained so cold and cruel a mistress towards him as to remove the revenues for the wines. I wondered at times if Essex truly convinced himself that the lies he told were true. Indeed, had he seen himself in a mirror which showed only his honest reflection, he might well have flinched. It might have been easier to believe his own lies, to believe that he indeed loved me and I was cruel, rather than to believe that he was simply trying through false flattery and cynical means to extract money from me, again; easier to believe I was wronging him than that he was a shallow, false and hollow man. Yet it might have done him good to see that truth, to face it. If he had managed to do such a thing, he might have understood why I had taken away this income, and why he had lost me as well as other friends.

But Essex could not see he had lost the income from those sweet wines because he was of no use to England anymore, and could not see that this was his fault. When Harrington went to see him, my godson left swiftly for Essex spoke so wild that Boy Jack feared to be around his talk. Knowing that nothing lay in his future but further ruin and disgrace, any self-control that Essex had possessed finally fled. Harrington's opinion was that Essex was tending towards madness. The Earl spoke in rage and of rebellion to my godson. Had Essex been of sound mind, he might have realised that saying such things to *my* godson was dangerous. Boy Jack wrote to Cecil saying, *"Thank God I am safe at home and if I go in such troubles again I deserve the gallows for a meddling fool! His speeches of the Queen becometh no man who hath Mens sana in corpore sano,"* showing he clearly believed Essex's mind was not healthy anymore. Harrington wrote to Cecil that Essex's soul *"seemeth tossed to and fro like the waves of a troubled sea."*

Boy Jack told Cecil something else. When Essex heard of the monopolies lost, he turned to my godson and told him my mind and conditions were as "crooked as my carcass."

"My mind is as crooked as my carcass?" I asked. Cecil watched me steadily, with some fear. I saw his feet twitch, ready to fly, thinking I would go wild, join the Earl in madness. "*Carcass*?" I said again with dreadful calm. "The Earl thinks of me as already dead, does he?"

Cecil was not about to be fool enough to answer that, so he went on to what else Boy Jack had reported to him. "Harrington warned that whilst he thought Essex had spoken out of sorrow and rage, Essex had also spoken thoughts of rebellion aloud." Cecil paused, gave a little cough which I suspected was more to ease his discomfort than dislodge a stuck particle of carp left behind from dinner in his throat. "Other disaffected men, who have little faith in you, Majesty, and no love either, have started to be invited to Essex's house. It would seem he is gathering men to him who have one thing in common; dissatisfaction with the realm."

I stared at Cecil, and simply nodded. I knew what he meant, what this meant.

"Would you have me arrest any of them, Majesty?" Cecil asked.

"Leave them be," I said, my tone cold, controlled. "Watch them close. I want eyes on Essex House, on Essex and on all these men flocking to him. I know where one traitor in my room is sleeping, I would know what others come to rest beside him."

I went to my window to look out on nature, a purer soul than the feckless, faithless ones of men. "Corrupt bodies," I said, echoing something I had said to Cecil earlier. "Corrupt bodies, the more you feed them, the more hurt you do them. An unruly horse must be abated of his provender, that he may be the more easily and better managed." I stared into the night. "I will take your feed, Essex," I said. "Enough have you fed, and well, at my hand. It is time to stand alone, or fall beneath my feet you will."

Chapter Eighteen

Whitehall Palace
Autumn- Winter 1600

As disaffected men gathered unto Essex, and Robert kept his spies upon them so we knew who they were and how many, there was good news. War in the Netherlands came to an end, at last, and it was a good end for our allies the Dutch. It had been a long time coming, but at last people could see that I had been right to support them all this time, for finally God had made up His mind, and settled upon the Dutch the rights I had thought should be theirs.

On my Accession Day of that year Essex was not at court but I had no rest from his chatter, for he was writing to me. His letters were as wild as his words to Harrington had been, and he sounded inflamed of mind and suspicion, certain that his recent misfortunes had been brought about by a plan put together by his enemies to utterly destroy him. He believed Cecil was planning to murder him and was conspiring with Philip III to put Isabella on the throne instead of me. It was *imperative* that Essex warned me, he declared, so I could rid myself of ministers who would betray me and England, and he needed me to reconcile with him, restore him fully to favour. There were hints that if I refused to listen, then he would make me do this for my own good. Essex seemed convinced that the only way back into my favour was to force his way in there, just as he had into my bedchamber.

I had a feeling, listening to reports from Cecil, that if I failed to restore Essex I would not just face one man this time, but possibly many. A veritable army of his friends and citizens who were disaffected with my reign were gathering to him at Essex House. An army, or a rebel force?

"The Earls of Southampton and Rutland are with him, Majesty," said Cecil, "as well as Sir Charles Danvers, his stepfather Christopher Blount, a recusant named Francis Tresham and Essex's secretary Henry Cuffe, who is the one who is pouring the most poison into his ears."

"I have had the displeasure of meeting Cuffe," I said shortly. "He does not place a high value on the lives of men."

"Lady Rich too appears to be with her brother, and his Welsh steward Sir Gelli Meyrick is with them also. Essex is writing all the time to James of Scots, telling him that I am trying to promote the Infanta Isabella as the next queen, or possibly as a queen to replace you, Majesty. I have been told by my men that James has been worried by this at last and has responded to Essex, sending a coded message."

"Can we get hold of this coded message?" I asked.

"Essex is carrying it with him at all times in a black pouch which hangs about his neck," said Cecil.

"If nothing else," I said, twisting my nervous sleeves. "The fact he has it on his person all the time is telling. Essex is no subtle man. That note sent by James must be inflammatory, or promises much to him, or both." I stared at Cecil. "We are watching the borders with Scotland? And your people will watch James?"

"We are watching both, Majesty, but I see no indication of an army to be sent in support of Essex."

"Let us hope it stays that way. I would not wish to have to exclude James from the succession at this moment when you have tried so hard to be his friend. It would be a grand waste of both our times."

"The conspirators are meeting at Essex House, also at Southampton's house of Drury," Cecil went on. "I have heard Essex is contemplating breaking into your apartments once more, Majesty, placing you under a kind of gentle arrest, and it is said he will rule England in your name. They are saying, Majesty, that you have forgot your good sense and judgement, and it is up to them to restore it."

I laughed bitterly. "Many a traitor has claimed he acts in the name and interests of his monarch," I said. "They convince themselves too, no doubt, for to face what they do truly and honestly must be a thing most hard, most unsettling. No man likes to look in the mirror to see a snake staring back."

My eyes drifted to the wall, staring at nothing. "I agree not with them, so they declare I have lost my mind. No doubt they will blame my age or sex, but the truth is I do not agree with them, so they will force me to. They mean to impose themselves upon me, my mind, body, my kingdom, because I will not do as they say. I never did react well to men trying to force me. These fools evidently think their plans original, but I have seen their kind often enough."

"What should we do?" asked Cecil.

"Continue to watch them," I said. "Continue to watch."

"This is dangerous, Majesty," said Robert.

"Of that I am well aware, Pygmy," I said, my eyes flashing to his face. "But continue to wait and watch, have your men listen. The Earl is not one to be silent about his plans, as we already know." I turned to him, smoothing my gown. "I want to know who is with him when this breaks, and I want to know all of them. We will capture Essex, and we will take his friends too. Wait we will, until the traitors have gathered all together, so we can see them plain in the light of day."

I sounded strong, and I meant to be so, but there are times the body expresses strains of the mind. I made a short visit not long after to Baynard's Castle, near Blackfriars, to see Robert Sidney. Travelling there I felt fine, but as soon as I started to talk to my host I felt so tired, so very tired of all of it, all of the meeting and greeting, playing and acting, all of the things that had, in truth, made up the game of my life. I was not sure I wanted to play anymore. I ate little at dinner, my stomach protesting it wanted no food, as though it too was sick of things that once had sustained us. I walked with my stick about the house, and suddenly noted that I was being flanked when going up or down stairs by two careful pages, who patently had been set this cautious task in case I fell. I chuckled when I noticed them, and even made a jest by swaying a little on purpose. Then, when their faces were worried enough, I turned to them and whispered. "Rest easy, young gallants. I shall not fall, not yet and not now." I smiled at them.

With no idea of what I was speaking, they simply smiled and bowed, humouring the old woman before them. But I knew. Sick of life and this tiring struggle I was that day, but there was still work for me to do, and as long as there was I could not fall. When my desk was empty it would be time to go, when I could no more pull another paper before my eyes. When I was lost to use for England it would be time for this Queen to crumble.

"But not before that time, no matter how crooked my mind or carcass be," I said to my reflection in the mirror that night. "And I will decide when it is time, and no other will for me."

That included a treasonous Earl, not so far away speaking words of rebellion to others. He meant to make me see reason? I would give him reason to regret, regret much, if he dared try to rise against me. Essex had no idea who he was dealing with. Of course he did not, for always he had underestimated me. Soon he would learn what folly that was.

Chapter Nineteen

Whitehall Palace
Winter 1600

As I walked down the corridor of Whitehall, my eyes were drawn to a window. Just visible beyond a layer of paint on the sill was the horn of a bull poking out. The emblem of a rose was painted over the top, but once a bull had stood on that sill. "No doubt with a lion or greyhound next to it," I said, stroking the tiny tip of the horn with my slim finger. "So Father could stand next to you, Mother, as once he always wanted."

The Boleyn bull. I had, both here at Whitehall where she had designed much of the palace with my father, and in other palaces, found tiny reminders of my mother. There were other memories of her that lingered. Here and there in plaster or brick would be a phoenix, Jane Seymour's badge, which in truth looked more like a falcon. My father had replaced badges of former wives with those of present ones, but sometimes the work had not been done well.

Here and there was a little of each wife, even of my mother, and her emblems he had tried the hardest to rid his palaces of. I had found many of Katherine Parr's, but hers had not been scratched away since she was his last wife and had managed to outlive him. Every now and then I found a pomegranate, a phoenix, sometimes a badge of Cleves or a crowned woman, and many were roses, despite Catherine Howard's disgrace and death. Her emblem was the easiest to alter in many ways, as it needed no alteration, being also the symbol of my father. My maternal cousin who died in the same way and place as my own mother, and was buried with her in the Tower, had always tried to be the most placating of my father's wives. Even in death she had not failed him. Her emblems must have been the easiest to disguise as something else, as another Tudor rose. So little of herself had Catherine left behind, and now all that once might have been a sign she had lived, been Queen, walked these halls, had been reabsorbed into the Crown, into my father, as though she never had existed, which in truth was what I think he wanted to do to her memory. "Poor child," I whispered.

It was odd in a way for me to think that I had grown to be far older than Catherine Howard ever had. When I thought of her I remembered a woman older than me, but of course when she had lived I had been a child, and had not understood that Catherine was a child too, just a slightly older one. Now nearing seventy years, I could see that anyone under thirty was still a child, no matter what they thought, and some would be children all their lives, never learning to grow up.

Catherine's emblems had simply been swallowed by the palace, surrounded by those of my father so they looked like his, so it seemed as if she never existed. Hers were the ones you would see most often, and my other step-mothers' too slipped in. But my mother's emblems were rare, and precious sights each were for that rarity. I liked to look up at the gateway as I rode into Hampton Court, see my mother's initial entwined with my father's, a missed mark of a love once strong. There was another in the chapel there, and here and there falcons, sometimes set into other scenes by painters of the palaces who had tried to save a little money for the Crown. My grandfather had been known as the miser, but towards the end of his life my father was in some ways the same. His meanness had saved memories, little hints of each of his wives left behind from his rush to destroy them, so it seemed each time he married it was for the first time, another chance to start again, build upon the destruction of the last marriage, make this one perfect. I imagine I was not the only one over the years who had found these marks, and to the women who followed my father's former wives each mark must have been vastly unwelcome reminders of what happened to women who failed my father, but to me they were sweet, lingering ghosts of women who all in their own ways I had admired. I had not lived their lives, so did not have to take sides. I believed my father had chosen remarkable women to love, and sadly, to destroy.

"Rest well, Mother," I whispered to the bull, the finger stroking it being the one on which my ring of secrets sat. It opened, had a portrait of my mother on one panel and of me on the other. No one alive knew of it but me. Kat had known, my goldsmith who made it too. Now both those secret-keepers were dead. I had never shown the inside to anyone, not even Robin or Cecil. It was my memory of my mother, my honouring of her, and it was for me and no other. Enough of my relationship with my parents had been commented on and judged by others. I held a complicated love for both of them that I never had reconciled and realised now I never would. I had accepted. One had killed the other, they had hated, had loved, had me and both were gone, and for their flaws and all they each had done, I still loved them. That was as it was. I could not change the past by wishing it had been different, so all I could do was accept my feelings for them and continue. It was a comfort, actually. I once believed that to love one must forgive all a person has done. I now knew that was not so. I had a large and complicated heart. It could love much and deeply, and be angry at the same time. There was room enough for all emotions.

"Come, come," I said to Helena, as though she had been the one dallying in the corridor, staring at an old splash of paint. "This will not do, we will be late for Cecil."

"Yes, Majesty," my old friend obediently said, as though she was indeed the one holding us up.

I was on my way to dine with Robert Cecil, and he had made great preparation, ensuring my present favourite dishes of plain pottage and good bread were upon his table. Although I never had been one, as my father had been, for consuming huge amounts of meat, my teeth were troubling me and ulcers in my mouth and throat caused pain, so soup and bread made soft by that same soup were more welcome to me now than roasted meat, no matter how tender, that I would have to chew. Sadly, and for the same reason, I had had to give up my sweet treats of gingerbread and marchpane. Doctors said the sugar in them, whilst beneficial most of the time for hale strength and energy, might be what was causing my teeth to go black and rot. Little stock did I put in the opinion of doctors, and their remedies were full enough of sugar in any case, so they could not have thought that badly of the substance, but it was true my teeth ached more after a treat of sugar, and the sweet was not worth the sour pain which followed.

"The ambassador from Muscovy will arrive tomorrow," Cecil informed me as we supped on chicory pottage.

"I will feast with him on Twelfth Night," I said. "And dance too."

"The Duke of Bracciano was telling me today how impressed he was by your obvious health and vigour, Majesty," Cecil said.

The Duke was on a private visit to my court, and no doubt also had been sent to spy on us, for he was the cousin of the new French Queen Maria de Medici. The Medici were notorious, risen from merchants to bankers to warriors and lords, and now they were marrying into royalty. Of course they had for some time; Catherine de Medici, my old adversary in France, had been one of the first daughters of that house to step up so far in the world.

I had danced many galliards before our visiting Duke, to demonstrate I was not as old in spirit as I was in years. "I am glad he was impressed," I said. "Although there are men not far away who I hear speak not so well of me."

"I am making lists of the men heading to join the Earl," Cecil said, playing with a strip of rabbit on his plate.

Many who were disaffected had gone to Essex, their new *King*. Friends old and new had flocked to his house like

Southampton, Blount, Tresham and Davies. Recently we had heard that the Governor of Plymouth, Sir Ferdinando Gorges, a cousin of Raleigh's, had joined them. There were now a number of lords short of coin and poor of purse with Essex, along with other gentlemen who had not done well in our society. Either they were second or third sons and had stopped short behind their brothers in the race of life, or they were just less lucky than others, or lazy. It seemed what they wanted more than anything was to become rich, quick, without need for much work. Usually that means through violence. Essex was their ruler. Perhaps these men should have noted that all the opportunities they had lacked Essex had had, and had achieved nothing more than they. But perhaps to men dissatisfied with life, this seemed to indicate that something was against Essex, and that something was most likely Cecil. That meant if Cecil could be removed then there might be opportunities not only for Essex, but for all men, and if I could be charmed or captured into submission, Essex would be the one handing out such favours.

He was the ruler of the rootless, oligarch of outcasts. Men embittered because they had not done well in their lives, and thought I or others with power were the cause rather than their own lack of industry, luck or talent, went to Essex, who after all believed the same as them, and to his new men Essex preached false prophecies of easy glory and fairy-tale happy endings. From all accounts they lapped them up, as well they might. Essex always was a charming teller of stories, and people want to believe in ease and happiness. The tale he was telling them was simple; England was being ruled not by a wise queen but by bad men who took advantage of her failing mind and womanly weakness, and were those men to be removed there would be more power for others, and other men might advise the queen better. In truth, they talked treason pretending it was patriotism. They thought me taken captive by Cecil and others, thought they instead should be my captors. My own freedom and wishes did not figure in their plans whatsoever. I would be but a mask they held in front of their treacherous faces, so they could pretend they were patriots.

Although it was a different situation in some ways, I was reminded very much of the time when I was a young princess, heir to the throne, and there was a plan hatched to force me to marry a crony of Phillip of Spain. That way, if and when I came to the throne after my sister, there would be a Spanish agent controlling me, as I would *have* to obey my husband. This felt the same. By capturing my body these men would control my power, my mind, the fate of my country. What woman can dare to rule on her own, without a man controlling her? That was how Essex had come to think; that I was feeble and making the wrong choices, so he should make them for me. If he tried to capture me, he would be violating all that was me and mine, a symbolic rape of my person.

I swore long before he was born that no man would know me, or control me. I was not about to allow that to happen now. The Earl would find no feeble old woman if it came to a fight. He would discover this old vixen had teeth left to bite, and bite I would, until the last of my rotten teeth crumbled into the soft, bloody flesh of his throat.

"The Earl is still trying to get James of Scotland to support him," said Cecil. "And still he opens his doors to people who resent and fear you, Majesty."

"Like calls to like," I said, whirling a spoon of silver in my pale broth. "He is planning a *coup*? An actual one this time?" I sat back and took up my small ale. The pottage was good, but I had lost my appetite again. When a man who once swore he loves you is planning to destroy you there is little enthusiasm to be found in the belly for food. When such comes we are hungry for other things, safety, and perhaps revenge. I wish I could say I was surprised, but I had been thinking Essex would rise against me eventually. Ever since he had burst into my room I had thought the day would come. That it had did not shock me, but it did sadden me. I would have welcomed being wrong.

"He still says he wants to reach you, Majesty, that we are keeping him away, but with him at your side you would be safe, as would England. He says he alone is loyal to you and to England."

"Bolingbroke kissed the hand of Richard oftentimes enough before he turned on him," I said. "He bowed to his King, swore to be loyal and true, then he locked him in a tower cell and starved the young man to death." I stared into my ale. "A little room he put him in, a little room where Death waited."

"Essex declares he is loyal, all the same," said Robert. "He says to all he wishes only to reason with you."

"To *dictate* to me, you mean," I said. "Essex would have me think as he does, speak as he wishes. He does not want a Queen or master, he wants a doll he can dress up.

"His arrogance is such that he believes me still under his spell," I went on. "That if he could but get close to me he could bend me once more to his will. He does not want to understand that it is I who do not want to see him, not that you are keeping me away from him." I straightened my shoulders. "And the information we had from Mountjoy's household?"

Mountjoy was in Ireland still, and still doing well. The Earl had sent his man Southampton to Ireland to tell Mountjoy he must muster his forces ready to invade England upon the order of the Earl, for England was in danger. Essex still thought himself overall commander of the Irish army, you see, and Mountjoy had spoken for him in the past. But that time was done. Mountjoy had said to Southampton that working to save the Earl if he was a prisoner was one thing, but doing such a thing just to restore the Earl's fortunes, which as he was well aware this was all about, was another.

Southampton, on orders from Essex, had told Mountjoy that the enemies of England, who were Cecil, Raleigh, Cecil's brother-in-law Lord Cobham, as well as Cecil's elder brother, Thomas, who was now Baron Burghley, were working to sell England to Spain, and set the Infanta Isabella on the throne in my place. He asked Mountjoy that if he would not muster a force to support Essex, to write to me and relay this information, for surely I was in the dark about this nefarious plot, and with the help of his loyal captains Essex would free me and arrest Cecil and the others who were trying to bring England down.

Mountjoy had refused to get involved, but we knew what had happened due to Cecil's spies. Essex was far from subtle in any case. He talked so much about this plot at his house that anyone could hear his ideas, festering and lunatic, seeping from the walls. Robert had placed men in his house, but we barely had a need. I think most of London knew what the Earl was telling his men.

"From spies about Mountjoy we know much, and not least of it that Essex lacks support that will be required if even half of these insane stories are true," Robert said.

"Have you reached James yourself?"

Cecil nodded. "I found him, as you said, Majesty, not averse to talking with me no matter that my father was instrumental in his mother's death. He told my men that the Earl has asked him to send an ambassador, the Earl of Mar, to your court, and Mar is to ask that you agree to formally name James as your successor and to reinstate the Earl at the same time. James said he was of course keen to be named successor, but was at a loss to know why this should be so linked to Essex and his fortunes. He said the Earl made many large and grand promises and said that I was working for Spain to succeed to the throne, but offered no evidence. So he found himself suspicious. Yet James was cheered to hear that I, who am still close to you, supported him."

"Tell James to send the Earl of Mar, or at least send word he will," I said. "That will make Essex believe he is in control."

Cecil smiled a little.

"You already did?" I asked and grinned back. "It is good to see your father's wiles are treasures you inherited, Pygmy," I said.

The trouble is that if one is to pull off a *coup* it must, by nature, be a surprise, and Essex was incapable of keeping his mouth shut. His followers were strewing rumours, wild and feral, about Catholic plots throughout London. It was being said already in the streets that if these plots were so, then loyal men had to make sure that the Queen was safe, and government as well. I was already hearing that Essex would approach me once the city and Tower of London had been secured. He would make me summon a Parliament, in which Cecil and his friends would be impeached and Essex would be named Lord Protector. Every one of these rumours I heard said that I should not be harmed, yet they did mean to harm me, for what they intended was to take away my power, my freedom, and my rights as a queen. But Essex no more cared for anything that was mine, that I knew well enough.

Yet Essex should have had a care for Essex.

Chapter Twenty

Whitehall Palace
Twelfth Night 1601

On Twelfth Night I danced for the Duke of Bracciano again, and he admired my jewels and the lightness of my feet. He said he was amazed I could dance with so many diamonds and pearls upon my clothing, and declared that my age was a lie. "You must be one of those women who, contrary to the rest of your sex, go about telling people you are older than you are, Majesty, so to amaze them with the brilliance of your youthful looks!"

I laughed. The Duke was young, charming and scandalous, which made me like him even more. There were rumours he had embarked on an affair with the new Queen of France, Marie, his own cousin, as he escorted her to marry her new husband, Henri IV. After years of fruitless marriage to the last of the Valois, Margot, another Queen of France with a less than virginal reputation, had agreed to be set aside, allowing Henri to marry again to gain an heir. The rumour was Margot now openly kept the lovers she had enjoyed before in secret, and that now they were not married she and Henri got on famously well. She even had made friends with Marie, and there were stories the old wife and the new at times shared a bed, sometimes with Henri in it too. Whilst there are always tales, particularly about the French, I privately thought it all sounded rather charming. People love to pass judgement on others, but I thought if it worked for them, what was the harm?

On Twelfth Night we also had the Lord Chamberlain's Men at court to perform a new play flown from Master William Shakespeare's pen, called, fittingly *Twelfth Night*, and the Duke was deeply enamoured of the slightly ridiculous plot full of women dressing as men, lost ships and twins and true love. Since the Duke of the play, Orsino, was obviously named for my guest Orsini of Bracciano, my guest was further bewitched.

"You are not as morose as this one, my lord," I said, waving a hand at the man playing the Duke as we watched the play. "I wonder if any damsel of the world could have you sitting about, a sadness on your face and in your heart."

"You think me immune to the charms of women, Majesty?" he asked and laughed. "It is the opposite. I am in love with *all* of your sex, and think them higher creatures than men. The problem and the sorrow of my life is that I find too much to marvel at in each and every one, so I am in love with the world of women entire, unable to offer my heart to one alone. Women do not like that, and no wonder. They treasure fidelity since they themselves are so often forced into it. So I am in love and I am alone, and that is my state until all virtues and vices be in one woman, and she shall have me as her slave."

"You think women want men to be pets, prisoners at their feet in chains?"

"Love is captivity," he said, his eyes roaming over the players strutting on the stage. "When it is true, that is, and yet love is a cage we enter willingly, knowing the pain it will cause. The bars are silk and the insides furnished in velvet. The food slipped through the bars is sugar and violet sweetness, but it is a cage, for it holds us to another, binds our hearts to them."

"Love is not a cage," I said. "Marriage is. Love when it is untrue keeps a person as its prisoner, but when true, when a heart may regard another honestly, for flaws and virtues and all that lies in between, and honours that heart, allowing its soul to do as it must in life, upholding its goals, love is not a cage. Marriage, my lord, binds one to another and allows neither to be free, but love is different. It is the wind that drives the storm, knowing the storm must roam and break upon shores unknown and unknowable. It is the sunlight of a winter morning, which allows frost to glimmer and ice to break, taking the water that comes from those fractures on, to run down hill and mountainside. Love is the winds of summer, freeing seeds to fly further than their parent plants could manage, so they might grow in new and undiscovered places. Love, when true, is no cage, my lord. It is a spirit of liberty, the essence of freedom that sees the potential in another being and honours it so greatly that it will help it to achieve all that it is capable of, and support it every inch of its way through life."

The Duke regarded me solemnly for a moment. "I think you have known great love, Majesty," he said.

"Once, for a man," I said. "And although it was not perfect, it was true. But many times I have known love for others, for friends, and the best of those loves were as I have said. They were not emotions that sought to possess and control, cages as you have spoken of. That kind of love is not love, it is something that believes it is love but is not. That kind of love is poison, and it destroys. It is the kind I have seen in many couples, and it does them no good. One person cannot possess another, one may not control another. We cannot change people to become what we want them to be. When we love true, we love the person as they are, and for what they may become, but that potential is not ours to bend or break. It is for us to surrender to, so we might aid that potential to become all that it can be. Love is liberty, pure freedom, when it is true, and when it is not it is the opposite. I know not much of this world, but that I do know."

"Perhaps this is why I have not found it," he mused.

"Perhaps you have not found love for you mistook her face for that of the false love that cages people," I said. "You have not been looking for love, but trying to flee her opposite."

"Is this the secret of your youth, then, that you have known such things as this perfect love?"

"With my country I have had perfect love," I said. "Of all who love me true, England was the one who set me free of the bonds of youth, and while I will not say she set me free from danger, she and I have known my destiny a long time, and she was my destiny as I was hers." I smiled at him. "The secret of my long life, my lord is simple; I will be here as long as England, my great love, has need of me. When the time comes that I am no more needed, she will release me, gently and with care, into the hands of death."

I breathed in, looking at the dark, shuttered windows of the palace. Far beyond, along many streets, was Essex House, where a man was plotting to strip away my crown.

"But useful I still am," I said. "And so I remain, England's Queen and England's destiny, her daughter and her love."

Chapter Twenty-One

Whitehall Palace
February 1601

If Master Shakespeare's play had been performed at court that winter, mine was not the only court displaying that young man's talents. We heard in February that the Globe Theatre had had its players bribed, and they had put on a production of *Richard II* for Essex and his men. A scene banned in the play when performed for my people was added in, depicting the deposition of the King. The message, unsubtle and crude though it was, was clear.

"Bolingbroke," I muttered, looking from my window. "You shall not have my throne, Essex."

I had other matters to deal with besides Essex. The year before, some men, including a merchant who had grievances about the ownership of several former slaves, had come to Cecil and made demands. There had been a dispute over the ownership of slaves who had come to England and subsequently become free. The merchant thought they were still his property and demanded them back, so he could take them to his plantations. He had been unsuccessful, despite many petitions, and now had joined with others to rouse more complaints.

They wanted people of Moorish or African descent to be either in their property, as slaves, or expelled from the realm. The reason they wanted them expelled, as I knew, was so they could then claim ownership of them as slaves. Saying such people had grown in number about England and were infidels and thieves, beggars who did nothing for the country, they wanted them deported. They were gaining support from those who, impoverished by years of bad harvests and high taxes, looked about to find someone to blame, and blamed people who had immigrated to England. These people were stealing their jobs and homes, they said, never thinking that this made no sense since the other claim was that all such people were beggars who did nothing for England. Which was it? What it was, was nonsense. People see trouble in their own lives and look for someone to blame, and the easiest people to spot are the ones who stand out, because their skin is a different shade, or their accent or clothes are different. Such foolishness has gone on since the dawn of time, and some never seem to learn. If anyone was to blame for high taxes, surely it was me. Would they demand I be deported, or simply join with Essex, and try to depose me?

"What nonsense is this," I said.

"I agree, Majesty," Cecil replied. In his own house he had a most valuable man who worked for him, Fortunatus, who was a Blackamoor and had a grand talent for the art of spyery. Cecil leaned on him, and considered him as much a friend as servant. Much we had found out over the past years had come through his contacts. I knew of many other children of England who once came from other lands, there were large groups in cities like London and Plymouth, and I knew not a one who was not employed. It was legal for men to keep slaves outside of England, but not when in England. All former slaves who had come to my kingdom were free, and worked as servants, merchants and traders. In my household I had had a fool, Thomasina, who sadly had died some years before, as well as other Moors, like Paul, my page. But as some men insisted all Jews should be flung from my kingdom, some also thought all who were not white of skin should be too.

"They want a proclamation to be put out," Cecil said, "saying that all Blackamoors carried into this realm after our troubles first started with Spain should be thrown out."

I shook my head. With all the troubles I had with Essex I hardly needed more men against me, yet this demand was ridiculous, and illegal. People living in England were English, no matter the colour of their skin. In England they had become free people, and it was not legal to treat them differently to others on the basis of their skin or the country they hailed from. I had briefly engaged with the slave trade for money, and had swiftly left, for guilt. I could do little about slavery outside of England, even my power had limits and the slave trade was used by many lords and merchants, too many for me to go against, but I would not allow former slaves now free, and now my children, to be abused.

"Draft something," I said. "To appease them for the moment, for I do not need any more men turning to Essex, but it will not be put out into the world, Robert."

It was drafted, but never was it proclaimed or promulgated. There was no expulsion, and if I had my way for the rest of my reign at least, there never would be. That draft was buried in Cecil's papers, and never saw light of day.

*

In the wake of this irritation of one group of men trying to dictate what would be in my kingdom, I turned back to another.

Sir Ferdinando Gorges suddenly became inspired with fright, I believe it was the performance of *Richard II* which alerted him to the truth of the situation he was now a part of. He came to Raleigh and told his cousin what was going on in Essex House. Raleigh informed the Council, but we already knew and Cecil was already prepared.

"I have set a rumour, Majesty, about London that Essex is about to be sent to the Tower," he told me.

I nodded. "And is that rumour now all over London and has reached Essex House?"

"It has, Majesty, and it is said it has frightened the Earl, so I think that he will move, and move before he is ready."

"Good," I said. "Let the rabbit flee and run straight into our snare."

The day of the night that play was performed, Essex had been ordered to appear before the Council. He had refused, as we thought he might. He believed that this command to appear before my men was the first stage in his arrest and he would be taken to the Tower, for Cecil's rumour was all over London by that time. Sending men to Essex and telling him to appear before the Council was a way to make things move. It was a test. We knew the end of his ramblings about power and control was coming, but wanted to test his resolution. It was also his last chance.

That night, after refusing to appear at court, he and his men watched the play where a king, the last of his line, was deposed by a man who carried royal blood, but was no more than a noble. That was the 7th of February, and that night his friends warned him to act, delay no further. I did hear later that he briefly considered fleeing the kingdom, but in the end his ambitions of controlling all of England and me overcame his fears that this was a trap. Greed reigned victorious over sense. Essex should have listened to his instincts. Instincts we so often ignore, yet they are so much wiser than we ever will be.

The royal messenger, sent to tell Essex that he was to come to the Council the next morning, was sent back to court with a message that the Earl could not attend. 300 of his followers assembled before him, and Essex, no doubt feeling again like a commander and perhaps as a king, told them that he had discovered that Cecil and Raleigh were planning his assassination, and therefore their rebellion would begin the next day.

I was not to be harmed, he said. Did he not know that through the body is only one way to hurt someone? He meant to strike at my soul, my heart. He meant to harm me.

But we had not been idle either. Levies had been summoned from nearby shires, and London preachers had been instructed to tell citizens to remain indoors when the morrow came. The guard was doubled at Whitehall, although the palace was not the easiest place to defend, being long and rambling. We knew that some of Essex's people were watching the palace, and we knew they must have warned Essex that there were extra guards, but it seemed to deter him not at all.

That night my Privy Council came to me, to discuss the rebellion we knew Essex would begin on the morrow. "Raleigh has the extra guards in place?" I asked, "and there will be defences in the city?"

"A row of carriages will block the way from Charing Cross," said Cecil, "and your Captain of the Guards assures me Whitehall is secure."

I nodded. I never had forgiven Raleigh for marrying Bess Throckmorton, who was as close as a ward and daughter as ever I had, but his return to his old post as Captain of the Guard was welcome. And he despised Essex. His men would not let anyone through to capture me. Whitehall, however, was vulnerable. It was sprawling, and there were many ways in and out. I had refused to move, however, thinking that it might alert Essex and he would stand down his plans, which I did not want for I wanted him caught now, seen by the world as guilty, and I certainly did not want him retreating this *coup* only to try again, perhaps better prepared. But I also did not move because I did not believe he had something he thought he had. Essex was popular in London, in England, but although this was true I thought he overestimated what the people would do for him. Grumble and groan about my treatment of him they might, but I did not think he had enough support to rouse them to rebellion. It was a gamble, but I was prepared to gamble on the love of my people, even if this was the last time.

"The mood of the people?" I asked.

"Baffled, mainly, Majesty," said Raleigh. "I sent men out to find what they thought and everywhere people said Essex should be reinstated, but they thought tales of him plotting against you untrue. Yet now he speaks wild and they hear of it, and know not what to think. There is no general mood of evil against either of you."

"They will not support him," I said.

"You are sure of this, Majesty?" Cecil asked nervously. "We are gambling a great deal on the loyalty of your people. If they rise with Essex, if only a small number of them rise even, we may be in trouble. It might be wiser to move you to St James's Palace, for it is easier to defend than Whitehall."

"I will go nowhere," I said resolutely. "And my people will not follow him. This is the moment they will see the truth that long I have been sad to see, and see Essex for what he is, a traitor and a villain. I am a daughter of England and of kings, mother of my kingdom and people, and I will be damned into the darkest pit of Hell if I will run before a wanton scoundrel like Essex."

I drew myself up. "I will stand, here, at my palace and I will not flee into the night. Essex is to learn a lesson tomorrow, by God, and one he should learn; Elizabeth of England was chosen by God, and God will smile on me tomorrow."

On the 8th, a Sunday, Essex began his *coup*. His friends and supporters, along with 200 soldiers, gathered in the courtyard of Essex House, and there was so much commotion that we could hear it quite easily from Whitehall. I sent Lord Keeper Egerton, the Lord Chief Justice Sir John Cobham, the Earl of Worcester, and Sir William Knollys to insist that Essex come and explain himself to the Council. Essex himself invited them into his library but behind them his friends and supporters crowded crying, "Kill them, kill them!" which scared my men quite considerably, as you may imagine. My four councillors were locked up in Essex's library, and Essex departed Essex House, his unruly, foolish rebels at his back.

The Earl was in normal clothing rather than armour, something intended to signify peaceful intentions and show that this was not truly a rebel rousing. Carrying his sword he marched through Temple Bar and into Fleet Street crying out, "For the Queen! For the Queen! The crown of England is sold to the Spaniard! A plot is laid for my life!"

But my people did little more than stare.

They did not join him in his mad and feckless plan, but did as they had been told by the London preachers, and remained indoors. Essex tried to force his way through Ludgate which had been locked against his men, and he failed. By the time he reached St Paul's Cathedral and his numbers had swelled no more, he was finally faced with the fact that London was not rising in his favour, or in his name. He began to panic.

As he turned into Cheapside it was said his face was almost molten with sweat and suffused with fear. When he reached the house of the Sheriff of London, Thomas Smith, who had offered support to Essex in the past, Essex was sweating so greatly that he had to ask for a clean shirt for his was sodden. Already his so-called loyal followers were fleeing from him, covering their faces with their clothes, trying to disguise their features. Thomas Smith, now regretting he had ever spoken to the Earl, ran out of his own back door and summoned the mayor, who was busy at that time ordering an injunction I had put out, which was to call all my citizens to arms in my name.

As Essex had marched fruitlessly through London, heralds had ridden abroad proclaiming him a traitor, and government troops had erected our planned barricade of coaches across the road from Charing Cross to Whitehall. Many of my people had rushed to the palace, some just to see what was going on and some to help defend their Queen. Ludgate had been closed by my forces and every one of London's seven gates had been locked.

There had been a skirmish in Ludgate, and one of Essex's men died. They rode back, calling for men to rise up and join them, free me from the clutches of my Councillors. People stared at the Earl, their darling, with confused and worried eyes. The people of England might have loved him, but they all could see he was lunatic. No one rose, no one followed.

That did not stop false rumour. At one point, as I sat down to a meal, for I had refused to interrupt the normal progress of the day for an ingrate like Essex, I was handed a note. It said the city had gone over to the Earl. I handed the note back and sent the messenger back to Cecil.

"Tell him I refuse to believe it, and think it false," I said, keeping my voice strong and sure. I believe I had paled, but under my white cosmetics the man was unlikely to see further pallor. "God put me on this throne and God will preserve me, and my people are loyal to the last."

It was a false report, as we found without much effort. I was glad of my boldness, for it looked now as if I was secure in my certainties and my kingdom. I was not, not entirely. I worried some might follow Essex, but I did not believe most would. If I could brazen it out, sound confident always, then he would win nothing from this campaign whether he won or lost. But I would. My people would know I was still brave in the face of trouble and rebellion, undaunted in the belief God was on my side. If I was to come out of this better than I had gone in, the situation entire had to be used for me. Essex might do me some good, in doing himself so much mischief.

By two of the afternoon Essex realised his revolution and attempt to gain power over England and me had failed. Abandoning those few who still remained with him, he fled to Queenhithe where he took a barge back to his house. He found that some of his supporters had released the four hostages from my Council and they had all returned to Whitehall together. Essex found himself abandoned by friends, and without any kind of leverage over me or my government. At Essex House, his last refuge, the Earl locked himself in, and the chimneys smoked busily all afternoon as he burnt important documents, one of them being the black pouch about his neck in which the message from James of Scots had been kept. I never would find out what my godson had written to Essex. In many ways I did not want to know. Before long my soldiers under the command of Lord Admiral Nottingham surrounded his house and trained cannon on it. They demanded Essex give himself up.

Essex, dramatic to the last, climbed onto the roof brandishing his sword. "I would sooner fly to heaven!" he cried.

From below Nottingham called out, "Very well then, I will blow the house up, my lord."

Essex came out.

It was just after ten of the evening when Essex surrendered his sword. He asked that his chaplain remain with him. By that night, eighty-five rebels had been arrested and taken to gaol. Their rebellion had lasted twelve hours.

Poor Essex. Poor sad little fool. His rebellion was as successful as all other endeavours he undertook. For one who feared failure so, he kept company with it often enough. He finally understood the depths of his fantasy as it was stripped away, one absent Londoner at a time, as no one rose to follow him.

"Take the shameless ingrate to prison, I will hear no more of him this day," I said.

I went to my chamber. People said I was sad, but marvelled at how brave I had been. They said I had believed in my people so utterly that I was granted courage, but in truth that is not courage. Courage is fighting or standing before an enemy when you know there is a possibility you might lose the battle. I barely needed courage that day. I was fearless, something I more often despised than honoured, but I was fearless because I knew I had nothing to fear.

We had been too well informed to be caught off-guard. I admit even I was surprised at how few had followed Essex when he called to them, but I had not thought, truly, he would gain a rebel force in London to rise against me. The people could see he was unhinged, and whilst I was sure many still loved him, I believe he also scared many of them.

The wheel had turned. I had been shamed and vulnerable before the Earl, but now it was opposite. He was cast down before me, and I hoped he felt as I had that day in my chamber, for no other reason than then he might understand the moment he had failed was not riding through the streets shrieking out his wild claims, but long before that, when he made an old woman feel every weakness she possessed, when he abused a friend to make her feel shamed, vulnerable and helpless, when he put his ambition above the wellbeing of another person, stripping all they had from them, hoping to make them cower before him.

There are many crimes that deserve punishment, and the reduction of the soul of another person is one. "You should have known, Essex," I said. "If ever it came down to a choice between your life and mine, I would always choose my life over yours."

There were plenty of people I would have given my life for. Essex was not one of them. Once he might have been, but no more. There comes a point in any relationship where we can give no more. That point had come.

"My sister kept me captive, held me first in the Tower and then Woodstock," I said to my reflection. "Then I swore I would never again be a prisoner, and I have not been, other than to the constrictions that my position, religion, and power put upon me. I was not a creature made to live behind bars, and whether those bars be of iron, or if they be made by the will of men who seek to subdue me, to make themselves great by standing upon my body, I will always resist those bars. Essex could not take me, so he attempted to destroy me."

Staring into the night, I shook my head.

Enough I had given, enough I had hoped, enough had been done to save the young man.

Enough.

Chapter Twenty-Two

Whitehall Palace
Winter 1601

"Take him to prison, try him and hang him at Tyburn," I said. "I have had enough of men trying to force me to do their will because they have not the power to persuade."

A Captain Lea, one of Essex's followers and the messenger he had used to communicate with Tyrone in Ireland, had been found in my kitchens. He had been stopped because he was pale, sweating profusely and had asked if I was at supper yet. When detained by Raleigh and his guards, Lea was found to have a knife on his person, and admitted he was on his way to my chamber where he intended to force me at knifepoint to release Essex.

I knew Lea for another reason. Some years ago he had given me one of the most unwelcome gifts I ever received when he presented me with the severed head of an Irish rebel, thinking I would be pleased by the bloody mass of flesh and bone. I knew not why. I never had called for any body part of any man who died at my orders to be brought before me. My father's first wife had thought to send the body of King James of Scotland, slain on Flodden Field, to her husband whilst he fought in France, but even then English lords had thought it a grisly matter and had sent his blood-stained shirt instead. Why any man would think I would desire to see a rotten, parboiled head, I knew not.

Yet soon I would have another head, if I wanted it. Essex was to be arraigned on the 19th of February. The appearance of a man like Lea in my palace, on his way to exert violence over me following the example of his master, made me only more resolved to act against Essex. It had been proved now. He wanted my power, and would take it if he could.

But my people still thought I would spare him. They thought I would, when I had been hurt and threatened, when I had been let down, assaulted and my love abused, forgive him. I might forgive him, in time, but that did not mean he would not answer for his crimes. I might forgive him when we met again in Heaven, but in this life he was far too much a threat to my life.

For all actions there are debts to be paid. Essex was in my debt, and I wanted our account settled. There was but one payment to make.

Enough times I had forgiven, and enough times he had shown me that such was useless. His rebellion, ineffective and desperate though it had been, remained a rebellion. Had he had more support, and less arrogance, it might well have worked. Fortunately my people had seen in that last moment, that last hour as they were called on to rise and support the lord they loved, that what he was doing was wild and reckless, and fortunately they had enough affection left for me, and enough sense to see a desperate man when he was before them, so they did not rise and so his rebellion fell.

But it might not have. Whitehall was vulnerable, almost impossible to secure, so had Essex had more wit and launched a surprise attack, or had he not talked so long and deep about his plans with other men, then we might have been caught by surprise. Had he taken possession of me, he might well have been able to convince the people of London and then of England after that he was doing so for my own good. Essex had been in their love, and he was a charming man. He might have convinced them, his rebellion might have succeeded. So I could not forgive him, and I had no wish to.

And he showed me, the moment he walked into the room in which his trial was to be held, no good would come of forgiving him. He and Southampton were together arraigned before a jury of their peers in Westminster Hall. They were charged with conspiring between themselves and with others to depose me, procure my death and destruction, and to subvert the government of my country. It was put to the people that they had issued into London with a number of unarmed men intending to convince citizens of London to join with them and rebel against me.

Both men pleaded not guilty.

Shameless, Essex faced his accusers. He spoke in arrogance and boldness, tried to excuse all he had done by blaming other men. Had he understood the gravity of the situation he should have known that the only sensible option was to admit guilt and throw himself on my mercy, but he did not. And for a simple, stupid reason.

"He does not believe he will die," I said.

He did not, indeed. People did not believe it either. No matter all that had occurred they said I would pardon him. My reputation for mercy was ahead of me, bounding around and telling tales of my great love for Essex, but it was not so this time. I had forgiven many people, it was true, and many had plotted against me. Many times I had shown mercy, but if anyone speaking rumours that I would forgive Essex had paid attention they would have noted something important; I forgave, until I was offered proof positive of treason. I never had hesitated to remove people I knew to be a threat. Only when I had not been sure had I paused and shown mercy. But not for traitors true.

Essex had risen against me. He and I could not both live.

Essex faced his accusers boldly, and some remarked that perhaps he was aware he was going to die and therefore he was attempting to leave a good opinion in the minds of the people now they were close to parting. But I do not believe he thought he would die, I believe he thought he would live and I would forgive him. Perhaps he convinced himself I loved him too much to take his life, for I had not the last time, after

Ireland. Perhaps he truly thought he had been trying to free me from evil men, had swallowed his own lies. I know not, but Essex thought he would live. That seemed plain enough.

"Pretty lies," I whispered, thinking of my sister. "We make up pretty lies and try to make them true. Perhaps this is life."

*

During the trial there was a confrontation between Essex and Robert Cecil which had been years in the coming. Essex stood and in defending himself accused Robert Cecil of trying to sell England to Spain. Cecil, who had been in a hidden corner, came before the jury and fell on his knees in front of the presiding judge. He challenged Essex to name and bring forth the sources for so foul an accusation. Essex attempted to pass this responsibility to the Earl of Southampton but Robert Cecil continued to press for details.

Eventually it emerged from the mouth of Essex himself that the idea that England was to be sold to the Spaniards was based on one casual, passing remark that Cecil had made two years before to William Knollys. Knollys and Cecil had been wandering the gardens at court during the early hours of one morning, and they discussed the book by Robert Parsons on the next successor to the crown of England. Cecil had observed aloud that it was odd that the man who had written this paper, who was at that time anonymous, had given an equal right in law to the Infanta Isabella as he had to any other claimant to the crown. This light and ridiculous statement had been taken by Essex to mean that in some way Cecil supported the Infanta Isabella for the crown. In actual fact, as Cecil pointed out, he had been saying the opposite, and that he thought it a strange thing that Isabella was given as much right as any other claimant to the throne.

"Well done, Robert Cecil," I said when I heard.

Robert had for many years backed down and away when Essex came rushing in. He had always known he was not a physical match for Essex, being a hunchback and much shorter than the Earl, who was an athletic demi-god to look upon. In mind Cecil was more than a match for Essex, but often when before Essex and when accusing him, his courage and will to accuse the Earl had stumbled, as did his tongue. In this last moment, this last hour, Robert Cecil vindicated his honour and at the same time made his old rival appear foolish, misguided, and wicked, for it was certain Essex had deliberately misconstrued what Cecil had said in that one conversation to make him appear an enemy of England. Since I was sure that Essex had done much the same with my beloved doctor Lopez, an act of jealousy which had directly led to the most bloody and painful death for a man who had worked for me and my body, and maintained both for many years, I was glad Cecil had found justice in this matter.

Two days after his trial, Essex decided to write a letter influenced by the interference of his favourite chaplain, who had been attempting to impress upon him the dangerousness of his situation. In a very long, sorry statement Essex drafted out all details of his and his companions' activities over the past eighteen months. He named everyone from Lord Mountjoy to Southampton, to Blount, all his friends, and incriminated them all. Every one of them now had been delivered into our hands and we could see every treason that we had known, and all we had not, because of Essex. Perhaps the fool thought it would save him.

Finally the self-same chaplain who persuaded him to write this letter which condemned all his friends, managed to convince Essex that he was indeed to die for his crimes. He had been found guilty. There had been no letter from me, no indication that I was to give mercy, no indication that he was to live. Lady Essex, pitiable Frances, had written to Cecil and to me asking that her husband's life be spared and saying that if he died, *"I shall never wish to breathe one hour after."* Both of us were sorrowed to see Frances brought so low, but her dramatic plea would not stop me. There was no way for me to spare Essex's life without endangering the security of the realm, and there was no way to save his life without risking my own. What I did grant him was private execution.

On the 23rd of February, after delaying to grant Essex time to make his last confession, Essex's death warrant was delivered to the Lieutenant of the Tower. I sent a message after it, ordering that the execution was to be postponed. On Shrove Tuesday, the 24th of February, I went to the customary feast at court and watched a performance of one of Master Shakespeare's plays. That night I sent a command to the Lieutenant of the Tower to proceed with Essex's execution on the next morning, and informing him that two executioners were to be summoned to dispatch the prisoner. If one fainted, *"... the other may perform it to him, on whose soul God have mercy."*

The fact I sent one executioner and a spare to carry out the deed should have told everyone the truth. Essex would die.

I retired to my apartments and remained there throughout the following day. It was not truly that I was sorrowful. What I felt was disillusionment in people, and the things they said, words that spewed from mouths that meant nothing. I wanted to be alone. I had been forced, in this late part of my life, to take life again. I never relished the taking of life as some did, always it strained on my soul, but I had no choice as far as I could see with this man. But I resented that I had been put in this situation, and so close to the end of my life. I was no fool, I knew I was older than most ever cared to live, so my years remaining were surely spare. In this late season, so close to God and the time I would have to answer for all I had done, I had been forced to take life again.

I could hope that after other lives I had taken, I had done some good, perhaps enough, for God to understand I wanted to be forgiven, redeemed. But now, with Essex, would I have time to make reparation for my sins? Would I have time to do penance for a life taken, with the time I had left in life?

On the night of the 24th he was told to prepare for death, and prepare Essex did, by apologising to his guards for having no means of rewarding them, "for I have nothing left," he said, "but that which I must pay to the Queen tomorrow in the morning."

There was a story told after, which flew about everywhere with people thinking it truth, that once I had given Essex a ring, told him if ever he was in trouble to send that ring to me, and I would save him. People said Essex dropped that ring from a window, into the hands of a boy who gave the ring to one of my women, and she, knowing how dangerous Essex was and how much I loved him, kept the ring and did not send it to me. So Essex went to the block thinking I had abandoned him, and I sent him there thinking his pride was too great to permit him to send me the ring. People said I was told this on the day that woman of my bedchamber died, a deathbed confession, and I said to her that God might forgive her but I could not.

A pretty tale, excusing me *and* the Earl of wrong, which was perhaps the object of its origins. People wanted to believe in our grand love, for the truth was uglier, not such a good tale. But there never was a ring given that I said would save him, and he never sent the fabled ring and my lady never kept it. People want to believe in such rubbish, at times, thinking it nicer than the real tale. The truth was, I never made promises I could not keep, so I never would have given a man, any man, such a ring, to save him from any fate no matter what he had done. I was not such a fool.

In the early hours on the 25th of February a small company of lords, knights, and aldermen arrived at the Tower of London. Although it was a private execution, there were always some witnesses to death. They took their seats around the scaffold, built in the courtyard of the Tower in front of the Chapel of St Peter ad Vincula, where the bones of my mother lay sleeping. Raleigh was there, required as Captain of the Gentleman Pensioners to attend the execution. Many people disapproved of this, for it was well known he had been Essex's enemy during life, and people thought he should not be there to gloat over Essex's death. Raleigh, sensing general disapproval even from those who did not like Essex, withdrew to the armoury in the White Tower to watch the proceedings from a window. He would later tell me he had been moved to tears. It might well be true. We can weep even for those who have done us wrong.

Flanked by three clergymen Essex came to the scaffold just before eight o'clock of the morning. He was in a black velvet gown, breeches of black satin, and a black felt hat. I am sure he looked handsome. He always had looked well in dark colours. He walked up the steps, took off his hat and bowed to those there to watch him die. All those who were to die were allowed to make one last speech before they departed, and in Essex's he acknowledged with thankfulness to God that he was, "justly spewed out of the realm."

"My sins are more in number than the hairs on my head," Essex told the crowd. "I have bestowed my youth in wantonness, lust and uncleanness; I have been puffed up with pride, vanity and love of this wicked world's pleasures. Through which, I humbly beseech my Saviour Christ to be a mediator to the eternal Majesty for my pardon, especially for this my last sin, this great, this bloody, this crying, this infectious sin, whereby so many for love of me have been drawn to offend God, to offend their sovereign, to offend the world. I beseech God to forgive it to us, and to forgive it me, most wretched of all."

Essex begged God to preserve me, "the Queen, whose death I protest I never meant, nor violence to her person." He asked that those present to see him die join their souls with him to pray. His speech ended with Essex asking God to forgive his enemies.

He took off his gown and ruff, knelt by the block. One of the clergymen standing with him pleaded with him not to become overwhelmed by fear of death, to which Essex replied that several times in battle he had felt a weakness of the flesh, and had asked God to assist and strengthen him. Turning his eyes upwards towards the sky, Essex prayed for the realm, and recited the Lord's Prayer. The executioner knelt and begged forgiveness for what he was about to do. Essex gave it willingly and repeated the creed after a clergyman.

Rising, Essex removed his doublet revealing a long-sleeved scarlet waistcoat, scarlet being the colour of Catholic martyrs, and the colour of petticoat my mother had worn to her own execution. I wondered if that was one last message from the Earl, intended to give me guilt for the rest of my life. I would not have put it past him.

Essex knelt to the low block and laid himself over it, putting his head on the wood. He told the man waiting with the axe that he would be ready when his arms were stretched out. Many of the crowd were weeping. He twisted his head sideways on the block and said, "Lord, into Thy hands I commend my spirit."

A clergyman told him to recite the 51st Psalm but after two verses perhaps it was too much to wait any further. Essex cried, "Executioner, strike home!" and flung out his arms. It took three blows to sever his head. They told me he died by the first strike, because after the first his body did not move. I know not if this was true. The executioner lifted that head by its long, dark red hair, and cried out, "God save the Queen!"

He was thirty-five years old.

He died well, a brave soldier at the end. Four weeks later his captains followed him, but as for the other men who had followed Essex, I showed mercy. Forty-nine were imprisoned or fined, but Lady Rich and thirty others were to go free. Frances Walsingham, my Lady Essex, swore she would die yet I believed she had her father's fortitude and would live. One of those who died was Charles Blount, which made Lettice Knollys, my cousin, once more a widow. People said I executed Blount out of spite, in return for Lettice stealing

Robin away from me, but I would have kept Blount happily had he not joined with Essex. The man had just been starting to show promise in command in Ireland when he joined the ridiculous rebellion.

Anthony Bacon, broken and sorrowed by the loss of his friend Essex, died three months after the rebellion. His brother Francis was rewarded by me for his services to the Crown with a large grant of money.

"Such waste caused by one wasteful life," I muttered as I stood at my window on the day Essex died. I put my hand to the cold window, ice melting against my palm, burning like fire. "Purge me with hyssop, and I shall be clean: wash me and I shall be whiter than snow. Make me to hear joy and gladness; that the bones which thou hast broken may rejoice."

I sighed. "That the bones thou hast broken may rejoice," I said again. "Make me to hear joy and gladness."

My people mourned him, of course. I mourned although I knew this for the death of a foolish man, but they mourned the dream Essex might have become. "Sweet England's pride is gone," people sang, but sometimes we are better without pride. Sometimes the loss of it stops us falling. The pride of Essex was wrapped about his feet as weights, and into the waters of fate he sank. But if the people of England mourned Essex, kings of the world celebrated me.

"She *only* is a King!" the King of France, Henri, said of me.

"I alone am King," I said to my window that night. "The usurper is dead, long live the heir."

For this was not about my reign so much as it was about the future, who would lead my people. Essex had been a man of tradition and stories, and such men are dangerous. Essex had been a man who had sought to overthrow his queen, and who had thought his will was more important than mine. He had been wrong and he had paid for it with blood, with life. Essex was a dangerous boy, and I could be his mother no more. He was not the man to lead this country into the future of its destiny. He was not the son of mine I would choose to care for my people.

I had no regrets, other than thinking the boy could have changed had he wanted to. He would have put me in a cage, and I had escaped enough of those.

Immediately in the aftermath of Essex's death I not only felt no regret, but no anger either. This would change as time went on, my emotions fluctuated as emotions often do, so at times I felt angry at him, at times bitter, at times wistful wishing all he had said had been true. But immediately after Essex died I did not regret, I was not angry, I felt barely anything. This was an old tradition, an old tale. He had been a pretender to the throne, we had fought for it, and he had lost. He had paid the price for his treachery, and I was still alive, still upon my throne, still in possession of my personal power, liberty, and my life. The pretender had fallen, the prince prevailed.

"It is done," I said to my clasped hands whilst at prayer one morning. "And, Lord in Heaven, if You hear me, let this be the last blood on my hands before my own end comes. I want no more."

Something in me whispered that no more blood on my hands would mean I was Queen no more. Part of the duties of the Crown are to rid the country of those who would strike down the one on the throne, disturb the natural order. *The place of a king is to kill*, whispered something in my mind.

"Then take me from life before I must kill again," I said. "Too much blood there is on my hands, too much I have asked sacred oil to wash from my soul. I have killed where I had to, stayed my hand when I could, yet still my soul and heart are unclean. Still I have been pushed to harm and hurt, to do wrong."

I looked up at the altar, at a shining silver cross, more papist than my men would like, glimmering with the light from the window. "The last life will be mine," I said. "And there will be the end."

Chapter Twenty-Three

Richmond Palace
Spring 1601

In the wake of death there is quiet, it always is the way. People do not talk loud or with brittle voice, devoid of care, laugh. There is a hush, and in that hush of death people consider that they too are mortal. In that silence we confront the truth that one day we all will end, our stories done, the tellers of the story and their audience bored with our tale, wishing for an end. Yes, it is the way. One day all, great or not, good or not, become memory and then lost to memory. One day all our worlds come to an end.

For a time people speak our names, remember our lives, because they knew us. Then because they heard of us once they speak our names, tell of our deeds, and if we were titled or rich, perhaps people are taught of us in lessons. If we are fortunate, we few famed for something, then tutors may teach our lives as they truly were to barely listening pupils, boys and girls nodding half-slumberous with boredom and wishing to be elsewhere, outside, in the air and under the sun. If we are not fortunate then lies will be told of us. But who can say? Lies may be kinder to our memory than truth.

Perhaps the lies will be sweeter than the reality of what we did, or perhaps history will be kind. It often is not, but sometimes it shows mercy. Sometimes those who speak of the dead, of dead they knew not, try to be balanced and fair, although often that does not make as good a story as wilder tales, stories of the worst and best times of our lives. Should we be judged only on the best and worst times? Should not all moments we tried and aspired for goodness in our everydays be counted? But often these times die with us and those who knew us, for how can history mark every single moment of a life, and without marking every single moment how can people of history be known, judged, and understood? We cannot, and so into the past the dead are set, half-figures, shadows of what they once were. Into that mist of memory we all shall pass, as those who knew us honestly and true pass too from life, and the great and small acts of our lives fade, the light and shadow which we cast upon this glorious world dissipating too.

Perhaps those who speak our names will remember we too were people, bound to fail more often than to succeed, and as caught up in the blindness of emotion as they are. If we are unfortunate people will expect us to have been perfect, and we will have failed them.

Eventually we are but names writ in rock that wandering people passing a tomb or burial place see etched in stone and read out. Mayhap some remember some things of our life, or laugh at what the most foolish thing was about us that they heard. I wonder how many dead cringe in cold tombs, hearing all they ever did reduced down to one foolish mistake, one heated moment.

In death there is no dignity. We try to offer it to those we love, concealing corpses in bold, grand coffins and carrying them in honour to their final place of rest and decay, but all we do is conceal the rotting flesh and bone of our loved dead ones. All we do is mask the scent of the end of life with rosemary and bay. We all rot, all go back to feed the earth, and from our fetid corpses flowers will spring, as people still alive carry on without us remembering only one or two things of our lives, and only then if we are lucky. How many millions who were good and sweet and were loved true have faded in memory and now never are thought of, their names never spoken? How many ghosts wail in the darkness, wishing someone would speak of them?

Then we become history, then stories, then myths. Only a fragment of the person who lived remains then, lost wandering in some tale meant to teach the young to do or not do something. Only a little shard of the character of the one who lived, of their heart and soul is retained in a story, for how can a story take on and show others the universe inside the mind of another person? How can a story possibly explain the wondrous expanse inside the mind of another soul? Death is the only true winner of life, for He cannot die.

This is why we fall quiet when death comes. We sorrow for the loss of the universe in the mind of another, as we know the wonders of our own minds will too one day be no more.

I spent time with my ladies after Essex met his end. We read and walked, and I reminded myself of what friendship looks like, what love looks like, when it is true. These women had served me for years and they were friends. I knew they cared for me, an affection genuine and honest, and that made me treasure them all the more since I had just spilt the blood of one who played me false. These women, my friends and protectors, would not seek to destroy me as he had. They would uphold me, shield my name and reputation, care for me when I was low. Perhaps false people are a lesson sent by God, to make us treasure truth and honest love all the more. Perhaps this is so, but the lesson felt dark and bitter to me. I did not regret that I had killed Essex, but I regretted having been put in a situation where I could do nothing else. At times I remembered all he had done, all he had not, and knew this end was one he crafted for himself. At other times I blamed myself, for I was old and wise and should have been able to better guide such a promising lad. In age I had killed youth, and at times I felt that had taken a toll I never would repay in my soul.

At times I felt I had become my father, for he had killed everyone who ever loved him and then wondered why he felt so alone in life. Was his solitary and untrusting soul so different to mine? He had sought love and destroyed it many times. Had I not done the same? I had worked Cecil and Walsingham to death, perhaps Parry too. Kat and Blanche had given their lives in my service, worn to the nub by their duties to me. Robin I had promised to God as a sacrifice,

Hatton never married, for he loved me. And Essex had died by my pen, like my cousin of Scots. A brief line of ink, a signature scrawled and a life was spent, gone. One strike of a quill and the precious world inside another was fallen, their empire of mind destroyed. My father loved and then destroyed that love, time and time again. Was I not the same? I had thought I was so different but was I too not going about, breaking hearts and minds and souls upon my wheel, upon my sword of love?

In better moments I did not blame myself for all and everything that ever had happened. In more rational times I did not believe I had become infused with some phantom fragment of my father. But I admit I went back and forth in the days and weeks after I sent Essex to die. Most times I knew I had done right, for he had wished me nothing but wrong. At other times, I wondered.

It would be easier if we could see into the hearts and souls of men. We want to love the beautiful, so beauty blinds us. We want to see something perfect on the outside and believe it is so on the inside too. But fair face often masks deep and worrying flaws, sometimes set in there by the love the beautiful see in the eyes of others when they watch them. If they who are beautiful realise they can use that love, use that hope that they are as perfect as they look, they become creatures most dangerous.

Oh, this fearsome world of strangers into which we are born! Never to know friend or foe until they strip away their mask, never to know if love is real or an illusion. Never to know friendship until it is tested.

It would be easier if all that was evil was ugly. It felt right that a rotten soul should decay the face, waste the eyes and fade the hair. Only in tales of fairies is it so. We wish life to be simple, the heroes in shining armour and the evil with horns sticking out bold and prominent from their heads, yet rare is the demon who looks demonic, or the angel who wears wings we might stroke a curious finger along, feeling the softness of heavenly feathers. Proof of what lies in a soul must be in our acts, in what we do. Even intentions are not enough, and our thoughts no one is master of, for all of us think wicked things. I never did agree with Christ on one thing; that to think sinful thoughts is as bad as doing them. Whilst it is true that some thoughts may lead us into attitudes of sin which lead to actions of sin, to think is not the same as to do. To think "I would he was dead! I would do it myself!" about an annoying neighbour roaring drunkenly in the night, stealing sleep from you and your family is one thing. To actually head out into the night and stab him through the temple is another.

So I always believed in actions to show soul, not intentions for they may be lied about, and not thoughts for they are where our wild, ancient and feral natures have a little liberty from the cultured people we pretend to be. The actions of Essex had been against me. By the words that came from his mouth you would suppose him my friend, my love even, but look at all he had done and the truth was plain to see. He had not been my friend.

I kept myself busy. My projects were many, and many were for Scotland. James wanted me to formally recognise him as heir, but I would not. If Essex had taught me anything it was that I still could be deposed, even at this late hour of life. I would not recognise James, but I worked in secret for his success. "When I am gone, tell him I asked you to do this," I said to Cecil as we talked of the "secret" growing friendship between him and James. "I would like the King of Scots to know he was tricked. It would tickle my ghost."

Cecil chuckled. Between him and James, England and Scotland, relations were good, whilst between me and James they were tense. That was well. I did not want my godson stirring trouble for me as Essex had, and indeed, given the Earl's hasty incineration of the note James had sent, I knew not if James had made promises that might have urged Essex on. In a way I did not want to know if James had played a part. I would rather think he had not, and if my godson was kept reassured on one side by Cecil, and on the other unnerved by me, we would keep James balanced, not daring to go too far one way or the other.

"Peace until my end," I said to Cecil. "That is what I want."

Yes, I thought. *Peace until the end of my life would be desirable*. Had I had my way in life in general, peace would have been my destiny for all time, for I never was one who desired war, all the glory some suppose comes from bloodshed. Yet the destiny of a Queen is rarely one of peace, for even if war comes not for other reasons a woman always will find herself surrounded by men, many of whom are addicted to conflict, thirsting to take her throne and debase her power. They do it to each other of course, too, but more eager are they to strip women of power. It goes against their idea of the natural order, and to those who are weak of soul a woman with power threatens their own, just by its existence. I had always tried to keep peace, had made war only when I had to.

Young men of my court, both when I was young and now I was old, lusted for war and battle, and perhaps it was because I was a woman and therefore could take no part in such tales of glory that I did not glorify it, or perhaps it was because I had never welcomed waste, and war is the most wasteful of all things, which can destroy empires that long stood glorious under the long, red sun, which can destroy the potential all men carry within them, which renders children orphans and women widows, and even after a battle is spent and the graves of men are full, war will continue to take and take and take from the country that has used it, for war creates a debt that never is repaid. I never saw the honour in men thumping each other over the head with wood, or drawing blood with metal. We glorify war to make men go to war, so rich men can become richer and large countries larger. We glorify warriors so we will not run out of young fools willing to die for a country that will forget them with speed. We lie to our own children, and we let them die.

"So peace with the Scots, with Spain, if they will leave us alone," I said to Robert.

As Cecil worked on making friends with James of Scots, another claimant to the throne but a weaker one was lifting her head into the murky mist of politics. Lady Arbella Stuart, James's first cousin, had been born in England, yet her claim was inferior to his. Despite the weakness of her claim, and equally weak nature of her character, some were willing to support Arbella because not everyone welcomed the idea of the King of Scots taking the throne of England. James was too the son of Mary of Scots, a famed Catholic, and Lady Arbella was clearly Protestant. Despite the fact she had been born in England, I did not favour Arbella for the throne. Her blood was noble not royal, and she was an arrogant, ignorant chit besides. To me it was obvious that James should take the throne, for he was twice descended from Henry VII, my grandfather and the first Tudor king, and he was my godson and cousin. Just because he had been born in Scotland did not negate the English blood that flowed in his veins. Just as Welsh blood ran in my veins, as well as French, I was seen as English, and in truth I was as English as James was. It is not the country one is born into which dictates one's nationality, especially when it comes to those who are royal. James, whilst Scottish, was as English as I was. We all are many things, nation upon nation rolling in our blood.

I had long regarded James as my rightful heir, and had safeguarded his position when his mother was executed and when she was my prisoner, and had taken care that he never was excluded from the throne by my Parliament, government or nobles. Not naming him my heir caused him to distrust me, but had he taken the time to look at all I had done to ensure he never was excluded, he would have known I wanted my sacred duty to be handed to him.

I trusted Cecil to work for his own ambitions as well as mine, for like as not he would outlive me, James would be his King, and where there was a king of England I had determined there should be a Cecil next to that king, to guide the prince and to care for them with all the wit that the Cecil family had within them. Between sacred blood and Cecil blood, England would be safe. But Cecil's task was not easy, for Essex had done much damage. He had caused mischief and had talked badly of Cecil to James. I did not doubt James was a little suspicious of Robert, for James was my godson and therefore had a high-tuned sense of self-preservation. But I was determined that James would understand the value of Cecil, and that he needed him. Robert Cecil would not do everything as William Cecil had, and therefore not as I had, but he loved England as I did and as his father had. I was certain in his hands the future would be safer than in the hands of James alone or the hands of any other claimant.

Once one is dead one cannot control the present or the future, unless it is by becoming a ghost and wailing warnings at the living from within the shadowed corners of a house once your body walked through. I was well aware that when I passed from life those who came to rule after me would do as they saw fit with England and with my people. But if I could have one last hand in guiding my country, attempting to choose what men James might trust in the future, then I would, as any parent, have sent my children off into the world, their bags packed with all the provisions I thought they might need.

I could not dictate what would happen in the future. I would not be here anymore to guide my people, my children, but hopefully, as they stopped along the path they were walking to drink some water, take some rest, they would open the bag I had packed for them and smile, seeing the last caring touch of a mother who loved them and now was so far away. They might be grateful for these last provisions packed so their journey might be easier, so they might get to their destination hale and unharmed.

Chapter Twenty-Four

**London, Reading and Hampshire
Summer 1601**

I headed out on progress, wondering if it was my last. I had found I often wondered that of late. Something had made me consider how long I might be here. I had reigned longer than any of my family, had beaten most other monarchs too, save Edward III and Henry III. I had survived, and continued to, but something was whispering in my ear, telling me it was not to last. No one wins at life, for all die. It is just a question of when. People think to live long is to succeed, to win this game none of us chose to undertake, yet all were blessed with. It is as though some think life a trial of endurance, and who endures the most wins. I was still standing, still in the game, but it felt now not as though I was winning. I felt I had run on long and ahead of others, but for small purpose. All souls I had loved had decided to finish already, and were taking refreshment in the shade as I burned in the sun.

Yet I retained a natural fear of death, and as I thought I heard Death creeping closer I found more and more to love in life, much I never wanted to lose. I found myself admiring the countryside more than I had before, noticing little things everyone else ignored. I think I was saying goodbye.

"Silly old woman," I muttered, scolding myself when I found myself tearful over a pretty patch of heather. Pink and white lights flittered over brittle leaves and twigs and flowers, lit by sunshine and dew. "You are hale and well, fit as a flea! There is no cause for this foolishness."

Yet something told me there was. Something whispered that I should appreciate the world more, for soon we would part company, and I would miss this world, this life that even I, the great survivor, had at times taken for granted. What greater crime is there than to treat one who loves and nurtures us so well, never asking for anything but our happiness in return, as though they do not matter? You may well say murder and rape are greater crimes and you might be right, but they stem from the same cause; failing to treat people and things as though they matter. We render much inhuman when we try to kill, when we rape, even when we rob, unless it is done because of hunger. We take, and do not think of the one we take from. And if I, in this great age, was coming to have any understanding it was that there is nothing and no one who does not matter. Life, and every life, is glorious and deserving of respect.

And I had just killed, in order to not be killed. Essex was in my mind much as I tried to put him from it. He always had possessed an annoying ability to resurrect old arguments so they went around and around, driving everyone spare. I was wondering if I had acted right, by destroying him. I could tell you it was done for England, for her future, and in part I would be right, yet in part not, as justification for horrors we work can always be found. It is so easy to call on one's country, say it was for the kingdom that I killed this man, those men, all these people, this entire race. Mankind has been for centuries justifying murder, and mass murder, by declaring it is for our countries, as though soil and water cry out for us to wage war and kill. The truth is it is always for ourselves. We sense we and those closest to us may be in danger, and we strike. The Pope called young knights to fight for Jerusalem not because it was a holy city, but because the men holding it were of a different religion, one in which he had no power. They called those wars the Crusades, but they were murders, just carried out in plain view, out in the open and in company with others, so people thought them honest and honourable. Whether done in public in war or execution, or in private by dagger or pillow, murder is murder. We make up stories, we justify sins. We go to bed and sleep, having convinced ourselves with our lies. I was not sure I wanted to do that. In truth although it might be easier, I did not think I ever had done that. The times I killed, and they were few compared to some princes, I had weighed up the dangers to me and to England, and I had struck only when I had to. I do not think I ever killed on a whim.

But I had to face a truth that this time, and every other time, I had killed out of self-preservation. I had to face that I had dehumanised someone, often someone I had loved, in order to kill them, in order to survive.

What troubled me more was I felt I had not just killed a man, a once-friend, but something more. We all have to watch our worlds crumble. Great civilisations have fallen time and time again, their peoples standing, staring in confusion and horror at the tumbling buildings, the collapse of kings and gods. Yet it comes in little lives, single lives too.

With Essex something died. It had been waning, a sick and broken being for a long time, but by fantasy it had kept living; a vampire feeding from the warm life-blood of the living, dragging itself along the road seeking veins to feed from. Now it was no more, and although ghosts remained howling in the castle in which it had once lived, the vision was dead. My father had struck this crawling thing many times without meaning to, and others too had wounded it, but I think it was I who killed it. I struck the final blow. I salted the earth, so never would it rise again.

No matter that it had been fantasy, Essex had stood for an ideal of chivalry, a thought of times when knights had been true and honourable and men had defended to the death that which was good and pure. Of a world where noble blood made men noble in character and deed. The idea of being governed by goodness, by one chosen by God, where virtue was the banner under which men rode to battle.

Of course it was a lie, chivalry was a code knights kept to keep themselves safe and never had much to do with women or children, or even goodness. There was no world governed by goodness, more often what was good came about by accident, or because it benefited someone on high. Yet Essex had shouted those values to the skies and into the ears of my people, and he had been perhaps the last man who truly believed in them. Gods, myths and ideals must have believers, without them they crumble like the cities of old, become forgotten.

I brought that old ideal to an end, I thought. *I killed it.* I had truly become a creature of the past, for I alone now could remember when those ideals had a chance to be real. Now all knew they were fantasy. I felt guilt for I had thought I wanted my people, my children, to grow up and to make this happen I had murdered their innocence. Perhaps I had been wrong.

*

Whilst we were on progress, at the beginning of August, William Browne the Deputy Governor of Flushing came to find me to update me on the situation in the Low Countries. The Archduke Albert was besieging Ostend, and I had asked for an update on our allies the Dutch and how they were using my troops against the Archduke. On a pretty, sunny Sunday morning after we had attended church I walked with Browne in the garden of Sir William Clark. I had been thinking of something I had seen at chapel that morning, two marks carved into the wood before me where I had stood to hear Mass. One had been a ship and the other a cross. They had been crude, the cross more than the ship which, by the style of its sails, I could see was old and must have been carved long ago. I had found myself wondering who had carved such marks in that church. It was not uncommon to find images people had drawn in churches. Some were made by people dulled into a stupor by the Mass or a tedious sermon and had tried to keep themselves awake through occupation. Some were blessings, prayers if you will, that a pilgrim might have scribbled on a particular church they had been trying to reach, to ask a saint for aid in petitioning God. Some were prayers thanking God for getting them to that church safe, or pleading for the same treatment on the way home. Some were marks made for sick people, so the saint of that church would remember to pray for them, make them well again. Such things some thought had died out when England became Protestant, but there are many traditions we keep that never will die.

Whosoever carved these crude pictures had made their mark and gone, left no name, just a symbol. Mayhap they were prayers of thanks or pleading, were marks made by the bored, or perhaps these artists simply wanted to leave a sign, make a mark to show they too had stood there, so even if their names ceased to be heard and their deeds became forgot this one moment of life, of their present, might become imprinted with them. One moment of life and memory remained, carved into wood or stone, so others like me would one day stop, look down and trace that image with my finger, uniting past and present in ways untold and unknowable, making strangers that never would become friends into persons linked, bonded in time. Once someone else stood where I had that morning. They had been there, they had been. Like as not they were no more. As, one day, I would be no more.

So I had taken out my eating knife and carved a symbol too, a little eye. Let my people know I still was watching over them, even when I was no more. The thought had made me smile. Who would look on that little eye and think Queen Elizabeth of England was naughty enough to have carved that symbol in a church herself? They would think it was some schoolboy or wandering, bored pilgrim. Few would ever look down at such a thing and suppose I had done a thing so mischievous. The thought made me want to laugh out loud.

This I was thinking of as Browne approached, so he came upon me smiling merrily, in a fine mood. He kissed my hand and I made him stand up. I spoke loudly to him saying, "Come hither, Browne," and he scurried to keep up with me. I always did walk fast.

As we began to march my train of ladies attempted to walk up, right on my heel or so it seemed, and I whipped around.

"Stand, stand back! Will you not let us speak but will you be here!" As we walked on a little I told Browne of how highly I thought of him and all he was doing in the Low Countries for us.

"You are most gracious, Majesty," he said, "and yet I feel I do not do enough."

"It is always the people who think they do not do enough, Browne, who do more than enough and always those who suppose their deeds to be mighty who in fact do not do enough."

We spoke for some time on the Low Countries and on the situation of the Dutch in general. I complained about the lack of support from the Dutch at present for my auxiliary troops, whilst Brown attempted to defend them. "Tush, Brown," I said. "I know more than thou durst. When I first heard about the actions of the Archduke Albert I knew no good would be done. Our allies should have come down near Ostend, or have taken some town in the part of Brabant or Flanders that might have startled their enemy, and that they did promise me or else I should not have let them have so many men."

We went on to talk of the French King and the support he had promised to the Dutch, and then failed to deliver. Browne said that the French King rather marvelled at our ally's foolish boldness in venturing their army so far, then said Henri was now declaring that he never gave them any assurance to join with them.

"Tush, Browne," I said, scolding him again. "It does not good, Browne, to believe excuses of Kings. They are naughty liars all. Do not I know that Bucenval was written to, and written to again, to move the army to go that way so he would help them? Help was promised."

"Surely," Browne said, "but if this was so, Majesty, then you it must think it was but a *French* promise."

I laughed. A French promise was a way of saying a false promise. "And the French would say such was an *English* promise, Browne."

I was happy enough with Browne, and he knew it by the end of that interview. I think thoughts of death, ever upon me at that time, had led to remind me that children cannot be governed by punishment and criticism alone. I felt I had been too hard on my men of late. They needed more praise when praise was due. It does no good for a leader to only say when things have been done wrong. People must know they are getting some things right, so they have enthusiasm for the future, so they want to do better and so they know they can and will succeed.

"Go to our allies and keep them well-advised," I said to Browne. "Believe the evidence of your own eyes and trust your wits, Browne. They are as good as any man's I have met. Know we love you, and do trust you."

His eyes were shining with affection when we parted, and it occurred to me that a carved scribble on the wood in a church might not be the only marks we may leave behind.

*

I gave praise to another faithful subject that same month when William Lambarde came to me once we had returned to Greenwich for a brief stop. He came to me in my Privy Chamber. A learned historian and lawyer, and also Keeper of the Records at the Tower of London, Lambarde had been working on a particular project, and had compiled an inventory of the documents in his charge which he intended to present to me through the Countess of Warwick, but I did not want that. He had done me a service and I wanted to accept it from his own hands, and thank him. When he presented the book to me I opened it, read the epistle and title aloud, and then at once began to question him about the meaning of technical terms within the book. "I would be a scholar in age as I have been in life, I think it no schooling to learn during life, Lambarde," I said.

I scanned much of the book but when I reached the reign of Richard II my heart seemed to stall within me. I looked up at Lambarde. "I am Richard. Know you not that?" My voice was quiet. I felt more like that young, foolish king at times, especially since Essex died, than I had before. Perhaps I had won, but sometimes I felt I had not, as though if Richard had starved to death in a little room, I was destined to wane too, in the eyes of my people if not by reduction of belly and body. As he had slowly disappeared, I wondered if that too was my fate. The truth of it is, all kings must be replaced in the end, whether by death or deposition, through law or lawlessness. Mayhap in the end it is all the same.

"Such a wicked imagination," said Lambarde, "was determined and attempted by most unkind gentlemen, the most adorned creature that ever Your Majesty made." He was speaking of Essex of course, as he knew I was.

"He that will forget God," I said, "will also forget his benefactors."

I hurried on to ask more questions about the text, not wishing to speak further of Essex. Although at first it was pretended interest, soon it became real for Lambarde's work was most interesting. Eventually, called away to prayer, I set the book against my chest and forbade the good man to fall on his knee before me. "Farewell, good and honest Lambarde," I said, "and thank you for making me a student again."

"You would wish to be a student again, Majesty?" said Katherine Hastings as the man left.

"Aye, old friend," I said. "All of mankind should all their lives be a student, always be humble enough to understand that we do not know everything. There are few joys as pure as in learning may be found, few things that spark the mind as greatly as reading something we find interesting and wanting to know more about that same something. If a man or a woman for life may be a student, and may at times too be a teacher, then they are the most fortunate of souls. It means they are always willing to learn more about the world, and there is so much to learn, too much for any life to contain all of."

"And yet you make it sound an impossible task, Majesty."

"Perhaps it is, old friend," I said, taking my gloves from a maid so I could wear them to chapel. "Yet mankind delights in the impossible, do we not? We are not creatures made for comfort and stability. We must have challenge, adventure, excitement, and we must live our potential to its full. If we assume we have learned all there is to know about the world, about ourselves and about other people, we lose so much that we could have known. And even though at the end of life all that is contained within a mind will no more be found upon this earth, we may write down words expressed from our souls, and read those of others and in such ways touch the past and the present and the future together as one, through the pages of a book and the words of those who came before us. Books are the only eternal, the only immortality we ever will know.

"So yes, old friend, I say we should be students all our lives, willing to learn, to pass on our knowledge, to discuss and debate and to discover all we can in the short time we have, and pass on all we can to those who come after us. In such ways our minds are enlivened during life and we know joy, and in death our knowledge may go on to aid those who come after us, and one never knows, it may make the world a better place for our children and grandchildren."

I smiled at her, stroking my soft leather glove along the gentle contours of her cheek. "Never cease to wonder, never do the world the disservice so rank and cruel of taking her for granted. Love her every day by wondering, by looking on amazed at all that is here to see. Never cease to learn, be a student always, for then you never lose the enjoyment and the joy of finding something new." I took her chin. "Promise me this," I said.

"I promise, Majesty," she said, her voice almost a whisper.

*

Sadly all was not pleasure that summer, and some people never are students and never learn. On Monday the 24th of August 1601 the *fifth* Armada Spain had sent set sail from Lisbon, bent on reaching Ireland. It was a fleet made up of thirty-three ships, nineteen of them warships and the rest armed merchantman and transport vessels. We had reports that 4,500 soldiers were upon those ships under the command of Don Juan de Aguila. We knew he was a man to be feared, who had attacked England before at Mousehole in Cornwall, and had established a Spanish garrison in Brittany. They were sailing out to support Tyrone. Our blessing, as always however, was the time of year they had set out.

"August comes, and yet another Armada," I said despondently. "At what stage do you think will all the Phillips of Spain cease to send ships against Tudors of England, and not that I would wish them to come at a different time, and therefore find the seas more clement, but why do they *always* set out at the end of summer, when the winds of autumn and the uncaring sea will be allies to England rather than to Spain? Are they simply stupid?"

No man had an answer for me, and many looked at me with strange faces for it was truly of benefit that Spain was so full of fools that they kept sending their ships at a time when the sea and the wind and the weather would be against them, but I just thought it odd. Odd that a prince who might have a mighty purse and mighty empire could be so wasteful with his men, his ships and his money. Sometimes it seems that no one in life does learn.

As we heard of the fresh Armada, lowness fell on me. Court was being neglected, people running off to take pleasure elsewhere, perhaps sensing time running out for me. It was for another reason too. I was having to cut spending for my court, so it was becoming less glamorous. People did not want a frugal court, a mean monarch, so desert me they did.

I sought solace and sanctuary in my darkened bedchamber, and at times there I would weep. I had a nightgown of tawny velvet lined with unshorn velvet. I wore it when I felt low, and at times it made me feel lower still, and at others its sadness comforted me. Sometimes we need to be surrounded by sad things when we are sad, it makes us feel less alone somehow, as though if there are sadnesses other than ours in the world we do not have to be lonely, in company with just our own sorrow. We can be in company with other sadnesses, and share them.

The nightgown had been a gift from Robin, and I had preserved it well. More than ten years it had lasted. My father's clothes had been fortunate to survive a year before he had them pulled apart and made anew or handed them to servants, but I mended mine and had my women do the same. Of course some items had wasted and some been given away as gifts, but in my great age I had an almighty wardrobe because I did not throw things away.

In that wardrobe now, when I went to see it, I could pick out gowns I had worn when Kat was alive, dresses I had worn while sitting beside Blanche as we went through my papers. I could tell you that a hem of one gown, or sleeves of another, had been put together from a much older gown I had worn when first Queen. Some parts of the gown being wasted and frayed, strips had been cut away to make new parts of new gowns. Nothing was wasted, so my wardrobe was a box full of memory. Sometimes it broke my heart to go there, stroke a finger over the embroidered snakes or doves or eyes on a gown, over honeysuckle that my mother had favoured, roses of my father. All gifts Robin ever gave me of cloth were in there. Some had already fallen apart but I would not part with them. Some, like this nightgown which he had chosen to match my colouring, were still worn though they were so precious. In a way, that cloth against my skin was like having him embrace me. His soul was in Heaven, but I hoped his phantom hands still could touch me here on earth, steal a kiss as he had when we were young and giddy and knew not how little time we had with one another.

It was not just clothes and material that reminded me of those I had lost. There were parts of people everywhere, as though in death they had been torn apart and bits of their souls were sprinkled about my life. I saw glimpses of memory and love lost everywhere, in a cup, in the shadow of a curtain, the memory of a friend asleep next to me in my bed. All these things of them held fragments of souls, little memories, fingertips of ghosts reaching out to touch me. Sometimes when I saw something that reminded me of the dead it was not even a memory clear that struck, but merely the impression of a person, of eyes, a smile, a flash that passed before me brief and cutting, bringing joy to have known them, along with sorrow to have them no more.

I felt alone often. My greatest confidants had gone and to replace the brightest stars of my time had come pale shadows. I was a ghost of an age long passed, a woman who was dead already, wandering the earth as Cain.

I felt drained and tired, sometimes became forgetful when attending to state affairs. The last two years had been hard, and I had lost much faith and many friends. That summer I told the French ambassador that I was tired of life, for nothing now contented me or gave me much enjoyment. At times I missed Essex. When he had been gay and bright, he had danced with me and I had felt young again. There were few left who could make me feel that, and even if they might be safer than that wicked child had been they were not so enthralling.

It was said the people were weary of an old woman's government, and that was why court had emptied. It would have been true to say that after the fall of Essex, even though many had understood why it had to happen, my popularity had declined still further. Some thought that whilst Essex had erred, his was not a capital crime. My country, having come through several years of famine, seven in fact, was under a time of hardship. War with Spain dragged on, and many were talking of a need for change; that England had grown old with its old queen. At the same time I was criticised most unfairly for making cuts in my expenditure. Courtiers who could not meet the rising cost of living at court wanted me to pay them wages, hand them monopolies on trade, and I could not. I had to make cuts to my spending, and make my court less than it was so that we could meet the costs of war, and so that the money could go back into my country. "Now the wit of the fox is everywhere on foot, so as hardly a faithful or virtuous man may be found," I complained to some of my women.

Yet I understood why they deserted me. I had sunk into sadness low, and was not a merry monarch to be around. People looked at me and that hush of death fell upon them, because of Essex and because of the weariness upon me. They saw something in my eyes, and in my air. They saw the end.

There comes a time in life when we know we are saying farewell, a time when we suspect this will be the last time we see a sight, a sunset or rise, a person. In truth oftentimes the last time sneaks up on us so we know it not. I did not know the last time I saw Robin or Essex was to be the last, but that year as I went on progress I had a sneaking feeling, a warning in my heart, telling me this might be the last. It might not, but it might be, and therefore if I wanted to start saying goodbye to this land, to my people, to all the beauty that I had been blessed to witness, now was the time.

Chapter Twenty-Five

Windsor Castle
Autumn 1601

On the 19th of September I was back at Windsor, progress over. I was glad of it in a way, it had not felt like a joyous break this year, more like a funeral procession. And bad news was waiting for me. The rumoured Armada was close to Ireland, taking the back way into England that we had always feared they might. By the 23rd they were disembarking at Kinsale, west of Cork.

"If they join with Tyrone we may say goodbye to all the good work Mountjoy has done over the last eighteen months!" I almost screamed as I heard. "Our men are outnumbered."

We all knew the next weeks were vital.

In addition to the worthy work Mountjoy had done, one of his captains, Sir Henry Docwra, had made a base in rebel territory at Derry, which had aided our campaign greatly. However, if this force from Spain managed to get to Tyrone, all the hard-won gains we had made since Mountjoy sailed would be for nothing.

What we did not know for a while was that the Spanish were cursed, some said from the very start of their mission. Many of the Armada mariners were conscripts from foreign lands who had been pressed into service. They could not understand their leaders, for they spoke not their language, and had no wish to be there. Being prisoners, they had no loyalty to their commanders. The men who led the Armada had, in truth, been handed enemies to command. When they landed, many deserted.

They also had a shortage of food on the journey, and when they arrived sailed into the midst of a great storm, which many of course claimed was sent by God. When they got to Kinsale they had only 1,700 men, all on half-rations. Eventually as their numbers grew with lost men drifting in from other ships, they had around three thousand, but when Mountjoy sent his man Carew to assess the danger, Carew thought it was a danger that could be beaten. Nervously we waited for news.

*

"I hope it will not be the last," said Cecil when I spoke to him of Parliament that year, the first I had called since his father had died. I had said it would be the last I called, and I meant it.

"I think it will," I said and smiled. "In truth, much like my father I always tried to only call on Parliament when I really needed them. The trouble with hearing people is they all want things, Pygmy, and I have little left to give now."

This time they wanted something else, which I at first resisted. But in time I came to see. They wanted me, or rather the Crown, to no more hand out favours to favourites. They had been crying out about monopolies on trade and imports for years, and now wanted resolution. Rich incomes like the sweet wine imports that I had handed to Robin and to Essex, and many other such favours the Crown could hand to men, they wanted to end. I resisted at first for I saw it for what it was, a strike on the power of the Crown. But in time, when I thought about it, I thought them right. I had given more power to Essex than he should have had, out of a misguided idea he might change, become a true man. That was my fault, a mistake on my part. If many men decided who would have those grants then perhaps better choices would be made. If many could trade and import such things, the prices would be lower for my people.

I prepared my speech for Parliament with care that year. I always did, but again something within me was calling, telling me that this time I should make them remember my words. I was to give concessions that I never would have given at any other time in my reign, but I had come to think they were right, and the ability to give grants and favours such as I had given to many men over the years perhaps should not be solely in the control of the Crown. I do not flatter myself that I was a clever woman, although not always wise. I knew I was remarkable. I also knew that I was not perfect. I had made mistakes, and many of them because I loved people. Love is something which can blind us. Mistakes such as a king or queen can make may have larger repercussions upon their people and their country than intended, than they were even aware might happen. I was clever, yes, I was at times wise, and yet if I was not perfect then I could not suppose that any who followed me would be perfect either or would make perfect choices for my people. Gifts then, such as revenues for great income which would give men power for many years, should perhaps not be decided by just one person, even if they were the king or queen, and perhaps should not be in the hands of just one man, no matter what he had done for his country.

Parliament had a point when it said that it should be down to the country to decide what happened with the wealth given to the few. It could not be said that they would always get everything right either, but the old saying that the more heads you have the better a decision will be, probably was true. My father and my grandfather would never have welcomed what I was to do, I believe my sister would have screamed into my ear for it. But I believe my men were right, and my children, through their representatives in government and Parliament, should decide where the money of the kingdom went.

As any parent must, when they see their children are grown, I surrendered some of my power to my children that they might make choices for themselves.

It did not seem at first that it would start well, this Parliament of this year. Due to some blunder of organisation a number of members of Parliament were shut out of the Lords and so missed the Lord Keeper's opening address. Due to more poor management, I was jostled in a crowd of commoners as I came out of the Upper House. I moved my hand, indicating I needed more room, for I never did like people too close. One of the gentlemen ushers said openly, "Back, masters, make room!" And one member of Parliament standing behind me shouted, "If you will hang us, we can make no more room!"

I lifted my head at that, and looked towards him that had spoken. I met his eyes and he dropped his head. Perhaps he felt ashamed of what he had said or perhaps he was in fear about what I would do to one who spoke so bold to the Queen. Perhaps he thought I would not agree to what they wanted, so was trying to make a point.

As I came to speak to my Parliament, I missed my dear Spirit; his experience in handling government affairs was missed greatly, and this was brought to my attention as a row blew up in the commotion over monopolies. These patents issued by the Crown granted to individuals the sole right to manufacture, import or export commodities, and were now a sticking point. They had always been a way for the Crown, for monarchs, to offer a way inexpensive to reward those who deserved it, or placate those who needed placating. Of course they had always led to abuses. Men had made false shortages and inflated prices, had curtailed freedom of choice of goods and exploited private enterprise to make money. I had always thought those crimes minor, and secondary to the benefits they brought, but others thought not so. One member of Parliament came to the stand to describe the system as ending only in beggary and poverty to the subject, and another attacked the monopolists, calling them "bloodsuckers of the Commonwealth." One enquired as to whether bread would be added to the list, something that would destroy the common man. I had not, until it was pointed out, thought the abuses so many, or so frequent, but of course I was not the one suffering from these abuses, so I would not know. But these were my people, and it should have been my business to know.

I understood what they said, but at first I was unwilling. I saw the granting of such monopolies as royal rights, for they gave power to the monarch, and if Parliament was to strip that away the Crown was surrendering power. My men knew they were on dangerous ground, for always I had protected royal prerogatives, but still they fought.

Over and over this matter was discussed in Parliament, and propaganda sheets were circulated in the city. The Commons would not drop this issue, and refused to vote through taxes I badly needed, in an effort to make me listen to them. I did listen, and as I listened, more and more I began to think they perhaps had a point. I had handed Essex power, too much, through the wines. Others abused the gifts they were given. The people, my people, were the ones who suffered for this. I had thought the monopolies a way to secure or reward loyalty, but if they were being used to exploit my people, make more money than a man might need, they were favours for one, abuses for others. And why would any man need so much money? What could he do with such money?

Perhaps this was a sign that this was what I was supposed to do. Perhaps at this last stage of my life, I was being asked to willingly surrender a power, just as someone had tried to force it from my hands before. That God was asking me to set power into the hands of my children rather than into the hands of the few who little deserved it. *Mayhap this is my redemption*, I said to myself. So I came to speak to them. There were many hostile eyes on me as I stood before them.

"Mr Speaker," I said, my voice ringing out, "we perceive your coming is to present thanks unto me; know I accept it with no less joy than your loves can desire to offer such a present, and more esteem it than any treasure or riches, for that we know to prize, but loyalty, love and thanks I count invaluable." I looked around at the House, saw many unhappy faces. They cared not for my words, not yet, for they were angry at me, but I would have them understand not only that I had heard them, but that I would act because I loved them.

"And though God hath raised me high, yet this I count the glory of my crown; that I have reigned with your loves. This makes I do not so much rejoice that God hath made me to be a queen, as to be a queen over so thankful a people, and to be the mean under God to conserve you in safety and preserve you from danger, yea, to be the instrument to deliver you from dishonour, from shame, from infamy, from out of servitude and slavery under our enemies, to keep you from cruel tyranny and vile oppression intended against us. For better withstanding whereof we take very acceptably your intended helps, chiefly in that it manifesteth your loves and largeness of hearts unto your sovereign.

"Of myself I must say this; I never was any greedy, scraping grasper, nor a strait fast-holding prince, nor yet a waster; my heart was never set on any worldly goods, but only for my subjects' goods. What you do bestow on me I will not hoard it up, but receive it to bestow on you again. Yea, mine own properties I account yours to be expended for your good. And your eyes shall see the bestowing of all for your good.

"Mr Speaker," I went on, "I would wish you and the rest to stand up, for I shall yet trouble you with longer speech."

There was a little laughter at that. They were thawing. I could almost hear them creaking as a river's ice cracking in spring.

"Mr Speaker, you give me thanks, but I am more to thank you, and I charge you to thank them of the Lower House from me. For had I not received a knowledge from you, I might have fallen into a lapse of an error, only for lack of true information. For since I was queen, yet did I never put pen to any grant but upon pretext and semblance made to me that it was for the good and avail of my subjects generally, though a private profit to some of my ancient servants who had deserved well."

I drew my shoulders up and looked into their faces, one set of eyes after another. "But that my grants should be made grievances to my people and oppressions to be privileged under colour of our patents, our kingly dignity shall not suffer it. And when I heard it, I could give no rest unto my thoughts until I had reformed it. And those varlets, lewd persons, abusers of my bounty shall know I will not suffer it."

Men began to allow rumbles of cheers for me to leave their mouths. Hands tapped on wood, showing approval.

"And Mr Speaker, tell the House from me I take it exceedingly gratefully that the knowledge of these things is come to me from them. And though amongst them the principal members are such as are not touched in their private, therefore need not speak from any feeling of the grief; yet we have heard that other gentlemen also of the House who stand as free have spoken freely in it, which gives us to know that no respects or interests have moved them other than the minds they bear to deliver to suffer no diminution of our honour and our subjects' love unto us. The zeal of which affection tending to ease my people and knit their hearts unto us, I embrace with a princely care.

"For above all earthly treasure, I esteem my people's love, more than which I desire not to merit. And God that gave me here to sit, and set me over you, knows that I never respected myself, but as your good was concerned in me. Yet what dangers, what practices, what perils I have passed! Some if not all of you know. But it is God that hath delivered. And in my governing, this I have ever had the grace to use; to set the Last Judgement Day before mine eyes and so to rule as I shall be judged and to answer before a higher Judge, to whose judgement seat I do appeal that never thought was cherished in my heart that tended not to my people's good.

"And if my kingly bounty have been abused and my grants turned to the hurt of my people, contrary to my will and meaning; or if any in authority under me have neglected or perverted what I have committed to them, I hope God will not lay their culps unto my charge."

I drew myself up, feeling my years heavy upon my shoulders. "To be a king and wear a crown is a thing more glorious to them that see it than it is pleasant to them that bear it. For myself, I was never so much enticed with the glorious name of a king or royal authority of a queen as delighted that God had made me His instrument to maintain His truth and glory, and to defend this kingdom from dishonour, damage, tyranny, and oppression. But should I ascribe anything of this to myself or my sexly weakness, I were not worthy to live, and of all, most unworthy of the mercies I have had from God. But to God only and wholly, all is to be given and ascribed.

"The cares and troubles of a crown I cannot resemble more fitly than to the confections of a learned physician, perfumed with some aromatical savour, or to bitter pills gilded over, by which it is made acceptable or less offensive which indeed is bitter and unpleasant to take. And for my part, were it not for conscience's sake to discharge the duty which God hath laid upon me, and to maintain His glory and keep you in safety, in mine own disposition, I should willingly resign the place I hold to any other, and glad to be free of the glory with the labours.

"For it is not my desire to be or reign longer than my life and reign shall be for your good. And though you have had and may have many mightier princes sitting in this seat, yet you never had nor shall have any that will love you better."

They cheered me then, men great and cold and old standing with tears in their eyes. They knew I was honest, and they knew I was on their side.

I smiled. "Thus, Mr Speaker, I commend me to your loyal love, and you to my best care and your further counsels. And I pray you, Mr Comptroller, and you of my Councils, that before these gentlemen depart to their countries you bring them all to kiss my hand."

I wanted to look each in the eye, say a word or two. They would lead my England when I was no more. I wanted them to speak of me when I was gone, boast they had met me on the day of my speech. Perhaps it was a fool's errand, but I wanted to leave a mark on each man present that day.

I yielded on the favours to favourites, and on the following day the Speaker rose to inform the House that I, having learned to my surprise and distress that the patents were proving grievous to my subjects, intended to embark on an order for the reformation of evil. Robert Cecil confirmed my royal message, and assured the House that a proclamation giving effect to the promised reformation would be issued within days. He went on to list monopolies which were to be revoked with immediate effect. Every man in the future would have salt as cheap as he could make or buy it, and so be able to make his meat more tasty. Vinegar would be set into liberty, as would *aqua vitae*. Starch, pot and bottles, blubber oil and salted fish too were no more in the control of just one person.

I had surrendered and I did so generously. The proclamation was due to appear in two days' time. It did contain a clause which retained the power and validity of the royal prerogative, and warned of penalties for those who would contemptuously presume to call it into question, which it made plain that I had not given way on principle, but I had given way in practice. The power of the Crown must not be questioned on all things, and all privileges, but in this particular case I had surrendered.

The Commons was rising in power, and it was well. Perhaps in the future the people would have more power, but I could not be the one to see this happen. I had been raised to know the monarch was Head of State and Church, chosen by God. This issue I had given way on, but I would not be the one to see the end of this power in all things. It was alien to every way of my thinking.

That did not mean I did not think change was coming.

I had ever thought myself a mother to my people, and perhaps the people were children no more. The times of old where only nobles counted and were counted in death were waning. The times of the monarch being the one with all power were coming to an end. That end would not be in my lifetime, but I had good instincts. I felt I could feel a breath of a future I would barely recognise on my face.

I had a feeling growing in me that I was saying goodbye, not only to my people and life, but to the way of life England had possessed for so long. I would be the last Queen who ruled complete in the ways of old. Perhaps this was well, but I was glad I would not be the next to take on the crown and have to adapt to the changing ways of this world.

"You have lived too long," I said to myself. "You have become a ghost in your own life, a memory of a time long since passed."

Chapter Twenty-Six

Richmond Palace
Winter 1601

That Christmas was quiet, but for the voices of men of my Parliament coming to thank me for upholding their request. My speech had done the trick, for on Saturday the 5th of December that year, four days after the Speaker made his report to the Commons, the House voted in the taxes I had asked for. In return I had made the concessions they desired.

Some still were not satisfied, but no men ever are fully satisfied. No more would my subjects accept that the monarch had the absolute right to dictate what goods they could trade or products they could import or make, an aspect of my God-given appointed royal power which long had been mine and my ancestors'. There were some problems that followed, some men who questioned whether I meant honestly to give up the right, but I did. I meant for the monopolies to end, eventually. Some were ended that very year, others would take time but it would come. I meant it to come.

It was a gift, given to my people, a last act of redemption. I surrendered something precious to me in the hope that God would be watching, would see what I had given up. I had retained power for the Crown, but what my people had asked for I had delivered.

It was a significant decision. There would be no monopolies anymore, and men could trade as they wished as long as they had licence under the law, of course. I had needed the taxes they had given me for Ireland, and I was still determined to defend many rights and privileges of the Crown and just as determined that the Commons were not to take this as a sign that any of those powers had waned, or that this was a sign they could disregard the Crown, but the Commons and the people were growing more powerful, and I thought this was as well. One by one members of Parliament and of my government came to thank me. I thanked them in return for voting through the taxes I needed to end the war in Ireland.

The times had changed. My father I could almost hear turning in his grave at Windsor, but I thought this right.

"Redemption, Father," I said to his ghost as December came. "And perhaps for you as well, for you took and took from your people, closing the monasteries, taxing them brutally, debasing their coin. I am trying to give that back. Rest easy. Perhaps this will aid your restless spirit too."

*

There were few people at court that Christmas. Many people were heading north, hoping to send messages to my godson. Others did not like that court had become so staid, for so much of my money now had gone back into my country that I had little to entertain my courtiers with. I found I did not mind the quiet that year, there had been a long time of riot and confusion beforehand so I welcomed a little peace, and it was also welcome too, to contemplate the power I had handed to the House of Commons and to my people.

I began to think I had indeed perhaps lived too long, yet I was glad I had. So many parents never get to see their children grow, men die in war, women in childbed. I was one of the few fortunate for I had seen my children grow from infant to child, and now into adulthood they were starting to break.

We had good news just after Christmas when a messenger arrived from Ireland to tell us of a battle on the 24th of December, in which Lord Mountjoy had won a great victory over Tyrone at Kinsale.

At the end of October, Mountjoy had pulled his land army together from all over Ireland and he went to meet the half-starved Spaniards. He had 7,000 men. Tyrone had ravaged Leinster, trying to distract my commander and, buoyed up by reports of a strange sickness in the English troops which had killed more than two thousand and had another two sick in their beds, Tyrone advanced towards my men, but just as Mountjoy thought he might become trapped between the Spaniards he was setting siege to and the Irish marching upon him, Tyrone and Mountjoy came to battle.

Before dawn on Christmas Eve the fighting began. Tyrone's forces were split by a cavalry charge of English knights. Some of his men on firm ground and some in a bog, the O'Neil retreated. Seeing the Irish fail, the Spanish broke from their base in Kinsale, and sailed out. By the end of that night a thousand Irish men lay dead, more wounded, and the Spanish threat was retreating.

"We lost a handful of Englishmen," Cecil reported happily to me and my Council.

I nodded, though I little believed him. It was such a common report; that the winning side of a battle had lost hardly anyone. What they meant was anyone of *name*. Countless commoners fighting in battle rarely were counted. Their lives thought unimportant whilst they were alive, were supposed even more anonymous in death. Better it was, many supposed, for England to claim a stupendous victory than it was for us to honour the countless common dead. I thought not so. To my mind every soul who had died should have been counted and named. We would have honoured our country more to remember her sons, who had given so much, than to forget them in order to bolster our reputation in the tomes of history. It was not the first time that this had happened in my reign. Sometimes I thought of the countless dead still drifting under the sea, who had lost their lives fighting the first Armada. Sometimes in dreams of darkness I saw those men, weeds dancing about their faces and fishes drifting through their gaping, grinning skulls, and I felt ashamed, ashamed for sending them there to die, and for all who had died after, wasting to death of starvation or disease because the country they had fought for could not afford to care for them when the battle was won.

"We all must answer for what we have done," I whispered.

Tyrone had escaped, but the commander of the Spanish army who had arrived to assist the rebels gave up his cause and sued for peace. We had word that the Spaniards remaining in Ireland were to surrender to Mountjoy. They would leave and go back to Spain.

"And so we are in control of Ireland, at last," I breathed as I rose from the table at which I sat, smoothing my gown. "Our back door is shut and locked, gentlemen, and I have the key."

As I went to walk to the window I was surprised by a noise. Upon the table knuckles were rapping. I turned to look into the faces of my Council, many of them old, but so many young, young men who had never seen the troubles we had. They were smiling at me. Their knuckles upon that table celebrated me and my decision.

"Thank you, gentlemen," I said. "I am now, and ever have been, honoured to be served by loyal men such as you."

It was true. I was not proud of the Irish and English blood spent to secure that part of our empire, but it was done. In order to keep the whole safe, I had spent blood and bone, taken life. The Irish had risen and they had lost, and that is war. It was not fair and I knew it, but it was done. Much like Essex, it was a campaign I wished I never had to fight, yet had been forced to. Left alone, Ireland would have joined with Spain and my people would have died.

"The choices we are called upon to make are darker than many suppose," I said to my men, "yet we make them hoping for light, praying what we do is good and honest. Sometimes the way is dark indeed, but we must always hope there is an end to it, and an end worth reaching."

*

As the New Year faded away and 1602 was upon us, there was news from Ireland. The Spanish had indeed surrendered and sued for peace. On January the 2nd they had sailed back to Spain. "Send congratulations to Mountjoy," I said. "This is one of the most acceptable incidents that ever befell us, and whilst I might have preferred the Spaniards to be killed or imprisoned that is a minor detail. Any offences which Mountjoy has given, especially in the late affair of my lord of Essex, are forgotten and forgiven. Let him know this and let him know his loving sovereign will ensure that he is rewarded for this."

We wrote often, Mountjoy and I, after that. There was so much to be done in Ireland. We became quite close, he and I, even to the point where there were jests between us. I usually signed myself *"your loving sovereign"* when ending letters, but once after he complained I was treating him like a scullion, I responded with a very long, supportive letter in my own hand and began with *"a greeting, mistress kitchen maid"* as a jest. After his first and main victory I wrote, *"we have forgotten to praise your humility, that, after having been a Queen's kitchen maid, you have not disdained to be a traitor scullion. God bless you with perseverance."*

In light of our victory in Ireland, for the first time in many years that spring I started to talk to men who wished to follow in the footsteps of the great Sir Francis Drake, my personal pirate. It had been a long time since I authorised any naval expedition, for the main part because of the numerous Armadas Spain kept sending to flounder upon our shores. But that year I was in talks with Sir Richard Levinson, that he might head out upon the sea to capture Portuguese ships laden with treasure. The one on which he had his eye, a rich prize, would be protected by galleys and troops but I thought it was time that Englishmen once more set sail upon the seas. For one thing, now that Essex was gone there were fewer men in charge of my army or navy who would take risks such as would endanger England in vain pursuit of treasure.

It was not only in Ireland that peace, however forced that peace might be, was coming to be seen. War was ending on many fronts. Spain was surrendering the idea of capturing France, the Low Countries had seen off the Hapsburg armies and come to terms with them, and Ireland was largely at peace.

"I could not have wanted more than that," I said. "France is free of Spain, the Low Countries are no more under threat or thumb. Our backdoor of Ireland is locked. It is a good thing, even though it took a decade and more to achieve."

It was not only the end of war that encouraged me. "Many civilisations, you know, Pygmy, saw off the threat of war and then crumbled anyway, for lack of trade."

But that was not so for us. Trade was getting better, new markets opening all the time, all over the world. The lack of trade with our ancient partners like Spain and France and the Low Countries that many had wailed would be our downfall had forced English merchants to go out into the world, and the world had opened. Quality of life was improving all over England, more girls and boys were in school, at least for a few years, than ever had been educated before. My personal purse might be depleted after years of conflict with Spain, but England was becoming richer, her people more secure, and of all the countries all over the world we were one of a fortunate few who had not seen widespread uprisings and civil war because of religion. My religious settlement had not been perfect, had caused strife, but the numbers executed for disobeying my laws on religion were far fewer than those who had died in the wars of religion in France, or been slain in Spain. People had called me lunatic for keeping steady on a path of general tolerance, turning a blind eye to those who did not flaunt their faith too obviously, a path undisrupted for many years until enemies of England sent Jesuit priests in to test me, but stuck to it I had. It had taken courage, and I thought now, looking back, it had been worth it.

It is easier to go along with the sweeping skirts of hysteria, brushing us all as loose rushes and herbs under the breeze of a gown so we become one, detritus swept along the ground, taking more and more with us. More strength does it take to stand alone and say that one does not believe all of other faiths are our enemies or monsters, that they may be men and women like us, some bad and some good, all flawed and none perfect, and be willing to offer them a chance to show what and who they are. Assumption is so easy, quick and simple, for we may place into the minds of other people all we want, all we assume and all we fear and in making them monsters we may fight our fears, and believe ourselves to be the righteous angels in comparison. More courage does it take to note that people are people, all of the same mothers born, all of the same race no matter if we were born in one country or another. More courage does it take to get to know people than it does to judge them in a flash, upon one act or deed. It took courage for me to think that not all Catholics were evil and wanted me dead, courage to not dig every one out of their holes of faith and throw them to the hounds. It took courage of my heart to believe that many could honour me *and* their differing faith, courage to see there are more colours than black and white in this stupendous and chaotic world God crafted for us all.

As I said, it had not been perfect, for some had died for faith and refusing to conceal it in order to maintain the peace general of England, but the number that had died was smaller than it might have been had I insisted, as my sister had, that all convert honestly to my own faith. And it was not faith alone that I had needed courage for.

In a world where men ruled all, it had taken courage to be a queen, and even more so as a queen who refused to wed. In a world where women are by their bodies judged, it had taken courage to refuse to have a child. Although I ever had been blessed with good men and women to guide me, it had taken strength to do so as a sole person, not as a couple or as a woman with a child to bring to the throne.

It had taken courage for England, a small and when I came to the throne impoverished nation, to stand against Spain, and to support men of the Low Countries against her. In part I had done this to protect England, but I had done good for other men and women of other lands too.

I had been vindicated. Peace there was upon France, the Low Countries, upon us, and in large part this was because I had made alliance with men of our faith and kept peace with them, had aided them against their enemies. They too had come to our aid. It never had been perfect, but peace had been made. To my mind there was no greater achievement.

I had too been vindicated in my own ways, for although I had remained unmarried England had not fallen to war or waste. I had borne no heir of my body, but there was a person to pass my throne to. Men aplenty had called me unnatural for not marrying or wanting a child, but in doing what was natural for me I had succeeded, brought goodness to my life, and those of others.

"Mistakes I have made," I said to my reflection in the window. "I am only too aware of them and the blood on my hands, but I took England into my hands as a young woman, and now I let her go from my old hands in a better state than I found her, many other countries too. In that I may rest satisfied, and hope history, when it speaks of all my failings, will say this of me; she kept courage in her heart, and left the world a little better than she found it."

I nodded. "That is enough for me."

Chapter Twenty-Seven

Richmond Palace and
Greenwich Palace
Winter - Summer 1602

"No one would believe her Majesty was as old as she is," I heard someone whisper as past them I whirled, carried like the breath of a ghost on the arm of the Duc de Nevers.

I laughed. The Duc thought I laughed out of enjoyment of the dance and joined in, lifting me into a perilously high leap, which I bounded down from gaily. People always found the fact that I was old *and* healthy astonishing. We learn to put certain things together and assume because they are common that they are universal truths. If one is old one *must* be infirm, sick, crotchety, and ugly. If one is young they must be hale, sweet-tempered and handsome. I was old yet I was well, and strong enough to still be dancing with handsome men, and outlasting the youngest of them on the floor of the dance. This was enough to confuse simple minds who took commonalities for truths.

It was April and the Duc was visiting court, so I had treated him to a performance of my skills at music, on my organ and virginals, and now this dance. The winter had passed quietly, Ireland subdued, many nations at peace. The youngest men of my court were not impressed by the peace fallen on the world since it gave them fewer chances to show off, or die in some ridiculous, supposedly glorious manner. But the elders of our old tribe breathed a sigh of relief, knowing the value of peace. A time to rest without some immediate threat was good, as we knew. The young, always seeking adventure and mistaking war, fear, and abuse for adventure, understand not. Sometimes living through a dull period of history is a good thing, and if you believe me not, go ask ghosts of Rome and Constantinople who were there when the barbarians invaded,

Egyptians when their ships of war fell before the wolves of Rome. Go ask the people of Troy as their city fell in flames and they watched their children burn. Ask the phantom of my father as he sent wife after wife and countless friends to death. Ask them if they would rather have peace than excitement. I know what their answer would be.

In this gift of peace, there was work to be done. War, you see, is easy in a way. Immediate threats must be dealt with immediately, so it grants a sense of purpose because of this. This purpose is false, for there is no longevity in it; rather it is like a city on fire. Flames burst from one rooftop to another, leaping just as I did in the dance that night, and people run hither to thither, putting them out. There is a sense of purpose and achievement, but both are false for if the fire was not there, destroying, there would be neither. When peace falls there is a sense there is no purpose, but there is. Plans can be made for a future, and plans can be laid in place that may come to fruition months or years ahead. There is less sense of immediate purpose and achievement, yet plans laid in peace have a chance to become true, for achievements completed in times of peace have a chance of actually lasting. Our plans bear more fruit planted in an orchard safe from the winds and storms of the world.

I made my schedule for the summer punishing on purpose. It would begin with a visit to Richmond for the May Day festivities, and from there unfolded into a summer progress made up of twenty stays in different houses of lords and nobles. I was to travel around London in a radius of thirty miles, see as many people as I could. At times the stops were brief, just a visit to dine or hunt, and at others I would stay days or even a week. At Oatlands we would end and there I would entertain ambassadors of many countries.

I had a sense of time running out, and there was much I had left to do. Sometimes I thought something of Essex had floated from the pools of his blood on the scaffold and infested me. I was high and full of restless energy, or I was low and wanted to do nothing more than lie in my bed, be let alone by everyone. There was nothing in between. The last restless energy of my life was upon me and I welcomed it. It was better than lowness. So productive was I when in a rush and hurry that I amazed people. It was like a fever upon me. I was sick with life.

One of those I met with was the Duc de Sully, who was Minister of Finance for France. That summer he came on a private mission to London, and much of it was to meet me and talk about the future that England and France might forge together now that France was free of the yoke of Spain. I took him to one side, so I could speak to him freely about the present state of affairs in Europe. Beginning with the Treaty of Vervins, I began to talk of history and then into the present reality of the peace between our people. I told him it was necessary to contain the power of Spain and the House of Hapsburg, and I went on to speak to him of my views on the ways in which other powers of Europe could work together, so that none of them might be capable of giving umbrage to the rest.

"I could not agree more wholeheartedly, Majesty," said Sully. "And I find myself most impressed by your reflections on the past and present of Europe."

In truth the man seemed to find me so sensible that he was quite filled with astonishment. He said it was not unusual to find princes who had formed great designs upon the world and their place in it, for that position often forces them to incline to do this, but what he found remarkable in me was that I was able to distinguish and form ideas that were reasonable. I could foresee obstacles that would come up put there by other princes and by other men. After our interview Sully went into court and told my people, "I cannot bestow praises upon the Queen of England that would be equal to the merit which I discovered in her in this short time, both as to the qualities of the heart and the understanding."

How sweet of him.

Perhaps I should have thought it odd that after all this time, and after all men's experiences with me one should believe me to be wise, but the truth of life is this; that we are ever seeking to prove ourselves to new people, we are always meeting people who do not know us, and they must come to know us not only by reputation but by soul and heart. I was glad to have met Sully; some people said he was dour and dull, but I did not find him so. Perhaps in my grey hairs I had come to appreciate dull men with sensible minds who cared genuinely about the world.

That summer in June a small fleet under the command of Sir Richard Levison set out upon the seas bound for the great Portuguese carack laden with treasure. We knew it was being protected by eleven galleys and 10,000 troops, but I had good hope that he would succeed. Sadly, he did not. The expedition returned empty-handed, as so many of the past had done. I sent word to Levison saying I was sad that the expedition had not succeeded, but in truth I was not overly surprised. The days of Drake, of truly wild men of the sea adventuring upon its waves, I believed were done, and enough times had even Drake returned empty-handed from an attempt to take treasure from Spain, so it was not remarkable that a lesser sailor failed to.

An epidemic of smallpox broke that summer too, dragging many into the shadow of death, but nevertheless and against many of my men's dire urgings of safety because of this sickness, I planned a long progress towards Bristol. Sadly, even as we set out the weather again that summer was wet, stormy and inclement, and I was persuaded that the visits of me and my court to the houses of my people would cause hardship to those who already endured hardship.

In the end all the dire warnings of my men came to little. God decided to smile upon us. The weather improved and the harvest that year turned out to be a good one. Years of suffering came to an end. As the harvest was good, and trade began to revive as peace fell upon so many countries which brought prosperity to their people as well as ours, the spirits of the people of England improved, as mine did. "You see," I said, "God smiles upon countries that make peace rather than war."

"Do you think then that God was punishing us and others with famine as we made war, Majesty?" Katherine Hastings asked me.

"I sometimes do not know if God means to punish," I said, "but sometimes I think that when the Almighty disapproves of something and frowns, a period of hardship falls upon the earth. Some say that God is a father who means to chastise and punish His children when they do wrong. I do not think of God as a father who holds a willow-whip in His hands, ready to use upon His children. But I do think that when God frowns rain falls, and I do think that when He smiles the sun is seen. I believe that now we have made peace God is in heaven smiling, and we are reaping the benefit."

Although at the beginning of summer I had felt quite low of spirits, by the end of August, knowing that that year the harvest was safe and my people would have full bellies come winter, I was happy to announce to my court and to my ladies that I felt in better health than I had done for the past twelve years. I set out almost to prove it that summer. During progress, on one single day, I rode ten miles on horseback and then went hunting. That night I arrived home exhausted, but the next morning I was up, taking a very, very long walk, in case all of my court heard how tired the previous day had made me. I slept better during those two nights than I had done for many years, the utter exhaustion of my body sending my mind into a realm where there were no dreams, no ghosts of past mistakes haunting me, where I slept in nothing but the vast deep darkness of a dreamless sleep. The next morning, Cecil came to me and presented me with a jewel. It was set with rubies and topazes which he said was to match the life of my eyes and the colour of my lips. I laughed. "Do you think me as beautiful as this jewel, Pygmy?" I asked.

"You are more beautiful than any jewel, Majesty," he said. "I do not say this to flatter. Stones, such as these gems within this jewel, shine forever as sometimes I do believe you will live on forever, outlasting every single one of us. Eternity is beauty."

"So the young always say," I mused. "Yet to me, Pygmy, eternity may be vast but I am not sure it is beautiful. I have lived a long time and I would not wish to live forever, as God and as the saints do. Mayhap in Heaven it is different where the chaos of the body and of the spirit have been removed from a person who is to spend all their time in that glorious realm, but for those of us who walk upon this earth, I do not think eternity is something we should ask for. It sounds a lonely existence to me, to live forever, for unless all those I love were to live forever too I would eventually be alone, and although in life we meet new people all the time, there are so many who are so precious to us as when we lose them we lose a part of ourselves to death as well. Therefore long life you may well wish upon me, and I would call it beautiful for I have seen many things and have treasured many people, but do not wish eternity upon me. I would not wish to live and lose people, lose parts of myself each time so I became a hollow husk. I do not wish to live alone as I believe those who are eternal do; they may have the strength for such a feat, but I do not."

"Then I wish you long life, Majesty," he said.

"That is a good wish, Robert," I said. "Easy to fulfil, for I already have had it."

*

That month I left Greenwich for Cheswick, then visited Lord Keeper Egerton at his Hereford Park in Middlesex. Despite constant rain I was entertained most lavishly and Egerton called me the best housewife in all his company, which made me laugh heartily. There were endless rounds of feasts, masques, performances of music, and allegorical pageants. Egerton even put on a lottery, rigged so that I would win the prize, which pleased me as I had ever been a relentless and feckless cheater at cards. Days after the festivities, pamphlets went on sale, printed in London, telling the tale of all our feasts and frippery which brought to life all that we had done for my people. Yet because of the rain, which did in the end subside, and the smallpox which too subsided, progress was not as long as I would have wanted that year, and for a time longer than planned I settled at the palace of Oatlands. There I began an energetic round of entertaining ambassadors, and speaking to many about a future that now could be formed in the name of peace.

But seeing so many men from so many lands brought some things to mind I had little considered before.

One day I stood at my window, my ladies about me, and I turned to Anne Dudley. "Did you know I have never been upon the sea?"

Without waiting for her to answer I continued. "My mother and father both travelled to France, to Austria and the Low Countries. To the court of Burgundy my mother was sent when she was a child to serve the Archduchess Margaret. And yet I, queen of this realm, have barely been beyond London for most of my life. I have never felt the sea beneath me, heard the cry of gulls over the expanse of the water. I have never seen a shore that was not part of England."

"Beloved to England you are, Majesty," she said. "And so England wanted you close."

"It is true that my duties little seemed to allow it," I said, "and mistake me not, I do not regret the time I have spent with England. Although I have little to compare her to, I think her the most beautiful of places, and I have known excitement and peace and delight in her company, but I think sometimes I would have liked to see France, Spain, Rome perhaps. I would have liked to set eyes on a crashing sea or a high mountain, would have liked to know the scent of other cities, or seen islands in the sun full of strange plants and people. I doubt now I ever shall.

"So little of this world have I seen, and yet so much do I love. In my everyday life, so small and contained, I have seen wonders and miracles. In my friends I have found heroes and villains, and in my long nights I have had a glimpse of the eternal and solitary spirit of God, touched a strand of His loneliness. In the dawn I have caught sight of the love of every parent as their child is born. So much have I seen and sometimes I know it is enough, as sometimes I want it to be more."

I smiled wolfishly at her. "I tried once to set sail upon the sea and go to the Isle of Wight, but William Cecil stopped me, for he feared I would die on the voyage. I have never seen the north of my country, I have never felt the snows of the northern parts of this kingdom upon my face. I have never been to the toe of England, to Cornwall. I have never been to the outer reaches of Wales. I have ruled this country for almost forty-four years, yet so little of it have I seen."

I turned back to the window. "All of my life I have spent in little rooms."

Chapter Twenty-Eight

Oatlands Palace and
Windsor Castle
Autumn 1602

"It is all over court," said Robert Cecil, a delighted smile on his plain face.

"That I was *walking* in my garden," I said dryly. "This is not an unusual occurrence, I do it every day."

"Striding like a lass of eighteen," he replied. "The speed and vigour were what amazed people, Majesty, especially the ambassador who reported this to all of court."

"What amazes people is I am still alive," I said.

"Your health amazes."

"I ever knew that I had to take care of my flesh," I said. "It was something learned from my father. He made the mistake of thinking he, a king, could command his body as he did his kingdom, that it would obey him as his people did. He did not see that he abused his flesh and his bones, eating and drinking so much that those foods became not sustenance but poison. When he was a young man he was hale, but by the time he reached years younger than mine he had polluted himself, and could not understand why." I paused, turning my coronation ring on my finger. "When I saw him, an old man and a broken one, both in body and spirit, when I saw him wheeled about his castles in a chair, striking at everyone with a stick, I swore, Cecil, that I would never become the same.

"Admittedly I was granted a more nervous appetite and belly than he had, and that aided me, but I could never give in to what he had, could never treat myself so badly. To my mind there were enough people willing to mistreat me, so I thought I should not become one of my enemies' allies. People criticised my eating and drinking all my life, telling me I should surrender and give in and eat and drink like there was no tomorrow, but I always wanted to be here to see another tomorrow. It was, for a large part of my early life, my only and sole goal, and now I am here and in my aged years, and still I can walk, unlike my father, and still I can dance and sing and I have my mind. My health amazes people because people take their bodies for granted, thinking they may, like a careless love, treat them any way they wish and they will manage, forgive them, carry on. They, like careless people in love, are surprised when the one long ignored turns on them."

"Your doctors complain they do not see you enough," he said.

I snorted indelicately. "They see me more than enough, and they are only worried for their purses, not my health. I tell you, never was there a person who became ill who was not made worse by a doctor. Few and far between are the ones who actually know their trade and possess skill in it; all others are slaves to superstition and arrogance, and do more harm than good. Another reason I have survived is because I let few doctors near me. Most are butchers and charlatans, and I would not trust the bodies of others to them, let alone mine."

I sighed a little. "You have told the Clerk of the Council what I said to you?" I asked.

Robert nodded. I had asked him to ask the clerk to read out letters to me. My eyes had grown too weak, at short *and* long distances now, to read well. It was a vast sadness to me, as reading had always been one of my greatest pleasures. My ladies read books to me now, but I did not like it as well as reading myself. There are inflections different people put on different words, for in truth when we all read the same book we read different ones, our minds finding meanings diverse in all words. The way my women read the words of books was not the same as I would have read them. I was grateful I had not lost my books altogether, but still I mourned losing my ability to read. Sixty-nine I had become, so perhaps it was not unexpected I was losing parts of my body to the ravages of time. What I worried about was my mind.

My mind was getting tired. I knew this for something had happened at Greenwich when we moved there in October. Officers of the court were presented to me, and while I could remember their names I clean forgot what posts they held. It was a strange moment. The offices were just not in my mind. They had gone. No matter how hard I tried to remember I could not. Cecil covered the incident up, but I could not forget it. It worried, shamed and scared me. My mind had always been my greatest treasure, a companion who had delighted and aided me always. I felt like a doddering idiot on that day, and it worried me. What if I, like Henry VI, should lose my mind? In my last years might my mind become lost in a mist of forgetfulness and blankness, might what I was and all I had been float away from me, leaving me in a shell which was, all agreed, so very healthy? What if it was *too* healthy and I might last for years, just a shell? Would there be some poor part of me still there, hidden at the back of my mind in a tiny chamber, screaming because she could not make herself heard or understood?

The thought gave me horrors which came in the night. Dreams where I stood alone, talking and no one heard me. Where I was in my chamber writing, and yet no one saw me or came to take the papers upon which my painstakingly wise orders for my kingdom were written. Where I became a piece of furniture, and people just walked around me.

More than death I think I feared the notion of becoming invisible, irrelevant, ignored.

*

Queen's Day came that year, the forty-fourth anniversary of the time I took to the throne. Despite my depression which had been coming and going, and largely depended on how much sleep and how well I was feeling, as lowness of spirit often does feed upon lowness of body, that day was gay.

"There are so many young here today," I said.

The tilting yard was full of them, young lads who, to my old eyes, looked like nothing more than boys. I did wonder that their mothers had let them out of the schoolroom to come to my court. "Why is it," I said, "that the older one gets the younger everybody else seems? It is not just the lack of wrinkles or grey hair upon them that brings this to my mind, it is the innocence upon their faces. So little of this world have they seen, but unlike others I would not that they would face it sooner and know hardship sooner, that they might be prepared for all those hard times of the world. I wish people would stay as innocent as they can for as long as they can, for I think innocence keeps us young, as does the hope that we may change the world and be good for it."

"You do not think then it is true that we may change the world?" asked Anne Dudley.

"All people change the world just a little at a time," I said. "Some manage to change it in large ways, for good or for ill. Some simply change the world a little for the people who live near them. Neither is a wasted effort, but sadly many of us will never change the world as much as we might wish to. What is important is that we try, and that is all God or anyone else can ask of us."

I was ably distracted from this talk of changing the world and of youth and innocence by my fool, Garrett, who was riding into the tiltyard just at that moment on a pony who was the size of a small dog. In a full suit of armour this little man, who was so willing to make fun of himself as well as others, gave a grand performance of jousting which if any had been paying attention, showed the whole grand spectacle for the utter foolishness that it truly was. Young men riding at each other with big sticks, that was all the joust was. We were distracted from the ridiculousness of the situation by the shine on their armour, by the grandness and greatness of their horses, by the noise and the dust and the thrill of watching fake war enacted before us, but my fool was there as all fools are; to bring men down, closer to the earth whence they came.

"A good show, well played, Master Garrett!" I cried, throwing him a bag of coin. My fool, a good man who made me laugh so often, and there is no greater gift you can give to anyone but laughter, bowed and fell over his own armour and made me laugh again.

But after this time and as autumn waned and winter started to fall, as I was reminded once again of the death of William Cecil, loneliness fell upon me once more and would not leave. I tried not to show it too greatly to my people, and I dined with people like Cecil at their houses, but small accidents, such as when I managed to strain my foot merely by walking upon it, made me feel lower in spirit again. Many of my injuries were not serious, but more frequent they were and it was so easy for me to inflict pain upon myself. Advancing age brought almost constant pain, and I knew that my time was waning.

I lapsed into a soul-depression. Lack of food did not help. My teeth troubled me again and often I was in agony, my gums stuffed with cloves to numb the pain. I felt I had reached that stage I said I wanted not, that I would become useless to my country. I feared I might end up a senseless baggage in a little room, unable to recall who she was or who others were, unable to talk or remember. A husk of a woman once great, now on display to people who would pass by and shake their heads, saying what a pity I now was what I was.

I think I feared the loss of my mind more than the waning of my body. I had always tried to maintain a regal presence, knowing it is important that the people of a kingdom and country may look to their ruler and know they are great. But as my body began to surrender to the ravages of time, I feared my mind might try to outstrip it in that race, and fail me. I did not want to become useless to my people, or to myself. My mind had been my greatest ally, and if it was to leave me, I wanted no more to live.

Chapter Twenty-Nine

Whitehall Palace
Winter 1602

"Chicory soup is good for all things," I said to my ladies, who were pressing me to eat other foods. "Do you think I know myself and my body not at all just because I am old?" Younger ones scuttled back as I glared at them. Why is it when a person gets old the young suppose them stupid? "I reached this great age because of the things I know, child, things still a mystery to you," I grumbled at one. "Try to listen to those older than you and you might learn something."

When I was young I had often wondered why the old people I knew were so annoyed all the time. Now I knew. It was because the young were fools all, and worse, thought me a fool.

I rose from the table, tired of trying to eat and of fending off the helpful who were no help, and took up my cane. My father had ended up in a wheeled chair at the end of his life, but I managed with a stick. My hip ached, especially in winter, as it was then. I leaned on the cane for aid, but I had found it had another, more amusing function, for I could hit people who annoyed me with ease now, even if they danced out of the reach of my arm. My father had done the same. Once I had despised this about him, but now I saw the sense in it. I took up the family tradition.

We had moved to Whitehall for Christmas and I kept it with the usual splendour, not cutting to save money that year. I felt my people needed a treat, and trade was going well so the royal purse was a little healthier. Besides, I needed fewer complaints. There was much dancing, and bear-baiting, and many plays were performed. If it was not for my women constantly trying to make me eat things that I did not want to eat I would be merry enough always.

One thing that should have cheered me was a visit from John Harrington, my godson, Boy Jack. I normally liked to see the cheeky young man, although he was not so young anymore, but I was low when I saw him. I could not disguise this, even to save his feelings. Whenever I saw my godson I was reminded of Essex and the Irish disaster, for he had had one of the last interviews with Essex before Essex lost his mind and decided to try to claim my throne. When I saw him a tear came from my eyes and fell upon my chest. John tried to distract me by reading to me from some of his wittier verses and I smiled but when he asked me why I looked so sad, I could not help but answer honestly. "When you feel creeping time at the gate, these fooleries will please thee less. I am passing my relish for such matters."

Harrington too tried to lecture me about my diet, for my ladies, traitors all, decided to tell him that I was hardly eating. "I eat well enough, Boy Jack," I said. "It is my mind I fear for more than my body."

"But who," Harrington said, "shall say to you, Majesty, that your Highness has forgotten anything?"

I laughed at that, but it made me sad too. I knew there was a truth in what he said and people might not tell me when I had forgotten things, and so I might not realise the progress of the disintegration of my mind.

But if Boy Jack came to see me, others were heading north. Many said they were visiting northern estates, but I knew they were going to see James. The most likely successor he was, all knew it, and all people wanted to be there first to become his friend. It tired me but I understood, and I wanted peace at court, and there was no peace with legions of people.

All the same, whilst I welcomed the peace I admit it made me sorrowful too. I had always known people would turn to a rising sun more than a setting one, but it was sorrowing to sense the dusk approaching and know there were few to watch the last lights with me. Sometimes it is good to share a sunset.

*

"And you have lost again, Pygmy!" I crowed, slapping my hand on the table. Others holding their own hands of cards laughed. Cecil managed to as well, despite his losses. All in all that Christmas he had lost nigh on eight hundred pounds, most of it to me.

People laughed all around me, for the people who had remained at court had enjoyed themselves, as well they might. I had kept Christmas well that year, made it a splendid Christmas for the first time in years, and managed for the most part to appear before my court in good spirits. There was good news from Ireland too, for Tyrone had offered to surrender if I would spare his life. Mountjoy was urging me to accept this condition of Tyrone's surrender, to bring the war in Ireland finally to an end. I said I would consider Tyrone's proposal.

The heat of the chamber was high, the scent of spices riding on perfume and candle smoke. Fires were roaring in all hearths, flooding the chambers of the palace with welcome warmth. By night I would hear men and women outside my window, secret walks taken under the cloak of concealing darkness, and I smiled to hear them speak love to one another, smiled to know the adventures of many were just beginning. It was a good Christmas.

But as the New Year came, blood of my blood was attempting to annoy me. "Can they not leave me in peace to see out the last years or months that I have upon this earth?" I asked no one in particular when I heard about Arbella Stuart's recent plan.

The last time Arbella had come to court was in 1587, but I was so offended by her that I had sent her away, and she had been at Hardwick with her grandmother Bess, Countess of

Shrewsbury, ever since. Arbella was by that time twenty-eight years of age and still unmarried, and she hated her grandmother more than anyone alive. She saw Bess as not her guardian but her gaoler. It seemed that the girl was so desperate to escape from the prison of Hardwick House that she sent a message to Lord Hertford, the widower of Katherine Grey, my cousin, and had offered herself as a bride for his grandson.

Hertford had recently been in trouble, for he had decided to attempt, against his own best interests, to have his marriage to Katherine Grey declared valid, therefore his sons might become heirs to my throne. Since I had all but informed him that I might send him to the Tower and take his head if he attempted to do such a thing, he realised he was not in good standing with me, and so when Arbella's message, offering herself in marriage to his grandson, came to him, he went immediately to my Council and informed them of the plan. Hertford knew that on no account would I allow these two young people who both held royal blood to marry.

I sent a collection of my deputies to Arbella, and they encountered a most annoyed Bess of Hardwick, who had known absolutely nothing of her granddaughter's naughty scheme. When Bess was informed of the plan, I was told she rounded on Arbella as though she might start beating the girl, but screamed at her instead. It would not be fitting to lash her granddaughter in front of my deputies, after all, although I doubt not it happened after. Bess penned me a letter, assuring me that she had been entirely ignorant of Arbella's vain doings and pleaded to be relieved of responsibility of being the girl's guardian. Bess clearly was not keeping Arbella out of mischief, but I did not want Arbella with another lord, who might well use her for some dynastic plan, and I certainly did not want the girl at court. I told her grandmother that she must make a better effort to control her, and keep her at Hardwick Hall.

In addition to the general annoyance that this caused me, it also caused people to talk of the succession. Anytime it came up, I hit the offending person with my cane. If I could no more rely on my wits to keep people in line, I would do as my father had before me, and quite happily beat servants who disobeyed.

"Why she would try to marry someone she knows not, I know not," I said to my women. "And in secret."

How many secret marriages had gone on when I was Queen? And most of them ended in misery as I foretold, without me doing anything against them. People thought they should be ruled by the heart, by love, never seeing that what they had was not love. They craved excitement, and mistook it for love, and ended up unhappy because they had fallen for a fantasy and not a real person at all.

Perhaps all of us do this, trying to make what we wish would come of life occur in reality. Perhaps I was doing it even then, trying to hang on to a life that was weary of holding me up, trying to remain one of the living, when I had in truth already started to walk with the dead.

Chapter Thirty

Richmond Palace
January 1603

We moved to Richmond on the 21st of January. I wanted to be in my warm box, as I had long called Richmond. On the way there my blood felt hot and I wore summer gowns, much to the horror of my ladies who thought I would catch a chill and die.

It was my aged friend Doctor John Dee who told me I should go to Richmond. Since the man was in communication with spirits and angels, I did wonder if he had been told by one who now stood at the side of God the Almighty and of Mary the Virgin that I should be sent to Richmond, and Richmond would see my end. It was where my grandfather Henry VII had died, my dearest Kat too. I was not unaware my end was coming, and I believed ghosts of my past had seen it too. They spoke to Dee and sent me somewhere safe, to wait for the end.

On the way to Richmond, Nottingham, riding at the side of my litter, was keeping me company and in conversation. "I do so enjoy my warm winter box," I said to him, speaking of Richmond. The weather was wet, colder than had been for years, with a sharp north-easterly wind blowing. My insistence on wearing summer garments and refusing to put on my furs had led many to think I was losing my mind. But I was warm enough in blood. I was to become warmer still.

As we rode and I spoke to Nottingham he took my friendly stance too much to heart and decided to ask me if I would name my successor. "My seat hath been the seat of kings," I snapped, "and I will have no rascal to succeed me. And who should succeed me but a king? Let that be enough for you, Nottingham."

Nottingham, amongst others, took this to mean that I wanted James of Scots to succeed me, but I would not confirm it, nor would I deny it. Now, as I felt the end approaching, I was even less likely to name a successor in case *all* my people decided to desert me. I had few enough left, only my truest friends.

The weather was exceptionally cold by the time we were at Richmond. Ice formed on water even in the palace, and there were many found to a bed, trying to keep warm. I spent my time by the fire in my rooms, walking in my gardens bundled in furs, and eating my chicory soup. Robert Cecil bade me not to go out, but I did. When I could, I still went to wander in the world. He spoke of the dangers of the weather, ice on the paths, demons in the air, and wanted me kept in my little rooms, but I knew what those rooms would become, not places of safety but seclusion. Spaces about me would grow smaller and smaller, so less of the world would I see and would see me, and soon enough those rooms would be not wall and brick. They would grow smaller and smaller still, until I was in a tomb, a coffin, a shroud.

*

In the first week of February I received Giovanni Scaramelli, the first Venetian ambassador ever appointed to my court since I had come to the throne. I dressed with care for the meeting, my gown of white and silver, a wig of light colour never made by nature upon my head, and I pretended to be in good spirits. I spoke to the ambassador in his own language, and at the end of the audience said to him, "I do not know if I have spoken Italian well; still I think so, for I learned it when a child, and believe I have not forgotten it."

The ambassador assured me that my Italian was perfect, and I smiled at him for I believe he did tell the truth and it was pleasing to me to know that my mind still was sharp, even though my body was weak.

Although I was most pleased to be at Richmond, and although my blood was warm, something came upon me that I could not cast off. I felt as though I had been infested with the spirit of Essex again, part of my soul high and willing to work and part of me low and feeling alone.

There came a restlessness upon me, as though I were a caterpillar and I was trying to shed my skin, transform into something else. I was not eating, barely sleeping. I stood at my window and I watched this world I had loved. Sometimes I thought I saw Death, and I started to whisper tales to Him.

My eyesight was so poor by that time that the sights outside my window were a blur. Something in me liked it, for it was as though all was drifting into one, lights and colours, the trees and the river and the boats and the people, all things separate blending, becoming one, a blaze of light.

I wondered if all things once separate and doomed to walk alone and be alone and suffer for loneliness, should in the end realise they are not alone?

Was the truth that all that is, and was and shall be, has always been of one spirit, and that spirit is most beautiful, entirely wondrous? That there was within all of us an immutable, ineffable light and darkness, and in the end those torches and flames and shadows would bond, and we would know we were not alone and never had been?

Chapter Thirty-One

Richmond Palace
February 1603

"Majesty, come to a chair, or the cushions at least."

"Leave me be," I said.

For days I had stood at the window, running a finger along my sore gums, refusing to sit down or go to bed. People had been talking in my ear, trying to get me to rest, take a seat or go to bed, and I would not.

They did not know. They thought I was mad and ill and perhaps I was, but I saw much they did not. They had taken a sword away from me, for I had thrust it into the shadow and they thought I had lost my senses, but they did not see.

If they knew what I saw, they would say it was because I had not eaten. They would say it was because I barely slept. But I did not believe that this was the truth. When people see things that other people do not, often they assume the person with visions is insane, or there must be some reason of body or mind or lack of rest that causes such visions to occur in the mind. But I did not think so. As the end neared for me I believed I had come to a place where the veil of death was not as dense as once it had been when I was close to life. Something of mist that ever had been about me whilst I lived had lifted. I was able now to see beyond, to see those who had passed from before my eyes when I lived, and now dwelled in death.

There were ghosts in the gardens.

I saw them. I watched them. Unwilling to take my eyes from them in case into my palace, mayhap my room they wandered, I watched. The dead were not gone, not lost, they all were here. All I had wronged were here, just below me, in my own gardens.

My cousin of Scots, Katherine Grey and her sisters, Norfolk, friends and enemies. All those I had wronged were there, out *there*, walking by night and light of moon as though it was day. Essex had linked arms with Mary, and the two strolled, laughing. Mary looked as she had when first I had portraits of her from France, so young and fresh and full of promise, and Essex too looked like a boy, one moment his face handsome as an adult, the next wavering, melding into the face of the cheeky young lad who had stood before me and forgotten to remove his hat.

Katherine Grey was dancing upon the lawns, her sister Jane not far away and in her company my sister, Mary. Strange those two should be together in death. Walsingham who I had worked to death was with Robin, who I had prayed into darkness. Cecil stood with Kat and Blanche, watching the river and the boats. Katherine Parr, poor wronged Katherine, was near her husband, Thomas Seymour. He seemed to be asking her to spend time with him and she would not. She took arms with Blanche and left him behind. At least in death she had selected better company to keep than his. Norfolk strolled the paths laughing with my father.

About them were dead men, legions of them, men I had sent to the Low Countries, to Ireland, France, Spain. Men whose hair moved as though they were under water; all those who had drowned fighting the Armada. Men were in the hedges, weeping, for their empty bellies hurt them. There were wailing people of Ireland before me, holding dead children, starved or stabbed through by English pikes. Slaves I had purchased and who had died in the hulls of sweating ships were there, their chains clanking, their mouths asking other ghosts if they could tell them where their children were. Catholic priests who had died upon my orders were preaching in the gardens, surrounded by flowers, blooms which must too have been ghosts, since it was winter. A woman pressed to death lay upon the lawns. My sister walked away from Jane Grey and took the arm of Phillip, her beloved husband who never loved her. Past Lopez they wandered, chatting gaily, as he opened his chest to spill his blood upon the cold earth.

And my mother was there, she alone looking up at me, disappointment in her eyes.

Ghosts of every mistake I ever made had come to haunt me. They all were there. The legions I had failed were before me, every mistake and enemy I had made, and it all had started with her, with my mother. Had I been a boy she would have lived.

"What can I possibly do to make amends for all this evil I have wrought?" I asked. None of them answered.

So I continued to watch them.

*

On the 16th of February 1603, a Wednesday, I called Cecil to me and accepted finally that if England was to keep Ireland safe in our possession then I would have to come to terms with Tyrone. Mountjoy had suggested it, saying if we did not then the war would drag on and on, only costing more and more blood. I had considered not taking Mountjoy's advice, as I had considered not coming to terms with Tyrone as he advised. But with my end approaching and feeling weak and sad and alone, I did not want to leave England in the same state as I presently found myself to be. I dictated a letter to Mountjoy, in which I said I understood I must yield.

"We conceive the world hath seen sufficiently how dear the conservation of that kingdom and people hath been unto us, and how precious we have been of our honour that have of late rejected so many of those offers of his, only because we were sorry to make a precedent of facility to show grace or favour to him that hath been the author of so much misery to

our loving subjects. Nevertheless because it seemeth that there is a general conceit that this reduction may prove profitable to the state by sparing the effusion of Christian blood... We are content to lay aside anything that may herein contrary our own private affections and will consider that clemency has as eminent a place in supreme authority as justice and severity."

I did however send word to my Lord Deputy of Ireland cautioning him to preserve our royal dignity in all circumstances. I told Mountjoy that Tyrone should keep his life and he would receive upon his surrender other conditions which would be honourable and reasonable for the Crown and Mountjoy to grant to this rebel. All it meant in truth was that Mountjoy was to send for Tyrone, but he promised that his life would not be taken if he humbly submitted to England and the Crown. For anything else Mountjoy needed my personal approval, or that of the king who would follow me. Essex had taught me enough to now know that giving commanders full licence to do as they wished was not a good idea.

But the next day I changed my mind, and wrote again offering Mountjoy more flexibility as he dealt with Tyrone. I said he could offer Tyrone life, liberty and pardon. He was not to discuss religion, but the rebel leader was not to be prosecuted even if he remained Catholic. Time he had to surrender his lands in Ulster but as soon as his garrisons had been dismissed and his fortified forts and places had been demolished he could have his lands back. The one thing I insisted on was that Tyrone must resign his title and take a different one. The name of Tyrone was the same as the name of rebellion. He would have to take another, or people would always see him as a rebel.

The next day I said to Cecil that I believed myself to be on a slippery slope to Hades for discussing terms with the traitor. But I knew that talks with the O'Neil were the only way to set Ireland to peace for good. "I do not think Tyrone will ever abandon his ancestral title, Majesty," Cecil said.

"Perhaps he will not, but I have to insist upon it," I said.

A canny light entered his eyes and I was aware that he was going to tell Mountjoy to pretend to follow my orders and then to disobey them. I was aware the reason Cecil thought he might get away with this was because he thought I would not last to punish him.

And yet although I managed to deal with these things I felt I was slipping away. "I am not sick, I feel no pain, and yet I pine away," I said to my ladies. When I could I would stand at my window and watch the ghosts. When I could not stand it I came away.

What I said was true in a way. The swelling of my fingers no longer hurt me, my gums sometimes pained me but not always. I was not in great pain but I did not want to eat and I did not want to rest. There was a sadness upon me that I could not shift anymore, not even by pretence by pretending to smile for my people. I was barely eating and not sleeping at all. And then my chest began to feel tight and my breathing became laboured.

"I am dying," I said, "and yet there is nothing truly wrong with me."

It is time, said something in the wind outside, but when I looked outside and saw the ghosts waiting, the judgement upon me waiting for me, I did not want the end to come. Always I had resisted Death, and I believed I had to then.

I was not ready. Is anyone?

*

Still at my window in late February, although I had sat down from time to time, they told me Katherine Howard, my great friend, was about to pass from life. I said nothing.

Katherine Howard had been not only my friend, she was the daughter of Lord Hunsdon, the man who possibly was my cousin and just as possibly had been my brother. When I heard she was close to death I went to her bedside, and I found her as low as I had been told she was. Katherine was barely able to talk by the time I reached her, but she held my hand and I held hers. I heard the last gurgle of her life and I wondered what it was she had wanted to say to me. I would now not know, not until we met again. "I will not keep you long waiting, old friend, and my niece," I whispered to her as the warmth drained from her flesh.

I ordered a state funeral for this woman I had loved, and I went back to my chambers where I sank into a lowness of spirits from which I would never emerge again. The day after Katherine died, my coronation ring was cut from my finger. It had to be sawn off for it had become embedded in the swollen flesh of my finger. I had tried to wait as long as possible before having the ring cut away, for to me it was the breaking of a sacred bond, the only marriage I had ever made in my entire life, to my people and to my country. As the ring came from my finger, I knew that death was not far away. I wrote that night to Henri of France. *"All the fabric of my reign, little by little, is beginning to fail,"* I wrote to him. As I sealed that letter I wondered whether when he opened it, he would be reading words written by a ghost.

That was the night I saw Him. Straight from Katherine's bed He had flown to mine. Death. He came that night, standing by my bed, waiting.

He knew the sadness would end me, that He would win at last. That night was when I started talking to Death in earnest, telling Him the tale of my life. It was how I would hold Him off, I thought, delay Him, and how I would appease the ghosts outside my window. If I could say how it had been, confess my sins honestly, and in context, dealing with each as they had come to me in life, perhaps those people, all those people I had wronged who were waiting outside for me, perhaps they would understand, perhaps they would forgive.

I talked to Death, trying to explain life.

*

Ambassadors were still asking for audiences with me, and I told my men to ask them to wait a few days because of the death of Lady Nottingham, for which I was still weeping, and from which I wondered if I would recover. I had no wish to again appear before them, before court, before my people or before the world. Little by little I drew into myself. I was sad and I was tired of feeling sad. I believed the end was coming and I wanted the end to come, and yet I feared it too, thinking these ghosts gathering outside my walls, and every time I looked there were more and more of them, that all these people I had failed would exact revenge upon me for all I had done and had failed to do. I was ready to die yet I feared to be judged, feared that God would not understand all I had done, and even if He did understand would punish me for every mistake, and forget any goodness I had managed to achieve.

*

"I told you my tale," I say, looking at Death. "And here now, it is the end."

Death looks at me and bows, a low and deep bow. If it came from a courtier I would think he intended to bestow respect. I can but hope this is what Death means to show me, but still I know not. I turn to the window. The ghosts are there, and they wander no more. Many are missing.

Some are still in the gardens, and they all stand under my window, looking up. And some are in this chamber, this little room. They too are watching me.

"The end," I whisper.

Chapter Thirty-Two

Richmond Palace
February - March 1603

"When Katherine died you came," I whispered to Death. My voice was leaving me. Mayhap it was the ulcers in my throat, or perhaps I had whispered so long and deep to Death, telling my tale, that I had no voice left. I knew not.

"I fear to climb into bed," I said to Him. "I fear the phantoms of my mistakes, there outside, are waiting to tear me apart."

Ambassadors asking for audiences had been told that I could not see them for I was in mourning, but I had in truth withdrawn into myself. With Katherine's death I lost the last enjoyment that I had known in life. I could not endure another death, another loss.

Robert Carey, youngest son of Lord Hunsdon and the brother of Lady Nottingham, came to court at that time. On a Saturday night he was admitted to my private apartments, for he looked so like his sister that I had wanted to gaze upon his face. He found me in one of my withdrawing chambers sitting up on cushions. I had ceased to stand at my window and stare at all the ghosts out there. I had taken two cushions, and there I stayed, refusing to get into bed. Robert came to me and kissed my hand. "It is my chiefest happiness to see you in safety and in health, Majesty, and I hope this might long continue," he said to me.

I took his hand and wrung it hard. "No, Robin, I am not well," I said. "My heart has been sad and heavy for twelve days and I think in truth it may have been heavy a long time before that and I did not notice." I sighed many times and his face became drawn with grief. Later he said to one of my ladies that he had never heard me fetch a sigh, except when Mary of Scots was beheaded.

The next day would be Sunday and I gave a command that the Great Closet should be prepared for me to go to chapel the next day. Everyone made ready the next morn, but by eleven o'clock I knew I was not going to make it to the chapel. I sent one of my grooms out, told him to ask the men to make ready the Private Closet for I could not go to the Great. There were many people outside waiting for my coming but at last I ordered cushions to be laid for me in the Privy Chamber, by the closet door and there I managed to crawl so I could hear the service.

I sickened.

My throat was swollen by ulcers, and my head was full of a cold. As March fell a fever fell on me and I could not sleep at all, and I could not swallow food with ease. Even my blessed chicory soup pained me as it went down. On the 9th of March I called my doctors to me and told them I felt a great heat in my stomach and a continual throat-thirst which every moment asked me to drink to abate it. There was hard and dry phlegm choking me. Up until that moment I had refused everything prescribed by my doctors, but the symptoms of whatever illness it was that was coming for me were growing worse. I was in great pain, and I was heavy of heart.

On the 11th of March suddenly I felt better for a day, there was less pain. I could breathe. I laughed a little as the day went on. Death seemed to dim. But then the day after I felt worse again, falling into a heavy dullness of spirit. I felt very, very old. Men told me to take remedies, and I wanted none of them. Cecil and Whitgift came to me and took to their knees begging me to do as my physicians recommended. "I know my own strength and constitution better than you, gentlemen," I said, "and I am not in such danger as you imagine."

But I would not eat anything. I spent all my days lying on the floor on cushions, staring at the gilded ceiling, trying not to look my ghosts in the eyes.

As I grew worse and worse, they tried to persuade me to go to bed. Cecil knelt by me. "Your Majesty, to content the people, you *must* go to bed."

I turned my head towards Cecil. "Little man, little man, the word *must* is not to be used to princes," I said sternly. "If your father had lived, you durst not have said so, but you know that I must die, and that makes thee so presumptuous."

My throat was closing in on itself. I stopped talking.

Eventually Nottingham came to see me. He had retired from court to mourn his wife, but men about me had obviously decided he was the only one who could convince me to get into my bed. He came and sat beside me on my cushions. I looked up at him. "They send friends because medicine fails," I said.

"I understand you will take none, Majesty," he said with a brief smile. "If you will not try it, you do not know if it would work."

I stared at him a while. "Nothing will work, old friend. I see in your eyes that you too have been keeping company with Death. I see the echo of His presence in your eyes, *there*." I touched his face, near his eye. "And you know as I do. People think Death should be feared, but we know, do we not, Nottingham? You and I know the dreadful comfort death brings, more dangerous than a thousand armies or assassins is that comfort, that creeping voice that tells us there is more for us to love in death than is left in life. There is more to tempt us to go there, than to stay here. They call to me too, old friend, the ghosts you see of the ones you love. Every day I too wish more and more to walk with them than to stay here, and yet I fear that path."

His hand clasped mine. "Courage, Majesty," he said. I was unsure if he was talking in truth to me, or to himself.

"My lord," I said. "I am tied with a chain of iron around my neck. I am tied, I am tired, and the case is altered with me." I told him there was a heat inside my breasts and a dryness in my mouth which stole sleep from me, and that all I really wanted now was to go to sleep.

"Come to your bed, Majesty. You would be much more comfortable there and you might recover sooner."

I stared at Nottingham. "If you were in the habit of seeing such things in your bed as I do when I am in mine, you would not persuade me to go there, old friend."

That was a pregnant pause in which Nottingham tried to wonder how he could convince me otherwise.

"I had a premonition, Nottingham," I said, "once I lie down, I never will rise again."

I looked over at the bed, and beside it Death stood, watching me.

*

The next day I allowed myself to be lifted into a low chair. I then found I was unable to rise from it to get to the privy. Attendants helped me to my feet. Once I was back on my feet, I refused to sit down again. I stood there unmoving for fifteen hours. People flapped about me and stared in horror as I stood there swaying slightly. Eventually when I was ready to faint with exhaustion, they took me back to my cushions. I stayed there for four more days.

They told me it was the 18th of March. I nodded. I was not speaking. Sometimes I did not speak for two or three hours, for my throat hurt me so. I held my finger in my mouth, with my eyes open and fixed on the ground, and I sat on my cushions, sitting still. I had grown thinner than I had ever been before, and now I was simply sitting there in my day clothes, the same clothes I had worn now for three weeks.

The next day I was so ill that I whispered to Cecil I thought soon I would die. "I do not think I will last three days," I said. "Write to Carey and tell him to write to James."

"Majesty, we have posted horses along the Great North Road," Cecil said, "and they are prepared for Carey to ride to Scotland, as you commanded. It will be blood of your blood that will inform blood of your blood of his destiny."

"That is well," I whispered. "You have done well, Robert."

Cecil was stopping the publication of any bulletins about my health, as he knew that my illness had to be contained until James heard I had died, until the kingdom was his. I had told Cecil to make sure that the kingdom passed cleanly from my hands to James, and he was doing so. His secret mission was almost ready to begin, with my end. On the 21st of March Nottingham finally persuaded me to go to bed. I felt my back could no more support me to sit up on my cushions, so protested but little as they put me into my bed.

I lay there for a few hours, then something burst in my throat. Although the matter that flooded down my throat was foul I felt better, my head cleared, and I asked for some of my chicory broth to be made. Prunes and dried currants were placed on a table at my bedside, and they brought my chicory soup to me, but soon after I had taken a little I began to lose the ability to speak, and from that time I ate nothing. I lay on one side without speaking or looking upon any person, although I made directions at some of my women that they were to read to me.

Archbishop Whitgift came, along with my own chaplains, and my musicians played softly in the background to soothe me, as Whitgift and my chaplains prayed.

On the 23rd my chaplain, Doctor Perry, held a special service of intercession in the Royal Chapel, and I could hear their fervent, compassionate prayers for me from my bed. I had been mostly speechless for two or three days. But I made signs that Whitgift was to keep praying, although I did not want to hear him speak of hope for my life left to be lived longer, but when he prayed or spoke of heaven I held his hand tight.

"Majesty," Cecil asked, leaning over my bed, "will it be the Scots' King?"

I lifted my hands, put them to my head. They all looked baffled. *Let them take it as they may,* I thought, wanting to laugh but having not the energy. *Let me be ambiguous in death as I always was in life.*

At six of the clock Whitgift came to pray at my bedside again, and I gestured with my hands for him to come close. Many people I loved were in my bedchamber, kneeling and praying next to me. I was lying on my back with one hand in the bed and the other outside of it. The Archbishop was kneeling beside me and asking me of my faith.

I answered all his questions by lifting up my eyes and holding up my hand. The good man told me what I was and what I was to come to, saying that I had long been a great queen hereupon earth, yet shortly was to yield an account of my stewardship to the King of Kings. I inclined my head.

I could avoid the answering no more, it was almost time to answer to God for what I had done, and for all I had failed to do.

*

They all have left, all but my ladies. As my women guarded me in life so they will in death, standing with me until the very end.

I can hear people moving outside. Cecil will be ready. I do not begrudge him preparing for my end. He can see it coming as I can. I hope he has indeed asked Robert Carey, as I asked him to some months ago, to be the man who would take the news of my death and of his ascension to the Scottish King, when I leave life.

It is ten of the evening, and it has started to rain, the noise of rain splattering against the windows of my palace brings soft comfort. I am tired, ready to sleep. Before I fall to sleep, and to death, I turn to the figure at my bedside.

The night is long, and I know dawn is coming. I will not be here for it, says my mind.

In my bed, unable to talk, I lie and Death is here. *Take me*, my mind says to Him. *Take me. If I must answer for all I have done to the people out there, I have tried. I have confessed. Take me, and I will face what will come.*

Death nods to me. He reaches out a hand and lightly He strokes it along my face. If He could speak I know what He would say. That all must pass, that the old and young must die so other steps can fall upon the world. That crowns are taken up by others. For good or for ill all must pass and all must change. Every dawn the stars fall back, and in the gloaming so too falls away the sun.

I understand, I say in my mind.

Things are blending together, words and memories and sights. The colours and light and darkness of the world are becoming one, one light, one shadow.

I see things I once saw when I was a child and things that are before me now. I see my mother, first her face watching me, a smile on her pretty mouth and then as an image in a ring, surrounded by gold. I see her hands reaching out to my father. I see my father stare at me, horror on his face for a moment, and I drop my eyes knowing the blackness in them reminded him for a moment of my mother, the only woman he truly loved, and the first he utterly destroyed.

I see my women crying, weeping for they love me, will miss me. They stand with me now at the end, and they will guard my body when I am dead. Cecil stands at my bedside, near Death though he knows it not, and his face is so sad. I think now I know; he did love me, as master and mistress, perhaps as mother too. I wish I could say to him that his destiny is to carry on, but that I think he knows.

I see my sister, my brother, both as children and as adults. I see Kat crying as we were to go to the Tower, and again on the day I was told I would be Queen. I see Blanche standing with me in the gardens, telling me I was the place where her soul felt content, and Robin making faces at me in the gardens too, when we were children and he did not want to read the book that was in his lap.

Walsingham grins, Cecil takes my hand and pats it. Parry is here, his canny eyes bright. Katherine Howard, Countess of Nottingham has come. So recently dead, she shines bright, smiling, waiting for me. Friends, so many lost friends, they gather at my side, waiting.

Half remembered things and well-remembered come, flooding my mind. The little rooms of my mind, all these compartments where different memories and people, different parts of myself were kept, they are falling, becoming one. There are no walls between them anymore, everything blends into one. Everything contained is no more contained. My empire falls and the palace of my mind wastes. Dust plumes into the skies from the buildings crumbling before my eyes.

And I smile, for I know it is well. We all must watch our empires destroyed, but if we understand the truths of death we can see, in all ends there is a chance to begin again. As my world tumbles another will be built. And as my kingdom falls into nothingness it becomes not separate but one. All that I ever loved is crashing upon me, and I flow into it, and I swim and sink at the same time in the waters of my own soul, and in the flowing destruction of my own life.

Take me, I say. Take me into dust and water, into this broken world of my world. I will drift in the ashes of my life and be free to wander with all that has fractured, all that now flies in the winds of time. Take me and I will be free with all this shattered kingdom, free to fly with all and everyone I ever loved, for the rest of time.

I fall, into darkness so vast. There is no end and no beginning to this darkness, and I am not afraid. It is warm and soft, and I am safe. I fall peaceful, I do not resist. The end has come, and I am glad of it. The little room in which life ends is gone, and before me the world opens, vast and wide, and beautiful.

Epilogue

I open my eyes and I find myself in shade, under a tree in a place where there are other trees scattered. A park, and not far away a house I know well.

"Hatfield," I say softly, not wanting to disturb the peace of the day. I put my hand to my throat; it does not hurt. My voice is in me again, my breathing pains me not. I stretch out my hands and toes, my legs. I turn my neck side to side and I feel no pain, anywhere. I laugh a little, relishing the simple joy we all forget, of a body that works and knows no pain or tiredness. And then I look around, taking great, beautiful, delicious breaths of the wild wind blowing past me.

It seems like summer, or early autumn perhaps, a soft wind blowing and flowers and grass bending to dance in the light breeze. The trees are brown and gold, flowers spare, so autumn it must be, yet it is one of those surprising days of autumn where it feels summer has raced back and seized control. Birds are calling in the trees. Not far away there is a wood pigeon cooing, a noise of awe as she sings to the skies. A good scent is on the air, a freshness of wind and grass, wetness and plants. I know not what I am doing here, or why, for I know not long ago I was not here, but I do not care. I sit in the dappled shade of the trees and I watch. Not far away there is activity.

A girl, her waist like a willow, her arms and hands long too, stands under an oak before the great house of my childhood. Red hair streams out, bright as blood from her head. In the wind it lifts and dances. Her skin is milk and snow, and her eyes are black as the darkness of death through which I have passed. She has no idea, this girl, no idea how very beautiful she is.

There are men standing in front of her, and more people at her back, watching. A rider is coming on a great white horse along the road, riding hard and strong. The girl spreads her arms. She thinks she has survived so much, that she has reached the end of her trials. I, looking on her, could tell her they are just about to begin.

"But, Elizabeth," I say to myself, this figure of this girl I once was, "what an adventure you are to have."

I envy her a little for all those years, those beautiful years and months, weeks, days and moments she would have with people who would steal our heart. All the people we had loved and all we would come to love, so many she had yet to meet. Yet I would not begrudge her a second of it. Those times and moments were hers now as they had been mine. She would not understand how precious they were, but they would stay in her heart, glowing memories of gold and silver, light and darkness, to lighten her days and make the endless nights pass in greater comfort. There is so much ahead of her, and so much she has faced already.

Perhaps I should warn her, tell her of all she will lose, of battles fought and blood that will spill, but I cannot. Tell her that and she will do otherwise and I think most times I did well enough. Not perfectly, that cannot be for anyone, but well enough.

I will know soon. I cannot imagine this is where I will rest for all time. I will be taken elsewhere and I will answer for all I did in life, the good and the bad, the wondrous and the evil. "So why take me here?" I ask, even though I know the answer.

There are in life many beginnings. It could be said my life began on the day I was born, or on the moment of my first memory. Perhaps it was on the day my mother died at the hands of my father, or the day I was taken to the Tower on the orders of my sister and thought I would die. But this day, the day they came to Hatfield and told me I was Queen, this was the day my purpose began. I had become Queen, guardian of England and her people, one of a line of so many. People search all their lives for the meaning of life, but I was handed mine; to keep my country steady, to give her people a chance to right themselves after the chaos of the past that my family had caused, and to hand this kingdom on to my successor, in as good a state as I was able.

"This is the Lord's doing," calls the girl, speaking to the men who have just told her she is England's Queen, "and it is marvellous in our eyes."

I smile as I watch the men before her fall to their knees. I want so much to chuckle, for she knows exactly what she is doing, bending this moment to make a memory in so many minds. I remember how I chose that psalm, selected those very words. She looks up at the tree, the glimmering lights of the sun behind the last of the leaves, and then she looks over, at me. I see her eyes narrow, her sight even then not as strong as others'. I smile at her.

"This is the Lord's doing," I echo.

I stand, my back against the tree. Good, strong oak of England presses into my back, holding me up. "Never cease to learn, Elizabeth," I say to the girl who stands before those men not so far away. "Be as the old hare who never is caught; learn, listen, trust in yourself. Stand out when you wish and hide when you have need. Love where you can, Elizabeth, and trust and love with all your heart, devoid of care. Love those who deserve your love, and cast off those who do not. Accept people as they are, Elizabeth, not as you want them to be, and you will live a happier life. Learn from the past, sweet girl, but do not live in it. Think of the future but do not rest your happiness there.

"Be of the present, my child. Enjoy the moment and surrender to joy for it is fleeting. And if you wish to survive, to live as long as I have, then listen to your instincts, Elizabeth, for they know much you do not. Learn, listen, and love and know in the end you will lose. And know that to lose is as well, for all stories must end, Elizabeth, so another can begin.

"It is time," I say, "for you to stand alone. And you will be well, brave girl. What adventures you are about to have, what a life you are about to lead, Elizabeth of England."

I rise from the base of the tree, and I walk into the woods. The purpose of our life is hers now. I have done all I can. Good and ill I have done, but I hope more good, enough to warrant me taking a peaceful stroll in these woods of the past.

I can hear voices not far away. There are people I know here, in these shaded paths. They are just out of sight, but I can see shadows flitting, light playing on headdresses and caps. I hear music, drums beating in the distance, hands clapping in time, and I know there will be dancing nearby.

They have been here all along, I think, these shades and shadows, ghosts made of silver and gold and green. These shadow-shades have long been at the corner of my eye, dancing for years beside me in life, and now in death they are waiting for me. They were not trapped in me, they always could come out. Little rooms of life are not the kingdom of death. They simply waited for me, with patience.

I never was alone. Always they were with me.

I hope if I walk far enough I will find them all, past the crackling bracken and the rustling briar. They will smile when they see me, my friends waiting for me. We will take hands, and take a last wander through the woods together, the clement warmth of autumn on our backs, and the setting sun before our eyes.

They are here to share the sunset with me.

I glance back at the girl, and she looks right at me, as though she sees me. I lift my hand, and I wave to her. For a moment I think she waves to me. I laugh, and I turn for the dark coolness of the woods. I walk into the freedom of the outside world, a space always I loved. There is nothing for me to do but wander where I want. There are no papers or problems waiting, no one I must watch for signs of treason. I am responsible for no one but myself. There are no more games to play but those I wish to play. My footsteps quicken on the path, crunching red-gold bracken and leaves. My heart races swift, excitement and anticipation filling my blood.

I walk towards the voices of friends. I will find them.

**Here ends *Little Rooms*,
Book Ten of the Elizabeth of England Chronicles,
And here too ends the Chronicles of Elizabeth Tudor,
Queen of England.**

Author's Notes

This is a work of fiction. Although I try to stick to known facts, there are certain elements I created in this book. All conversations are fictional, although where the words of the characters were set down in historical record, those words are used. The characters of the people involved are my invention, although based on study of their lives and actions. I used a great deal of sources for this book, which I have included in the bibliography. For clarity, I will explain here what I altered or added from the historical record and why.

There is no proof that Elizabeth asked Robert Cecil to secretly approach James of Scots, or see him safe to the throne. This is my invention. Cecil, like many other men of influence, was in touch with James during the latter years of Elizabeth's reign to forge a relationship with the man most likely to be the next king, but there is no evidence Elizabeth asked this of him. It is, however, something I could easily see her doing. On the same vein, there is no evidence Elizabeth asked Francis Bacon to warn Essex of the dire and very real trouble he was in during his trial, but I could imagine Elizabeth giving him one last chance to redeem himself. And someone *must* have warned him, for although Essex was a complex man in many ways, his behaviour during this part of his trial was out of character, leading to the notion that someone must have talked to him and managed to impress the danger he was in upon him. All of this is supposition, however, I have no proof. I should add as a side note, I'm not a big Essex fan. There are advocates for the young man aplenty, and they can stick up for him, but to me he was a man who boasted too much and did too little. I fully believe he may have struggled with some kind of bipolar disorder, as it is often said in many reports about him that he suffered from high, productive periods followed by very low, crippling depressions. Essex had the potential to go far, yet never did, and whilst some of this could be explained by a disorder, more can be blamed on his character. I'm afraid until someone convinces me otherwise, I see him as a spoiled, entitled, selfish child, someone who talked big, produced little, wallowed in self-pity and hurt people who loved him.

The play performed on Twelfth Night, whilst the Duke of Bracciano was visiting I have listed as Shakespeare's *Twelfth Night*. I should point out that although the timing of the visit and the fact that one of the characters appears to have been written to honour the visiting Duke both fit with this time period, this is a hotly contested point with those who study Shakespeare, for reasons best known to them.

I have mentioned before that Elizabeth's pet names for her men and women were not what we would deem suitable or appropriate now, and "Pygmy" for Robert Cecil is one of the worst. But it was what she called him, and in many ways was a gesture of affection, so I have not attempted to alter it.

One event in this part of Elizabeth's life always has astonished me when I read about it; the invasion of Essex into her bedchamber. Many historians take this event not seriously at all, and many more ascribe her later behaviour, since in many ways this marks the start of Essex's fall, on vanity. People say she did not like that he saw her without her make-up and wig, and that is why he fell from her affections. I saw something quite different.

I saw Elizabeth at her most vulnerable, and in her most private space. I saw how this event could be full of fear, since she was physically vulnerable, and indeed without her clothes and cosmetics she was not in her costume of Queen, which (at least psychologically) was very important to Elizabeth. She had few guards, and her ladies could not help her. She knew of other kings and princes who had been taken in similar ways. Indeed, her brother was almost kidnapped once by his uncle, Thomas Seymour, in a manner most similar to this.

I saw her as a woman of advanced years, who knew herself to be physically weaker than a man who had just invaded her rooms, and a man she was unsure of, given his late behaviour in Ireland. I do not believe that event or Essex's fall had anything to do with vanity. I think he scared her, and I believe at least a part of him *intended* to scare her, as it would have given him power over her. That Elizabeth, in this book, goes over the worst that could happen to her, captivity, rape and death, is not outlandish either. The worst that could happen always runs through our minds when we are scared. I believe the secret to the start of the fall of Essex was that by bursting into that room he showed her how fragile her power, and her life was. I do not believe she welcomed that knowledge. I also believe she understood in that moment that Essex did not love or respect her. Up until then she had gone back and forth, but no one who loves someone truly tries on purpose to scare them, intimidate them and lessen them through fear, and I think that was what Essex was doing, knowingly or not, when he burst into her rooms. It was a show of force, power and an attempt at domination. That moment to me is one of the most telling of the character of Essex, the moment when all that lies beneath a pretty face and charming ways is revealed. I do not think Elizabeth liked what she caught a glimpse of under that mask.

And as for the end... Some contest that Elizabeth was signalling that James of Scots should be King when she lifted her hands to her head on her deathbed. Some say she was indicating a crown, that he should be her successor, and some say not. Elizabeth was certain that no one but a King should follow her and had worked hard enough to ensure that those of merely noble blood were not about to succeed her. James was the only choice really, who could fulfil the correct criteria, and Elizabeth always made sure if he was not named successor, he was never excluded either. I believe she wanted him on the throne, and although a lot of her reasoning I believe was because of all she said of him and who should succeed her, there is another reason for which I have no proof. I believe Elizabeth never forgave herself for the death of Mary of Scots. There was proof enough of that in the years following Mary's execution, and of the lengths Elizabeth went to to avoid being blamed or held responsible for it. I think in

James coming to the throne she felt perhaps a little redeemed for what she had done to his mother. This is only an idea, and I am sure many will disagree with me.

Elizabeth Tudor was a remarkable woman, who had many flaws and just as many outstanding virtues to her character. She was a canny, intelligent survivor, often a compassionate and forgiving monarch, and she had a wild temper and a lasting one when she thought herself betrayed. I find her fascinating. I think I always will, and I hope, in these books covering her long life I have done justice to her memory and brought to you a woman who was by no means perfect, but was in so many ways extraordinary.

Select Bibliography

Ackroyd, Peter. *Shakespeare the Biography*
Aesop. *The Complete Fables*
Alford, Stephen. *The Watchers*
Baker, Margaret. *Folklore and Customs of Rural England. Discovering the Folklore of Plants.*
Beer, Anna. *Patriot or Traitor*
Bicheno, Hugh. *Elizabeth's Sea Dogs*
Borman, Tracy. *The Private Lives of the Tudors. Elizabeth's Women*
Brears, Peter. *All the King's Cooks*
Breverton, Terry. *The Tudor Cookbook*
Brigden, Susan. *New Worlds, Lost Worlds*
Brotton, Jerry. *The Sultan and the Queen*
Budiansky, Stephen. *Her Majesty's Spymaster*
Castiglione, Baldesar. *The Book of the Courtier*
Chainey, Dee Dee. *A Treasury of British Folklore*
Champion, Matthew. *Medieval Graffiti*
Childs, Jessie. *God's Traitors*
Cook, Judith. *Pirate Queen, the life of Grace O'Malley*
Cooper, John. *The Queen's Agent*
Curley, Michael. J (translator). *Physiologus*
De Bray, Lys. *Elizabethan Garlands*
De Lisle, Leanda. *The Sisters who Would be Queen*
Doran, Susan. *Elizabeth I and her Circle*
Duffy, Eamon. *The Stripping of the Altars. Fires of Faith, Catholic England under Mary Tudor*
Erasmus, Desiderius. *A Handbook on Good Manners for Children*
Evans, Victoria Sylvia. *Ladies in Waiting: Women who served at the Tudor Court*
Falls, Cyril. *Elizabeth's Irish Wars*
Fraser, Antonia. *Mary Queen of Scots*
Goodman, Ruth. *How to be a Tudor*
Gristwood, Sarah. *Elizabeth and Leicester. Arbella, England's Lost Queen*
Grueninger, Natalie. *Discovering Tudor London*

Guy, John. *Elizabeth the Forgotten Years*
My Heart is my Own: The Life of Mary Queen of Scots
Handley, Sasha. *Sleep in Early Modern England*
Hanson, Neil. *The Confident Hope of a Miracle*
Haynes, Alan. *The Elizabethan Secret Services.*
Sex in Elizabethan England
Helm, P.J. *Exploring Tudor England*
Herman, Eleanor. *The Royal Art of Poison*
Hieatt and Butler. *Curye on Inglysche*
Hilton, Lisa. *Elizabeth, Renaissance Prince*
Hogge, Alice. *God's Secret Agents*
Hutchinson, Robert. *The Spanish Armada*
Kaufmann, Miranda. *Black Tudors*
Lacey, R. *Robert, Earl of Essex*
Loades, David. *The Tudor Queens of England*
Lovell, Mary. S. *Bess of Hardwick*
Lipscomb, Susan. *1536: The Year that Changed Henry VIII.*
A Visitor's Companion to Tudor England.
Luke, Mary. M. *Gloriana, the Years of Elizabeth I*
Markham, Gervase. *The English Housewife*
Matusiak, John. *The Tudors and Europe.*
A History of the Tudors in 100 Objects
McGowan, Margaret. M. *Dance in the Renaissance*
Mortimer, Ian. *The Time Traveller's Guide to Elizabethan England*
Neale, J.E. *Queen Elizabeth*
Norton, Elizabeth. *The Lives of Tudor Women*
Norris, Herbert. *Tudor Costume and Fashion*
Norwich, Edward of. *The Master of Game*
Onyeka, Narrative Eye. *Blackamoores: Africans in Tudor England, their presence, status and origins*
Parry, Glyn. *The Arch-Conjuror or England, John Dee*
Picard, Lisa. *Elizabeth's London*
Plat, Sir Hugh. *Delightes For Ladies*
Plowden, Alison. *Elizabeth Regina.*
Danger to Elizabeth.
Marriage with my Kingdom.
Tudor Women: Queens and Commoners.
The House of Tudor

The Young Elizabeth
Porter, Linda. *Crown of Thistles*
Porter, Stephen. *Everyday Life in Tudor London.*
Shakespeare's London
Reynolds, Tony. *St Nicholas Owen, Priest-Hole Maker*
Ronald, Susan. *The Pirate Queen.*
Heretic Queen
Roud, Steve. *The English Year*
Rowse, A. L. *The England of Elizabeth*
Sass, Lorna. J. *To the King's Taste*
Singh, Simon. *The Code Book*
Sim, Alison. *Food and Feast in Tudor England*
Masters and Servants in Tudor England
Pleasures and Pastimes in Tudor England
Skidmore, Chris. *Death and the Virgin*
Soberton, Sylvia Barbara. *Medical Downfalls of the Tudors.*
The Forgotten Tudor Women
Somerset, Anne. *Ladies in Waiting*
Spearing, Sinead. *Old English Medical Remedies*
Starkey, David. *Elizabeth*
Starkey, David and Greening, Katie. *Music and Monarchy*
Stone, Lawrence. *The Family, Sex and Marriage in England, 1500-1800*
Sugden, John. *Sir Francis Drake*
Tallis, Nicola. *Elizabeth's Rival*
Thomas, Keith. *Religion and the Decline of Magic*
Tudor, Elizabeth. *Elizabeth I, Collected Works*
Veerapen, Steven. *Elizabeth and Essex*
Weir, Alison. *Elizabeth the Queen.*
Henry VIII, King and Court.
Britain's Royal Families: The Complete Genealogy.
The Lost Tudor Princess.
The Children of Henry VIII
Traitors of the Tower
Mary, Queen of Scots
Weir, Alison and Clarke, Siobhan. *A Tudor Christmas*
Whitelock, Anna. *Elizabeth's Bedfellows.*
Woolley, Benjamin. *The Queen's Conjuror*

Thank You

…to so many people for helping me make this book, and all those I have writer about Elizabeth possible… to my first proof reader Brooke Aldrich, and my present proof reader, Julia Gibbs, who gave me her time, wonderful guidance and also encouragement. To my family for their ongoing love and support. To my friend Petra who took a tour of Tudor palaces and medieval places with me back in 2010 which helped me to prepare for this book and others; her enthusiasm for that strange but amazing holiday brought an early ally to the idea I could actually write a book, begin a career as an author. To my friend Nessa for her support and affection, and to another friend, Anne, who has done so much for me. To Sue and Annette, more friends who read my books and cheer me on. To Terry for getting me into writing and indie publishing in the first place. To Katie and Jooles, Macer and Heather, often there in times of trial. To Lew, for being there when I needed someone. And to all my wonderful readers, who took a chance on an unknown author, and have followed my career and books since.

To those who have left reviews or contacted me by email or Twitter, I give great thanks, as you have shown support for my career as an author, and enabled me to continue writing. Thank you for allowing me to live my dream.

And lastly, to the people who wrote all the books I read in order to write this book… all the historical biographers and masters of their craft who brought Elizabeth, and her times, to life in my head.

Thank you to all of you; you'll never know how much you've helped me, but I know what I owe to you.

Gemma Lawrence
Wales
2021

About The Author

I find people talking about themselves in the third person to be entirely unsettling, so, since this section is written by me, I will use my own voice rather than try to make you believe that another person is writing about me to make me sound terribly important.

I am an independent author, publishing my books by myself, with the help of my lovely proof reader. I left my day job in 2016 and am now a fully-fledged, full-time author, and proud to be so.

My passion for history began early in life. As a child I lived in Croydon, near London, and my schools were lucky enough to be close to such glorious places as Hampton Court and the Tower of London, allowing field trips to take us to those castles. I think it's hard not to find characters from history infectious when you hear their stories, especially when surrounded by the bricks and mortar they built their reigns and legends within. There is heroism and scandal, betrayal and belief, politics and passion and a seemingly never-ending cast list of truly fascinating people. So when I sat down to start writing, I could think of no better place to start than a subject I loved and was obsessed with.

Expect *many* books from me, but do not necessarily expect them all to be of one era. I write as many of you read, I suspect; in many genres. My own bookshelves are weighted down with historical volumes and biographies, but they also contain dystopias, sci-fi, horror, humour, children's books, fairy tales, romance and adventure. I can't promise I'll manage to write in *all* the areas I've mentioned there, but I'd love to give it a go. If anything I've published isn't your thing, that's fine, I just hope you like the ones I write which *are* your thing!

The majority of my books *are* historical fiction, however, so I hope that if you liked this volume you will give the others in this series (and perhaps not in this series), a look. I want to divert you as readers, to please you with my writing and to have you join me on these adventures.

A book is nothing without a reader.

As to the rest of me; I am in my thirties and live in Wales with a rescued cat. I studied Literature at University after I fell in love with books as a small child. When I was little I could often be found nestled halfway up the stairs with a pile of books in my lap and my head lost in another world. There is nothing more satisfying to me than finding a new book I adore, to place next to the multitudes I own and love… and nothing more disappointing to me to find a book I am willing to never open again. I do hope that this book was not a disappointment to you; I loved writing it and I hope that showed through the pages.

This is only one of a large selection of titles coming to you on Amazon. I hope you will try the others.

If you would like to contact me, please do so.

On Twitter, I am @TudorTweep and am more than happy to follow back and reply to any and all messages. I may avoid you if you decide to say anything worrying or anything abusive, but I figure that's acceptable.

Via email, I am tudortweep@gmail.com a dedicated email account for my readers to reach me on. I'll try and reply within a few days.

Thank you for taking a risk with an unknown author and reading my book. I do hope now that you've read one you'll want to read more. If you'd like to leave me a review, that would be very much appreciated also!

Gemma Lawrence
Wales
2021

Printed in Great Britain
by Amazon